For my mum, Tania,
My husband, Adam,
And my daughter, Aurelia:
Three generations who taught me what love really means

# The Dead Wife's Handbook

HANNAH BECKERMAN

PENGUIN BOOKS

PENGUIN BOOKS

Published by the Penguin Group
Penguin Books Ltd, 80 Strand, London WC2R ORL, England
Penguin Group (USA) Inc., 375 Hudson Street, New York, New York 10014, USA
Penguin Group (Canada), 90 Eglinton Avenue East, Suite 700, Toronto, Ontario, Canada M4P 2Y3
(a division of Pearson Penguin Canada Inc.)
Penguin Ireland, 25 St Stephen's Green, Dublin 2, Ireland (a division of Penguin Books Ltd)
Penguin Group (Australia), 707 Collins Street, Melbourne, Victoria 3008, Australia
(a division of Pearson Australia Group Pty Ltd)
Penguin Books India Pvt Ltd, 11 Community Centre,
Panchsheel Park, New Delhi – 110 017, India
Penguin Group (NZ), 67 Apollo Drive, Rosedale, Auckland 0632, New Zealand
(a division of Pearson New Zealand Ltd)
Penguin Books (South Africa) (Pty) Ltd, Block D, Rosebank Office Park,
181 Jan Smuts Avenue, Parktown North, Guateng 2193, South Africa

Penguin Books Ltd, Registered Offices: 80 Strand, London WC2R ORL, England

www.penguin.com

Published in Penguin Books 2014

001

Typeset by Firstsource Solutions Ltd
Printed in Great Britain by Clays Ltd, St Ives plc

A CIP catalogue record for this book is available from the British Library

ISBN: 978-0-718-17814-7

www.greenpenguin.co.uk

MIX
Paper from
responsible sources
FSC
www.fsc.org   FSC™ C018179

Penguin Books is committed to a sustainable
future for our business, our readers and our planet.
This book is made from Forest Stewardship
Council™ certified paper.

We are such stuff
As dreams are made on; and our little life
Is rounded with a sleep.

Shakespeare, *The Tempest*

# Prologue

I didn't mean to die so young. I don't suppose anyone does. I don't suppose many people would willingly fail to reach their thirty-seventh birthday or their eighth wedding anniversary or see out their daughter's seventh year on the planet. I suspect there aren't many people who would voluntarily relinquish all that, given the choice.

But that's the point; we don't get a choice, do we? One day you're leaving a restaurant with your husband, conscious of the future only so far as your certainty that it will arrive and you will be part of it, preoccupied with the promotion you've just been celebrating and the summer holiday you've been planning and the child's progress you've been discussing. An evening when your happiness is due only in part to the bottle of champagne you ordered but is mostly a result of those rare occasions when the pieces of the jigsaw slot into place and you see with clarity the picture of the life you've been trying to create for the past weeks, months, years. And the next moment you're slumped on the floor, with only the briefest awareness of how you got there and yet the sharpest recognition of the hot, tight pain invading your left arm and marching on towards your chest.

I remember thinking that no one survives pain like this.

After my heart had decided it was no longer for this world – long before the paramedics arrived, long before that night even began it turns out: a heart that had been secretly destined to expire prematurely for as long as it had been beating – I found myself here.

I don't actually know where here is. If I believed in heaven then I'd have been disappointed if this was it. There's no one else around, no reunions with loved ones, no winged beings checking people in or out. I'm completely alone. And lonely. More lonely than I ever knew possible. There are no gardens, no rainbows, no magical worlds like those at the top of the Faraway Tree. Just whiteness spreading out into the infinite beyond, as far as the eye can see, in every conceivable direction.

The only respite in this interminable void is when occasionally, sporadically, the whiteness beneath me clears, like fog receding begrudgingly on the coldest of winter mornings, and I'm granted a dress-circle view of the living world to watch my family getting on with life without me.

Who grants it, or why, or how, I've no idea.

It's both a blessing and a curse, being able to see and hear the people I've left behind, the people I love, but in silence, invisible, impotent. I'm lucky, I know, to be able to observe fragments of their lives, to listen to their conversations, to pretend – even if only fleetingly – that I'm a part of their lives still. But it's painful, too, the inability to console them when they're sad, to laugh with them when they're happy or, simply, to hold and be held by them, to give and take refuge in the comfort of physical intimacy.

Perhaps it wouldn't be quite as bewildering if it weren't so unreliable, this incomprehensible access I have to the living; sometimes my time with them can last a whole day, at others just a matter of minutes. Sometimes I'm kept waiting only a few hours between visits; at others long, solitary weeks go by without so much as a glimpse of the real world. I spend inordinate stretches of time alone in the impenetrable whiteness wondering what I might have missed in my enforced absence although, in truth, I have very little conception of the passage of days here.

And it's frustratingly unpredictable too; sometimes I'm allowed to observe that which I most want to be a part of, while at others the air clears suddenly and I've no choice but to witness that which I'd most like to miss. It can be cruel like that.

I wonder, occasionally, when I let my fears and fantasies get the better of me, whether my presence here is a privilege or a punishment. Whether it's a passing phenomenon or is set to continue for all eternity. Whether there may be a future in which I'll be something other than a passive spectator of a life I no longer lead.

Sometimes I wonder whether any of what I'm seeing is actually real. In moments of desperation, I find myself questioning whether I am, in fact, dead at all. I begin to hope that I'm in a temporary coma and that the whiteness and the loneliness and the lives of the living I'm observing are nothing more than products of my unconscious fantasies.

I have a lot of time to think about these things.

I wonder, too, whether it's more distressing to watch your family in mourning for you or whether it will be worse when, one day, they stop grieving and start living painlessly without you. I try to imagine how I'll feel when I begin to occupy that place which all dead people must dread: that distant, rarely visited corner of someone's mind, neatly packed away in a box marked 'Memories'.

I often find myself thinking back to those conversations couples have about death, the conversations where each proclaims that should they die first they'd want their bereaved to carry on with life, meet someone new, be happy. I know now how delusional those conversations are. How untruthful. I know now that the only thing in the world worse than dying is the fear that one day you'll be replaced and that life will continue with only the faintest echo of your existence.

Because to our loved ones, at least, we're all irreplaceable, aren't we?

# Shock

# CHAPTER 1

Today is my anniversary. Not my wedding anniversary or my engagement anniversary or the anniversary of the day Max and I first met at a friend's wedding and knew immediately that this could be something special in a way that I'd always imagined only ever happened in movies.

Today is my Death Anniversary. A year ago today I was still alive, with fifteen hours remaining before the arrhythmia I'd been oblivious to for the past thirty-six years would fatally disturb the supply of blood to my left ventricle, which in turn would cease pumping blood to my brain which would, in a matter of minutes, kill me.

Anniversary probably isn't the right word, is it?

I've wondered a lot over the past few days, ever since I heard Max and his parents discuss it, what Max and Ellie and my mum and all the other people whose lives I used to be a part of will do today. I've wondered whether it's maudlin and self-indulgent and even selfish of me to hope that they'll commemorate it somehow. But I also know that I'll be devastated if they don't.

I'm often full of trepidation when the whiteness dissolves and I wonder what, on each occasion, I might discover on my return. Especially after lengthy absences dominated by fear and speculation about what I may have missed in my time apart. Not that time has any clear, linear definition for me now, not in the sense that I knew it back then. I rely on fragments of information each time my access is restored to determine how long I've been absent, like a detective searching for clues to fill the missing gaps in the timeline of the living world. For me now, instead of time, there's space and silence and often, despite the loneliness, an inexplicable tranquillity. But that doesn't stop me worrying about how they are, about what they're up to, about how they've been coping during my absence. I think worrying's just a mother's prerogative isn't it, dead or alive?

Today appears to be starting much like any other. The clouds have cleared to reveal the illuminated digits of a bedside alarm clock – the very same clock that woke me, every single morning, for the last seven years of my life – telling me it's a little after six-thirty. Ellie is scrambling under the duvet where Max is only just beginning to stir towards consciousness. She burrows under his heavy, sleeping arm and absent-mindedly twists the sparse hairs on his chest around her fingers. He takes hold of her hand, only in part to stop the tickling, but mostly to reassure her he knows she's there.

I think this is the time of day I miss them most. I miss the sensation of Ellie clambering on to our bed and the gentle weight of her lithe body awakening me each morning. I miss her obliviousness to the adult limbs she crawled over in her bid to locate the smallest of gaps between us where she'd slip, feet first, under the duvet. I miss the smell of her hair and watching her dozing eyelids flutter and the warmth of her limbs – exuding heat after a long night under her Hello Kitty bed linen – intertwined with mine.

8

Max and I each used to wrap our arms around her, holding her tight between us. An Ellie Sandwich we'd call her, and it would make her giggle. We'd tell her she was the best breakfast anyone could wish for.

'Daddy?'

Max emits a deep groan and pulls Ellie into a secure embrace by way of a response.

'Daddy, are you awake?'

Ellie struggles to free herself from Max's arms and gently pokes at his eyelids.

'No. I'm still asleep.'

Ellie giggles. It's a game they seem to play almost every morning and yet one Ellie never appears to tire of.

'You are awake, Daddy. You talked.'

'I'm sleep-talking, munchkin. I'm definitely not awake. See.'

Max produces a loud, exaggerated snore. Ellie is still laughing.

'Daddy, be awake. It's morning.'

'Only just. Stop poking me in the eye and I'll almost certainly wake up faster. How did you sleep, sweetheart?'

'I slept all night. I didn't even have to go to the toilet.'

'That's very good, angel. And did you have any nice dreams?'

Max asks about Ellie's dreams every morning. It's his way of continuing a tradition, our tradition, a tradition which began just weeks into our romance, in which I'd share with him the intricately recovered details of stories I'd told myself during the night. He said he'd never known anyone remember their dreams with such vividness, that he couldn't believe someone could be so affected during the day by events that existed only in the unconscious depths of night. Occasionally I'd dream that he'd been unfaithful to me and in the morning I'd feel as unnerved as if he really had betrayed me.

*You can't blame me for infidelities I commit during your dreams,* he'd say, laughing, comforting, reassuring me that even my most potent fears didn't have the power to make something real.

Now I don't dream at all. I don't sleep so I can't dream. Dreaming is just one of the many experiences that I miss about being alive. I miss the magic of it, the knowledge that I'm still thinking, fearing, desiring and despairing long after I'm conscious of it. I miss the chance to escape.

'Can't remember. What did you dream about, Daddy?'

'Well, sweetheart, I had a dream about Mummy. You were in it too. We were in a little boat on the sea, like that one we had in Greece, and it was really hot and sunny. Do you remember that boat we hired for the day, when we sailed around all those pretty bays?'

'Was that when I wanted an ice cream but you said you couldn't get me one?'

Max laughs. She's right. She spent the whole day on a boat desperate for ice cream, unable to understand why we couldn't magic her one out of thin air. It was a blissful holiday. Two idyllic weeks in Greece – first Athens and then Naxos – with Max as our personal tour guide. I'd worried when we'd booked it that Ellie would get bored, scrambling over ancient ruins and exploring historical landmarks, but she seemed to have inherited Max's passion for history and was spellbound by his tales of gods and goddesses, of war and revenge, of love and honour.

It had been the first holiday when Ellie, still only five at the time, had nonetheless been a proper travelling companion, staying up late with us to banquet on plump olives and pan-fried halloumi, fresh grilled sardines and oversized prawns, reminiscing about the day's events, discussing tomorrow's possible adventures and developing her own, individual hierarchy of aesthetic pleasures: her preference for clear blue waters over dusty olive groves, for hills over flatlands, for sunsets over midday blue skies.

It was our last holiday together as a family. I wonder if she'll have any memories of it at all in years to come.

'Trust you to remember the one time I failed to find you an ice cream. I'm a pretty good ice-cream hunter usually, aren't I?'

Ellie giggles and flings her arm across Max's chest. I close my eyes and imagine it's me she's clinging to, the warmth of her breath on my neck a memory still recent enough that for the briefest of moments I believe I can actually feel her: the plumpness of her cheek on my shoulder, the weight of her body in my arms, the softness of her hair against my lips, the air from deep within her breezing softly over my skin.

I ache, physically, to hold her.

I open my eyes to find Max gently prising Ellie from his body. He holds her face in his hands and studies her with a seriousness at odds with the conversation they've just been having.

'Sweetheart, do you know what day it is today?'

I feel the tectonic plates of panic shift. For the past few days I've thought of nothing other than the hope that he'd remind her, but now that he is I find myself wishing he wouldn't. I know it's not fair on her to keep invoking the memories, but equally – selfishly – I can feel the pre-emptive disappointment should he allow her to forget.

'Er, it's Wednesday, Daddy. I went to school yesterday, and the day before, and before that it was the weekend.'

'Yes, sweetheart, you're right. But today's also a special day. Shall I tell you why?'

Ellie's expression combines confusion, suspicion and hope. She hasn't remembered. Of course she hasn't. She's only just seven, after all. It's a relief, to be honest, to know that she hasn't been counting down the days towards the anniversary of the night she was told her mummy's never coming home again.

'What's special today? Are we having a party?'

'No, munchkin, we're not having a party. Do you remember this time last year when we were all really sad because Mummy got ill and she wasn't going to be with us any more? Well, today it's exactly a year since Mummy died. So I thought it would be nice if, after school, you and I visit the place where she's buried. We could maybe take her some flowers to let her know that we're thinking about her. Do you think you might like to do that?'

I'd love you to do that.

Ellie doesn't seem so sure. She buries her head in Max's chest, her eyes scrunched closed, as if wanting to shut herself off from the whole world and from this conversation in particular.

Max strokes the top of her head.

'What's wrong, sweetheart? Does it make you sad to talk about Mummy? You know that's okay, don't you?

I feel really sad when we talk about Mummy. We miss her, don't we?'

Ellie's only response is the tensing of her body into an even tighter ball, her eyes still firmly closed.

Perhaps that's my answer. Perhaps it's all too much for Ellie. Perhaps both Max and I are forgetting just how young she is, how vulnerable, how fragile still.

'Angel, I'm sorry. I know it's hard. Really I do. I'm not going to make you do anything you don't want to. I just thought it might be nice for us to remember Mummy in that way today. Is it talking about Mummy that's making you upset?'

There's an almost imperceptible shaking of Ellie's long, brown curls. It's at moments like this that I most question what I'm doing here. Why let me witness what's going on in the world without enabling me to scoop up my baby girl and make it all better for her?

'Do you think you might be able to talk to me, sweet-heart? I think we're both really sad today, but maybe it'll be a bit better if we tell each other how we're feeling. Do you think you can do that?'

Ellie's unresponsive. I don't know what to do. I know there's nothing I can do. But then I'm not sure I'd know what to do if I was Max either. I'm not sure there's anyone who can teach you how to make the world right for one who's already had so much go wrong.

'Is it that you don't want to go to the cemetery? Is that it?'

Ellie exhales a heavily burdened breath and tentatively nods her head.

It pains me even though I know it shouldn't. Rationally I know that no seven-year-old would relish the prospect of visiting a cemetery. Maternally I know that she's too fragile to suffer repeated grief. And yet I still fear the possibility of getting lost in the labyrinth of Ellie's memory, of becoming nothing more than a word spoken without remembrance or thought or feeling attached. But I'm not sure what more Max could possibly do to try and keep alive in her mind the mother who loved her so very much and who never wanted to leave her.

'Sweetheart, can you look at me?'

Max tries to pull Ellie's head from where it's still burrowed against his body, but it's as if she's stuck to him with glue, such is her determination to shield herself from the grief she's so far from being ready to face.

'Okay, you stay there. But do you think you can tell me what it is you don't like about the cemetery? Because I think if you can tell me it might not feel so bad.'

There's a long pause while Ellie considers Max's proposition.

'It's scary.'

The words, mumbled into Max's chest, are only just audible, as though to say them clearly, out loud, may bring upon the speaker some bad fortune even worse than the one she's already endured.

I'd thought that there was no greater guilt beyond that of dying and leaving your daughter motherless. I thought I'd accepted that I had no control over my death, that it wasn't in my power not to leave Ellie, that sometimes there's simply no correlation between the things we feel guilty about and our complicity in their cause. I'd thought perhaps the guilt might begin to erode with time.

But guilt, it would seem, is the titanium of emotions.

'Angel, I think everyone finds cemeteries a bit scary. Why don't you tell me what scares you most and maybe we can make your fears go away?'

Max manages to prise Ellie's head from his chest where she's finally ready to open her eyes and face the world that's betrayed her.

'It's all those dead bodies. They're horrible. How do you know they're not going to come out of the ground like in *Scooby Doo*?'

Ellie's more assertive now, confident that the cartoon world must surely mirror her own.

'In *Scooby Doo*, it's never really a monster or a zombie that goes around scaring people, though, is it? It's always just a person dressed up like that, like at Halloween. You know there's no such thing as people coming back from the dead, don't you?'

I can't help but wonder if it wouldn't be preferable to Ellie if the dead were to come back to haunt the living. At least in that case death wouldn't be final. At least then she might not have lost me forever.

'But it's so quiet there. It really gives me the creeps.'

Ellie's looking at Max imploringly now. Maybe they should just wait until next year, or the year after that, or whatever time in the unforeseeable future she's ready to face the inanimate commemoration of me. It's not as though my headstone's going anywhere, after all.

'I know cemeteries can be a bit spooky, sweetheart, but I'd be there with you. How about this: how about we just pop along after school and if you really don't like it after five minutes, we'll leave. How does that sound?'

That sounds like the perfect solution, Max.

'Mmm . . . okay, Daddy. If you find it scary too then I don't want you to have to go all by yourself. But you promise that if we get creeped out we can leave?'

'I promise, angel. Hand on heart.'

And hope not to die.

As Max and Ellie settle into the final few minutes of their morning embrace, Max pulls Ellie into his arms and kisses her, protectively, on the top of her head.

I always knew Max would be a great father. I just hadn't been prepared for the extent to which my own love for him would multiply when I witnessed quite how great. I'd thought, during those first few years together when it was just the two of us, that it wasn't possible to love him any more than I already did. I thought I knew the unrivalled depths of his patience, his generosity, his compassion, of his uncanny ability to make every situation – however difficult – seem manageable. But then along came Ellie and with her the proof that even those you think you know best still have the capacity to surprise you, as I witnessed the tenderness and awe with which he greeted our little girl into the world.

And now, here he is, parenting our child without me. I'd never really considered that possibility when I was alive. I don't suppose anyone does. I don't suppose many people can bear to acknowledge the chance, however remote, that they may not be around to guide their children into adulthood.

As the seven o'clock beeps ring out from the bedside alarm clock, the whiteness begins to gather beneath me and I know, for this morning at least, that my access is coming to an end. I watch Max and Ellie slowly fade out of view, leaving me with the image of them huddled under a duvet together, sharing the cosiest of morning rituals, a sight that would fill any mother's heart – even my defunct one – with love and with longing.

# CHAPTER 2

The clouds clear to reveal Max sitting in a coffee shop around the corner from his school with an overpriced chicken-and-pesto panini and my best friend, Harriet. This is an unprecedented event; I've never known Max leave the school premises for lunch during his sixteen years as a history teacher, and Harriet's job as a corporate lawyer rarely releases her with sufficient time to get home before midnight, let alone traipse across town from her office in Holborn to our life in Acton in the middle of the day. I can only assume that my absence has been just a matter of hours and that this unparalleled lunchtime get-together has something to do with the day's commemorative date.

Harriet's been my best friend since university. I'm sure to most outsiders it's an unlikely friendship, but I'd always known – from that very first term when we confided secrets to one another that we rarely dared acknowledge, even to ourselves – that our differences were only skin deep. Despite Harriet's confidence and her apparent brashness and her refusal ever to admit being in the wrong – all characteristics which I've no doubt make her a fantastic lawyer – she and I aren't that different, really. Perhaps she's done a better job of concealing her insecurities than I ever did but I think we both knew somehow in those early days of our friendship – unconsciously, perhaps – that there was an affinity between us that transcended the superficial personality differences. It wasn't until later that we discovered the absent fathers we had in common, whose disappearances had fashioned the people we'd become and the lives we aspired to, albeit in different ways.

When Ellie was born, there was never any question in my mind that Harriet deserved a more meaningful role than the ubiquitous 'auntie' epithet, and so the woman who'd vowed for two decades never to want a child of her own became godmother to mine instead. And now that I'm dead, I couldn't be more grateful that she is. Because not only is she everything you'd want a godmother to be – doting, devoted and defiantly unconventional – she's also one of only three women whose presence in my daughter's life doesn't now overwhelm me with feelings of envy and exclusion. And of those three, Harriet's the only one who isn't related to Ellie by blood.

'So, how are you doing?'

It should be Max answering the question but instead he's asking it. Even today, of all days, he's playing the stoical role as he's done so much over the past twelve months, putting everyone else's feelings before his own.

'Oh, you know, it just feels weird, doesn't it? I mean, she was my best friend and I miss her like hell but that doesn't mean I have a clue how I'm supposed to act today. Is it enough that we've got together to talk about her? It doesn't feel like enough but then I'm not sure what else there is to do. But how are you doing, more importantly?'

'Honestly? I think I feel pretty much the same as I did this time last year. All that stuff about time being a great healer? It's rubbish. I still think about her all the time.

I think about her when I'm awake and I dream about her when I'm asleep and then my dreams wake me up and I spend half the night just missing her. I don't think I can remember the last time I had a proper night's sleep. I never imagined grief would be so exhausting.'

That's one thing you and I have in common now, my darling. People always talk about the dead being at rest but I don't remember ever being this tired in my whole life.

'You know, I never really appreciated before how sleep deprivation totally destroys you. I look back to when we first had Ellie, when Rachel was feeding her two or three times a night, and I genuinely don't know now how she coped during the day without going mad. I feel like I'm constantly on the verge of insanity these days. Quite a lot of the time I act like I am too. Do you know, the other day I took Ellie round to my mum and dad's and when I came home I realized I'd left the keys in the front door. It was a miracle we hadn't been burgled.'

That's not the first time Max has escaped a minor disaster in the past year. There was the time he forgot the food he'd left cooking in the oven until the hallway smoke alarm furiously alerted him to the impending danger. There were the times he'd get up in the middle of the night, convinced it was morning and head for the shower, often not realizing his error until he switched on the radio to discover an eclectic mix of World Service programmes filling up the twilight hours instead of the morning news bulletin. And then there was the time he went out for an early morning run one weekend Ellie was staying with my mum, returning home an hour later to discover that he'd left the bath taps running, the contents of which had since flooded the kitchen below. It was a mess. He was a mess. His dad had to come over the next weekend to help him redecorate both rooms. That was at the beginning, though. He's definitely been less dazed and confused lately. At least, I think he has. But perhaps that's just my own wishful thinking.

'Don't beat yourself up, Max. Things like that can happen to anyone. It doesn't make you a nut job to forget the odd thing now and again.'

'So when was the last time you did something like that, Harriet? I can't see you being that forgetful.'

'Of course I'd never do anything so stupid as to leave my keys in the front door but that's because I'm a control freak with mild OCD who has to check that everything's locked a dozen times before I'll so much as close the garden gate behind me. Don't go judging yourself by my standards, Max, because therein lies a whole different path to Crazyville.'

Max raises a wry smile. I do too. Harriet may be the most exacting person I've ever known, but you can't accuse her of lacking self-awareness.

'Talking of crazy decisions, I'm taking Ellie to the cemetery later. I thought it was important to mark the day somehow. She doesn't really want to go and I don't know whether I'm doing the right thing in coercing her into it. I'm not sure if I want her to go because I think it's right for her or because I think it's right for me or because I think it's right for Rachel, and I know that sounds ridiculous because it's not like Rachel's going to know if we go or not.'

Max pauses for a second to consider the implication of what he's just said, as if saying those words out loud reminds him again and afresh that I really am dead.

'I don't know, Harriet. Am I doing the right thing? What do you think? God, welcome to the world of widower parenting where every decision you make is almost certainly the wrong one.'

And to the world where a single sentence has the power to break my heart all over again.

'I think you've got to stop being so bloody hard on yourself, Max. Everyone tells you what a great job you're doing, all the time. For god's sake, even I tell you how great you are with Ellie and I'm not exactly renowned for handing out compliments just to make other people feel better. You're like the poster boy for single fatherhood.'

It's true. Max has been amazing. I just wish I could be the one to tell him that. Actually, that's not true. I wish no one were telling him that. I wish there was no need for him to be told that in the first place.

'That's good of you to say, Harriet. Really, I do appreciate it. I'm just not sure it stops me feeling guilty.'

'Guilty about what, for god's sake? You're doing the best you can and, let me tell you Max, that's pretty damn good by anyone's standards.'

Max looks down at the solitary remaining mouthful of his sandwich and doesn't look up again, even as he begins to answer Harriet's question, slowly and quietly.

'How did I not know? That's the question that keeps going round and round in my head, all the time, day and night. It's driving me mad. If I really loved her, how on earth can I not have known?'

'Not known what?'

'That she was ill. That her heart was broken, literally broken. I still don't understand it. There was no sign, not even on that last night. How can I not have noticed there was something so catastrophically wrong? What kind of husband does that make me? Really, Harriet, what kind of husband?'

I've never heard Max talk like this before. Maybe he has and I just haven't been there to witness it. Or maybe he hasn't and this is the first time these feelings have found a voice.

'Max, it makes you the kind of husband who doesn't also happen to be a cardiologist. Seriously, you can't actually be blaming yourself for Rach's death? No one knew there was anything wrong with her. No doctors, not her mum, not even Rach herself as far as we know.'

Harriet's right. No one had ever identified that fault line in my most vital of organs. Four and a half thousand beats an hour, over a hundred thousand a day, and yet no one had ever detected that a few of mine – enough to matter – were missing. I try not to get angry about it, about the fact that not a single doctor I'd seen for thirty-six years had ever discovered that critical imperfection. I try but I don't always succeed.

Harriet's right as well that I'd been oblivious to the signs. I'd thought that the shortness of breath and the tiredness and the occasional dizzy spells were the result of nothing more than my own lack of fitness. I'd been promising myself, even as Max and I headed out for dinner that last evening, that I really was going to join a gym. I'm not sure whether it would have made any difference if

I had. I suspect not. I suspect it was already too late by then.

'I can't help thinking, if only we hadn't gone out that night, perhaps she'd still be here now. If only I hadn't ordered that bottle of champagne . . . I was just feeling celebratory, you know, and I'd just wanted us to have a really special evening. Rachel had put up with so much from me in those weeks I was gearing up for the deputy head interview . . . I'd been so preoccupied with the prospect of not getting it and what that would mean. I wasn't sure I'd even stay at the school if they didn't give me the job. And then I got it and all I wanted to do was give Rachel a great evening to thank her for her support. But now I can't stop thinking that if we'd stayed home that night perhaps none of this would have happened.'

'Hey now, Max. You've got to stop thinking like that. You know as well as I do that a single evening out wasn't the difference between life and death. You've got to stop beating yourself up. It's not going to bring Rach back. None of this is your fault, you must know that. You didn't know Rach was ill, you couldn't possibly have known, and so there's nothing you could have done to change what happened.'

'I should have been able to save her.'

Max almost whispers these eight words and by the end of them he seems spent.

These are the moments when I most want to be able to shout through the invisible barrier that separates us, to make my voice heard to Max, to let him know just how little I blame him. To tell him how sorry I am for inflicting this on him. To reassure him – to implore him to believe – that he has nothing whatsoever to feel guilty about. To acknowledge that if anyone should feel guilty it's me; for failing to identify the signs of that internal time bomb, for being unable to save myself, for leaving my husband without a wife and my daughter without a mother.

People say that hindsight is a wonderful thing. It seems to me that the purpose of hindsight is simply to taunt us with our own failings.

Max and Harriet have been sitting in silence for a minute or so now, Harriet's hand resting on the arm of Max's grey suit jacket, him still head bowed, her staring out of the window knowing – rightly – that there are no words of comfort to offer.

'I'm sorry, Harriet. I shouldn't be offloading all of this on you. I'm sure you'd have thought twice about traipsing across town to meet me today if you'd known you were going to be fed a lunch of self-indulgence. God, I hate myself for being like this.'

'For being like what? For being miserable? For grieving? Honestly, Max, I'd think you were weird if you weren't upset today.'

'For not being able to haul myself out of this trench of self-pity. It feels pathetic. I feel pathetic.'

'Max, if there's one thing you don't need to do, it's apologize. To be perfectly frank, I'm surprised we haven't had more of these conversations over the past year. I didn't want to push you and I assumed you were talking all of this over with other people. Have you?'

'Honestly? Not really, no. It hasn't seemed fair to dump it on anyone else. My mum would only worry and Celia would find it too upsetting – it's enough that she's lost her daughter without bearing the emotional brunt of her grieving son-in-law too.'

'What about Connor?'

Max nearly manages a smile.

'That's very generous of you, Harriet, but we both know that my brother doesn't exactly top the emotional literacy charts.'

'Well, you need to talk to someone, Max. You can't keep all of this bottled up.'

'Why not? I thought I was doing everyone a favour by keeping quiet. I think most people would rather talk about any subject under the sun than listen to someone whine on about their grief. I remember when Rachel first died, and it was as if those words – death, dead, died – had been obliterated overnight. People kept saying how sorry they were for my loss as though Rachel were a puppy I'd mislaid in the park and if only I'd put up posters offering a reward perhaps she'd be returned to me. Or they'd say they were sorry that Rachel had gone, as though she'd popped to the shops for a pint of milk and decided on a whim not to come home. It was shocking, really, people's inability to face reality. I was the one dealing with her death and yet no one else could even cope with saying the word out loud. So I think I realized pretty early on that it was my job to make sure other people didn't feel too awkward about the fact that my wife had died.'

Max's voice is seeped in frustration and I want so much to be able to hold him, to soothe him, to stroke the back of his neck until I've caressed away the resentment that's so out of character for him.

I know exactly what he means, though. I remember having the same feelings when my dad died. Half my school friends couldn't even look me in the eye any more, let alone speak to me. Even their parents seemed wary of me, as though death were a contagious disease and proximity to me carried with it the very real danger that their own loved ones might die prematurely, abruptly, in tragic circumstances too.

'Max, don't ever feel that you can't talk to me about Rach. Really. You know how much I miss her too. I'm not suggesting for a second that it's anything close to what you're going through but I can cope with you being miserable now and again.'

'I know, I'm sorry. I suppose I just still haven't got used to the general indifference. In the early days especially I remember the sense of shock that the world could carry on as normal, as though nothing terrible had happened. I couldn't believe other people could go on with their lives ignorant of what I was going through. I'd look at the kids in my classes, or the other teachers in the staff room, or just random strangers walking past me in the street and I'd want to shout at them for going about their daily lives while I couldn't imagine surviving the next second without her. So I suppose I've learnt to shut myself off, keep those feelings private, become indifferent to their indifference.'

'But I'm not indifferent, Max, and I'm not the only one. There are loads of people who'd happily talk to you about Rachel if only you'd let them in.'

'I know you're right. But sometimes I worry that if I start talking about her I may never stop. Every day there are so many things I want to tell Rachel. Things that I know would make her laugh or that she'd find interesting. And then I get angry that I can't switch my brain off, that it keeps allowing me to forget for a few seconds that she's dead, only to punch me in the face with a renewed rush of loss all over again. It's like a Groundhog Day for the grieving.'

'God, I'm not surprised you're exhausted, Max. It sounds exhausting. But it will get better. You know that, don't you? I've no idea when, but it will.'

'Will it? Isn't that just an empty platitude so that people like me have the prospect of a respite from it all? I can't imagine a time when I don't miss her so much that I can barely breathe. It's like I'm living a life in suspended animation, that nothing's real because Rachel's not here to share things with. I feel like I'm in perpetual limbo.'

That's one thing Max and I have in common, that feeling of being stuck in a place we never agreed to go to and from which we can't now escape. And that feeling, too, of needing to share every experience with one another if those experiences are to have even a semblance of verisimilitude.

'You know what you need? You need a change of scenery. Or at least a change of scene. When was the last time you went out for an evening?'

I can answer that. It was, as far as I know, a year ago to the day.

'I haven't felt much like socializing, Harriet. I'm not sure I'd be great company. And anyway, I've got Ellie to think about.'

'Ellie would be asleep if you went out for an evening, Max, and it's not as if your parents wouldn't babysit.

Hasn't Connor tried to get you out with him? Do I need to have a word with that brother of yours?'

'Please don't, Harriet. I'm really not up for a night out right now, particularly of the Connor variety. I'm fine, really. You're just catching me on a particularly bad day.'

'You're clearly anything but fine, Max. Imagine I was telling you about someone who'd lost their wife, who hadn't socialized for a year and who was feeling like their life was stuck in – what was it? – suspended animation. What would your advice be to them? You've got to break out of the limbo, Max. Trust me. You need to try and have some fun.'

'Harriet, I know you mean well, really I do, but believe me when I say I'm just not ready for fun. Not yet.'

'That's because you haven't tried. I think you'd feel guilty if you even contemplated having fun. I think you'd feel it was some kind of betrayal. But it's not. I know it's probably hard to imagine right now but you're going to need to start thinking about moving on – or at least beginning to move on – at some point in the not-too-distant future, Max.'

Max is beginning to disengage from the conversation, I can tell. It's his way of avoiding conflict and it was, I've no doubt, the reason he and I hardly ever rowed in our ten years together. I'd ask him sometimes how he managed it, how he so rarely rose to whatever bait was dangled before him. He'd just smile and tell me, matter-of-factly, that he couldn't see the point in arguments because, in the end, they'd almost always be resolved, so why not just skip the row and head straight for the resolution. I loved him for that logic, and even more so for being able to act successfully on it, time after time.

'Who else other than Connor could you go out with? I'd invite you out for an evening with my friends but we both know you'd hate it. What about all those people who came to Ellie's last birthday party?'

I know what Max is thinking even before he says it.

'They're not people I want to see, Harriet. Please, can we just drop this now?'

'Why don't you want to see them? They all seemed perfectly nice. Not necessarily my cup of tea, admittedly, but just what I'd have thought you need right now.'

Max takes a few seconds to respond. I think he's unclear as to how candid he wants to be.

'I don't want to see them, Harriet. They're people I used to see with Rachel. They're people who remind me of some of the best times I had with Rachel. They're people whose perfect relationships and perfect families make me so envious that I don't even want to be in their presence right now. Do you have any idea how many kids' birthday party invitations I've turned down in the past year? I can't be around other families' happiness right now. I just can't.'

Harriet has the good grace to give Max's outburst a moment's contemplation. But only a moment's.

'Well, in that case, you know what you need? You need some new friends, people who don't remind you of Rach, people who you can go and have fun with and forget about everything else. You know what we should do? We should sign you up to a website where you can meet some new friends.'

Max looks at Harriet incredulously.

'Do you mean a dating site?'

Harriet raises an unintentionally disdainful eyebrow.

'God, Max, stop being so 1990s. They're not just about dating. All those sites are for people who want anything from long-term relationships to friendship. You'd only have to tick the friendship box for now.'

For now? What's Harriet playing at? Isn't she supposed to be my best friend? Why's she encouraging my husband to think about a time when he might be ticking anything other than the friendship box? If this is her idea of providing emotional support, I think both Max and I can survive without it.

'Harriet, I'm sure that works for some people but I can't imagine anything I'd like to do less right now than meet a total stranger in some random pub and spend an evening exchanging dull, polite small talk with them. I find it exhausting enough spending a lunchtime with you, for goodness sake.'

Harriet laughs. I'm not laughing.

'Well, I know you think that right now, but that's because you haven't tried it yet. You're so hopelessly out of the habit of interacting with grown-ups it's no surprise that the prospect of spending an entire evening in the company of someone who's not related to you by blood and is legally old enough to drink scares the living daylights out of you.'

Max allows Harriet a smile. He probably doesn't realize how dangerous that is, how much encouragement it will give her.

'I really am only thinking about what's best for you, Max. What's best for you and Ellie. And I do think you need to start focussing on the future, be proactive about your life again, start thinking about moving on. I don't suspect either of us imagines Rach would want to see your life frozen in suspended animation forever, would she?'

Forever's a long time, Harriet. I've only been dead a year and I'm just not ready for Max to move on – whatever that means, to whatever that is – just yet.

'Harriet, I know you mean well, really I do. But if you're seriously asking me what I think Rachel would have wanted, I think she'd have wanted me to be allowed to grieve in my own good time. I'm not ready to embrace a life without her and neither is Ellie.'

Thank you, Max. Thank you for knowing me better even in death than anyone else knew me when I was alive.

'Okay, okay. I give in. For now, anyway. But I can't promise not to mention it again. So do think about it. You don't want to leave it too long or I may have to establish your social life as my personal project, and I'm woman enough to know that's the last thing you want.'

Max laughs. He's never been one for holding grudges, even when his opponent is a Harriet-shaped bull in a grief-ridden china shop.

'So, when are you going to come and see Ellie? It's been nearly three weeks and she misses you.'

'Well, if I forgive the blatant change of subject, it's not going to be for a fortnight or so, I'm afraid. I've got a hellish case on at the moment but it'll be over in a couple of weeks so some time that last weekend in May?'

'Perfect – that's the beginning of half term. Come for Sunday lunch. Ellie will love that.'

The perfect Sunday lunch. What I'd give for just one more of those.

There's a sudden loud clatter, so immediate I assume it must have come from my world rather than theirs. I look around and above me, squinting my eyes in a bid to stretch my field of vision far into the void beyond, unsure whether I'm hoping to discover something or nothing, fearful of what an intruder may bring into my solitary, lonely, vicarious world. I call out into the vacuum, my voice filled with the ambivalent combination of hope and fear, unsure of what I'll do should my entreaties be returned. But there's nothing and no one there. Just another momentary fantasy that I may not be alone.

When I return my gaze to the café below to investigate the cause of the calamity, I discover that the living world has disappeared, replaced by three hundred and sixty degrees of nothingness.

# CHAPTER 3

Ellie and Max are standing in front of my gravestone. It's a beautiful late spring afternoon, the cherry blossom only just beginning to scatter like confetti on to the grass, the sun still suspended above the trees as if auditioning for the months ahead.

Ellie is clutching a bunch of pink peonies, holding on to them tightly as though they're a newly acquired security blanket. I wonder if she remembers that they're my favourite or whether her choosing them at the florist on the way here was nothing more than a coincidence.

Max and I had peonies at our wedding – white rather than pink but peonies nonetheless. I'd have chosen peonies for my funeral too, had I had the forethought or the self-indulgence to write a plan for the final party I'd inadvertently host. Instead I had roses chosen by my mum, or rather agonized over by her, as if to pick the wrong flower might have undone a lifetime's good parenting.

I don't think Max has brought Ellie here since the funeral. I think that's the right decision. The funeral had overwhelmed her. I'm not sure she quite understood what was happening or why she was there or the fact that her mummy's body was laid out inert in the big box at the end of the church. I think it was other people's grief that had disturbed her, the sight of all those adults in tears turning the world as she knew it on its head. She'd clung, silently,

34

to the hands of Max and my mum throughout, as though in the midst of an earthquake and all she wanted was for the ground to stop shaking beneath her feet.

It's one of life's great paradoxical fantasies, isn't it, the desire to be present at one's own funeral? To hear eulogies composed by heartbroken relatives and read by fractured voices emerging from tear-stained faces. To discover the plethora of humankind's virtues attributed to you and to learn your value to those who had so often failed to proclaim it during your lifetime. It's supposed to be the moment, isn't it, when all the various elements of your life coalesce to provide the one true, fully formed picture of you that will ever exist? A picture of life from the cradle to the grave.

I'd been unprepared, though, as I'd hovered above the altar with a bird's eye view of a congregation in mourning, for just how wretched it would be, witnessing the people I most loved and cared about in distress. Particularly when one of the distraught was my six-year-old daughter. Far from being a moment to revel in the collective approbation of my all-too-short existence, it had been a day on which I'd cursed my access ever having been granted.

'How are you doing, munchkin? You're not feeling too scared are you?'

Ellie shakes her head unconvincingly, reduced to shyness in these unfamiliar surroundings.

'Do you want to give Mummy the flowers you got her? She's going to love those, you know – they're so pretty. Shall we put them on her grave?'

Ellie doesn't move except to cling ever tighter to Max's leg. Max hauls her into his arms, where her head rests on his neck and the peonies embrace him.

'I think Mummy would like it if we gave her the flowers. Do you want me to put them down for you?'

Ellie nods, tentatively, unsure whether that's the right answer. Max prises the flowers from her fingers, bends down with Ellie still in his arms, and rests the flowers against my headstone.

'They look pretty, don't they? I think Mummy will think you've chosen really well.'

Ellie pulls her head up to look at Max.

'Will Mummy come to look at the flowers later, after we've gone?'

Max lets out an achingly pained breath, seeming to fill the air around him with the sorrow of someone who knows they're destined to disappoint.

'No, sweetheart. Mummy can't come back any more. Do you remember? That's why we had the funeral, when we came here last time with Granny and Grandpa and Nanna and all our friends, so we could all say goodbye to her.'

Ellie looks thoughtful. I wonder whether she's trying to remember or trying to forget.

'But if she's not going to come later then how's she going to see the flowers?'

Max eyes Ellie intently, as if assessing the avenues of response open to him.

'Well, some people believe that after you die, some part of you still lives on and that maybe, although we can't see people who've died, they might still be able to see and hear us.'

'Like ghosts?'

'Not really like ghosts, no. Because you're scared of ghosts, aren't you? Whereas you'd never be scared of Mummy, would you?'

Ellie looks confused. I wonder how long she's been contemplating these questions, whether they're only coming to mind now because of the gravestones surrounding her, or whether she's been bottling up these existential enquiries for the past twelve months.

'Do you think Mummy can hear us?'

Max hesitates, and I wait to see which path he'll choose: the path of honesty, a route which he knows will make Ellie even sadder than she already is, or the path of benign reassurance.

'It would be nice to think so, wouldn't it? The thing is, sweetheart, we can never really know, so we should keep on talking to her if that makes us feel better, don't you think?'

Ellie runs her hands absent-mindedly through Max's hair, her head still nestled against his shoulder, her eyes darting rapidly from one impossible question to the next.

'Why did my mummy die and other mummies don't die?'

It's a question asked in the most plaintive of voices, as if Ellie knows even before Max replies that there's no comprehensible answer.

'We've talked about this before, haven't we, sweetheart? Do you remember? Mummy had a poorly heart and that's why she died. But I don't know why her heart was poorly when other mummies' hearts are okay. It was just really, really unlucky.'

Ellie pauses for a second, as if to digest Max's uncertainty and contemplate her response.

'Georgia at school, she said that her mummy says mummies don't die if you're good because God only punishes bad people. Did Mummy die 'cos I did something bad?'

I'd weep if my anger didn't intervene. Instead, the shock of other people's insensitivity continues to astound me, even from an entire lifetime away.

'Which one's Georgia? Do I know her?'

The tensing of Max's jaw betrays the fact that he's as incensed as I am. I remember Georgia, not because Ellie's particularly good friends with her, but because her mother was always a domineering force in the playground. The kind of parent who views all other children as impediments to their own child's success. I never liked her.

'She's in my class. She doesn't sit on my table but she's in the red team for PE like me.'

'And she said that to you? When?'

'The other day when we were doing games.'

'Well, she's talking rubbish, angel. I promise you – I promise you with all my heart – that Mummy didn't die because of anything you did. I know it's really hard to understand and I can't promise you that you'll ever understand it completely, but I can promise you that none of this is your fault. Can you believe that for me, Ellie? Please?'

Max holds Ellie tight in his arms as if only by fusing her body to his can he protect her from the emotional elements.

Ellie pulls away from him.

'But Georgia said that if I was really good then maybe Mummy would come home.'

Grief and impotence combine to create the Molotov of emotional cocktails. I know I'm dead and yet still it's incomprehensible to me that I'm powerless to shield Ellie from the toxicity of others' stupidity.

'Sweetheart, you have to trust me. Georgia doesn't know what she's talking about. Will you promise me that next time Georgia or anyone else says anything about Mummy you come and tell me straight away so that we can talk about it?'

Max is unable to hide his annoyance. Not with Ellie, but with Georgia and her mum and all the other people with their injurious proclamations from whom he can't protect Ellie, despite his best intentions.

Ellie doesn't pick up on Max's frustration. She's too lost in her own world of confusion.

'But does that mean Mummy's really never coming home? Really never? Not even if I brush my teeth every night and every morning and go to bed on time and keep my room really, really tidy?'

Ellie looks at Max pleadingly, willing him not to destroy her most precious of fantasies. I wonder who wishes the most that he didn't have to: Ellie, Max or me? I also wonder if this is why she's been so well-behaved these past few months, whether she's been engaged in a private pact, drawing an invisible correlation between her own good behaviour and the likelihood of my return.

'Sweetheart, you have no idea how much I want to be able to tell you that Mummy will come back to us one day.

I wish it were true as much as you do. I'm sorry, sweetheart, really I am. But you've just got to remember, Mummy loved you so much and you still have lots of people who love you and we'll always be here for you.'

Max squeezes Ellie's limp body even tighter. She doesn't seem to have the will to hug him back.

'But if you couldn't stop Mummy from dying then how do you know you won't die too?'

It's the sixty-four million dollar question and it's taken a year for her to ask it but now that she has I can't help worrying that it may have been preying on her mind all this time. I hate to think of her connecting the two, fearing the worst, imagining her own orphanhood. I hate it because I know how terrifying it is. I'm not sure at what age one stops feeling that to lose both parents would be the most painful of abandonments. I don't think I'd quite got there by the time I died, even as a grown woman with a child of my own.

'I'm not going anywhere, angel, I promise.'

'But how do you know?'

'I just know, sweetheart. There's no way I'm leaving you, not for a very long time.'

Sometimes lying to your children is the only option. The kindest option. Or the selfish option, the one which allows you to keep the grief-stricken wolves from your family's door just a little longer.

'If Mummy's really never coming home again then will I ever get a new mummy? Like Tom got after his mummy moved to Australia?'

Ellie's question jolts every fibre of my defunct being in a single, debilitating instant.

*Tell her, Max, please tell her no.*

'Sweetheart, people only ever have one mummy. And yours loved you very, very much. No one can ever replace her, and we'll never forget her, will we?'

Ellie shakes her head vigorously. There are tears in her eyes. Mine too.

Perhaps Max was right; perhaps it was selfish of him to bring her. Selfish of us both to want her company here today.

I probably should have known better, shouldn't I? I was three years older than Ellie when my dad died but my memories are still sharp enough for me to recall those feelings of confusion and fear and doubt. So perhaps I should have known that Ellie's presence here today would reignite the emotional flames, that it would rekindle the unanswerable questions, that it would reprise the endless whys.

Sometimes I wonder whether it's a help or a hindrance that I've been through the same experience as Ellie, whether it renders my empathy more poignant or simply more comprehensible. I think perhaps I was luckier than her in many ways because at least I had someone to blame. I could direct all my anger towards the middle-aged drunk who got into his car that Saturday afternoon after a liquid lunch in the local pub and, moments later, failed to stop at the red light of the pedestrian crossing that my dad just happened to be walking over at that very moment. Ellie doesn't have that. I can't imagine what she'll do with her blame, once she's old enough for the anger and the resentment to kick in. Perhaps there's some way Max can mitigate against her ever having those feelings. I hope there is. I don't want her ever to know that rage.

Max puts Ellie back on her feet and gently wipes away her tears. He leans a hand against my headstone. I almost believe I can feel his tear-stained fingers on my face.

'I've got an idea.'

Max is speaking brightly now, clearly wanting to change the tone of this visit. Would that he could, or else Ellie may never want to return.

'Why don't you tell Mummy what you've been doing at school today?'

Ellie looks relieved to have some guidance but not altogether convinced about the suggestion on offer.

'But how do we know if Mummy can hear us?'

'Well, we don't. But I'd like to hear about your day anyway.'

Ellie holds on to Max's hand as she begins to talk, her words directed in turn between the daddy by her side and the headstone in front of her.

'Well, today we had PE and Miss Collins was telling us about Sports Day and me and Megan want to do the race where you tie your legs together but Miss Collins says she's going to put all our names in a hat.'

'That's the three-legged race, isn't it munchkin?'

'Yes, the three-legs race. And then we did Art and Miss Collins told us to draw a picture of our favourite animal so I did a white rabbit but then there was nothing for me to colour in so I coloured him pink.'

White rabbits. Max was reading her *Alice in Wonderland* at bedtime last week. She was mesmerized by it, her fascination with rabbit holes and magic potions and returns from another world perhaps provoking some of her questions today.

'And why don't you tell Mummy about the spelling test you did this morning? You did so well, didn't you angel?'

'Well, we had to learn ten words and Daddy tested me every day after dinner for a whole week and when we had to do them in class I got them all right. Miss Collins gave me a gold star and a smiley face sticker for my jumper. See?'

Ellie leans towards my gravestone and pulls her bottle-green sticker-adorned jumper towards it, as if showing her trophies to a living being rather than an inanimate lump of granite.

I'm here, sweetheart, and I'm so, so proud of you.

'Is there anything else you'd like to tell Mummy?'

'Erm . . . I don't think so.'

'Well then, how about we play a game?'

Ellie's eyes light up. Max sits down, cross-legged, on the grass in front of my headstone and pulls Ellie on to his lap.

'Why don't we play a game where we each have to say something we love best about Mummy. Listen, I'll go first. I love Mummy's meringues, the ones with all the gooey cream in the middle and the strawberries on top and the special raspberry sauce round the edge.'

Ellie thinks for a few seconds, brow furrowed with concentration, as though it's critically important that she recalls the best possible memory.

'I love Mummy's roast potatoes.'

It's true. She did always love my roast potatoes. Max keeps trying to recreate them but he always forgets the drizzle of lemon juice. Everything else he remembers – the onion, the garlic, the fresh rosemary, the salt and pepper –

but never the fresh lemon. Ellie keeps gently reminding him of his omission, telling him that they're 'almost perfect, just not quite', as if painfully, unconsciously aware of the necessary encouragement she's giving Max for his unexpected, new-found role in their lives.

'I love Mummy's singing and how she makes up words when she doesn't know the lyrics so she ends up singing a lot of gibberish.'

'Gibberish. That's funny.'

Ellie giggles infectiously and then goes quiet for a second, seemingly lost in her own world of memories.

'I love Mummy reading me bedtime stories and doing the silly voices of all the people in the book.'

'Yes, Mummy's story voices are the best. You're good at story voices too, sweetheart. Mummy always said you'd be a good actress, didn't she? Oh, I've thought of another one. I love Mummy's hair when she's just washed it and it goes all curly and bouncy.'

'And I love Mummy painting my nails. Especially when she does my fingers and my toes all matching. Pink and red are best. They smell nice too. Can you paint my nails when we get home, Daddy?'

'I can try but I think you might be better off asking Granny to do it for you later. You know one of the things I love best about Mummy? Her laugh and the way her eyes go all crinkly when she smiles. Although she never liked me saying that. She thought I meant she looked old and had wrinkles. But Mummy never had wrinkles, did she, munchkin?'

'No. Mummy was the most beautiful mummy in the whole world ever.'

If there are a million ways to break a heart, then hearing myself relegated to the past tense has to be one of the most painful. And listening to the people I love best honouring the simplest quotidian pleasures of our shared lives one of the most bittersweet.

I wipe away the tears that are blurring my view, only to discover that they're not alone in obscuring the scene before me.

As the white mist gathers, I leave Max and Ellie sitting in front of my headstone embracing one another with memories, while the last of the day's sunshine begins to fade, casting my inscription into shadow.

# CHAPTER 4

Max's dad is watching *Channel 4 News* as Max's mum comes down the stairs from where she's been tucking Ellie into bed after an early dinner. It had been right of Joan and Ralph to invite themselves over tonight. I'd been unsure when Joan had suggested it last week, wondering whether it might be important for Max and Ellie to be allowed time on their own together today. But after their trip to the cemetery earlier, I think they both needed the kind of oxygenation that only fresh company could provide. Anything else and they'd have been in danger of becoming locked together in a hermetically sealed world of mourning.

Joan brought over a home-made lasagne, one of Ellie's favourites. She brings them supper two or three nights a week usually, not to eat with Max and Ellie but simply by way of culinary support. We could never have envisaged when we moved to Acton eight years ago, pregnant and craving stability, just how important Joan and Ralph's proximity would eventually become. I'd been ambivalent about returning to Max's childhood suburb, fearful of the ramifications of living quite so close to my in-laws and nervous that it would forever feel like we were camping in their back garden rather than establishing grown-up lives of our own. And I had, in all honesty, been concerned about the message it would send to Joan, the mother who could never quite believe that Max and his brother weren't in need of her daily involvement in their lives any more.

When Max and I were first dating I was surprised and, occasionally, irked by just how often his mobile phone would ring only to reveal his mum's name flashing up yet again. I couldn't understand why she wouldn't allow her boys to be men, to fly the nest without wanting to ride on their wings, to acknowledge that she was feeding her own desire for closeness, not theirs.

But I didn't have Ellie then.

Because then Ellie arrived to turn our own lives upside down and I realized that I'd known nothing about motherhood until that moment, nothing of that deep, primal, inarticulable drive to safeguard your child and ensure their happiness. And I'll never know now what kind of parent I'd have been to Ellie in her twenties, thirties, forties, whether I'd have encouraged her independence as Max and I always vowed we would, or whether I'd have given in to those urges towards protectiveness too.

But our return to Max's old stomping ground swiftly transpired to be the best move we could possibly have made given that Ellie's birth brought with it the realization that there's simply no overestimating the importance of a family network for first-time parents. We relied on Joan and Ralph more than I'd ever imagined. And then I died and their presence three streets away gained a value that none of us could ever have predicted.

Because here they are, in my sitting room as they're so often to be found, on a day when Max and Ellie need them most.

Ralph moves from the sofa to the armchair, an action which may be motivated by the fact that it's the seat closest to the television or it may be because it's the chair furthest away from where Joan is grilling Max about his current state of emotional well-being.

'So, love, how was it today? Did Ellie cope all right? She seemed fine this evening, all things considered.'

'I don't know, Mum. We ended up having quite a tough conversation. Ellie was asking about whether Rachel was ever coming home so I explained everything to her again. But if I'm honest I felt like a bit of a fraud. Even I still fantasize about Rachel coming back one day so I don't know how I'm supposed to convince Ellie she's not.'

'I'm sure you did just the right thing. You mustn't be too hard on yourself.'

'But that's just it. I feel like I never know whether I'm doing the right thing any more. I've no idea if going to the cemetery was a good idea, whether it's right to keep reminding Ellie or whether it just emphasizes the fact that Rachel's not here any more.'

'Of course it's right, Max. It's about honouring Rachel's life, and that's exactly what you did today. I'm sure Ellie will be grateful for it in years to come. How long did you stay?'

'About an hour in the end. I got Ellie to tell Rachel about what she'd been up to at school. I just felt like she needed something . . . I don't know . . . active to do. But I think it might have confused her even more, the idea of talking to someone who's not really there, who can't talk back. She did it though. You should have seen her, Mum. She was so sweet, holding on to my hand, chatting away. She really is amazing.'

'She's a treasure, Max. And you're doing wonders with her. I know you don't like me telling you, but I'm ever so proud of you.'

Max's humble gratitude is conveyed with one of his goosebump-inducing smiles and I'm transported back in an instant to the very first time I saw that smile, grinning at me across the table at a friend's wedding, one of those tables tucked away in the far corner of the marquee reserved exclusively for singletons who come without even the hint of a plus-one to accompany them. Max had caught my eye pretty early on, that smile drawing my attention towards him despite the littering of flowers, glassware and rapidly depleting wine bottles between us, the two of us exchanging the kind of silent, visual communications usually reserved for husbands, wives or – at the very least – lovers, an unspoken flirtation all the more exciting for its surreptitiousness. Max had been the life and soul of that table of strangers, delivering wry observations on the day's events, cracking jokes and creating an atmosphere of inclusion to an occasion that can so often leave one feeling like nothing more than an extra on a film set.

It was only later, when we knew one another infinitely better, that I learnt how out of character it had been for him, how Max would never willingly place himself centre stage at a social gathering, how he'd done it purely in the hope of attracting my attention.

I think I'd fallen a little bit in love with him there and then.

'It's just a suggestion, love, but have you thought about taking up a hobby, something to get you out of the house a bit? Why don't you do some photography again? You used to be so good at taking photos.'

It's true. Max is a brilliant photographer. He never used to go anywhere without his trusted Canon. He must have taken thousands – literally thousands – of photographs of Ellie and me over the years. I haven't seen him pick up his camera once since I died, not even to take a picture of Ellie.

'I don't think so, Mum.'

'Why not? Think of all those lovely pictures you took of Rachel. Some of those are good enough to be professional.'

'Because they're pointless, Mum. They're pointless, pathetic lies.'

'What do you mean? Don't be silly. They're lovely memories, those photos.'

'But they're not going to bring her back, are they? If you want the truth, I can't stand to look at them these days. It's as though the more I look at photos, the less I can remember Rachel as a real person. I hate them for reducing her to nothing more than a hollow image on a piece of paper. I'd burn the lot of them if it weren't for Ellie.'

There's a ferocity in Max's voice that I suspect has shocked Joan as much as me. I wish I could be real for him once more, to stroke his warm naked skin, skin that never seemed to chill even on the coldest day, and to kiss the lids of his eyes which he once said was like me kissing directly into his soul.

'I'm sorry, love. I didn't mean to upset you. I just thought it might be . . . I don't know . . . therapeutic for you to do something you were so good at, something to take your mind off things. I just worry about you, you know I do, and I think it would do you good if you got out and about a bit more. Maybe you could see some of your old friends? You haven't had an evening out for ages.'

Twice in one day. There are provocations that not even Max's legendary calm can withstand.

'Really, Mum? You really want to have this conversation, today of all days? What is it with you and Harriet? I've had her on my case all lunchtime haranguing me with unsolicited advice about moving on. I promise you, both of you, when I'm ready to start doing whatever it is you think I should be doing a year after the death of my wife, you'll be the first to know.'

Joan looks taken aback. I'm not surprised. I don't remember him ever raising his voice to her before. She's touched a nerve rawer than any of us knew it to be.

'There's no need to jump down my throat, Max. I'm only trying to help.'

A wave of guilt washes over Max's face.

'I know, Mum. I'm sorry. I shouldn't have got angry. I suppose I've just had my fill of uninvited suggestions today, what with Harriet and now you.'

A look of irresistible curiosity peeks above the parapet in Joan's eyes.

'So what's Harriet been saying now? Don't tell me — she's been meddling in things that don't concern her yet again.'

This is a conversational opportunity I wouldn't expect Joan to relinquish lightly. I've never quite understood the mutual enmity between my best friend and my mother-in-law, whether it emanates from a simple generational

51

misunderstanding or a deeper disapproval of each other's life choices: the conventionality that's so unpalatable to Harriet, the childlessness that's incomprehensible to Joan. There've been many a family get-together when Joan's comments have veered just an inch too far over the line of social acceptability, or when Harriet's barbed retorts have threatened to shatter the veneer of collective harmony, forcing Max or I to intervene. I wonder whether their paths cross at all these days.

'Believe it or not, she was saying exactly what you just said: that it's time I started thinking about moving on, that I need to get out more, that I need to find new friends. She seems to think I should join a website where I can meet new people – a dating website, basically. It's okay – I've made it crystal clear to her that she's barking up the wrong tree.'

Joan looks thoughtful for a second before patting a maternal hand on Max's knee.

'Max, I know Harriet can be a bit tactless, but I don't think her suggestion's complete nonsense. I mean, would it do you any harm to meet some new people and have a bit of fun?'

I'm not sure what's more shocking: Joan actually agreeing with Harriet or my former mother-in-law advocating that my husband join a dating agency on the first anniversary of my unexpected departure from their lives.

'Are you being serious?'

'Well, why not? It's not good for you, cooped up at home every weekend.'

'I'm not cooped up. Ellie and I get out and about plenty at weekends.'

'I don't mean with Ellie. I mean by yourself, with other adults. You're still a young man, you know. You've got your whole life ahead of you.'

'Honestly, I can't believe I'm hearing this. I can't believe anyone's suggesting I so much as contemplate dating again, least of all Harriet and least of all you. I'll say to you what I said to Harriet: I'm not ready and I think it's much too early — for me, for Ellie and for Rachel.'

Joan raises a defensive eyebrow.

'Well, since you've brought her up, do you think it's best for Ellie, you shutting yourself away like this? I worry about her, really I do, Max. It's hard enough that the poor little mite hasn't got any siblings to share all this with. I think it would do her good if you had some friends over now and again.'

For the few seconds it takes Max to respond, I panic that he's going to tell her, that he's going to divulge the story I most want him to keep sacred. It's our secret, one I don't want him to share with anyone, ever. The fourteen months of trying and not succeeding, of deluding ourselves, month after month, that this would be the time. The plotting of dates and the obsessive observation of a sign, any sign, that this month we may not have let one another down. It was never the recurrent defeat that depressed us, it was the continued hope. Towards the end I'd spend hours on the internet, frustrated that no one could give me a simple remedy, berating myself that our decision to delay a second child, to allow Ellie time to savour us on her own, might now result in her never having siblings at all.

And so now there's that guilt too, to add to the guilt about deserting Max and abandoning Ellie, the guilt that I've left Ellie not only without a mother but without a brother or sister with whom to share this burden. I've been an only child dealing with my own grief alongside the premature responsibility for a parent's well-being and I wouldn't have knowingly inflicted it on Ellie for anything.

'Fine, Mum. If it'll get you off my case, I'll have a think about it.'

He'll have a think about it? Surely he's just saying that to placate her, to bring the conversation to an end, to minimize the opportunity for further disagreement? He can't actually mean it. Can he?

'Really, Max, will you? Because I think it would do you good. I wouldn't be pushing you if I didn't think so. Maybe Harriet's right, maybe one of those online websites might be a good idea. I mean, it can't hurt to meet some new people, can it?'

That depends. It depends on whether you're the dead wife of the man everyone's cajoling into dating other women under the auspices of him making some new friends. Then it might hurt a bit.

'Honestly, Mum. I'm not going to pretend I'm ready yet but I will think about what you've said. For goodness sake, if you and Harriet are agreeing on something then there might actually be some truth in it.'

The shock destabilizes me with a vertiginous blow that leaves me desperate to hold on to something but in the full knowledge that there's not a single tangible object within imaginable reach.

How can Max even begin to contemplate moving on in that way? How can he even suggest he might think about it? How can he not know that it's much, much too soon?

His words course through me like an electrical charge, straight into the chest that used to house my faulty heart. I never imagined that the dead could feel pain, physical or emotional. I feel like I never knew anything until now.

I close my eyes tightly, willing myself away, and for once the worlds cooperate.

For the first time in a year, I understand the full horror of dying. It's not just the guilt and the abandonment and the loss. It's the realization that I'm on my own. That my loneliness isn't imagined or exaggerated but is fuelled by the absence of the glue that secures each and every human bond: the bond of empathy. And it's the knowledge – the shocking knowledge that's only just hitting me now – that my life, love and relationships won't be preserved in aspic just because I'm not there any more.

It turns out that the only thing more unexpected than dying prematurely is the unpredictability of the life you leave behind.

# Denial

# CHAPTER 5

As the empty void gives way to reveal the activities of the living world, I see that my daughter and her godmother are in the back garden of the house I used to call home. They're playing a game involving a blindfolded Harriet and an overexcited Ellie running literal rings around her as Ellie giggles irrepressibly, refusing to be caught. The air must be as warm as it is bright, given Ellie's bare feet flitting over the lawn's freshly cut grass and the pale, smooth skin of her uncovered arms flapping energetically in the breeze.

She's wearing one of my favourite outfits, a knee-length jersey dress in navy blue decorated with tiny white butterflies, a dress that might be nondescript if it weren't hanging gracefully from the lithe limbs of my beautiful girl. Her long brown curls bounce in time with her body as she gambols from one foot to the other, her cheeks flushed with exertion. If I was down there rather than up here I'd scoop her into my arms and kiss her neck a hundred times, Ellie counting each and every one to ensure I didn't miss a single caress, just as we've done innumerable times before.

'You can't catch me, Hetty!'

Ellie's the only person I've known who's ever been permitted to give Harriet a nickname. Harriet pretends she merely tolerates it but I think, secretly, she rather loves the special moniker created by – and reserved exclusively for use by – her goddaughter.

'I don't doubt you're right, gorgeous girl. Do you think you might have had enough of this game yet?'

Harriet pulls the blindfold from her eyes as if to answer her own rhetorical question, although the tone of her voice infers the likely response.

'Oh. Put the blindfold back on, Hetty, or it's too easy for you to get me.'

'I'm not sure that's true, darling, not in these heels.'

'Take your shoes off and then you'll be able to run faster. The grass feels all lovely and tickly between my toes.'

Harriet laughs.

'I'd rather not put dirty feet back into these little beauties, if it's all the same to you. Do you like them? I treated myself to them yesterday.'

Ellie squats down to inspect the shoes more closely. She's always been fascinated by Harriet's extensive footwear collection, spending countless happy hours ensconced in the floor-to-ceiling shoe cupboard in Harriet's dressing room, a methodically catalogued selection of over a hundred designer pairs resembling something out of a fashion magazine. Sometimes Ellie and I used to retreat to Harriet's on weekend afternoons when our sitting room played host to the screening of a football match. Harriet would let Ellie loose in that cupboard and she'd put on a show for us, shuffling across varnished wooden floorboards in shoes too big with heels too high for her little body to balance on, describing in the meticulous detail of a five-year-old the defining features of whichever pairs she'd chosen to model for us that afternoon. I remember, on those cosy afternoons, thinking how lucky Ellie was to have Harriet in her life and how much I'd have loved to have someone like her around when I was growing up: the not-quite-aunt who's nonetheless so much more.

'Mmm, they're quite nice. I like the colour. I'm not sure about that pattern, though. They're not my favourite.'

'Well I'm very sorry to hear that, young lady. I'll endeavour to choose ones more to your liking next time.'

Harriet grabs Ellie under the arms and swings her into the air, causing Ellie to dissolve into uncontrollable, unselfconscious giggles.

They're lucky to have each other, those two.

'Come on, Hetty. Just one more go. *Please.*'

'Oh go on then, you little tyrant. How could I possibly refuse?'

Harriet blindfolds herself and begins to totter precariously towards the ever-changing direction of Ellie's laughter. I'm not sure if it's the game Ellie's finding amusing or the sight of Harriet teetering around the garden on three-inch Jimmy Choos in a Diane von Furstenberg dress. Either way, it's indicative of Ellie's powers of persuasion that she's got Harriet playing this game in the first place. That or it's proof of Harriet's adoration for her goddaughter. Or, more likely, it's a combination of the two.

Ellie's teasing Harriet, poking her from different angles and then running away out of reach until finally Harriet manages to grab her arm and keep hold of her long enough for this round to be over.

'Right, that's my lot, madam. I'm afraid this godmother needs a cup of coffee and some room-temperature oxygen in her lungs.'

Harriet pulls off the blindfold to discover Ellie already presenting her tried-and-tested disgruntled pose: arms folded, head down, brow furrowed and lips pursed in a caricature of what she thinks disappointment should look like. It's an expression I always failed to resist because it made me laugh so much I'd feel it was churlish then to refuse whatever she wanted.

'Awww. But I don't want to go inside yet. Just one more go? Please. I'll let you catch me much quicker this time, I promise.'

'Now, gorgeous girl, you might be in possession of persuasive techniques that would put most lawyers to shame but I'm afraid you've met your match here. Maybe we'll play some more after lunch. Why don't you run around here for a bit and burn off some of that incomprehensible energy. We'll call you when lunch is ready, okay?'

Harriet kisses Ellie on the top of her head before joining Max in the kitchen where he's in the process of basting a tray of potatoes. I love seeing Max in the 'Keep Calm and Carry On Cooking' apron that I bought him for his birthday as a joke a few years ago – a joke because back then his food preparation skills extended to emptying a tin of microwaved beans on to two slices of heavily buttered toast and referring to it as cooking. I'd never have believed it if someone had told me then that here he'd be now, oven gloves in hand, overseeing the roasting of a leg of lamb coated with fresh garlic and rosemary, just one dish on his long list of newly mastered culinary achievements.

'Bloody hell, where on earth do kids get all their energy from? I'm knackered and I've only been out there for half an hour.'

'More like fifteen minutes, Harriet. But it's true. And children are pretty shrewd when it comes to coercing their godparents into playing energetic outdoor games with them on a Sunday morning.'

'Very funny. You know I can never resist her. And so does she, unfortunately. Honestly, I don't know how you do it. A ninety-hour week in the office is a breeze compared to a weekend of full-on childcare. It makes you wonder whether there's something ever so slightly insane about the desire to have kids, especially people who do it on their own.'

Harriet pauses long enough for the tactless penny to drop.

'God, I'm sorry, Max. I'm such a klutz. Just ignore me, will you, and I'll try to think before I speak for the rest of the day.'

Max laughs as he returns lunch to the oven.

'I don't think we can expect you to change the habit of a lifetime in a single day, Harriet. Don't worry about it. You're right — it is totally exhausting. Sometimes I find myself wondering if I'll ever have the energy to go to bed after nine o'clock ever again.'

'Ah, well, speaking of which, there's something I wanted to discuss with you. You know what we were talking about a few weeks ago? You know, the blindingly obvious fact that if you don't engage in some kind of adult interaction soon, you're going to turn into the sort of strange old man whose house children are scared to walk in front of after dark?'

I probably could have guessed that Harriet wasn't going to let this one lie. I love her to bits, really I do, but I suppose you don't get to be as successful as she is by giving in gracefully to the first sign of opposition.

'How could I forget, Harriet? And I did think about it, honestly, but my feelings haven't changed. I'm just not ready for that yet.'

A wave of relief surfs over me. I've spent the past fortnight fearful he was going to reach a different conclusion. I should have known better. I should have known Max better.

'Yes, I know what you said, but that doesn't mean you're right. Anyway, I figured that since you're probably not going to do anything about it yourself, I'd better do something about it for you.'

'God, what have you done, Harriet? Please don't tell me you've fixed me up with one of your terrifying lawyer friends? If you have, you'll just have to cancel it. I'm not going.'

'Don't be ridiculous, Max. I'm not that stupid – even I know that would be a date from hell for you. No, I've taken the smallest of baby steps. Not even you can object, really.'

I wouldn't bank on it. I object, your honour, and I don't even know what the crime is yet.

'Enough with the suspense, Harriet. What've you done?'

I'm not sure whether I want to know or whether I'd prefer to remain in the kind of blissful ignorance that doesn't involve overhearing my best friend discussing possible dating strategies for my widowed husband. It's a bit like overhearing your parents talk about the intricacies of their sex life; it just simply shouldn't ever happen.

'Well, you probably won't know this given that you and Rachel started dating practically before the internet was even invented, but there's this really great introduction website where you don't have to do a thing. Well, not yet anyway. I do it all for you. It's a site where people recommend their friends – write their profile and tell the virtual world how wonderful they are, so that you're spared the embarrassing bit I know you'd hate. All you have to do is wait for the hordes of women who'll be drawn to my exceptionally eloquent and glowing portrayal of you to get in contact. And then you take your pick. It's genius. What's not to like?'

Harriet beams at Max with the sense of triumph I imagine crosses her face every time she wins a case. Except Max looks less than ecstatic.

'Harriet, it may well be the world's greatest website but I'm just not interested. If it's that fantastic I'm sure it'll still be up-and-running in a few years' time when I might actually be ready to start considering all that stuff.'

'I knew you'd say that. Which is why, in anticipation of that auspicious day, I went ahead and created a profile for you.'

You did *what?*

'You did what?'

'Don't be mad. It's not like you can't take it down if you really hate it. But I think it might just give you the proverbial kick up the butt you need.'

Max's shock gives way to annoyance before morphing into an expression that's as close to anger as Max ever gets.

'Take it down, Harriet. Right now. You can't go around doing stuff like that without even telling me.'

'I'm telling you now, aren't I? I didn't tell you before because I knew you'd be weird about it. Just come and take a look. Aren't you even a little bit intrigued to know what I wrote about you?'

'No I'm not, Harriet. In case you can't tell, I'm not exactly over the moon you've done it at all.'

'Well, you might be a bit miffed now, but wait till I tell you how popular you are with the ladies. I only put it up on Friday night and when I checked this morning you already had four messages. Four messages, Max. That's pretty damn good, especially for someone your age.'

Max breathes deeply as he puts a pan of water on the stove to boil.

'Harriet, please just take it down. Right now. And we'll pretend it didn't happen. I know you think you're trying to help but you've got to allow me to do things my own way, in my own time.'

'Okay, okay, but at least let me read out what I wrote about you first. You must be just the tiniest bit curious.'

Before Max has a chance to protest, Harriet pulls out her phone and begins tapping away with a focus that clearly signals she has no intention of capitulating to any opposition.

'Okay, here goes. *I've known Max for eleven years. He might be a bit uptight and he can sometimes be a party pooper and if you get him started on the War of the Roses he may never stop, but he's solvent, sane (mostly) and stable and, quite honestly, what more can you expect of a bloke who's only just the right side of forty? Give him a nudge and see if you can't relight his fire.* There you go. What do you think?'

Max looks as flabbergasted as I feel.

'You didn't seriously put that up about me? In a public place? What if someone I know sees it, someone from school? For god's sake, Harriet, what on earth were you thinking?'

'Of course I didn't write that, you idiot. What do you take me for? Calm down, will you, before you have a fit. It was just a joke.'

'You mean you haven't created a profile? That's not funny, Harriet. You could see how annoyed I was.'

'Oh no, I have created a profile for you. That's just not what I wrote. God, you're having a severe sense of humour failure today, Max.'

'I have a sense of humour when something's funny, Harriet. And this isn't funny. So have you put up a profile of me or not?'

'I have. And you're going to love it. Come on, let me show you on the laptop so you can get the full effect.'

'I don't want to see it, Harriet. How many times do I have to say it, I'm not interested.'

Max is professing a lack of interest while nonetheless allowing himself to be dragged across the kitchen towards the open laptop on the table.

'Just let me get it loaded. I don't think you're going to stay angry at me for long when you see how well I actually sold you.'

Sold him? Has Harriet swapped the modern world of corporate law for good old-fashioned pimping?

'See, how nice is that photo? Have you ever seen it before? I thought probably not. My lovely friend Philippe – you remember, gay, French, accent to die for – took it at my birthday lunch a couple of years ago. Even I'd say you look passably good-looking in that picture.'

Harriet loads the photo full screen. Max looks gorgeous. His thick, brown hair is a bit longer in the photo than it is now giving it a very slight wave on top which I always thought managed to make him look both suave and dishevelled at the same time. He's laughing at something someone's saying and his smile seems to fill the frame, embracing you from without and drawing you in. It really is a lovely picture.

'You know I don't like photos of myself, Harriet. Admittedly, that one's less offensive than most but that's not saying much.'

'But wait till you see what I wrote. Don't look – let me read it out to you.'

Max does as he's told. There are times when the extremity of Harriet's bossiness can be almost comical. Today, though, I seem to be missing the funny side.

*'I've known Max for eleven years. I know this isn't all about me, but I think it's worth you knowing up front that I don't suffer fools gladly and I'm not one who's generally given to waxing lyrical about other people's attributes. Max, however, is an exception. To cut to the chase, he has what people commonly refer to as "the whole*

*package": he's smart, funny, kind, patient and – for a bloke in his late thirties – looks surprisingly acceptable in a pair of swimming shorts. He can cook, he doesn't have any unappealing habits that I know of (apart from his modesty which I find annoying but I'm sure other women wouldn't) and he's genuinely a man of multiple interests and endless good humour. He's the man, to coin a cliché, with whom women want to share their problems and men want to share a pint. He also happens to be the world's best dad to his gorgeous seven-year-old daughter. And right now, lucky ladies, he's all yours.* How's that for a testimony, huh?'

It's a wonderful testimony, there's no denying. I never knew my best friend thought so highly of my husband.

I think about all the things I'd have added if I'd been writing that profile instead of Harriet. I'd have described Max's broad shoulders that reassure you he could carry the weight of the world on them if he had to, and his beautifully solid hands that encase yours in security when he holds them. I'd have mentioned the muscle definition in his calves – cyclist's calves – that imbue his every stride with a sense of purpose, and the oversensitivity of his bare skin that renders every human touch potentially ticklish. I'd have talked about how the tip of his nose quivers when he talks, engendering even the most fractious conversation with an air of comedy and how, last thing at night, after a difficult day, he'll stroke your head with the gentlest of touches – so gentle it's like the air of an angel passing through your hair – until such time as he's caressed away the day's frustrations and soothed you into slumber.

I think if I'd started writing that profile, I might never have been able to stop.

'Harriet, I'm flattered, really I am. But that doesn't change the fact that I don't want it up there.'

'Hang on a second, Mr Risk-Averse. Before you go jumping the apocalyptic gun, just have a look at some of these women who've messaged you already. Look – there's one here called Sophia who's a doctor – actually, she's a bloody surgeon – and, though I hate to admit it, she's got even better legs than me. Look at them – they go on for-ever. What's not to like about a surgeon with legs like that? And there's another really pretty one here too – let me find her – yes, here she is. Sarah, she's a social worker – possibly a bit earnest but she's still pretty hot.'

Max looks over Harriet's shoulder with disconcertingly more interest in this collection of female admirers than befits a man who insists he's not ready for all of this yet.

'You haven't even got my height right here, Harriet. Since when was I six foot? And my eyes aren't brown – they're hazel. And while it's very kind of you to have described me as "very good-looking" I think it might have been more honest to have ticked the average box.'

'Stop obsessing over the details, Max. You're almost six foot and anyway – what kind of freak is going to get out a tape measure to check? I said your eyes were brown because I always think that hazel sounds a bit – I don't know – indeterminate whereas everyone loves a man with brown eyes. And given that it's standard practice for peo-ple to upgrade themselves at least one rank on the looks leader board on these kinds of sites, if I'd said you were average I'd basically be implying that you're ugly and I'm assuming you wouldn't have wanted me to communicate that to the virtual world, would you?'

Max looks contemplative. I wish I could know what's going through his mind. I wish I could discuss this with him, face-to-face, even though I know that if that were possible, the conversation wouldn't be necessary.

'I'm sorry, Harriet. I can see you're just trying to be helpful and that you've gone to a lot of trouble. But it's just not the right time.'

'Oh come on, Max. You and I both know that left to your own devices you'll still be saying it's not the right time come Doomsday. Some of these women look genuinely nice. What's the worst that can happen if you give it a go?'

Max leaves the kitchen table and begins wiping down work surfaces that were already spotlessly clean.

'It's not that I think something bad will happen, Harriet. It's just that I look at the pictures of those women and I'm sure they're all perfectly nice, but they're not Rachel. In fact, when I look at them, all I can think about is how little they compare to her, to Rachel's beautiful bright eyes and her quizzical expression and her eloquent mouth. I know it's stupid and I know it's not going to happen, but Rachel's is the only face I want to see right now.'

Max has spoken slowly, quietly, the smallest of wistful smiles upending the edges of his lips as though there's an entire movie of memories spooling through his mind that he'd rather view alone.

'But, Max, Rach isn't here any more. I know how much you miss her – or, at least, I think I have some sense of it – but you refusing ever to go out with anyone else isn't going to bring her back.'

Max takes a deep breath that he lets out slowly, wearily.

'That's not the point, Harriet. You're missing the point. It's not about thinking I can ever have Rachel back. It's about not really being able to cope with her being gone. There's a big difference. When Rachel died, I didn't just lose her. I lost the amazing, intangible thing that Rachel and I had together. It's like there was me and there was Rachel and then there was this third entity, the alchemy of the two of us combined. And when you have that thing – call it a good relationship, I suppose – you get so used to living slightly outside of yourself in order to inhabit this other place with this other person that you forget how to live on your own, with only your own thoughts and opinions for company. It's not as simple as losing a partner. It's losing the part of yourself that went into creating that relationship. And that's what I don't ever expect to have with anyone else. I know how lucky I was to have it once.'

There's a look of appeal in Max's eyes, the hope that Harriet's going to understand something he's perhaps only just beginning to come to terms with himself.

'I get it, Max. But it's not like you can't think for yourself any more, or make decisions on your own. You're still a grown-up capable of making your own choices.'

'Of course it's not that I can't make decisions for myself any more. It's just that I'm out of practice and, quite honestly, I wish I didn't have to. When you've been used to sharing your thoughts with someone else for over a decade, and used to having those thoughts come back to you reworked, improved, often more comprehensible than they were when you set them off, it's hard – it's really hard – to live without that. I keep trying to invoke Rachel's voice in my head. I know it probably sounds stupid but I ask her opinion on things and try to hear what she has to say about Ellie and work and how she thinks I'm coping without her. Sometimes I manage it and that's great and I feel like I still have a little part of her alive in my head. But a lot of the time I feel that she's just out of reach and that's when it hits me all over again that I've lost her. That I'm never going to be able to talk to her about anything ever again. That she'll never give me advice or help me out or laugh at my stupid jokes or tell me off. And I can't imagine anyone else ever filling that space. I can't imagine ever having that alchemy with anyone else. So if I can't have it with Rachel, I really would rather just be on my own. Just me and Ellie.'

Max drops his head, as if exhausted by so much honesty. There's a hint of salt water in the corner of his eye that he tries and fails to blink away inconspicuously.

I'm sorry for doubting you, Max, even for a second.

Harriet stares out of the patio doors, feigning absorption in Ellie's antics in the garden, leaving her gaze averted just long enough for Max to compose himself.

'I'm sorry I overstepped the mark, Max. You know I'd never do anything to piss you off deliberately, right?'

'I'm not angry, Harriet. I'm just sad and I feel quite private and I think it's going to be a while before I start to feel any differently.'

'Well, listen, I won't do anything with that profile, I promise. I'll just leave it there, untouched, gathering virtual dust until such time as you're ready for it, whether that's in a few months or a few years' time. Okay?'

Before Max has a chance to respond, Ellie comes bounding in from outside. Harriet snaps the laptop shut.

'Is it lunchtime yet? I'm starving.'

'You're bang on cue, angel. I'm just about to serve.'

As Max swings open the oven door and pulls out the loaded tray, I'm reminded of the smell of roast lamb I can see steaming in front of him. I'm not hungry – I don't get hungry any more – but the recalled smell is one of nostalgia and longing, a smell that warms me from the inside out and makes me yearn to be part of that nourishing domesticity.

The steam from the oven begins to thicken excessively into an impenetrable white mist and before I've had a chance to savour a final view of Max and Ellie today, I find myself back alone above the clouds. Not even a spectator's invite to Sunday lunch for me today, it would seem.

I wonder what Max's reply would have been, had Ellie not arrived to interrupt the conversation. I wonder whether Max will agree to leave the profile online or whether he'll insist on Harriet withdrawing him from the virtual dating pool. I wonder whether it will take only one bored, lonely evening for Max's curiosity to get the better of him and for him to begin surfing the profiles of women who may one day wish to replace me.

I try to console myself with all that I know about Max, about the man he is and the relationship we cherished.

I recall his hatred of blind dating and how, when we'd been together just long enough to confess such things to one another, he admitted his relief at being liberated from anxious evenings in the company of hopeful strangers.

I hear his words to my mum on the evening of my funeral, after the guests had left, after the dining table had been cleared of haphazardly constructed sandwiches, after Ellie had been tucked up in bed, when he'd told her he wouldn't have been able to continue without me if it weren't for Ellie's existence.

I recollect his words to Harriet today, sentiments that aren't, surely, those of a man on the brink of contemplating a romantic life without me.

I think about all these things and, eventually, I manage to entrench myself in reassurance.

Max isn't any more ready to move on than I am. I have to trust him, trust the legacy of our marriage, trust that if time is a great healer then we are both yet in need of a longer passage.

I have to trust all of that because there is, after all, little else I can do.

# CHAPTER 6

Trust, it transpires, can often be misplaced.

Max is sitting alone in a pub on Portobello Road, tapping his fingers on the table in rhythmic succession, betraying his nerves to anyone observing him with anything more than fleeting attention. Given that it's Friday night in an overcrowded Notting Hill pub populated by people a decade younger and a generation cooler than Max or I, luckily no one else seems to be taking much notice of him at all.

It's been over a month since my last visit, a fact of which I'm aware due to the frustrating tail end of a conversation between Max and Harriet I was privy to last night during a tantalizingly brief few minutes of access. I discovered that Max has been doing a lot of thinking lately which has, inexplicably, led him to the conclusion that it's time he 'took the plunge' into the murky waters of the online dating pool. Harriet, unsurprisingly, endorsed the decision, reassuring him it's 'best to get it over with sooner rather than later', like 'the ripping off of a well-worn plaster'. Joan, meanwhile, has apparently continued to 'encourage' Max to 'get out and about' more, hence the purpose of this evening's arrangement is as much to 'get Mum off my case' as it is to dip his own tentative toes into the dating waters.

It was horrible listening to that conversation last night. It was one of those rare times I wished my access had done me the favour of maintaining my ignorance. There are some things a dead wife is definitely better off not knowing, and right at the top of that list is undoubtedly the stomach-churning thought of your husband on a date with another woman. I honestly think Max isn't ready. I think he knows he's not ready. But I suppose if there's one predictable aspect of grief, it's the promise to make people behave unpredictably.

During my protracted weeks of absence – weeks that feel so much longer now than when I lived and breathed them – I've assumed that if Max did at some point in the distant, unimaginable future decide to start dating again, my feelings about it would be unambiguous. I expected there to be simple, unadulterated jealousy and a possessive desire for nothing short of social disaster. But watching Max now, witnessing his profound level of discomfort, remembering – just about – what it's like to be meeting a stranger for the first time with all the accompanying hopes, desires, fantasies and fears, my overriding feeling is the simple wish that Max wasn't putting himself through this. That I wasn't putting him through it. That none of this – for either of our sakes – was happening.

I know frustratingly little about the woman Max is about to meet. I know that she's a vet and that Max thinks her photo makes her look 'friendly'. I know that her name is Dodie, which seems strangely fitting for a vet and yet equally inappropriate for anyone living in the twenty-first century. I know that she's thirty-four, which is younger than me but thankfully not quite young enough to be threatening.

I also know that the woman who eventually walks through the door that Max can now barely take his eyes off for more than a few seconds may bring with her the best or the worst of evenings. That she may be the woman with whom Max spends the rest of his life. Or she may not.

Either way, I don't believe that any of us are ready for this.

The pub's double doors swing open and a woman halts hesitantly for a second, scanning the room in search of the swiftest of rescues before her eyes eventually settle on Max, who stands up clumsily at a table devoid of enough space to fully erect himself, and offers her a comforting wave.

'Hi. You must be Dodie.'

Max stretches out his hand to be shaken while simultaneously inching his head towards her in anticipation of an introductory cheek-kiss, a movement which fails to be reciprocated, leaving him bobbing in and out of Dodie's personal space like an inconclusive jack-in-the-box until, finally, accompanied by a nervous laugh (from him) and an awkward smile (from her) he touches his lips to this woman's cheek. It's hardly a consummation of the relationship but already my stomach's somersaulting with the violence of envy.

'What can I get you to drink?'

'Just a coke would be great, thanks. I'm driving.'

A flutter of surprise stumbles across Max's face. I can understand why. He told Harriet he planned to traipse here via two separate buses this evening under the relatively sensible assumption that blind dates and alcohol are inextricable bedfellows. Now Max must decide whether to continue to drink alone and order his third pint of the evening or join Dodie in her sobriety.

Max elbows his way to the bar where he spends an uncomfortable few minutes endeavouring to attract the barman's attention while simultaneously offering Dodie a series of awkward, reassuring smiles. After the third of these, Dodie turns to face the opposite direction, affecting an impression of interest – however improbable – in the antiquarian maps hanging in frames on the wall. With Max free to devote his efforts to getting served, I turn my attention to a closer study of Dodie; I know that once Max returns it'll be impossible for me to concentrate on anything other than the most microscopic signs of possible flirtation.

Dodie is what I suspect *Country Life* magazine might describe as 'hearty': tall, broad-shouldered and on the stocky side of slim, she's the kind of woman whose appearance welcomes the image of her elbow-deep in blood and placenta, yanking a foal from a horse's belly. And the clothes she's chosen to wear for a blind date might be better suited to life down on the farm too; there's a knee-length brown corduroy skirt, fitted just a fraction too snugly across her ample hips giving the impression that she and the skirt are engaged in a not-so-private battle for supremacy. She's paired this with a bottle-green crew-neck jumper that looks like it's had a few too many dates with detergent and is now in dire need of one of those gadgets you see advertised in Sunday supplements promising to de-bobble your sweaters. Her calves are encased in sturdy brown leather biker boots that wouldn't look out of place on a signed-up member of Hells Angels, while her shoulder-length hair doesn't seem to have encountered any form of electronic drying, curling or straightening device in recent days, protruding defiantly from her scalp as if each and every strand has its own, individual statement to make. It would be fair to say that the whole appearance would be better suited to a pub quiz in Ambridge than a first date in a Notting Hill bar.

As I'm studying the woman my husband has chosen for his first date in over a decade, she suddenly dispatches her right index finger into the far reaches of her upper left jaw, picks at something for a second or two, extracts it, inspects whatever was lodged in her teeth that now sits under her nail and then, without so much as a moment's surreptitious survey to check she's not being observed, pops the retrieved morsel back into her mouth for consumption.

Even from this far away, it's enough to turn your stomach.

I check back to where Max is finally getting served and there's no indication at all that he's seen what I saw. If he had, I'm not sure how he'd cope sharing a single drink with her let alone an entire evening; if there's one thing Max can get endearingly neurotic about, it's people displaying in public the kind of personal habits that really ought to be kept private. He absolutely hates it. And it's not even as if I can warn him about what I've seen. Honestly, what's the point in life after death if you can't alert your husband to the objectionable habits of the woman with whom he's about to spend the evening?

Max returns with Dodie's alcohol-free drink and a wise third pint for himself. As he tries to squeeze into the Lilliputian gap Dodie's left between him and the table, his arm knocks against a picture frame, spilling the top quarter-inch of lager on his hand which he subsequently licks off while trying not to spill any more. I catch Dodie raise an offended eyebrow as though he's the one with the uncouth manners.

'So, you drove here. Did you manage to park okay? It gets so busy round here on Friday nights, doesn't it? I remember when hardly anyone ever ventured out this way for a night out, when it was all about the West End. Now you can barely walk to the end of the street in this neck of the woods without a new bar popping up.'

Max is attempting to sound socially savvy but the truth is, neither he nor I have been out drinking to a trendy new bar for almost as long as Ellie's been alive.

'Yeah, I parked just up the road. It's free after six-thirty. Even the resident bays.'

'So you don't live round here, then?'

Dodie studies Max slightly nervously, as if weighing up the likelihood of him being a serial killer who's assessing whether to slit her throat at his house or hers.

'No, I'm a north London girl. How about you?'

'I'm in Acton. Have been all my life. Well, most of it anyway. I grew up there but my wife and I started out in a rented flat in Kentish Town. She was never that keen on the area, though, and it never felt like a place we'd make a home together. She always thought it was a bit – what was the word she used to use? – grimy. It's funny how areas change so quickly isn't it? I'm not sure I could afford to buy there now even if I wanted to. Anyway, when it came to thinking about starting a family and buying a house, we headed back to Acton. My mum and dad are still there and it's where I teach so it all worked out pretty well, really.'

Max is gabbling, as you might expect from someone who hasn't had to make polite conversation with a total stranger in these circumstances for over a decade and who's probably spent almost as long under the legitimate assumption that he'd never find himself in this position ever again. But Dodie doesn't appear to be giving a conversational inch. She simply nods, disinterestedly, just the vaguest acknowledgement that Max has spoken but reciprocating nothing, not even an encouraging smile.

Doesn't she realize how lucky she is to be sitting just inches away from him, sharing the very same table, close enough to touch him if she so chooses, although I sincerely hope she doesn't?

'So, you're a vet. What made you want to do that? They say never work with children and animals and yet here's us doing exactly that. We must be mad.'

Max smiles at her broadly, signalling – in case she hadn't realized – that he's made a joke. Dodie eyes him earnestly.

'I've just always loved animals. My dad's a vet and I grew up around animals so it was never really much of a decision for me. More of a calling, I guess.'

I laugh out loud and it's probably a good thing there's no one to hear me. She takes care of household pets, for goodness sake; it's hardly discovering the existence of the Higgs Boson, is it?

'That's a bit like me with teaching. Although the calling there more often involves kids shouting at each other across the classroom.'

Dodie finally manages to raise the corners of her lips into something approaching a smile, although it could just be a grimace.

'Yes, well I've always preferred animals to people. They're just so much less demanding.'

Dodie slurps a long, voracious gulp of her coke while Max looks at her expectantly, as if waiting for the punch-line to what he assumed was going to be a joke. Dodie remains silent.

'Yeah, my wife, Rachel, she always used to joke that to be a teacher you either had to have loved school so much you never wanted to leave or hated it so much you wanted to punish the next generation. She was a marketing direc-tor for Visit Britain and I did sometimes wonder whether being in an office surrounded by adults all day might not be an easier option. Not that I'm saying her job was easy. Not at all. A lot of the time it was much harder than mine. And much longer hours. And she was great at it. Brilliant, in fact. It's just . . . well . . . you know what I mean?'

Max shifts uncomfortably in his chair, possibly unsure whether even he knows what he means.

'So, what are you . . . like . . . divorced or separated or something?'

Max looks pained. I feel pained. He must have known the subject was likely to arise, but he still doesn't seem prepared for it.

'The "or something", I'm afraid. Rachel – my wife – she died. I'm a widower, although I hate that word. Makes me feel like I should be pottering around in tartan slippers and a tweed dressing gown, smoking a pipe and listening to Benny Goodman.'

And that's exactly what you should have been doing by the time I left you, my darling, if only I'd left you at a reasonable hour in our life together, rather than deserting you when we were still in the adolescence of our marriage.

'God, that's awful. What happened, if you don't mind me asking?'

It's the first inkling of interest she's shown in the conversation so far and it is, of all things, death that's sparked her curiosity.

'She died of a heart attack. She'd had an irregularity her entire life that she hadn't even known about. And then one day it just gave way. There wasn't any warning. She hadn't even been ill.'

'Really? Sorry, I don't know what to say.'

'It's okay. There's nothing much you can say. One minute we were out having dinner together and the next she was slumped on the floor. I don't want to sound clichéd, but it just all happened so fast.'

'So you were there? You actually saw it happen?'

Dodie seems a little too excited about the horror of this story for my liking.

'The paramedics told me that she'd died within minutes, before they even arrived. She died in my arms which, if you read enough books about coping with grief, you soon learn is everyone's ideal death fantasy. I suppose I should be grateful for small mercies.'

I don't think I'll ever stop finding this story unbearable, however many times I hear Max tell it. I remember so little about it myself. I've got no memory, in fact, of anything from the time I felt that first sharp stab of pain and realized that my throat was constricting with a determination so clearly against my best interests, to the time I found myself here, a little while later, watching Max cope with the rawest moments of his grief and contemplating whether an afterlife I'd never believed in existed after all.

'So when did all this happen?'

'Just over a year ago. Still early days, as everyone keeps telling me. Well, when they're not telling me to get out and start living my life again. It's amazing how everyone becomes an expert on grief the moment someone close to you dies.'

There's an uncomfortable silence. This is beginning to sound less like a date and more like a therapy session. It unnerves me that this woman who may yet have romantic designs on my husband has inadvertently encouraged him to open his heart to her. Who knows what she's planning to do with its contents?

'Sorry. I don't know why I'm telling you all this. It's not really date-chat, is it?'

'It's fine. It sounds like you've been through the mill a bit.'

Well, that's one way of putting it, I suppose, but only if you're hoping to win a prize for understatement of the year.

'This is the first time I've been out since Rachel died. I wasn't really sure what to expect. Maybe I'm not ready after all. I'm sorry.'

'Don't worry about it. Better out than in, as they say.'

Dodie chews ferociously and unselfconsciously on her thumbnail, ripping it off with her teeth before extracting it from the tip of her tongue and flicking it on to the wooden floor. Max doesn't seem to notice, lost in his own train of thought, as though now he's opened the floodgates he doesn't know quite how to stem the tide of storytelling.

'Sometimes I think it would be so much easier if I only had myself to worry about. But there's Ellie too and most of the time I have no idea if I'm doing the best things for her.'

'Ellie?'

'Yes, my daughter. I think she's mentioned on my profile.'

She hasn't clocked that he has a daughter? Maybe she'd have paid more attention if his profile had referenced a family pet instead.

'Yes, right, of course. How old is she?'

'She's seven now. She was six when Rachel died. There are times when I wonder what on earth I'd do without her. It turns out the needs of a young child are a great leveller when it comes to keeping your grief in check.'

Max suddenly stops talking and reddens slightly before taking a long, deep gulp of his pint. I wonder what Dodie's thinking, whether she's wondering how quickly she can escape this unconventional internet date with her dignity and her evening still intact, or whether she's perversely enjoying the provision of her ample shoulder for Max to cry on. There are, I've no doubt, some women who'd find nothing more attractive than a vulnerable man in need of rescuing and even I have to admit that Max falls into that category right now, however out of character it is for him.

'And so how's she doing – sorry, what's her name again?'

'Ellie. I don't really know, to be honest. Most of the time I think she's doing pretty well, all things considered. She's an amazing little girl. I'm sure all parents say that but Ellie really is: she's so thoughtful and perceptive and kind. And she's great fun to be with. I hear people complain about what hard work parenting is and they're right, sometimes it is, but most of the time with Ellie it just feels like – I don't know – a privilege. I'm lucky, too, that my parents live just round the corner from us and they're great with her. Not only in the sense of helping out. It's more than that. I used to think Rachel was the daughter they never had; now I think it's Ellie. They pick her up from school every day so they're really like second parents to her. I suppose my mum is actually the closest Ellie's got to a mum now.'

'Well, not everyone would be so lucky to have their parents on tap. You're pretty fortunate, in the circumstances.'

Dodie's tactless platitude hangs in the air like a lonely phrase in need of companionship but with little hope of finding any. Wouldn't she be better to remain silent and have people think she's emotionally incompetent than to speak out and prove that she is?

'Would you like another drink?'

Max clearly does. Or maybe it's just that he needs one.

'Um . . . that would have been nice but I've just noticed the time and I said I'd meet some friends for a late supper. I really ought to head off.'

So it's to be the emergency rescue package for the failing economy of her evening. Dodie must be aware that no one believes the late-supper story, that everyone knows it's the oldest trick in the dating book, that even Max, who hasn't dated for over a decade and hasn't spent the intervening period watching Hollywood rom-coms, will know that this is nothing more than the lamest of get-out clauses.

'Yeah, right, course. Sorry. I didn't clock the time.'

Stop apologizing, Max. It's not even eight o'clock. She's been here precisely twenty-five minutes. She should be the one apologizing to you.

'No worries. Thanks for the drink.'

'Don't mention it. I hope you enjoy the rest of the evening.'

'Yeah, you too.'

She's out of her chair and into her jacket faster than Max can stand up without almost knocking over the table again.

'Well, it was really nice to meet you. I hope all those animals behave themselves and, er, have a good weekend.'

I can see Max isn't sure how to end this unfortunate encounter, but before he has a chance to decide on the most appropriate course of action, Dodie finalizes what is sure to be their one and only meeting with a verbal goodbye, an ill-disguised sigh of relief and a decisive departure.

Max stands by the table, looking slightly confused as to what just happened. I don't know whether her swift exit has upset or angered him, humiliated or simply bewildered him. Possibly all that, and more.

Max goes to the bar and orders a fourth pint before returning to the empty table where he sits in solitary silence, dejection and bemusement etched in the lines across his forehead.

I wish there were some way of me finding out what Max is thinking, some way of him knowing that he's not alone, some way to reassure him that I'm still here by his side. I wish I could convince him that tonight's debacle was in no way his fault, that Dodie just wasn't right for him, that what he needs right now – if he needs anything at all from imperfect strangers – is empathy and patience and understanding about just how hard this is for him. And that while he may be the one feeling despondent at this moment in time, it is he who's had the greatest escape from this failed venture, not her.

Max finishes his pint in student-record time and heads out into the still-bright, early-summer's evening to make his way home, concluding his inaugural night out just as the regular Notting Hill-ites are beginning theirs.

As Max wanders with just the faintest air of tipsiness towards the first of the two bus stops which will see him back to Acton, where he'll collect Ellie from his mum and dad's before heading home, an opaque mist begins to cloud my view and within seconds my access has disappeared altogether.

I really wanted to stay longer with him tonight. I wanted to see that he got home safely, wanted to reassure myself that he wasn't too upset, wanted to remain close to him even though I know there's nothing useful, nothing tangible, I can offer.

Instead I just have to wait as I so often do until I can return to see how he is. And hope, in the meantime, that he'll be okay.

# CHAPTER 7

Music greets me for a few tantalizing seconds before the clouds disperse, and I feel the familiar lump in my throat that's been the spontaneous accompaniment to these lyrics for the past eight years.

As the scene pulls into focus, I find myself in the darkened sitting room of my house, the flicker of the television screen the only light illuminating the lone figure of my husband on the sofa, Dean Martin informing him, as if Max didn't already know it, that he's nobody till somebody loves him.

And there we both are, on the screen, proving that we've found somebody to do just that, Max looking the most handsome I've ever seen him, in a charcoal-grey morning suit with powder-blue tie, me in his arms draped in multiple layers of floor-length ivory satin that I'd only that day mastered the ability to walk in, let alone dance. The moment we took to the floor to confirm our status as the newest of formally committed couples.

I hear a swallowed sob and pull my eyes away from the television to see another version of Max, so different from the beaming, dancing, newly-wed on the screen. He's sitting on the sofa with tears streaming down his face, his cheeks streaked with the evidence that he's been here, like this, for too long already. There's an empty wine glass in his hand, tilted precariously against his leg, the last remaining dregs of red sediment clinging to its sides, the half-empty bottle resting on the floor by his feet. He's wearing the same clothes that I left him in after his date earlier and I suspect that only a matter of hours have passed since my last visit, that this video trip down memory lane may have been prompted by the disappointment and disillusionment of the evening's events.

Max wipes his face with the back of his free hand and I realize that this is only the third time I've ever seen him cry, a sight I've only ever borne witness to since I died. I want to be able to hold him and for him to feel the endurance of my embrace. I want the love that I have for him – that I'll always have for him, however far away I am, whatever worlds separate us – to envelop him in security. I want it not to be over, this relationship that neither of us could ever quite believe – even after we'd rented our first flat, even after the wedding, even after creating a new little person together – that we'd been lucky enough to have discovered in one another. We'd often say – in private, never out loud, never in earshot of others for fear of appearing smug – that relationships like ours just don't happen every day, they don't happen to everyone. I don't think either of us ever doubted the rare fortune of having chanced upon one another in that vast sea of human interactions, two lone boats bobbing on the water whose navigational charts just happened to coincide on a day when each of us thought there'd be nothing but empty ocean for nautical miles around.

As Dean Martin concludes his paean to the merits of romantic love, I turn back to the television screen just in time to watch Max whisper in my ear as the next track begins and a swarm of guests join us on the dance floor. I'll never forget what he said; I can hear the words right here and now, as clearly as if Max had been wearing a microphone and the cameraman had managed to pick up that most private of triumphant sentiments:

*We did it, baby. It's just me and you and the adventure of the rest of our lives together now.*

And it was an adventure, a wonderful adventure, however short-lived.

We're laughing now, amidst congratulatory friends and upbeat music, but the celebratory tone on the screen does nothing to lighten Max's mood in the darkness. He chokes back a deep, guttural sob and pours another lonely slug of wine from the bottle into his glass.

Please don't do this to yourself, Max. I love you reminiscing about our past but I want those reminiscences to bring you happiness, to reignite our relationship for you so that you can experience it even in my absence, not to reduce you to alcohol-infused heartbreak. Perhaps you're just not ready to watch this yet, perhaps this is one collection of memories that does need to be stored away a little while longer, perhaps tonight just isn't the night to be recollecting happier evenings from a life we no longer lead.

But my silent entreaties have as little hope of reaching him as if I said the words out loud. There's no possibility of me whispering reassurances into his ear, of wrapping my arms around him, of kissing away his sadness.

The empty wine glass tumbles sedately, as if in slow motion, from Max's hand to the rug under his feet. His eyes are closed, his heavy breathing audible above the disco that continues to play in miniature in front of him, where he's twirling me around the floor with amateur enthusiasm, both of us grinning ecstatically, high on love and adrenaline, in full confidence that this was the first day of the rest of our lives together. Which it was, I suppose. Just not the lives we imagined might unfold.

Max emits the gentlest of snores, his head tilted back on the edge of the sofa, his face still damp with tears and his lips tinged with the pigment of fermented grapes.

I'm reminded of all those times I've watched him sleep in the past, of all those mornings I'd rouse before him or nights when I'd lie awake after nursing Ellie in the darkness, and I remember how peaceful it's always made me feel. How peaceful and safe and secure. There's an echo of that serenity now too, shadowed only by the knowledge that tonight he's wept – and drunk – himself to sleep, rather than slipped into that unconscious realm at peace with himself and the world.

As Max continues to snuffle softly in response to whatever netherworld of his own he's currently inhabiting, the white mist begins to gather and I know that I'll imminently be back in my own private existence too.

I savour one last glimpse of my slumbering husband, that familiar surge of love sweeping through me as it always has, as it always will while I watch him sleep, before he's gone from me altogether.

# CHAPTER 8

'Oh, come on, mate – there have to be some single women here, surely?'

Max's brother, Connor, surveys the scene in front of him: adults politely jostling for position on inconveniently low mahogany benches, colourful plastic equipment of various shapes and sizes being assembled in the field beyond, children in uniform white T-shirts and navy blue shorts chattering impatiently amongst the preamble. It's an event that's almost certainly being replicated all over the country this week.

And sitting on one of those benches is Max, looking incredulously at his brother and laughing.

'Is that why you came? Did you seriously expect there to be a pool of school mums you could hit on? Honestly, you're incorrigible. Sorry to disabuse you of your sordid little fantasy but we're here to watch Ellie, not to provide you with the opportunity to meet women. As if you needed that anyway.'

'You underestimate me, little bro. I can do both at the same time. It's called multitasking. You might like to try it some time.'

'Yeah, well, I think I'll leave that particular brand of multitasking to you, thanks very much.'

I sometimes have to remind myself that Max and Connor did actually emerge from the same gene pool, albeit three years apart. I imagine that's one of the revelations that come with having more than one child; that a shared genetic inheritance can nonetheless produce two such distinctive characters. It's remarkable that, in spite of those differences, Max and Connor still get on so well. I've often thought how lucky they are, not just in the fact of one another's existence, but in genuinely liking one another as much as they do too.

If you didn't know Connor as well as I do, I'm sure it would be easy to caricature him as a walking cliché: a hedge fund manager with an incomprehensible salary, an annual bonus that I've no doubt would extinguish half the mortgages on our street, a Farringdon bachelor pad equipped with every gadget imaginable and a string of unfeasibly beautiful – if not particularly long-lasting – girlfriends. On paper, at least, he reads like someone most of us would try to avoid in a City bar on a Friday night. But they're just the headlines and that's far from the whole story. He conceals it well, behind the bravura and the status and the steering wheel of his Aston Martin, but there's an endearingly soft centre to Connor's self-aggrandizing exterior. I'd known him for years before I saw it for myself. It was seeing him with Ellie, in fact, that helped Connor's hidden depths first surface for me.

I remember a friend telling me, after she'd already given birth to her first child but before I'd even conceived of – let alone conceived – Ellie, that when you have children the prism through which you view your friends shifts focus from how you feel about them to how they feel about your child. I'd thought at the time it sounded self-absorbed and slightly crazy and I remember vowing that

I wouldn't become the kind of parent who expected my child to be at the centre of everyone else's lives. But when Ellie arrived I realized it's a feeling that surpasses rational thought, that it mines the most primitive of instincts, beyond your control – that feeling of being drawn to people who are interested in, engaged with, invested in your child. It's primordial, I'm sure, that urge to surround your progeny with people who'll help them navigate their journey successfully through life.

That's when Connor became more than a peripheral, two-dimensional character for me; when Ellie was born he embraced his new-found avuncular role with such joy, such enthusiasm, such unexpected commitment that it gave birth to a new relationship between us too. I can't think of a single time he's ever let Ellie down. And that's why, I'm sure, Max has invited him to her school Sports Day today.

I spy my little girl bounding across the field towards her daddy and her uncle, where she throws herself on to Connor's lap and into his arms.

'Hello, princess. You're looking particularly fetching today, if I might say so. Like a perfectly edible piece of pink candy floss. Much prettier than all those others in their drab uniforms.'

Ellie frowns, first at Connor, then at Max and then back at Connor.

'I'm supposed to be wearing my PE kit but Daddy forgot to wash it and I couldn't wear it 'cos it had blackcurrant all down the front.'

'Guilty as charged, m'lord. I'm so sorry, angel. I did explain to Miss Collins, didn't I, and she was fine about it?'

'But I really wanted to wear it today. Miss Collins says that wearing your PE kit shows that you're part of the team.'

'Of course you're still part of the team, princess. Just the prettiest member, that's all. I bet everyone would rather wear what you're wearing, given half the chance.'

Connor tickles Ellie's tummy, transforming her frown into peals of giggles.

'He's not going to forget again, though, are you, Daddy? 'Cos now we've got the chart on the fridge.'

'A chart on the fridge, huh? That sounds very organized.'

'We can but hope. Ellie's gone through the calendar highlighting all the days she needs her PE kit so that I have advance warning of when to wash it. Although there are only a couple of weeks of term left now, aren't there, angel, so we'll have to remember to do it again in September?'

'Don't worry, Daddy. I won't forget.'

'So what's on the line-up for today, then? Are you going to win some races and make your daddy and me proud?'

'Um, I don't know. I'll try. But Miss Collins says it doesn't matter who wins. She says it's all just for fun.'

'Well, Miss Collins clearly hasn't learnt yet that it's a dog-eat-dog world out there. Just remember, you don't get one of those nice shiny medals if you come second.'

Max rolls his eyes and pulls Ellie on to his lap.

'Don't listen to Uncle Connor, sweetheart. He doesn't understand that not everything in life is a competition. You just have a good time and enjoy yourself. Do you know who you're doing the three-legged race with yet?'

'Yes, Miss Collins let us choose so me and Megan are doing it together.'

'That's great. You two will make a great pairing. And who's giving out the prizes this year?'

Now it's Ellie's turn to roll her eyes.

'Mr Baxter, like always, Daddy.'

'Which one's Mr Baxter, again?'

'Aw, Daddy, you know Mr Baxter. He does all our games lessons. He's my favourite. He's really funny.'

'Yes, I remember now. Isn't he the one you say looks like a Labrador puppy?'

'Shhhh, Daddy. What if someone hears you? Then we'll get into trouble.'

'Oh, I think we'll be okay, munchkin. If anyone tells Mr Baxter what we said I promise to take the rap and say it was all my fault.'

Ellie giggles and kisses Max squarely on the lips. I close my eyes and remember the feeling of her soft, plump lips on mine.

'Look, I think Miss Collins is calling you all back over. Hop off, munchkin, and we'll see you in a bit.'

Ellie tightens her lithe, T-shirted arms around Max's neck.

'Can't I just stay here with you and Uncle Connor for a bit?'

'What, and miss out on all the fun? Don't be silly, angel. The first race will be starting soon.'

'I don't want to go yet.'

Ellie buries her plaintive voice under Max's chin, tightening her grip further.

'You don't want to hang out with us old fogeys when you could be with your friends, do you? And if you stay here with your daddy and me you don't even stand a chance of winning one of those medals.'

Ellie doesn't answer Connor, burrowing her face further into Max's shoulder, an attempt, perhaps, to render herself invisible so she'll never have to move. Max encloses her in his arms, as if to protect her from the sadness he'd do anything to alleviate.

I'd been hoping she wouldn't be plagued today by memories of last year, that they wouldn't impede her enjoyment this time around. I'd been confident that Connor's presence might provide enough of a distraction to allow Ellie to experience this annual school ritual afresh.

Because last year's Sports Day had been horrendous. I'd been dead for just over two months and Ellie was too confused and withdrawn still to interact with her friends, let alone compete against them. She'd burst into tears spontaneously and repeatedly and no one – not Max, not the teachers and certainly not the other parents – had known how to console her. Max had taken her home early in the end, where he'd tucked her under a blanket on the sofa and watched *Monsters, Inc.* with her, the film that Ellie had viewed repeatedly in the months after I died. Later Max had confessed to his mum that he'd felt more angry about my death on that day than any other in the nine weeks prior; that he'd been enraged by the lack of empathy from other parents, whom he'd felt had looked upon him and Ellie with silent, detached judgement; that he'd felt overwhelming resentment towards me for casting him as the tragic widower, upon whom all curious eyes were surreptitiously cast; and that, worst of all, he'd hated himself for his own discomfort, for his embarrassment at

Ellie's behaviour and for his wish that she could have abandoned her grief for just one afternoon. He said he'd yearned to be part of a normal, inconspicuous family, whose personal tragedy wasn't the topic of trackside conversation, where gossip and speculation masquerade as sympathy and understanding. And that, at the end of it all, his guilt about all those feelings had been almost intolerable.

Max prises Ellie's head gently from his shoulder and holds her face in his hands.

'It's fine, sweetheart. You're going to be just fine. We'll be right here, cheering you on. We won't move from this spot, I promise.'

Ellie looks deep into Max's eyes with an intensity so much greater than befits her years.

'You promise you're not going anywhere? You're going to stay right there, all afternoon?'

'We promise, angel. Don't we, Connor?'

'Scout's honour, princess. Where else could we possibly want to be when there's our favourite little girl competing all afternoon?'

Ellie grants them a wistful smile, seemingly more for their benefit than her own. She slips warily from Max's lap, turns to leave and then circles back for one additional paternal hug before walking across the field to rejoin her classmates. Halfway over she halts for a second, revolves to face Max and Connor and gives them an almost imperceptible wave of insecurity. Her daddy and her uncle respond with exaggerated reassurance, Connor blowing kisses and Max waving enthusiastically back.

'She's still a bit clingy, then?'

Connor and Max both keep a watchful eye on Ellie's completed journey.

'To be honest, she hasn't been too bad lately. No bed-wetting for ages now and she generally only comes in with me just before the alarm goes off. I thought she'd been a lot more settled until just now.'

'One day at a time, huh?'

'Yeah, I know. I just don't like seeing her so insecure again.'

They lapse into a respectful silence, as if in honour of Ellie's adversity.

'She'll be okay, Max. It's going to take some time, but she will.'

'I hope you're right. I suppose, if I'm honest, I knew today might trigger something in her. It's hard enough for me not having Rachel here for events like this so I can't really imagine what it's like for Ellie.'

And it's hard for me too, to be here but not be here, to hear you but not be heard, to see you but not be seen. To want to make things better for you and Ellie but being powerless to do so.

'It's tough, there's no doubt about it. It's no surprise she'll have moments like that, given everything she's been through. Two steps forward and one back, I reckon.'

'You're probably right. That's why I was so pleased when you said you could come today. She might not have both her parents here and it's unfortunate timing that Mum and Dad are on holiday, but at least she's still got the two of us supporting her.'

'Hey, I wouldn't have missed it for anything. Not even for a client lunch at Nobu.'

'I'm sure that's not too much of a sacrifice, is it, given the number of client lunches you seem to go on every week?'

'It's all work, Max, whatever you might think. In fact, the bloke I was supposed to be meeting today owns a massive TV company, the one that made the new comedy show on Channel 4 last Friday that everyone's been raving about. Did you see it? I couldn't figure out what all the fuss was about. Didn't think it was funny at all.'

Max hesitates for a second and I can almost hear the contemplative cogs whirring in his mind, deciding whether or not to risk a confidence.

'No, I was out. On a date, for my sins.'

'On a date? Bloody hell, you kept that one quiet. Who's the lucky lady?'

'Well, not-so-lucky, as it turned out. It was a complete disaster. I don't really want to talk about it.'

A light flush of humiliation grazes Max's cheeks.

'Come on, mate. You're probably just a bit rusty. It has been a while since you tested out the old Myerson magic, after all.'

'The only magic I was capable of was making my date disappear in record time. Seriously, she couldn't get out of there quick enough.'

'It can't have been that bad.'

'Trust me, it can. I found myself talking about Rachel the whole time, telling this woman I'd only met five minutes before about the night she died. Honestly, I cringe just thinking about it.'

Connor tries – and fails – to restrain the look of amused disbelief on his face.

'Okay, you win, that does sound pretty bad.'

'I know, Connor. That's why I didn't want to talk about it. The whole time I was there I could hear this voice shouting in my head, telling me to shut up and change the subject, but for some reason I just couldn't. All this stuff about Rachel and Ellie kept coming out, like the verbal equivalent of projectile vomit.'

'Well, I suppose there's an argument that if you do end up dating someone, they'll find out about Rachel sooner or later so it's probably better to get it out in the open early on?'

'I'm not sure. It was obvious that I didn't have anything in common with this woman and it was never going to go anywhere so that wasn't really the issue. It was more that I felt so guilty about it, like it was some kind of betrayal of Rachel, to be confiding about her to this total stranger. But even though it felt wrong I still couldn't stop myself.'

It's a relief, albeit maybe a selfish one, that it's not just me who feels that my death and its aftermath aren't yet ready for public consumption. The last thing I want is for Max to feel guilty on top of everything else he has to contend with, but I do want to believe that our marriage – including its untimely end – is still a sacred thing, not yet sufficiently digested to be used as conversational fodder, certainly not with random strangers.

'How did you meet this date anyway? Did someone set you up?'

Max looks sheepish, as though this is one part of the confession he was hoping his brother might overlook.

'It was Harriet's idea. And Mum's. I shouldn't have listened to them.'

'What was?'

'It was an internet date. Harriet set up a profile for me. I didn't ask her to. She just went ahead and did it without me even knowing.'

Connor laughs at Max's defensiveness. In response, Max turns an even deeper shade of pink.

'What on earth are you doing taking dating advice from Mum? I mean, I know it's been a long time, bro, but it's been practically a lifetime for her. Why didn't you come to me if you were thinking of getting back out on the dating scene?'

'Because I wasn't thinking about it. I didn't have any inclination to go out at all, let alone on dates with complete strangers. They just somehow talked me into it. You know what Mum's like when she gets going, and Harriet's even worse.'

'But isn't there something a bit – I dunno – desperate about internet dating?'

'Well, maybe I was desperate. Desperate to get Mum and Harriet off my case, at least. But I was right before – it's far too soon.'

I couldn't agree more. Perhaps there'll come a time when we'll both feel differently. Right now, though, I can't imagine when that time might arrive and what it might feel like if it ever does.

'Hang on there a second. There's no need to throw in the dating towel just yet. Just because you had one bad experience doesn't mean to say the next one, or the one after that, will be the same. Like I said, it's early days.'

'There won't be a next one. That's my lot. I should have listened to my instincts. Rachel's only been gone a year. It wouldn't feel right to be seeing someone else. Not yet. Maybe not ever. I just don't know.'

Max has spoken rapidly, almost tripping over his own words in a bid to get them out before Connor has an opportunity to argue with him.

'Look, I get that you've been burnt by one bad experience. But you haven't got anything to feel guilty about. It's not your fault Rachel died. And there's no reason you should be on your own forever as a result. You can't seriously want that?'

'Connor, I can barely think about what's going to happen tomorrow, let alone years in the future. All I know is that it feels too soon. And I'm sure that other people – people who knew Rachel and me – would think it was too soon too.'

'Who cares what other people think? I knew you both and I don't think it's too soon. I read something online the other day and it made me think of you. I should have sent you the link. It was an article about how long it takes to get over the end of a relationship. Apparently, the going rate is a month for every year. Now, you and Rachel were together – what, ten years? – and it's been over a year that you've been on your own already, so technically you've every right to start seeing other women now. In fact, if you want to be pedantic about it, you've already lost a few legitimate months.'

Max stares at Connor with the incredulity I'm feeling.

'Are you for real? A month for every year? That's crass, Connor, even for you.'

'Okay okay, don't shoot the messenger. I'm only telling you what I read online. It was supposed to make you feel better. Jesus. I'm just trying to reassure you that you don't have anything to feel guilty about.'

'It's not just about feeling guilty. It's about being honourable. I don't expect you to understand.'

'You're right. I don't understand because it hasn't happened to me. But I don't think you're doing yourself any favours by burying your head in the sand. What's your plan – to spend the next forty-odd years in a state of perpetual denial?'

Max and Connor fall into a silence of passive irritation against a backdrop of cheering from the playing field as the first race begins. It's one of the older classes, not Ellie's, allowing the two brothers to remain locked inside their respective grievances.

It's not Connor's fault that Max is angry. It's not anyone's. Connor, like Harriet and Joan before him, is just trying to say what he thinks are the right words in the right order. His only fault is not knowing that there simply aren't any right words, right now, in any order, to make any of this okay for Max.

It's Connor who, to his credit, eventually breaks the silence.

'Look, Max, I know how much you loved Rachel. And you know how much I loved her too. She was awesome. I told you that right from the get-go, that very first time I met her. Do you remember? That dinner party she and Harriet put on when you two were first going out?'

Of course I remember. It was in that tiny top-floor flat in Earls Court that Harriet and I shared when we first moved to London. We could only afford a one-bedroom place so Harriet took the sitting room as her bedroom, while the kitchen – just large enough for a four-seated table – sufficed as our only communal area. That dinner party had been Harriet's suggestion, a way for me to have her moral support when I first met Max's brother, the sibling I'd heard so much about and who sounded so much more grown-up than any of us. I think Harriet and I had been desperate to prove our cosmopolitan credentials, although whether to Connor, Max or ourselves I was never quite sure. We cooked pasta and had salad with avocado in it and bought wine on a deal in the supermarket that we assumed must be good because the entire label was written in French, and I remember us thinking how sophisticated we were to be hosting a Saturday night dinner for my new boyfriend and his wealthy elder brother. It had been an undeniable success, that evening, Connor far less intimidating than I'd imagined, he and Harriet intellectually sparring all night, Max stroking my hand under the table both as reassurance of the evening's triumph thus far and a promise of what was to come later.

Of course I remember. I'll never forget it.

'I know you did. I know Mum did. I know Harriet did, for god's sake, because they'd been best friends for decades. That's why I can't understand why any of you are pushing me to start dating other people when you must all know that Rachel wouldn't like it. In fact, it's more than that. She'd hate it.'

'Really? You really think she wouldn't want you to be happy? Because the Rachel I knew would. Remember when Ellie was only a few months old and you got invited on that stag weekend and you said you wouldn't go, that it wouldn't be fair to leave Rachel on her own but she talked you into it? Didn't she say you deserved a break even though she was the one who was up every bloody night with Ellie? Or all those evenings she flew solo that year you were doing your photography course and became totally obsessed with your camera? And what about all those Saturday afternoons she was cool about us hanging out at the football when I'm sure she'd rather you'd spent time with her and Ellie? Seriously, bro, I think you underestimate just how generous that wife of yours was. I used to think that if only I could meet someone half as cool as Rachel even I might succumb to the marriage bug. So don't do her a disservice now by forgetting any of that and making out that she wouldn't want you to be happy.'

I don't know whether to feel gratified that Connor remembers all of those episodes or guilty that I don't, in truth, live up to his elevated image of me. Not right now, anyway.

Max takes a few seconds to consider what Connor has said.

'But there's a world of difference between day-to-day selflessness in a marriage and being cool about your husband dating other women. A world of difference. And if I know Rachel I'm pretty damn sure that she'd be horrified at the prospect. I'm just not willing to do that to her.'

Max folds his arms conclusively and I issue a silent declaration of thanks for his acceptance of my imperfections even after I've gone.

'Listen, you're probably right, you're probably not ready to meet random strangers yet, and internet dates are likely to be the most random there are. All I'm saying is I don't think you should close the dating door altogether. I think you just need to be a bit more selective, a bit more careful about who you spend time with. Why don't you let me fix you up with one of my friends? I know quite a few women who'd love that whole intellectual, thoughtful, creative thing you've got going on. How about I don't even send you out on your own? I'll organize a good old-fashioned double date with a couple of the more discerning women I know. At least then you'd have someone to vouch for the fact that the woman's not a total psycho and someone else to talk to if it's as disastrous as the last one. The worst it will be is a fun night out with your big brother. How can you possibly argue with that?'

Connor embraces Max with the neck-lock that substitutes for physical affection between them. Max responds with a mock endeavour to free himself and they struggle playfully for a few seconds in a pantomime that isn't at all out of kilter with the playground setting.

'Okay, fine – if it'll get you to release my neck before you strangle me. But only if it's essentially just a night out for me and you. And if the women you bring along aren't the kind you usually date, who think three-syllable words only come in foreign languages. And only if you swear that you won't disappear halfway through the evening leaving me to make awkward small talk on my own. Agreed?'

'That's one long list of conditions but whatever you say, bro. I'll rack my brains to find us the perfect female companions and I won't even expect thanks after we've had a fantastic night. Well, not much anyway.'

The boys laugh together in a spirit of fraternal camaraderie, leaving me in a state of exiled confusion. I can't understand why Max has agreed to it. Not when he'd seemed so resolute.

And I can't understand either why everyone's suddenly so keen for Max to start dating again. Perhaps they are actually doing what they think is best for him, what they think will help him recover, but I can't help fearing that everyone's desperation for Max to move on is more about alleviating their own discomfort than helping Max overcome his grief. I keep coming back to the gnawing suspicion that it would be a damn sight easier for everyone around him if Max stopped playing the part of the grieving widower and rediscovered his fun side. If he started living more freely without my shadow darkening his every conversation. If he allowed everyone to forget that tragedy is lurking silently and oh-so-closely in the wings of all our lives at any given time.

I can't help wondering whether everyone's entreaties are intended to make Max's life easier or their own?

'Right, stop congratulating yourself for a second, Connor. It's Ellie's first race up next.'

I look towards the racetrack and there's Ellie, pigtailed-hair and skinny legs in pink shorts with an incongruous look of determination on her face. It seems to be the fifty-metre sprint, two dozen seven-year-olds lined up alongside one another, with Ellie in the middle, appearing to be taking it all very seriously indeed.

The teacher blows the starting whistle and all the children simultaneously scramble across the chalky white line, intense concentration on their faces. Max and Connor are cheering from the benches, shouting Ellie's name with enough volume to drown out the other parents' encouragements. Ellie is running fast, faster than I've ever seen her, and she's heading up the pack with two other girls. One of her main competitors glances sideways to assess her place in the contest and, failing to realize that running forward in a straight line when you're seven necessitates looking ahead without a fraction's deviation, loses her footing, stumbles momentarily, and sets herself back a couple of paces, into the trailing mob of children. It's Ellie and another girl now, Ellie red-faced and puffing, her face a picture of single-mindedness, illustrating the determined recognition that, whatever her teacher or Max may have told her, winning does matter. And then they're coming up to the finishing line and both girls drive themselves forward with one last push of concerted effort but it's Ellie's eager shoulders that make it over the finishing line first.

Max and Connor are high-fiving each other on the sidelines with the same degree of celebration as if QPR had just won the premiership. Mr Baxter places a plastic gold medal on a red ribbon around Ellie's neck. Beaming with pride she runs immediately to her supporters and jumps straight into Max's arms.

'Did you see, Daddy? I won! I won the race!'

'Of course we saw, sweetheart. Couldn't you hear us cheering? You were so fast. Well done, my angel.'

'I've never won a race before. Not even in PE when we're just messing around. Look, I got a medal.'

'Let me see that. Now that is one very good-looking medal. We'll have to hang that up in your bedroom when we get home, won't we?'

'I've still got more races to do yet, Daddy. I've got the relay and the three-legs race. I might win more medals.'

Max laughs.

'Yes, you might. But even one is very, very good.'

Ellie grins, pride sparkling from her chocolate eyes.

'Mummy would like my medal, wouldn't she?'

Max returns her thoughtful gaze and smiles tenderly.

'She'd love it, sweetheart. She'd have been so very proud of you. Just as Uncle Connor and I are.'

Ellie flings her arms around Max's neck with contented reassurance, the happiness on her face a world away from last year's melancholy and it's evidence enough that history won't repeat itself today as I'd so feared it might.

As I watch Ellie tighten her grip around Max's neck, a warm breeze grazes my face, appearing from nowhere and having no discernible source. I close my eyes and relish the comfort of this rare phenomenon, the sensation of something, anything, touching my skin, even though it's impossible to decipher its origin.

The warm breeze fades away and I open my eyes to the discovery that I'm back alone in the whiteness. Ellie, Max, Connor, the sports field: they've all disappeared.

For a fleeting moment, there's the familiar ache of sadness and the wish to have been allowed to stay for longer. But then I think back to the sight of Ellie's triumphant smile as she crossed the finishing line, to the look of euphoria on her face when the medal was placed around her neck, to the delight in her eyes when she showed it to Max, and I remember just how lucky I am to have been there at all today, to have been privy to events from which I know I should, technically, be excluded.

I'm reminded of the first day I arrived here, of the first time my access was granted and subsequently denied, of my terror then that my bird's eye view of the living world might have been a one-time-only opportunity or, worse still, nothing more than the product of an over-active imagination. And yet here I am, over a year later, watching another of Ellie's Sports Days, sharing in the joy and triumph of my daughter's success, and I feel grateful, not just for today but for the confidence I now have that I'll be revisiting her again, sooner or later. I still don't profess to understand where I am or why I'm here but I do now feel able to ride that ambiguous wave until such time as I understand what – if any – meaning there is to all of this.

# CHAPTER 9

I hear a bell ring and, as the opaque mist finally diffuses to expose what's underneath, I see I'm in the hallway of my house and Ellie's running to answer the front door. She opens it to reveal my mum on the other side and I'm not sure whether it's me or Ellie who's more thrilled to see her.

It was quite some time after I died before I realized that everything I saw in the living world had to be channelled through Max or Ellie's presence; I never have access to anything that doesn't involve either one or both of them. So I only ever see my mum or Harriet or anyone else I used to know if their interaction with Max and Ellie happens to coincide with my access to the living world. And given that Ellie only visits Mum once a month, those coincidences are far less frequent than I'd like.

'Aren't you all grown-up, answering the door to Nanna. How are you, darling girl?'

'I'm okay. I was just watching cartoons on TV. What are we going to do at yours this weekend, Nanna?'

Mum still hasn't quite got her jacket off but she's used to Ellie chattering away the second she arrives.

'Well, by the time we drive back to Salisbury it will be nearly lunchtime, so I thought we could go to that café you like for a sandwich and a hot chocolate. Then I thought maybe you'd like to go to a farm for the afternoon – there's one we haven't been to before where you can ride horses. How does that sound?'

'Can I really go on a horse? I'd love that.'

'I thought you might. And then tomorrow, if the weather's good, which the BBC says it will be, I thought we could have a nice long walk along the river before I cook you your favourite Sunday lunch.'

'We're having roast beef?'

Mum nods, smiling with pleasure at Ellie's excitement.

'And roast potatoes and your special gravy?'

'Not only that, I've also made chocolate brownies for dessert, if you think you might be able to manage all that?'

'I can definitely manage all that. I'm going upstairs, Nanna, 'cos I've got to finish packing my bag.'

Ellie scampers up the stairs on all fours and disappears into her bedroom. Max calls Mum from the kitchen, where he's already in the process of making coffee.

'How are you, Max? Ellie seems to be in very good spirits.'

'That's the end of the school year for you. It's a relief for both of us, albeit for different reasons. She'll be bored by the end of next week whereas I'll only just be starting to recover.'

So it's the start of the summer holidays. That means no more than a couple of weeks have elapsed since my last visit, since Ellie's Sports Day triumph.

'Yes, I remember it well from Rachel's schooldays. Those first couple of weeks of feverish activity before a month of restlessness kicks in. I know you teachers need a break but I do think six weeks is too long for children.'

'As both a teacher and a parent I don't disagree with you on either count. But spending a few days with you will be great for her. She's been really looking forward to it.'

'I have too. It'll be lovely for me to have her to myself for more than a single night.'

I don't think Mum means to sound pointed, but she does nonetheless. It's been an unspoken bone of contention ever since Ellie was born, the fact that Max's parents get to see her almost every day in contrast to Mum's monthly visits. I know she'd never say anything, and I'm sure she'd rather she didn't even feel it, but I've always suspected that she wishes I'd never moved to London. I think she'd rather I'd stayed living in Salisbury, found a job locally and provided her with the proximity to her grandchild that she'd been selfless enough to give her own parents.

'So, Max, what have you got planned with four days of freedom ahead?'

'Oh, you know, just seeing some friends, catching up, maybe a beer or two. It's been a hellish term and the summer holidays really couldn't have come soon enough.'

'That's nice. Are you seeing anyone I know?'

'Yes, I'm going out with Connor and a few of his . . . um . . . friends this evening. He's organized a bit of a night out.'

Mum doesn't clock the significance of what Max has just said, but I do. It's actually happening. He must actually be allowing Connor to take him out on that stupid double date. Perhaps this isn't even the first. Perhaps they've been hitting the town on dozens of double dates in the fortnight I've been absent.

'That's nice. A boys' night out, is it? I'm sure you could do with one of those.'

'Er, kind of. Well, not really. No, I don't suppose it is.'

Mum raises an amused eyebrow as though Max is simply being vague.

'So what have you got planned?'

Max looks decidedly sheepish. Shifty, even, I'd say.

'Connor, he's . . . er . . . he's arranged for us to go out with a couple of friends of his. A couple of women he knows, through work I think. Although I'm not sure exactly how he knows them, I haven't really been paying much attention to be honest.'

Max keeps his back turned to Mum as he gabbles nervously, evading her gaze for as long as he can so he doesn't see – as I do – the changing expressions on her face from confusion to deduction to surprise to incredulity.

'Do you mean to tell me you and your brother are going out on dates together tonight?'

Max hands Mum the mug of coffee but he still isn't ready to look her in the eye.

'It's nothing serious. It's just a bit of fun, you know. Connor thought I could do with getting out of the house.'

Max feigns a half-hearted laugh but Mum's face remains stony.

'I can't believe I'm hearing this, Max. You're actually going on a date tonight? With another woman? When Rachel's only been gone just over a year?'

'Celia, please don't take this out of proportion. It's really not a big deal if we don't make it one.'

'Well forgive me, but I think it is a big deal. It hadn't even occurred to me that you'd start dating again. Not so soon. What on earth possessed you, Max?'

'I'm not dating. Not really. I don't know why I even mentioned it. It was stupid of me. I'm sorry.'

I know why Max mentioned it. It's his full disclosure gene, the congenital predisposition to tell people the truth even when it's not in his – or their – best interests.

'So is that why you wanted me to have Ellie for longer this time? So that you and Connor could go out on these . . . on these dates? God, I feel like such a fool. I suppose I'm the last to know, am I?'

'There's nothing to know, Celia. Please, you have to stop seeing this as more than it actually is. It's just one night out with my brother and some of his friends. Nothing more.'

'I wish that were true, Max. But it's not, is it? It's not just a normal night out. It's a night out with a woman who I suspect will be hoping for a little more than polite, platonic chit-chat. That's generally the purpose of a date, isn't it, or have things really altered that much since my day?'

Max falls silent momentarily. I detect a ripple of frustration furrow his brow before he blinks it away and lets out a long, slow, patient breath.

'I'm not looking for anything other than a vaguely entertaining evening with my brother, Celia. It's just that most people seem to think I need to get out of the house. Start engaging with the world again. That's all I'm trying to do.'

'I don't disagree, Max. I've told you myself that I'm worried about you getting stuck in a rut, that I think you need a change of scene. That's why I keep asking you to come and stay with me more often, just to get out of London for a few days. But you kept telling me you're fine. Now I discover you're so fine that you're about to go on a date with an unknown woman when my daughter's been dead barely a year.'

Mum stares questioningly at Max, as if daring him to contradict her, and I feel a wave of gratitude to her for being the only person to voice my concerns, for being the lone dissenting voice amidst the Pro-Dating Brigade. It's not that I want Max to be on his own forever, or to be unhappy, or to spend the rest of his life in mourning for me. I just wish I had some control over the timeline of his recovery. Don't they say that divorcing couples should move at the pace of the slowest partner? The same, surely, must be true of the bereaved? And right now the prospect of him dating other people feels painfully premature.

But perhaps I'm deluding myself. Perhaps I'd be saying the same thing in two years, in ten years, in twenty. Perhaps I'll never be ready to contemplate the possibility of Max being romantically involved with someone else. I can't predict the future. All I can do is know how I feel now, and now feels much, much too soon.

'I don't want to row, Max, but surely you can see why I'm upset? It just seems very . . . precipitate. I couldn't have conceived of going out with another man a year after Robert died.'

It's true. She couldn't. In fact, Mum never went out with another man ever again after Dad died, in spite of plenty of people asking her, in spite of the fact that she remains, to this day, an attractive woman, in spite of my encouragement, particularly after I left home, that she seek happiness in a new relationship. It was never too late, I used to assure her, but Mum was resolute: she'd had her love, she'd lost it prematurely and that was the end of it. As I got older, and my own romances came and went, I became convinced that Mum's decision was irrational, that it didn't make sense to keep alight a long-gone flame to the extinguishment of all others. I remember telling her on more than a handful of occasions that nothing lasts forever, that Dad wouldn't have wanted her to be alone, that she had the rest of her life yet to live.

It's only now that I realize how ignorant I was, and how arrogant.

It's only now that I realize how much I wish Max were as resolute as Mum.

'Everyone's different, Celia. I'm just trying to do what I think might be right for me. If you want the truth, I'm not sure I'm ready for this yet, either.'

'Why do it then? I don't think I'm the only person who'll find it strange. How's it going to look to other people if they see you out with another woman so soon? They'll think that you never really cared about Rachel, that you and she didn't have the wonderful marriage I know you did. They'll think it odd that you seem to have recovered so quickly. Doesn't that worry you in the slightest?'

'Celia, you're preaching to the converted. I've had exactly the same anxieties. But somehow Mum and Connor and Harriet have all managed to persuade me otherwise. You were right, I was in a rut and now I feel I have to do something to get out of it.'

'But I don't understand why that means you have to take such ... such drastic action. It almost sounds like you've forgotten what you and Rachel meant to each other, how much you loved one another, how special she was to you. How can that have disappeared so quickly?'

Mum has begun to weep slow, lonely tears and I don't know whether she's crying for me or Max or Dad or herself. Perhaps it's just not possible to distinguish one load of grief and pain from another.

Max slumps into one of the kitchen chairs, his shoulders hunched forward in resignation. Sadness, frustration and defeat are written on his face as clearly as if in indelible ink. I watch him sitting there, no doubt wondering how on earth he got himself into this conversation, and I can't help thinking that here is a man for whom it's impossible to do right by everyone, however hard he tries.

'Forgotten her? Why would you even say something like that, Celia? This is Rachel we're talking about. The woman I loved, the woman I married, the woman I thought I was going to spend the rest of my life with. But now I'm not. And I have to find a way to try and deal with that, every minute of every day, for as long as I live.'

'I know you loved her, Max. I know you did. That's why I can't understand how you're even contemplating seeing other women so soon after she's gone.'

'Because she's never coming back. I'm never going to see her again. It's taken over a year for that to sink in, but I finally get it. Now all I want to do is collect together whatever shards of life she's left behind and try and rebuild something that in some small way resembles normality, whatever that may be.'

I'm never coming back. It's the first time I've ever heard Max say it and the feelings of fear and anxiety and incapacity are akin to finding myself here for the first time all over again. He's starting to move on with his life, and there's nothing whatsoever I can do about it.

I think of all the thousands of hours I've filled with fantasies about what I'm doing here, about whether the reason I can still keep an eye on the living is because I won't always be part of the dead, about whether this vicarious, impotent, semi-existence is an endurance test before I'm proved worthy of a return. But now I discover that not even Max hopes ever to see me again.

'I'm sorry, Max. Of course you've got to do whatever you think best, whatever's right for you. It's just come as a bit of a shock, that's all. The last thing I want is to fall out with you over it.'

Max sighs, whether out of relief or forgiveness, I'm not entirely sure.

'Of course we're not going to fall out, Celia. I just think no one really understands how hard this is. I spend all my time weighing up every last decision to figure out what's best for Ellie and what's best for me in this odd little two-person family we find ourselves in. It's bloody hard work so I suppose I take it pretty personally when people tell me I'm getting it all wrong.'

Mum places a prominently veined hand on top of Max's.

'Max, you should know that if there's one person who understands precisely what you're going through it's me. I have been exactly where you are. Of course I know how hard this is for you. That's why I keep offering to help out more. It's why I keep suggesting that I come and stay for a while – to help out, to look after you both. I think it would do you both good and you know how much I'd love to.'

'I know, and it's not that I don't appreciate it. I just think it's important for Ellie and me to adjust to living together, just the two of us. And it's not as if I don't have a lot of help on hand, what with Mum and Dad just around the corner.'

Mum's face tenses almost imperceptibly but I know every nuance of her expressions too well not to read it. I can see how much more there is that she wants to say, how much hurt there is that she wants to share and how strong the self-containment needs to be for her to hold on to it all.

'Well, the offer's there if you need it.'

'Thanks, Celia. And I'm sorry about today. It was insensitive of me even mentioning it.'

Mum doesn't respond for a few seconds as she lowers herself slowly, carefully on to one the kitchen chairs. For the first time I see how much she's aged, not just the greying hair and the additional lines of grief she wears under her make-up but the tiredness of her limbs that no longer seem imbued with the energy or the inclination to move with any great alacrity.

'I just miss her so, so much, Max. I still talk to her all the time, you know, sometimes without even being aware of it. I'll be in the kitchen or the garden and I'll realize suddenly that I've been chatting away to her, as though she were still right by my side. She was my rock for such a long time and now I just don't know what to do without her.'

Mum drops her head into her hands and weeps quietly as I hover nearby, just a few feet above her and yet infinitely out of reach. Max pulls up a chair beside her and puts a gentle arm around her shoulders.

'It's hard, Celia. No one knows quite how hard unless they're going through it with you. That's probably why I've kept such a close rein on the group of people Ellie and I spend time with now. So few people understand.'

'You'd have thought I'd be better at dealing with it this time around, though. I should know how to cope by now but this is so much worse than I ever thought possible. I thought I knew the worst that grief had to offer when Robert died but this . . . I just don't think I'll ever recover from this.'

'It's going to take time, Celia. It's going to take time for all of us.'

'I'm not sure there's enough time in the universe for me to get over losing Rachel.'

'I know. I feel it too. Every day.'

'I know you do, Max. And I'm sorry, I shouldn't be burdening you like this.'

'You don't have to apologize. Of course you should be sharing this with me.'

Mum squeezes Max's hand and smiles gratefully before the lines around her eyes deepen and she begins shaking her head as though to eradicate whatever image has come into her mind.

'I just wish it had been me. It's all the wrong way round.'

'What do you mean?'

'It's all so cruel, Max. No parent should ever have to bury their child. I'd give my life a thousand times over for Rachel to have hers back. I wish it every single day.'

I choke back my own tears as I watch Mum's head drop into her hands. I had no idea she was still so raw. I hadn't realized because I haven't seen her in such a long time, though that doesn't make me feel any less guilty for not knowing.

It's only now, seeing her like this, that I'm able to acknowledge to myself just how much I miss her too.

When I was alive, Mum and I would talk on the phone almost every day, just as we had done since I first went to university, when I'd guiltily left behind the person who'd nurtured me single-handedly for the past nine years. It's a different bond, I'm sure, that between a parent and a child where there's a loss or an absence or a vacuum that you're both trying to fill. There's a responsibility to one another, a responsibility to make good the loss and to be that much more to one another to accommodate it, a closeness that I suspect is unnecessary in families with both parents present. It's a responsibility that I sometimes found over-whelming, on days or nights when I'd be out with friends worrying about Mum at home alone in ways that my peers never seemed burdened by. But it was all I'd ever known, and one's life as a child inevitably feels normal if you've never experienced anything different.

I remember the feeling, from such a young age, of wanting Mum to be proud of me. It's always felt like the very least I owed her. Even my move to London was, to my mind, about fulfilling that ambition, about repaying the debt of my upbringing through achievements I knew she valued: a loving partner whose company she appreci-ated, a successful career she could tell her friends about, a comfortable home she was keen to visit, a stable family with whom she could enjoy spending time. Perhaps that's a part of every child's ambition. Perhaps all children – whatever their endeavours – are in some way hoping to prove that a lifetime's parenting isn't in vain. Perhaps mine was merely exacerbated by the loss that Mum had already suffered, by the disappointments that life had already apportioned her, by the knowledge that I really was all she had left.

Looking at Mum now, head in her hands, shoulders hunched with the weight of accumulated grief, I can't imagine how on earth she's borne yet another of life's tragedies, how she can manage to forgive the world that's robbed her of so much.

I spent my life not wanting to disappoint her and yet, in the end, I inflicted on her the worst form of punishment any child could.

Ellie appears in the doorway suddenly, complete with Scooby Doo rucksack on her back, ready for her Wiltshire adventure. She stops in her tracks, swiftly surveying the scene before her, a look of consternation settling unnervingly on her face.

'What's wrong? Why's everyone sad? What's happened?'

Max immediately picks up on her concern, attuned to the instinctive connection Ellie now makes between weeping adults and proximate tragedy.

'Nothing's happened, sweetheart. Nanna was just feeling a little bit upset and I was helping make her feel better. But you know what's going to make her feel so much better? You two going to Salisbury and having a lovely four days together.'

Ellie smiles and climbs on to Mum's lap where she wraps her arms around her grandmother's neck and envelops her in the strongest clinch a seven-year-old could possibly muster.

'You smell nice, Nanna.'

'Thank you, Ellie. That will be my perfume. It's called Chance by Chanel. Maybe we could let you put a little bit on when we get back home.'

That's the perfume I used to wear too.

Ellie pulls her arms from around Mum's neck and smiles impishly at her.

'When we get to the café, can I have a jacket potato with melted cheese and a cake for afters?'

Mum returns her smile and pops her back on her feet.

'Of course you can, darling. Now, have you got everything? Your nightie? And your toothbrush? And your special bear?'

'I've got everything. Daddy helped pack most of my things earlier on.'

As Max stands on the doorstep to see them off, I feel the familiar fluctuation of air that signals I'll be leaving soon too. I catch one last glimpse of Ellie in the front seat of Mum's car, perched up on a booster cushion, blowing goodbye kisses to Max and waving excitedly through the window.

The clouds begin to gather beneath me, concealing Max from view and leaving me with nothing but anxious speculation as to what his evening ahead may hold in store.

# CHAPTER 10

'So, you're an artist, Connor tells me? What made you decide to do that rather than something more – well – a bit more conventional, I suppose?'

Sadie, the 'artist', flicks her long, artificially blonde hair over her shoulders with a degree of affectation that suggests she's expecting to be photographed by a swarm of paparazzi at any moment rather than what she's actually doing, sitting anonymously at a small round table with my husband in the corner of the kind of nightclub Max has always hated, with its self-regarding clientele and its ostentatiously aloof barman. I've no doubt it was Connor's choice of location given how much fun he seems to be having, lining up shot glasses at the bar in the company of a conspicuously beautiful woman.

Sadie, meanwhile, smiles at Max as if in deep contemplation of her answer, before waving her blonde locks around again like she's auditioning for a shampoo commercial. She's repeated this hair-tossing display several times in the few minutes since I arrived, which has proved more than long enough for me to deduce that Sadie's the kind of woman for whom flirtation is as imperative as breathing.

'Well, you know, in my humble opinion, becoming an artist isn't something you choose. It's something – I believe – that chooses you.'

She smiles coquettishly as though the idea that her opinion could be perceived as anything even vaguely resembling humble is clearly absurd.

'And I can't pretend to feel anything other than privileged that I'm one of the chosen ones. I do know how lucky I am. When I think of all those poor people traipsing off to their offices, you know, for their dull nine-to-five existences, I thank my lucky stars that my talents lie in other directions.'

As if to display – for the avoidance of any possible doubt – what one of her many self-confessed talents might include, Sadie pushes her chair back from the table, extracts her long, slim legs from underneath it, bare legs concealed only at the nether regions of her thighs by a skirt which might more accurately be described as a wide belt, and crosses them slowly, deliberately and – undeniably – seductively, for all the world to see.

My jaw would be on the floor if there was any chance of it reaching that far. Subtlety, it would seem, is not one of Sadie's apparently numerous attributes.

'Yes, well, you'll have to tell me more about it. But can I get you another drink first?'

'Ooh, yes, go on then. I'd love another gin and tonic. But go easy on the tonic.'

She flutters her faux-demure eyelashes and raises the corner of her lips just enough to suggest that it's universally acknowledged that going easy on the tonic is the world's best-known euphemism for morally questionable sexual practices.

Max potters off to the bar, seemingly oblivious to the fact that his date is emulating every clichéd characteristic employed by the stars of late-night, pay-TV movies.

Sadie is exactly the kind of woman I'd have expected Connor to set Max up with. In fact, if I had to pick out one of Connor's female friends – or, who knows, former conquests – from a line-up of a hundred women, I'd have bet pretty good money on identifying Sadie. Not only artificially blonde, she's also impeccably groomed and – I'd wager good money on it – surgically enhanced; those breasts can't possibly be the ones nature bestowed upon her and I'm sure it's rare to witness lips that plump if they haven't seen the spike of a surgeon's syringe.

If that weren't enough, her outfit leaves so little to the imagination that she might as well be wearing a sandwich board advertising precisely what's on offer. Except a sandwich board would cover up significantly more than she's willing to conceal. She's paired the teeny brown leather mini-skirt with a transparent cream chiffon blouse underlaid with nothing more than a lacy, cleavage-enhancing bra. A bra that I suspect was deliberately bought two sizes too small precisely for the effect it's now creating.

She's the kind of woman from whom most other women instantly recoil and to whom most men are instinctively – infuriatingly – attracted. But Max isn't most men. Or at least in this regard, anyway, I sincerely hope he's not.

'So, how's it going, Maxy? Are you charming the literal pants off our young Sadie, then?'

Connor drapes one arm around his date who looks like she's walked straight out of the casting book of a leading modelling agency, while clasping the back of Max's neck with his other hand.

'We're having a perfectly civilized chat, actually.'

Max's inability to pronounce his consonants properly is as much indication as ever I've needed that he's a little bit tipsy.

'She's a corker, though, isn't she? I told you you could count on me, didn't I, huh? You've got to trust your big brother on the really important things in life, haven't you, Maxy?'

Connor ruffles his little brother's hair, a fraternal tic that Max usually hates, but they both seem too drunk this evening to have remembered that.

'You're a very, very good big brother, Connor. Now, let me get to the bar so that I can get us some more drinks. Although it looks like you two might already be well catered for.'

Max edges his way past Connor and waits far too patiently for one of the unnecessarily handsome European barmen to acknowledge his presence. After he's finally been served a few minutes later, he returns with the easy-on-the-tonic gin for Sadie and an overpriced bottle of lager for himself.

As he sits back down at the table, Sadie leans over and plucks what I'm almost certain is an imaginary piece of fluff from Max's shirt, just to the right of his left nipple. As she theatrically flicks the non-existent detritus on to the floor, she smiles invitingly at him, as though she's just saved him from a fate worse than death and is in need of some form of gratitude.

Max looks a little taken aback at having had his nipple unexpectedly fondled by this relative stranger, but he's too well-mannered to do anything except smile politely.

'So, what kind of art do you do?'

'Well, my art is, you know, not really art in any conventional sense. There's no stretching of canvases where I'm involved. I'm a performance artist.'

Sadie says this with a flourish in her voice as though delivering information that could only possibly be received with awe and admiration.

'God, that's different. So what kind of performances do you do?'

'Well, you know, my art is all about challenging the objectification of the male gaze. So essentially it's a dance performance which I combine with the power of undress, and with photography and video, to create a deeply subversive experience. Just as I'm down to my undies and they think I'm about to give them the full monty, I project images of women's suffering throughout the ages around the room. The photos and videos interfere with my choreography and it creates, you know, a really unnerving juxtaposition between conflicting views of female empowerment and femininity. I suppose you'd call it feminist performance art but, you know, I prefer to eschew those kinds of labels.'

Sadie's 'performance art' sounds disarmingly like burlesque to me. Or, to give it its proper, old-fashioned name: stripping.

'So where do you do these performances? In galleries and stuff?'

'No, my view has always been that art shouldn't be confined to galleries. That it should be, you know, at the heart of the public arena, that it should be discovered rather than anticipated, that the element of surprise is key. I don't think you should wait for people to come to art, but that art should go to the people. So I go to pubs and clubs – sometimes even working men's clubs – and cabaret nights. I think I have the most impact where, you know, I'm least expected.'

I wonder if Sadie says 'you know' every other sentence precisely because she's aware somewhere – however deep down – that people haven't got the foggiest idea what she's going on about.

'That sounds like powerful stuff. Very challenging. I mean, that's what art's all about, isn't it – challenging perceptions?'

That's another thing I love about Max: his ability to engage in topics he has absolutely no interest in. Because I'm pretty sure that fairly close to the top of the list of subjects Max would like never to have a conversation about is feminist performance art.

'Yes, well, I like to think that I'm, you know, pushing boundaries and making people think about important issues while at the same time giving them something beautiful to watch.'

Sadie licks her lips, slowly and purposefully, just in case there was any doubt that the beauty she was referring to was her own. It's as though she spent her entire adolescence at Seduction School and is now determined to put each and every lesson into practice.

Max's eyes widen with a rabbit-in-the-headlights expression that suggests even he – who's only been on one date in over a decade – is finding it impossible to ignore the blatant onslaught of flirtation being directed at him. What on earth was Connor thinking when he extracted Sadie from his little black book and decided she'd be the perfect date for my husband? I can't imagine how she could possibly be less his type.

'Anyway, aren't you a bit of an artist yourself, Max? That's what Connor led me to believe, anyway.'

Max looks perplexed as though perhaps Sadie's got him confused with someone else she's in the process of being fixed up with by Connor.

'Me, an artist? No, I'm afraid I'm just a humble history teacher.'

'Oh, come now, you're being modest. Connor told me you're an amazing photographer. He thought we'd have artistic proclivities in common.'

So that's the connection? Connor assumed that because Max used to like taking the odd photo in his spare time, he'd discover a natural affinity with a feminist performance artist?

Sadie appears to have given up on hair flicking in favour of twirling various strands around her red nail-varnished fingers, as if to demonstrate what might be possible should Max choose to let his own hands loose in it.

'Well, I think my brother may have exaggerated a bit there. I used to dabble but really I'm just a rank amateur and I haven't done much at all lately, to be honest.'

There's a further, unspoken clause at the end of that sentence but Max elects to leave it unsaid. I'm relieved, on this occasion, not to be the topic of conversation with one more capricious stranger. Especially one whom I suspect wouldn't have much patience with another woman encroaching on her territory, even conversationally, even if the other woman in question were dead.

'So what are your favourite subjects? What most turns you on when you're gazing down that long lens?'

Sadie draws Max's eyes down towards the table where her hand is wrapped around the tall, slim, perspiring tumbler in front of her, rubbing it up and down in what can only be described as a simulating – if not necessarily stimulating – gesture.

It's so absurd I don't know how Max finds the self-restraint not to laugh.

'Portraits mainly. Some landscapes, but generally only as a tourist – a nice sunset or a dramatic mountain range will invariably catch my eye. Mostly I'm interested in people's faces.'

'And what would you make of *my* face, if you were photographing me?'

Sadie turns her body away from Max and looks back over her shoulder at him in a deliberately exaggerated imitation of a model's pose. She laughs at herself with affected embarrassment.

Does she really imagine – for a second – that anyone's buying this faux-demure act?

'I'd say that you were a very fine subject. Great posture, clear skin, captivating eyes. I wouldn't even need to light you to capture those cheekbones.'

Is it my imagination or is Max actually flirting with her?

Sadie bows her head and looks up at him, Princess Diana style, through almost certainly false eyelashes.

'Perhaps we should collaborate artistically? Maybe I should, you know, commission you to take some photos of me for one of my shows? We could be like Lee Miller and Man Ray.'

Max smiles at her in response, a smile imbued with invitation and appeal, and it delivers the awful, nauseating confirmation I don't want to receive. He's actually attracted to her.

How can I have judged this one so poorly? How can Max, for that matter?

'I'm not sure I'm quite in Man Ray's league, but that sounds like it could be fun. We should make a date. But right now I need a trip to the little boys' room – just excuse me for a sec, will you?'

The little boys' room? Since when did Max start expressing himself in childish euphemisms?

On his way out, Max grabs Connor and I follow the pair of them into the toilets. I don't generally make a habit of eavesdropping on urinal-based conversations but these are exceptional circumstances and there have to be some advantages to being a dead wife, after all.

'I think she might quite like me. Do you think she likes me?'

'Of course she likes you, little bro. What's not to like? Just call me Cupid and thank me later.'

'What do you think I should do? God, it's been so long I don't even know what the protocol is any more.'

'Just carry on doing what you've been doing for the past three hours. It seems to be going down a treat if her flashing her thighs at you every five seconds is anything to go by. Trust me, Max. You're in there.'

'You really think so? You don't think she's – you know – out of my league?'

Max checks his reflection in the mirror as if to remind himself what he's got on offer. I don't know whether to be annoyed that he fancies her or irritated that he might imagine for a second that she's a better catch than he is.

'What are you talking about, Maxy? There's no one too good for my little brother. I wouldn't have set you up with her if I thought she was out of your league, would I?'

'But she's so . . . I dunno . . . self-assured. I've never really met anyone quite like her before. What on earth is she going to see in me?'

'Not a lot if you carry on acting like such an idiot. Just go for it, Maxy. What have you got to lose? It's about bloody time you had a bit of fun.'

Connor issues a gesture of encouragement in the form of a drunken man-hug while the two of them declare their love for one another in an exchange I doubt either of them will recollect in the morning.

I think I'd throw up if there was anything left in my stomach to purge. He can't really be about to make a pass at her. Can he? What will I do if he does? What will I do if he does and she reciprocates and I'm there to see it in all its gruesome technicolour glory? Watching him flirt with her has been nauseating enough. Witnessing him going any further – that's got to be every woman's worst nightmare, hasn't it, dead or alive?

As Max and Connor stumble out of the toilets, I spy Sadie sitting at the table, head down, deep in clandestine conversation with Connor's date. I hurry ahead of the boys just in time to catch the final snippets of Sadie's confession.

'He's a nice enough guy but he's not, you know, electrifying. Not really my cup of tea at all, to be honest. I'm not sure what Connor was thinking. Guess he just felt, you know, sorry for his little brother. If you don't mind I think I'm going to head off soon. You'll be okay with Connor, won't you? Looks like you two are really hitting it off, lucky thing.'

Sadie and her friend giggle conspiratorially as they're joined by my hopeful husband and his misguided brother.

I hang uselessly above them, racking my brains to determine if there's any way — any way on earth or beyond — that I can warn Max about what I've overheard. There must be some means I can employ to communicate with him or what's the point of my being here? What's the point of being able to see and hear all of this if not to help protect Max from a humiliation he's so far from being ready to suffer?

Maybe there's some telepathic way I could contact him, like an extrasensory equivalent of the silent looks we used to give one another across dinner-party tables or at crowded birthday parties, the looks that conveyed we were ready to go home or that we wanted a drink refill or that the person we were talking to was a bore and we were in need of the swiftest of rescues.

I close my eyes and visualize Max arriving back at the table and making the politest of excuses before heading home alone. Perhaps if I focus really hard he might just pick up on some signal from beyond the grave, a signal that might just spare him imminent embarrassment.

I open my eyes to see Max picking up not his coat but Sadie's glass and handing it to his brother by way of ordering another round of drinks. He's flushed and grinning, just edging over the precipice of tipsiness into the swell of inebriation.

'Come on, you. Let's leave these two lovebirds alone.'

As Connor shepherds his date back to the bar, Sadie looks at her friend with the faintest of frowns that only someone attuned to her intentions would detect.

'You know what you were saying earlier, about us collaborating some time? Well, maybe we should start by me coming to see one of your performances? Maybe I could get a personal invite?'

Max places a hand on top of Sadie's and looks directly into her eyes with a combination of lust, hope and fear. He's flirting with her. He's actually flirting. A little unsubtly and definitely drunkenly, but he's flirting nonetheless.

I don't know what's more uncomfortable: watching Max flirt with a woman I'd never have imagined him finding attractive in a million years or watching Max flirt with a woman I pre-emptively know is going to reject him.

Whichever it is, I feel woefully unprepared to witness this.

I close my eyes and try to will myself away, hoping that the rarity of the wish will increase the likelihood of it being granted. But when I open them again, I'm looking down on the table where my husband is still in the process of grinning inanely at the woman with whom it would appear he'd like to spend the night.

Sadie glances down at his hand on hers and then back at Max with an expression of sympathy. As she pulls her immaculately manicured fingers from under his and back into her lap, she smiles at him, not her coquettish smile this time, but rather the consolatory smile, the one that tells him he hasn't won first prize this time.

'Now, I wouldn't want to be seen to be giving out special favours, would I? You've no idea how jealous my fans can get. Just look up dates and venues on my website and I'll expect to see you in the audience soon.'

She opens her clutch bag and pulls out a compact which she flips open to obscure Max's view of her before theatrically powdering her nose.

Max looks momentarily confused. I don't blame him. Every discernible sign has been pointing him in the direction of mutual attraction, only for him to find himself rebuffed at the eleventh hour. It would confound even the most confident of suitors and Max is far from that at the moment.

Who does this woman think she is? And how dare she not be interested in Max, how dare she not think him 'electrifying' enough, how dare she pull her hand away from his when I'd give anything – anything at all – to be touched by Max just one more time.

I could strangle Connor right now.

'Well, I might just have to do that. And perhaps, maybe, I could take you for a drink afterwards?'

Max doesn't seem to have understood the conclusiveness of the rejection he's already suffered and it's hardly surprising. Connor's led Max into an exaggerated state of romantic confidence while Sadie's led him into a false sense of flirtatious security; it's a lethal combination. No wonder he thinks there's still a chance of a happy ending.

Sadie looks at her watch.

'You know, it's getting pretty late. I think I might head home, if that's okay with you?'

'Oh, really? I think Connor's getting us some more drinks. Won't you stay for one more at least?'

Sadie bites her bottom lip coquettishly before producing yet another of her dazzling smiles aimed at masking the hypocrisy of the brush-off she's delivering. This woman can't put a lid on her flirtations even when she's in the throes of a dismissal.

'Not for me, sadly. I've got work to do tomorrow. There's no rest for wicked artists at the weekend, you know. You'll say goodbye to the others for me, won't you?'

Max nods, half-heartedly, as he stands up to help her on with her coat.

'Enjoy the rest of your evening. And I'm sure I'll see you around, you know, at one of your brother's infamous parties.'

Sadie places a patronizing hand on Max's arm who responds with a stoical smile, albeit perhaps a little too apologetically for the sake of dignity on either side. He leans over to kiss Sadie goodbye, but she turns her head away dismissively, leaving Max no option but to kiss the air beside her cheek instead. And with that she sweeps out of the club and out of Max's life, almost certainly forever.

As Max stands by the table, engulfed by his own bemusement, Connor bounds over with a bottle of champagne in one hand and two glasses in the other.

'I thought I'd help spice things up for you two. Where is she? Gone to the ladies to freshen up for you, has she?'

Max looks blankly at his brother as if only semi-aware of his presence.

'Max. What are you looking at me like a moron for? Just take the bottle and the glasses and enjoy a late night tipple on me.'

As Connor bangs the bottle down on the table, Max emerges from his private reverie.

'She's gone.'

'What, to the loo? It's fine, it'll still be cold when she gets back.'

'No. She's gone home. She's left. I don't get it.'

'Nah, you must be mistaken. She's probably just gone to powder her nose. You know what women are like. I'll get Saskia to go and check on her if you like.'

'No, Connor, you're not listening. She's gone home. She told me she was going home. As soon as we got back from the toilets she couldn't get out of here quick enough. I don't understand.'

Now it's Connor's turn to look perplexed. He stares at the door for a few seconds, then at Sadie's empty chair, then at Max before repeating the drunken charade twice more until the penny finally drops.

'Well that's bloody weird. Sorry, mate. Don't know what happened there. I thought you and her were a dead cert this evening. But don't look so miserable. The night's still young. Let me retrieve Saskia from the bar and we'll do a quick tour of this place to find you someone else.'

Max shrugs Connor's heavy arm from where it's slumped over his shoulders and pulls his coat wearily from the back of his chair.

'I don't think so. I'm going to call it a night.'

'What? Don't be stupid. This place doesn't close for hours yet.'

'I'm going home. I should never have come in the first place. I don't know what I was thinking letting you talk me into this. I knew it was a mistake.'

'Hey, bro, don't be so down on it all. So one woman gives you the brush off? So what? Plenty more fish in the sea. Especially in a place like this. Come on, have a glass of champagne.'

'No, thanks, I've had enough. I'm an idiot. I acted like an idiot and I just want to go home.'

'Don't be soft. Course you didn't. It's just the way these things roll sometimes.'

'No, it's not. Maybe it's me, maybe I'm just not ready for all this. Maybe I've been out of the game too long to know how to play it any more. And after tonight I'm not sure I can be bothered to relearn the rules. Thanks for trying, really, but I think I'm just going to sit on the bench a while longer.'

Max starts to put his coat on but Connor pulls it out of his hands and takes his brother by the shoulders.

'Listen, you cannot get freaked out by one single rejection. I know it's been a while but you'll soon get into the swing of things again. Tonight was just supposed to be a bit of fun. You didn't expect to be running off into the sunset together, did you?'

'No, of course I didn't. But I didn't expect to get it quite so wrong either. I don't want to get back into the swing of things if those things involve dates with women who are impossible to read and pretending that I'm in any way over Rachel, because I'm not. I should have listened to myself. I'm just not ready.'

'Okay, bro. Go home and get some sleep and we'll talk tomorrow and perhaps you'll feel a bit more upbeat about things.'

'I don't think so, but thanks anyway. You can't say I didn't give it a go. But I think it's best all round if I just give up on all this dating malarkey.'

The boys have one last hug before Max heads for the exit and out into the streets of Mayfair.

As he pulls out his phone to check for messages he stops in his tracks, phone in hand, staring at the screen in his palm. I hover over his shoulder and am greeted by my own smiling face beaming back at me, Max to my left and Ellie on my lap, the three of us grinning in the face of the windswept Dorset beach we're sitting on. I remember us asking a sweet elderly couple to take the photo, him insisting he knew how to use the 'newfangled' camera phone, his wife raising an affectionately doubtful eyebrow and proving to know his capabilities better than he did as he fiddled frustratedly with the buttons until finally, possibly more by luck than judgement, he took that lovely shot. The shot that Max must still look at every time he makes a phone call and which he's gazing at now with only his own, private thoughts for company.

It's been a tough night for both of us, in different ways, but I suppose if there's one thing this evening has taught us, it's that neither Max nor I are ready to move on yet. That our first instincts were spot on; it's too soon to live life so definitively without one another. And even if Max were ready, it's going to take more than a random internet introduction or a blind date to find a woman worthy of Max's attention. I mean, he's not just any bloke. He's Max. It'll take someone pretty special to win him over, if being won over is something, one day, he might want. And someone even more special ever to be allowed into Ellie's life.

After weeks of worry and hours of disconcerting fantasies alone in the whiteness, I think I can finally rest assured that I'm not on the verge of being replaced. That neither Max nor Ellie are in serious search of a marital or maternal substitute. That I still have a place in the centre of their lives, even though I'm no longer there to share it with them.

And with that reassurance I close my eyes and allow him to travel home alone, confident that Max and I are still bound together in spite of the worlds that keep us apart.

# Anger

# CHAPTER 11

I can't believe it. I can't believe I was so naive. I can't believe I've been stuck here, on my own, for day upon endless day, blithely reassured that Max had abolished any immediate thoughts of dating from his mind. And then I return to find this.

We're in a low-lit restaurant somewhere I don't recognize, probably because it's the kind of achingly trendy place that Max and I stopped going to after Ellie had transformed us from a couple into a family. From what I've been able to glean so far, which is far less than I'd have liked but probably about as much as is humanly possible in the few minutes since my access was restored, Max is on another date. Except this date is unlike any date he's previously had, both since I died and no doubt before he and I ever got together.

She's beautiful. Painfully beautiful. Painful for me, that is, but probably not so much for her. Her long hair is naturally blonde and super-humanly glossy, the kind of hair you imagine exists only in shampoo commercials, and then only when it's been digitally enhanced. Her eyes are the colour of sapphire with a sparkling intensity you want to dive into. Her skin appears to be foundation-free and yet devoid of a single blemish in its pale translucency. She has the kind of body I've always envied: willowy, slim, delicate, a figure that undoubtedly withstands extensive guilty pleasures without revealing an ounce of evidence. Even her hands are beautiful: long, elegant, piano-playing fingers adorned with a single, antique marcasite ring on the middle finger of her right hand. And, as if that weren't challenge enough to my already burgeoning envy, her clothes are flawless too; she's wearing a loose patterned blouse over tight dark-brown jeans, accessorized with a pale green chiffon scarf, a combination which on me would have looked frumpy or comical, or both, but on her looks simple, effortless, chic. To add a final insult to an already impressive array of injuries, she's also almost certainly at least a decade younger than me.

Max says something apparently comical which I fail to hear, engrossed as I am in my study of the woman who's currently sitting stomach-churningly close to my husband and whose hand has a disturbing habit of making lingering contact with his arm by way of reassurance or encouragement – or both. They're seated side by side on a banquette, giggling like two childhood friends sharing nostalgic memories after a decade or two's absence rather than the relative strangers they must surely be. There's an ease about their interactions, a familiarity which sends alarm bells clanging loudly in my ears. The date, clearly, is going incredibly well. Worryingly well.

This wasn't supposed to happen. Where's Max's conviction – the seemingly intractable conviction I last left him with – that he's just not ready for all this yet? What happened to his resolve that he's retiring from the dating scene for the foreseeable future? What – or who – has persuaded him back into territory I thought he'd so definitively withdrawn from?

The clock on the wall tells me it's just gone nine o'clock. Given that the last vestiges of evening light are illuminating the window, it must still be summer and therefore only a matter of weeks since I was last here.

It's ironic, really; this has been the only absence I can remember during which I haven't been consumed by fearful fantasies of what I might discover on my return and yet it transpires to be the one time I really should have been.

When did they meet? Where, how? Who is she and what does she mean to Max? And is this their first date or one of many?

'So, Eve, might I be able to tempt you with a dessert?'

Her name's Eve? Really? It's not enough that she's beautiful, elegant, stylish, she has to be named after the first woman in the world ever?

'Well, I did see someone else with the chocolate cheesecake and it did look pretty delicious. Maybe we should order one to share?'

So now they're sharing desserts. One spoon or two?

Max grins with unadulterated pleasure as he walks towards the bar to order Eve's decadent dessert. I can't remember the last time I saw him this relaxed. I don't think I've seen him this content since I died and it's uplifting and unnerving in equal measure. I want Max to be happy, of course I do. I'm just not sure I'm ready for him to be quite this happy just yet. Or that I want Eve to be his inspiration.

Eve leaves the table too, to make her way to the bathroom, stroking a disarmingly over-familiar hand across the small of Max's back as she passes him at the bar. Even her walk is exquisite.

I look at Eve's face as she saunters, gracefully, towards the stairs. If someone told me that she was, indeed, the archetypal woman and that after her creation they'd thrown away the blueprint, I wouldn't struggle to believe it. And it's impossible for me to ignore the fact that not only is she beautiful but she's also my exact physical opposite. I don't know whether to be insulted or relieved. I'm not sure whether it's tactful of Max to be on a date with someone so distinctly different from me, whether it demonstrates his desire to ensure some clear blue water between the past, the present and a possible future I'm not yet ready to contemplate. Or whether it's tactless and insensitive of him, an indication that he's spent the past decade wishing I were blonde, blue-eyed and congenitally slim rather than brunette, brown-eyed and in possession of the kind of body that spent its relatively short life denying itself all the foods it wanted but couldn't have.

The two of them return to the table at exactly the same moment – even their timing is perfect – and resume their adjacent positions on the banquette.

'I've got to say, Eve, I'm having a really good time. You know, I'd almost given up on dating altogether – internet dating in particular. But my brother – he's a bit of a law unto himself – hacked into my profile and found you. That'll teach me to be a bit more imaginative with my passwords in future. Although for once in my life I find myself grateful to have a sibling devoid of any moral compass whatsoever.'

So this is their first date. That's almost more disconcerting than if it were their tenth; because if this is how cosy they've become after a couple of hours together, I dread to think what may transpire by closing time.

Eve laughs. It's the sound of tropical rain falling on the warm shallows of ocean. It's a laugh you'd have to be mad not to want to listen to again and again.

'To be fair, we do have quite a bit in common. Your brother did well in getting you back on the site, but I'm sure if you'd been on it yourself you'd have found me anyway.'

'Mmm . . . well, I'm not sure our common professional interest is necessarily the reason my brother was so keen for me to meet you.'

Max pauses for a second, surprised possibly at the confidence of his innuendo. I'm surprised too. Max was never this smooth when I was first dating him.

'Actually, we never really finished that conversation earlier. How exactly did you become a head teacher so young?'

She's a head teacher? How is that even possible? She can't be long out of sixth form herself.

'Well, I'd been teaching for about four years and was already running the English department when my head there suggested I apply for the fast-track scheme. So I did, and I got a place.'

'But, still, to make it to head by the time you're thirty – that's really impressive. Surely not everyone on that scheme has such a meteoric rise?'

She's thirty. Older than I thought. But still younger than I'd have liked.

'I think I just got lucky. I hadn't expected even to apply for a headship so soon, but then this job came up at a specialist Arts and Humanities school and I realized it was such perfect territory for me that I'd be mad not to put my hat in the ring, at least. I genuinely never thought I'd get it.'

'So how long have you been there now?'

'This year was my first. A baptism of fire, you could say. But I've loved every minute of it. The kids are great and there's a real energy about the place. I'm lucky, I know, to have landed on my feet in such a great school.'

Max smiles at Eve as though he can't quite believe how lucky he is to have landed himself a first date with her. His smile is so open, so hopeful, so inviting that I can't imagine anyone resisting the urge to fall into it.

Max runs his fingers through his thick, wavy hair as he's done repeatedly with an OCD-like frequency in the past few minutes and it's confirmation, as if I needed it, that he's awash with nervous excitement. It's a spontaneous tic of his and one which I've always loved. He'd fiddled with his hair incessantly throughout our wedding ceremony, looking to anyone who didn't know better as if he was vainly checking that it was all still in place, rather than the simple, absent-minded quirk I knew it to be. By the time I came to put the ring on his finger, his hands were greasy with misplaced hair wax. We'd giggled, secretively, no one but us knowing what we'd suddenly found so funny: a private moment in the most public of ceremonies.

'Yeah, the first year in senior management is tough, for sure. Mine was made that much tougher, I guess, by the fact that Rachel died so soon before I started my deputy headship. It did cross my mind that perhaps I should have postponed it a year, that I was never going to be able to invest in the role in the way that I'd have liked after what happened. But this last term has definitely felt a lot easier.'

The way he drops my name into conversation, so nonchalantly, with so little fanfare, I realize that this must not be the first time I've been discussed this evening. For Max to have made that comment, they must have talked about me before I arrived. Eve must already be fully appraised of my life and death and the beautiful years I had with Max before I unexpectedly left him.

The thought fills me with a violent sense of vertigo, that feeling you get when you inadvertently overhear an unflattering conversation about you that you know was meant to be private and which you wish had stayed that way. It's compelling and destabilizing in equal measure. Except here I can only imagine what was said, how I was described, which parts of our story Max chose to share and which he declined to mention.

It's left to my imagination, too, how Eve chose to respond. Did she listen patiently, sympathetically, demonstrating a great capacity for empathy? Or did she tolerate the very mention of my name with her eyes fixed firmly on a future in which she may choose to eliminate all references to me?

I'm snatched from my speculations by the sound of Eve's laughter. She's laughing at a story Max is telling and I can see that he's basking in the attention.

'And then the kid said, "But Sir, I'm not being funny or anything but, like, do you even know what Grime is?" I think he actually believed I thought he was talking about dirt. Really, what is it with every generation thinking they've reinvented the cultural wheel?'

'Oh, come on, we were the same in our day. I remember listening to Blur and Oasis and my parents telling me it wasn't music, it was just noise. And now I find myself thinking the same about the stuff my students listen to. It's the inevitable generational shift – we're all past it before we even know it.'

'I suppose you're right. I used to drive my mum and dad mad listening to Run-D.M.C. and the Beastie Boys at full volume, bass turned up to the max, wondering why the hell they couldn't understand how revolutionary it was. I think we just have to hold our hands up and accept the fact that we shouldn't be allowed to listen to contemporary music any more, let alone comment on it.'

Eve laughs again. I wish she'd stop finding Max so damn funny. It's too dangerous. I know where laughter at Max's jokes can lead.

It was Connor who told me that when Max confided his intention to propose to me, Connor had asked – with the incredulity of a man who was destined still to be single in his early forties – what on earth possessed him to think that one woman could be enough to satisfy a lifetime. Max had replied that one of the reasons he knew he wanted to marry me was because I laughed at all of his jokes, even the unfunny ones.

But now it's Eve laughing at Max's jokes, and I can see in his eyes and his smile just how much he's enjoying entertaining someone again.

'Maybe that's partly why we got into teaching in the first place – to try and hold on to our youth a bit?'

'Speak for yourself, Max. My intentions were entirely honourable.'

'Seriously, though, what did make you want to become a teacher?'

'Seriously? Okay. Without wanting to sound earnest – and I can talk about this till the cows come home, so feel free to stop me whenever I start boring you – I genuinely think it's one of the most important jobs in the world. Educating the next generation, preparing them to head out into the world, ensuring that they contribute in some way to society – I can't think of many more worthwhile things to do. Now that I'm a head I really miss that daily contact with students. They can be infuriating but I can't imagine another job that's quite so energizing.'

As Eve concludes her speech, I see that Max is gazing at her with something approaching reverence.

'I couldn't agree more. It's just rare to hear someone articulate it so passionately. Most teachers, even after just a few years in the job, tend to succumb to the cynicism bug, however hard they might try to fight it. I think it's great you're still so enthusiastic.'

Eve laughs.

'I know what you mean about the Cynical Brigade – we've a fair few littering the staff room at my school. I just don't see the point of staying in a job if it doesn't excite you any more. Life's too short.'

Max doesn't respond and I wonder if he's thinking what I'm thinking. Eve, meanwhile, continues where she left off.

'Without wanting to eulogize, I suppose for me it's about recognizing the value in what you're doing. Parents entrusting you all day with their children – there aren't many greater privileges.'

Max smiles at her reflectively and it pains me to see because I know what's behind that smile and I know what's precipitated it. I can see the flame of enthusiasm lighting up his eyes again, the way it used to, the way it's failed to for over a year now, and I can't help but wish it was me who'd managed to ignite it.

'It's great talking to you about all of this. It's so easy to forget why you're doing what you're doing, particularly when you've got a child at home to take care of too; being a parent definitely shifts the priorities, makes you use every minute that much more efficiently. But I'm sure you'll probably find that out for yourself one day.'

Eve looks at Max slightly quizzically and I wonder whether he's crossed a line, whether he's misread the signals, whether he's getting too personal for a first date. But it's the lightest expressive breeze before her face restores its composure.

'Speaking of Ellie, I can't really imagine how you manage everything – a demanding job and a seven-year-old child. It must be incredibly hard.'

Just hearing her say my little girl's name already feels like she's more ensconced in our lives than I could ever be ready for.

'It's getting easier but I won't deny it's been the steepest learning curve I've ever climbed. It's the level of organization required – who knew that children's lives were so busy? Honestly, Ellie has a more vibrant social life than I do and nearly every day there's an activity after school that requires me to remember some sort of special equipment or outfit. You need the organizational skills of a military general just to keep up. I'll be honest – Rachel used to take care of most of that stuff and it's only now I realize quite how impressive she was in keeping track of everything.'

I smile to myself as I think back to when Ellie first started school, an initiation that brought with it a raft of extracurricular activities and play dates. Max and I were astounded that someone so little had such stamina. He used to say it was like she'd inherited the aggregate of both our energy reserves and then some quirk of DNA had doubled it. He used to say that she'd turned out better than the best of each of us combined. And he was right.

'It sounds like you're doing a great job, taking charge of it all. It can't be easy, doing the job of both parents.'

Max pauses for a second and I wonder whether he's weighing up just how much to share, whether he's wary of disclosing more than she's ready to embrace, whether he's remembering the humiliations of previous dates. I urge him, silently, to be cautious. I don't want him getting hurt again.

'It can be pretty tough, I'd be lying if I said otherwise. The truth is, when you live with someone, it's not so much that you take things for granted as things just kind of slip into a routine and you each take on different responsibilities. You know what it's like.'

Eve pauses for a second.

'Well, I don't actually. Not really.'

'What do you mean?'

'I . . . I haven't ever lived with anyone before.'

Eve smiles nervously as if embarrassed to admit it.

'Oh, right. But I don't just mean with partners. It was the same when my brother and I used to share a flat back in the day.'

'No, I mean I haven't lived with anyone before – not flat-shared or cohabited or anything. I've always lived by myself, ever since I left home.'

'Really? God, I'd have been hopeless living alone in my early twenties. Connor and I could only just manage to pay the bills on time between us. I think I'd get pretty lonely living by myself too. Have you just never fancied sharing with anyone?'

'It's not that. I suppose it's just never worked out that way. And after a while you do get used to being by yourself – I've no doubt it's made me hideously intolerant of other people.'

Eve laughs, just fractionally too hard.

'Anyway, it sounds like Ellie's social life hasn't suffered too much with you at the helm.'

'No, that's one thing I can definitely attest to. She's incredible, really. She has her moments of insecurity, as you'd expect, but she's amazingly resilient given what she's been through. And she's great fun to be with. I'm lucky to have her.'

'It sounds like she's pretty lucky to have you too.'

Eve gazes at Max with a look I can't quite decipher; it's a deep, introspective expression that seems lost inside itself. A few seconds of silence follow that seem loaded with something they're both unable to articulate and I'm unable to interpret, before Max breaks the mutual reverie.

'God, I've just realized we're the last people here. The staff will be cursing us. I guess we ought to be making a move.'

The wall clock reveals that it's a little after eleven. Eve slips on a beautiful pale green mac and together they wander outside, both very slightly tipsy, Max's arm swung loosely, protectively, across the small of her back; somehow they already look every inch a couple.

'I've had a fantastic time, Eve. You've restored my faith in internet dating.'

'I'm glad to hear it. Although I hope that doesn't mean you're going to be back online as soon as you get home this evening.'

Her smile is playful but I can hear the undertone of insecurity in her voice. She likes him. She really likes him.

'I'm kind of hoping I'm not going to need to. I'd really like to meet up again, if you'd like that too?'

And he likes her too. But I knew that already, before he made claim to a second date, the very moment I arrived this evening and saw the smile I know is reserved for these rare moments of alchemy.

'I'd like that a lot. Believe me, I've done my fair share of internet dates and blind dates and awful set-ups with friends of friends, and evenings like this don't come along very often.'

As Eve looks down, shyly, perhaps taken aback by her own forwardness, Max cups a hand around her cheek and gently, slowly, moves his face towards hers until they're so close they must be able to feel the heat of one another's breath and his fingers are grazing her hair and then their lips are touching and I'm witnessing, for the first time, my husband kiss another woman.

An intense, uncontrollable nausea swells inside me and I feel dizzy and sick and I fear I'm going to faint. I close my eyes to shut it all out, to shut them out, and I remain there, in self-imposed darkness, for what feels like an eternity of self-preservation, until I dare finally to open my eyes again, hoping they'll be gone, hoping it will all be over, praying that I'll be back on my own in the whiteness. But I open my eyes and they're still there, they're still kissing, and it's not passionate, nor energetic, but rather soft, affectionate, gentle and somehow that's far, far worse. It's tender and romantic and indicative of a confidence and a desire that there will be much, much more to come.

Finally it's over and they giggle together, conspiratorially, as if embarrassed by their own uninhibited desires. Max hails a passing cab and for a split second it occurs to me that they might get into it together, that there might yet be more horror ahead, and I know I can't bear it.

But Eve steps in alone and the torment, for now at least, is over.

As Max waves her off and wanders away in the opposite direction, white clouds begin to gather over the dark night sky and before I've snatched one last look at Max's face I find myself alone in my stark wilderness, with only the plague of recent memory for company. Just a few seconds earlier and I'd have been spared that scene. Instead I'm here momentarily too late, trying to purge that punishing image from my mind, but it assumes a life of its own, burning into the screen behind my eyes so that all I can see, the only picture in the world I seem capable of painting, is the sight of Max kissing the beautiful blonde.

I implore myself to think about Max with me instead, about that last kiss we shared, about that final evening we spent together, celebrating his promotion. I remember how we'd been in the restaurant, sitting across from one another, when suddenly he'd leaned over the table, taken my face in his hands, and kissed me tenderly on the lips. I recall how unexpected it had been, how happy it had made me, how at the time it had taken my breath away. But now I can't seem to locate any feelings attached to it. I can only remember it as if a scene from a movie, as if a memory that might as well belong to someone else. The only feelings I have right now are this evening's, the feelings I'm desperate to eradicate, the feelings no one should ever have to bear. The feelings that come with having watched my husband in the arms of another woman.

I can't believe that Max has done this to me. I can't believe he's gifted me this execrable image that I know will haunt me for days to come. And that, in doing so, he seems to have obliterated the memories I have of us being together.

Just one more kiss. That's all I want. Just one more. To feel his lips on mine, to feel our breaths intermingle until we don't know whose is whose any more, to know once again the intimacy that never failed to assure me that in Max's presence I was always going to be safe and loved and desired.

Now when I close my eyes it's not me Max is kissing. It's Eve.

I feel as though something profound has happened this evening. Something irreversible. I feel as though a part of Max is emptying out of me, or perhaps it's me emptying out of him.

And I feel angry, too. Angry that Max is alive and I'm not, that his life continues where mine has ended, that he's able to go on dates and flirt with beautiful women and kiss them outside restaurants late into the evening. Angry that he gets another shot at life, at love, at success, at parenthood. Angry about the naive, presumptuous certainty I had that there was so much more of my life yet to come.

Angry that of all the people in the world who had to die that day, one of them had to be me.

I just want to be with him. And with Ellie. And the knowledge that I can't is the lone atom of truth that makes me wish right now that dying really had been the end of everything.

# CHAPTER 12

I hear the living world before I can see it. There's cheering, shouting and chanting, a rabble of male voices that are at turns excitable and angry. As real life comes into view, I'm disorientated for a second, hovering high over a large stadium I don't think I recognize, before my vision instinctively zooms in on the person I'm here to see.

Max is standing in the terraces with his threadbare QPR scarf around his shoulders. I look next to him, expecting to see Connor, his regular football sidekick, but instead of Connor there's Eve, conspicuously radiant amidst the testosterone-fuelled crowd.

'Only five minutes to go. All we've got to do is hold our defence and the game's ours. You don't mind, really, do you? I know it's not the most romantic of fifth dates but I thought it might be fun and I wanted you to see why I always get so excited before a match.'

Fifth date? And he's taken her to see QPR? Only once in ten years was I afforded the privilege of accompanying Max to see his beloved football team play live, and then only because Connor was ill and the dozen friends he'd phoned to replace him had been unable to make it at such short notice, so it had made sense for me to go rather than 'waste the ticket' as he'd so gallantly put it. Football has always been sacred as far as Max is concerned; sacred amongst men, a masculine exclusion zone to which

165

women are never admitted. It was Max's only adherence to male stereotypes and I'd always counted myself lucky that of all the ways in which relationships can become polarized, one afternoon a week of agreed separation really wasn't anything to complain about.

But that was before Eve was invited to a football match on their fifth date. They can't have been seeing each other for more than a few weeks and yet already she's managed to inveigle the space that Max kept separate from me for a decade. It's hard not to feel affronted. Not only is this woman beginning to live my life, the one I'd be leading if I hadn't died, already she seems to be negotiating her way through it with greater success than I ever did.

The final whistle blows and Max hugs Eve with the adrenaline of sporting victory. It's a visual assault, seeing their bodies embrace, his arms around her, their torsos touching with a familiarity and a freedom that for so long has been the preserve of him and me.

As they file, slowly, out of the packed stadium, they're holding hands and laughing together, indisputably relaxed in one another's company. The first date had been promising, admittedly, but there's clearly been some progress since. Not for the first time, I curse the unpredictability and irregularity of my access. If it serves any purpose whatsoever, surely it should at least do me the courtesy of keeping me fully apprised of my husband's romantic liaisons. That should be the very least of a dead wife's prerogatives, shouldn't it?

Max and Eve reach the tube station and stand together, hesitantly, outside. They stop talking, stop laughing and an inexplicable awkwardness emerges between them but how or why or from where I've no idea. There's something going on here that I don't quite understand, some unspoken collusion between them from which I'm excluded, and it pains me to be outside of their intimacy, both physically and emotionally.

'So, what are your plans for the rest of the evening? Is Ellie waiting at your mum and dad's for you?'

'No, she's actually staying at theirs tonight. Mum's got some kind of baking extravaganza set up for the pair of them. They'll have a whale of a time.'

There's a pause in the conversation that feels suspiciously loaded. I think I know what's coming but if I'm right I'm pretty sure I don't want to hear it.

'So, given I'm child-free for the night, I could always come back to yours. Unless you've got other plans, of course.'

Eve hesitates for just a beat longer than Max can bear.

'I'm sorry. Forget I said that. We don't have to. How about we just grab a quick bite to eat and then I'll head home.'

'No, no. It's not that I don't want to. It's just . . .'

Eve intakes a lungful of air as if steeling herself to continue.

'It's just that it's been quite a while since I . . . since I had someone to . . . you know . . . stay over.'

There's just a hint of surprise in Max's eyes and I couldn't agree more. It's hard to believe that Eve doesn't have a string of suitors knocking down her door.

'It's fine. Please let's just forget it. I'm sorry. Do you think we can rewind this conversation a couple of minutes and start again? I'm not very practised at all of this.'

'Please don't apologize. It's not your fault, really. It's mine.'

Eve offers Max a conciliatory smile which lapses into another charged silence.

'Right, where do you fancy heading for supper? Greek or Italian or curry? Your wish is my command, madam.'

Max is desperately trying to inject some jocularity into the conversation but the awkwardness is palpable even to me.

'No, why don't you come back to mine. We can stop off at the supermarket on the way and I'll cook us supper.'

Max looks confused as though he instinctively wants to say one thing but chivalry is going to force him to say another.

'No really, Eve, it's fine. Let's eat out.'

'Honestly, Max, I want you to come back with me. Genuinely. I was just thrown for a second there. I suppose I didn't expect to be in this position just yet.'

'God, if it's too soon, we can wait. Seriously. There's no rush. You're probably right. Please let's just forget I ever mentioned it.'

Eve laughs and her laughter brings with it a decisive break in the tension.

'Please let's not forget it. It's just been a while and even though I knew this was coming somehow you still caught me off guard. But I want you to. Really.'

'Really?'

'Yes, really. I promise.'

Eve leans in and kisses Max tenderly on the lips and it's the kiss of a multitude of possibilities, each one reeling through my imagination in unnecessarily graphic detail, each scenario more distressing to envisage than the last.

'If it makes you feel any better, it's been a while for me too. I haven't been with anyone . . . with anyone like that since . . . since Rachel. I guess we'll just have to stumble through this clumsily together.'

Max laughs now too and I can hear the catharsis in his voice and I don't think any sound has ever made me feel so far away from him.

'Well, if there are awards for cringeworthy conversations, I think we can both share top prize for this one. I think we'd probably give some of our students a run for their money in the embarrassment department, don't you?'

Eve smiles and Max takes hold of her hand and looks directly, calmly, confidently into her eyes.

'Let's start this evening again shall we? So, Eve, how do you fancy us going back to yours for a quiet evening in?'

'Well, since you ask so nicely, that sounds like a wonderful idea. I may even have a spare toothbrush for you if you're really lucky.'

They grin at one another, conspiratorially and intensely, oblivious to the throngs of football fans circling them to enter the underground.

I take a deep breath to try and steady myself against the emotional tidal wave I can feel approaching. He's actually going to do it. He's going to sleep with another woman. He's going to get naked with her and caress her breasts and marvel at her tight, flat tummy, devoid of the evidence of childbearing, and he'll wonder whether he can remember when he last saw a tummy as beautiful and blemish-free and smooth as that. He's going to kiss her bare neck and stroke her exposed thigh and taste her skin and the taste will be like nothing else he's ever encountered before. He's going to run his fingers down her naked back and cup her perfect, rounded buttocks in his hands and look into her eyes as they make love and it's going to be a revelation, like he's making love for the very first time, because there's been a part of him for so many months, for over a year, that's believed he'd never make love to anyone again. He's going to spend the entire night entwined with her, sleep by her side, listen to her breathing and watch her dreaming and in the morning he's going to wake up next to her and realize that today is the first day of the rest of his life. His life without me.

I'm overwhelmed by panic. I can't watch this. I can't go with them. I don't want to see how the evening pans out. I know what's going to happen without the torture of having to watch it with my own eyes. Surely that's more than any wife can be expected to witness, dead or alive?

Max and Eve start walking towards the underground entrance, hand in hand, almost skipping with mutual excitement into the tube together as they head towards Eve's house for their very first night together. I feel sick, hysterical almost, like I can't breathe and I have to escape but where to and how I just don't know. I squeeze my eyes tightly shut, so tight it hurts. Maybe, I think, maybe if I focus on thoughts about Max and me, maybe they'll disappear.

I keep my eyes firmly closed and try to replace the graphic fantasies of what lies ahead with images of what lay before, with memories of Max and me instead, of us curled up in bed on Sunday mornings in the days before Ellie was born, naked, surrounded by Sunday papers and a swiftly cooling cafetière of coffee, our own favourite time for making love, both of us immersed in the weekend without the pressure of time or tiredness or work to invade that most private of spaces. I think about Max standing behind me when I was cooking in the kitchen, sweeping my hair on to one side of my neck while gently kissing the other. I think of us lying together in the bath, our much-relished pre-bed ritual, discussing the day's events while washing them off one another, cleansing ourselves of everything outside our own, exclusive cocoon. And I think about the time we made mid-afternoon love on the sofa of that New York hotel room, the full-height, twenty-third-storey windows overlooking the Manhattan skyline welcoming the early-summer sunshine into the room and warming our already-overheated bodies, and both of us knowing afterwards that something special had taken place, something exceptional, something we wouldn't comprehend until three weeks later when I took the test and we learnt for the first time that a brand new life would be completing our family.

When I open my eyes, finally, there's nothing but whiteness. I don't know how but I've managed to will myself away from the scene that I know would otherwise have haunted me for as many days as this afterworld exists. I'm grateful, more grateful than I ever thought possible, to be back on my own in the nothingness.

But pernicious images of the evening's possible events continue to spool through my mind like a speeded-up Super 8 film. My stomach churns with envy, eating away at me from the inside out like a cancer metastasizing in record time.

I imagine Eve's naked body and Max's certain appreciation of it and then I look down at my own body – a body no one else but me can see any more, with a face that even I haven't seen for over a year, so who knows what kind of state it's in – and I'm pierced by the sharpest stab of inadequacy. Did Max spend our entire marriage wondering if he might have done better for himself, whether he might have stood before a registrar declaring vows to someone who looked like Eve rather than me? Will he begin to question that now? Will he lie in bed with Eve and wonder why on earth he wasted a decade in my naked company?

For the first time since I met Max eleven years ago, I find myself questioning whether I was ever good enough for him. And whether Eve's perfection is about to relegate me to the Inadequate First Wives' Club.

All I can think about is Eve. Eve making love to Max, Eve stealing the heart of my husband, Eve and Max embarking on the exciting journey of a new relationship, with no idea where that road might lead them except that it seems, right now, to be heading in a direction they both want to go.

# CHAPTER 13

Max is walking jauntily down the path of his parents' front garden with what looks suspiciously like a morning-after-the-night-before spring in his step. I can tell it a mile – or even a thousand miles – off. Post-coital Max couldn't be more transparent if he ripped off his shirt, began beating his chest and howled a time-honoured chant of sexual conquest into the jungle.

My mind surrenders to an army of schizophrenic thoughts. Rationally I know that I'm dead, that Max is a widower, that he's free to pursue other relationships. Rationally I don't want him to be unhappy, in mourning and lonely forever. But those rational feelings aren't sufficiently robust to repel an onslaught of irrational impulses: that Max has betrayed me, that he's moved on too quickly, that he's desecrated the memory of our marriage with this act of emotional and physical treachery. And stoking the flames of envy's fury are those repetitive, invidious images of what I presume took place last night.

As Max lets himself into the house, Joan calls out to him from the kitchen.

'Come in here, quickly, will you love?'

Max saunters through, not quickly at all, his thoughts clearly a long way from his mother's kitchen.

'Close the door. I need to talk to you about something before Ellie comes downstairs.'

The tone of her voice and the frown above her eyes indicate concern. A small flutter of anxiety begins working its way tentatively from my stomach up to my throat.

'Sit down, Max. You know it makes me nervous when you loiter around me.'

Max does as he's told, still grinning, seemingly oblivious to Joan's preoccupation.

'It's about Ellie. We had a bit of an accident last night.'

Oh god. Please say she's okay. Please.

'What kind of accident? What happened? Is she okay?'

'She's fine. Not that kind of accident. She wet the bed. Stayed in it all night, poor little mite. Said this morning that she hadn't wanted to wake us up.'

My poor angel. My poor little girl. I can't bear the thought of her lying all night in a wet bed without me to comfort her, to change her sheets, to settle her back to sleep.

She used to wet the bed occasionally when she was a toddler. She'd come into our room in the middle of the night and gently – oh so gently – prod my arm until finally I stirred and she'd whisper, 'Mummy, I'm wet again,' as though what had happened was entirely out of her control, which I suppose, in a way, it was. I'd get up and we'd go to her room, collecting clean sheets from the airing cupboard on the way, and she'd stand silently, clutching her brown bear, watching me discard the soiled bedding and replace it with freshly ironed linen. I'd tuck her back in, often snuggling in beside her until she managed to fall back to sleep, constantly reiterating that it didn't matter, that it wasn't something to worry about, that all little people wet the bed sometimes. I didn't want it to be something she became too self-conscious about.

She started wetting the bed again in the months after I died but she hasn't, as far as I know, been troubled by it for a long time now. If she's started again, Joan's right to be worried.

'God, Mum, you nearly gave me a heart attack. Is that all? I thought there'd been a real accident. Honestly, I can't believe you can be so melodramatic sometimes.'

'I don't think I am being melodramatic, Max. Ellie hasn't wet the bed for nearly a year and then all of a sudden she did it again last night. Forgive me, but I think there's a question to be asked as to why now.'

I agree with Joan. Of course it's suspicious. Why isn't Max taking this more seriously?

'Well, clearly you have the answer to that question, Mum, so instead of us playing guessing games, why don't you just tell me what it is?'

Joan frowns at Max. I don't blame her. He's being rude and abrupt and it's not like him. And she, unlike me, isn't privy to the knowledge that she's inadvertently burst his post-coital bubble. He's behaving like a teenager after his first all-nighter, sullen and resentful that he's being pulled back to reality against his will. It's really not very becoming.

'It's obvious, isn't it? It's you going out all the time. You've been out more in the past few weeks than in the last eighteen months put together. It's unsettling her, Max. I think you're just going to have to give all this socializing a rest for a while.'

The mood in Max's eyes — which has already metamorphosed from pleasure to petulance — now undergoes a further transformation. Now he's plain angry.

'You're really having a go at me for going out too much, Mum? Isn't that just a tiny bit hypocritical since it was you who was hassling me to — what was it? — get out and about in the first place. You can't have it both ways.'

I think it's highly probable — however unsavoury the thought — that Max didn't get enough sleep last night. He so rarely behaves like this and when he does it's invariably the result of a severe hangover or chronic sleep-deprivation. This morning it could well be both. I try to stop my mind from running out of this conversation and into fantasies about what kept Max awake all night. Those kinds of thoughts aren't going to do anyone any good, least of all me.

'I never suggested you should be gallivanting around town every weekend till goodness knows what time and with goodness knows who. A couple of months ago you didn't even want to leave the house and now it looks like you haven't been home all night.'

'Mum, I'm a big boy now. I don't need your permission for a late pass.'

'Don't be silly. You know that's not what I'm saying. I'm just surprised — very surprised, if you want to know — that you don't seem to be taking last night's incident seriously.'

So am I. I'm surprised too. And I'm beginning to feel a bit annoyed as well. I'm trying really hard to put my feelings about last night aside, for them not to infect my thoughts about this morning's revelations, and what I'm left with is frustration that Max is so wrapped up in his new relationship with Eve that Ellie seems to have slipped down, overnight, from the top of his priority list where she belongs.

'It's one night of bedwetting for god's sake. I just don't think we need to be calling in the child psychologists yet.'

'There's no need to be sarcastic. Honestly, I don't know why you're so irascible today.'

I do, and I know who's to blame, too.

'I'm not irascible. I just don't want to get hysterical about one tiny mishap, that's all.'

'What if it's not only one? What if she gets into a pattern again, like she did after Rachel died? It was awful then, you know it was. I just want to try and nip it in the bud before it gets out of control.'

'Out of control? Really, Mum, you've got to stop over-dramatizing everything. It's only one night. It's really not a big deal.'

I don't know what's happened to Max, to the Max I know and love, to the Max who used to joke that he'd wrap Ellie up in cotton wool – quite literally – if he thought it would protect her from all of life's dangers. How can he ignore the fact that her bedwetting is a means of communication, whether she's conscious of it or not? How can he dismiss whatever it is she's trying to tell us, whatever feelings she has that she can't otherwise articulate? How can he belittle the possibility that our daughter might be suffering?

I've left him with one job that really matters – one job only – and that's to make sure Ellie's okay. That she's safe and loved and that she's compensated as far as is humanly possible through the love and support of everyone around her for the fact that she's lost her mother. That's all I want from him. To take care of our daughter and ensure that she makes it through childhood and adolescence with minimal emotional scars. Does he not realize how important – how critical, how absolutely imperative – it is that he should be able to achieve that? For all I know Max may have more children in the future, he may have an entire rabble of them. But Ellie's all I've got. And she's all I'll ever have now. She's my sole discernible legacy to the world, my only link to a future I'll never have. She's all the life I have left.

How can Max not see that? Is he really blind to the fact that if he fails Ellie, he fails me? And that if he fails her, I'll never, ever forgive him.

'I don't want to criticize you, Max. You know I don't. I'm just worried about Ellie, that's all.'

'And you think I'm not? Where is she, anyway?'

'She was upstairs in the spare room just before you arrived. Are you going to talk to her?'

Without bothering to answer, Max charges out of the kitchen and up the stairs, where he finds Ellie sitting on the edge of the pink bedspread Joan bought specially for her. He stands in the doorway, surveying our daughter, her head bowed and her shoulders slumped forward with dejection.

'Is Granny cross with me?'

'Of course not, sweetheart. She could never be cross with you. She was just sad that you had a bad night. Are you okay now?'

Ellie nods her head, unconvincingly, unable to raise her face to look Max in the eye. His tone has softened, at least;

he seems to have managed to leave his own frustrations downstairs.

Max sits next to her on the bed and puts a protective arm around her shoulders. Instead of finding comfort inside her daddy's embrace, Ellie bursts into tears.

'What is it, angel? What's the matter?'

Ellie sobs – grave, visceral sobs that seem too powerful to emanate from such a small, fragile body.

'You weren't here, Daddy. I wanted you and you weren't here.'

It's an accusation that shouldn't, by rights, land solely at Max's door and it brings with it a fresh wave of tears. I want to hold her, to haul her on to my lap and rock away her anguish.

'I'm sorry, angel. I thought you liked staying the night with Granny and Grandpa? You know they wouldn't have minded at all if you'd woken them up.'

'But I didn't want them, Daddy. I wanted you.'

Max draws Ellie's tear-stained face on to his chest and strokes the top of her head.

'I'm sorry, sweetheart. I won't leave you again until you're sure you're ready. Is that okay?'

Ellie's body begins to relax into the crook of Max's comforting arm, but the whimpering continues to punctuate her words.

'Do you . . . do you promise?'

'Of course I promise, sweetheart. You know I'd never do anything to upset you. You're my special angel and I love you so, so much.'

Max pulls her face up towards him and begins kissing her all over, making silly munching noises as he goes. It's a game we've played with Ellie since she was a baby, covering her face with kisses, counting as we go to reach the magical hundred, making her laugh with the sensation, the repetition, the playfulness of it. And Ellie laughs now too, feigning an attempt to free herself from Max's embrace while ensuring that some part of her skin is nonetheless free to enable him to reach his goal.

'Ninety-nine, one hundred! How many times in total do you think I've kissed you in your life so far, munchkin?'

Ellie grins into the air, a frown of comical thoughtfulness replacing her tears.

'A million.'

'Oh, I think at least a million. More like two million, I reckon. And there's a lot more where they came from.'

Max begins tickling her and kisses her face some more as she falls back on the bed in fits of giggles.

'Be careful, Daddy. I don't want to scrunch it up.'

Ellie sits up and I can see that she's holding something in her hand, something small and tattered. A cloud eclipses the sunshine in her eyes, and suddenly a lone, fat tear trickles down to the end of her nose and on to whatever it is she's guarding so vigilantly. With an instinctive, protective response Ellie swiftly wipes it away with the sleeve of her cardigan.

'What have you got there, munchkin? Can I see?'

Slowly, tentatively, Ellie removes her top hand to reveal what's underneath, not yet prepared to relinquish whatever it is to him altogether.

It's a small, passport-sized photo. In it are Ellie and I, our faces pressed close together to ensure we both fit into the tiny frame, laughing ahead into the automatic lens. It's a picture of perfect happiness.

'That's a lovely photo. When was that taken, do you remember?'

Ellie shakes her long brown curls. I remember. It was when we went into town, Christmas shopping together, the year before I died. We'd been to Hamleys and Selfridges, we'd looked at the Christmas lights, we'd had lunch in her favourite pizza restaurant and we'd carefully and collaboratively selected all of Max's gifts. There'd been a photo booth set up in one of the big department stores and after we'd posed for the single shot, we'd waited impatiently for the four identical images to emerge and when they did, Ellie had asked if she could keep one to put in her puppy-shaped purse. I can't believe she still has it. That was almost two years ago. I could cry at the thought of her having treasured that photo, all this time.

'Daddy?'

'Yes, munchkin.'

'Sometimes I really, really miss Mummy. Like last night, when I wet the bed. With Mummy I always knew that she wouldn't get cross with me, even if I woke her up in the middle of the night. I just really, really wanted her here.'

Max pulls Ellie on to his lap and into his arms. His eyes are bloodshot and I can see he's holding back the tears too. I'd give anything to be able to cradle Ellie right now, to let her know that I'm here, to reassure her that even though I'm no longer capable of changing the sheets and taking her back to bed I'm still looking out for her, still loving her, still hopeful that there may be some way I can protect her. I can't imagine there can be any greater torture in the world – in this world or any other – than to know that your child's in distress and to be powerless to do anything about it.

'I know, angel. I miss Mummy too. She loved you so, so much, and she'd never, ever have left you if she'd had a choice. You know that, don't you?'

Ellie shrugs her shoulders and it's the most painful gesture I think I've ever witnessed. She has to know, surely, how much I loved her, how much I love her still? Max has to make her see, he has to make her know, deep and indelibly in her heart, that I never, ever wanted to leave her.

'Look how happy the two of you are in that photo. We had some lovely times with Mummy, didn't we? We need to try and remember those and that way we can hold on to Mummy in our minds, all the time, every day.'

Ellie remains silent. She doesn't want memories. She wants a real, live mummy, who plays with her and laughs with her and takes her to school and does her homework with her and celebrates her achievements and encourages her endeavours and who tucks her back in bed at night after she's soiled the sheets.

She wants a mummy like all her friends have. Like all children deserve.

'Can I tell you a story?'

Ellie sighs at Max's question and it's a sound full of the resignation of someone with far greater weight on their shoulders than anyone of her age should ever have to bear.

'As soon as Mummy knew that you were in her tummy, which was a whole eight months before you were born, do you know what she did?'

Ellie looks up at Max, inquisitive now, and shakes her head.

'She started talking to you. She'd chatter away to you all the time, telling you all sorts of things about the world that you couldn't yet see for yourself. She'd talk to you about what she was doing that day and where she was going and what she could see and hear and smell. She'd describe what she was eating so that when it reached you, through the special cord in her tummy that used to feed you, you'd know what you were tasting. She told you about everyone in our family, about Granny and Grandpa, about Nanna, about Uncle Connor, about Harriet, because she wanted to be sure that when you finally came out to join us in the world, you knew about all the people who already loved you.'

Ellie looks thoughtful.

'Could I hear Mummy, when I was in her tummy?'

'Maybe not right at the beginning, although that didn't stop Mummy chatting away to you. But near the end, when you were getting big, we were sure you could hear her then. She'd sing you songs – so many different songs – and sometimes when she did, Mummy would feel you moving around in her tummy. And do you know what? After you were born she kept singing the same songs to you and often they'd stop you crying and Mummy was convinced it was because you remembered them from when you were still inside her.'

Ellie unselfconsciously puts a hand on her own tummy, as if imagining what it must be like to have another person in there.

Ellie, my gorgeous girl, it's the most wonderful feeling in the world and it's one I hope – I'm sure – you'll know for yourself one day.

'But why did Mummy talk to me if she wasn't even sure I could hear her?'

'That's a good question, munchkin. I asked her that myself once, right at the beginning when she started doing it. And do you know what she said? She said that whether or not you could hear what she was saying, she felt sure that you'd know she was talking to you and she wanted you to know, right from the moment you came into being, how much she loved you.'

Ellie snuggles her head tighter under Max's arm and I detect the faintest tremor of her bottom lip. Max looks down at her face and I can see he's noticed it too.

'Do you know what else? Sometimes she'd even talk to you on the bus, and she said people would give her very funny looks, like maybe she was a bit crazy, because they couldn't understand who she was talking to.'

Ellie giggles, skilfully brought back from the edge of an emotional precipice.

'What about when I was born, Daddy? What happened then?'

'Well, sweetheart, I know Mummy told you this story lots of times, but given that it's my favourite story in the whole world I'm very happy to repeat it as often as you like.'

Ellie smiles at him, comforted by the promise of a familiar narrative.

'The day you were born was the sunniest, brightest March day we'd had so far that year. It was a Friday morning and I was just about to leave the house to go to work when Mummy called me from upstairs in the bedroom and I knew straight away that something important was happening.'

'How did you know?'

'I could tell by Mummy's voice. She sounded excited and breathless and a little bit scared all at the same time. So I rushed upstairs and Mummy told me that she thought you were ready to come out and that we had to get to the hospital.'

'And did you go in an ambulance?'

Ellie never fails to ask the same question, however many times she hears the story. I think she's hoping that one day the details will change to comply with the image she has – drawn from TV and films and books – of how people are supposed to travel to hospital. I know it's always disappointed her that her journey into the world didn't include flashing blue lights, noisy sirens and an army of paramedics in dark green uniforms working dramatically around us.

'No, it wasn't an emergency so we didn't need an ambulance. I drove us there. When we arrived, we were put in a room and visited by lots of doctors and special nurses called midwives. And although all the signs were in place that you were ready to come out, like Mummy having strong tummy pains, you were a little bit stubborn even then, munchkin, and you didn't really want to make an appearance just yet.'

Max tickles Ellie under her arms and she laughs at what is always her favourite part of the story.

'Do you know how long Mummy and I were in the hospital before you started to come out?'

Ellie knows this already, but that's not going to stop her playing the game.

'How long?'

'Forty hours. That's nearly two whole days. Mummy was very, very tired. But then finally the midwife said that you were almost ready to make your grand entrance and she told Mummy that every time she felt a big pain in her tummy she had to push really, really hard. So Mummy kept pushing for nearly two hours and then all of a sudden I could see the top of your head.'

'What did I look like, Daddy? Was I ever so small?'

'Well, at that stage you were still mostly in Mummy's tummy, but then she pushed a few more times and then suddenly there you were. It was like a miracle. The midwife put you straight on to Mummy's chest and you gave out your first big cry and it was the most amazing sound I'd ever heard. And, yes, my angel, you were tiny. I don't think I'd ever seen such a tiny person in my whole life. As you lay in Mummy's arms I stroked your head and held your tiny fingers in mine and we marvelled that something so small could be so perfect. It was and always will be the most wonderful moment in my life, ever.'

Max kisses the top of Ellie's head. I remember every second of it – all one hundred and fifty-odd thousand of them – as if it were happening right now. I remember hour after interminable hour of midwives matter-of-factly informing me that I wasn't yet far enough dilated and my incomprehension that I could be in this much pain and yet still so far from the end. I remember examination after examination culminating in the same apologetic news that still I wasn't ready to start pushing and the feeling, heightened by pain and fear and anxiety, that I must be the world's worst childbearer. I remember the relief when I was finally told that I was ready, that we were entering the final stage, that this was the beginning of the end when the real work started and feeling so bone-shatteringly exhausted that I couldn't believe I had an ounce of energy left to give. I remember those final ninety minutes and my incredulity that the human body could withstand such violence, repeating to myself, over and over again, like a lifesaving mantra for both of us, that millennia of women had managed this since time imme-morial and there was no reason I should be any different. And then, finally, she was there, naked in my arms, her mucus-coated skin bare against my chest and I knew that our lives would never be the same again.

People often say that the only way women are capable of having more than one baby is by eradicating the experience of childbirth from memory, that only by entering into a form of self-denial can anyone tolerate giving birth more than once. But I remember it all, every last detail, and I'd do it all again, in a flash, without a moment's hesitation, to have Ellie at the end of it.

'And shall I tell you something else, munchkin? Before you were born, I thought I loved Mummy as much as it was possible to love anyone. But watching her give birth to you, seeing how brave she was, being by her side while she was working so hard for all those hours to help you come out, I loved her more than ever. I was so, so proud of her.'

I look at my little girl nestled in my husband's arms and I yearn to be able to turn back the clock, to be with Max and Ellie in that delivery suite, the three of us embracing one another for the very first time, hearing him say those words to me and feeling that elemental compulsion of wanting, above all else, to protect this new family from every imaginable harm.

'And do you know the first thing that Mummy said after you were born?'

Ellie shakes her head. This is a new end to the story, one she hasn't heard before. It's Max's ending, not mine.

'I thought she was going to tell me how tired she was or how hungry because she hadn't eaten anything for hours by then. But she held you in her arms, and I held her in mine, and she looked into my eyes, her face beaming, and said, "Now our family is complete." And she was right. It was. And that was all down to you, sweetheart.'

Ellie is quiet now, allowing herself the space to absorb this new epilogue to an otherwise familiar story.

'That's how I know just how much Mummy loved you, angel. Because I saw her face when you were born, and I'd never seen anyone so happy in my whole life before. And I know it's really, really unfair that you only had Mummy with you for such a short time, but she loved you as much in those six years as it's ever possible for anyone to be loved.'

Ellie emits a muffled sob as Max tightens his arms around her vulnerable shoulders.

I'm not sure I could be any more grateful to Max right now. All the frustration and the resentment and the sense of betrayal about last night have evaporated and I feel guilty for doubting him, for being so angry with him, for thinking, even for a second, even in the heat of the moment, that he wouldn't do his best for Ellie. He's Max. He'll always do his best for her.

'I know how hard this is for you, Ellie. But you're doing really, really well, sweetheart, and I'm so, so proud of you. And I'm going to use all my special daddy powers to make sure you're okay. Because you're the most important thing in the world to me – my special girl – you know that, don't you?'

Max rests his head on top of Ellie's, his fingers gently stroking her forehead.

'So, munchkin, about last night. I don't want you to worry about what happened. It's just an accident and no one's to blame for an accident. But will you promise me that if anything like that happens again, wherever you are, whether at home or here or Nanna's, you'll let someone know straight away?'

Ellie nods her head as she lets Max wipe away the last of her tears.

'There's one more promise I need from you, sweetheart. Whenever you're sad about Mummy, will you come and tell me? And if I'm not around, and there's no one else you want to talk to about her, will you promise me that you'll close your eyes and picture you and Mummy in that photograph, and remember just how much she loved you?'

Ellie smiles, sniffing away her grief and raising her head to look at Max with a maturity far beyond her years.

'Okay, Daddy. I promise.'

'Good girl. Now, why don't you go and wash your face and get your things together and I'll see you downstairs. I think we deserve a Sunday afternoon on the sofa with a duvet, a movie and possibly even one of my special ice cream sundaes. What do you think?'

Ellie grins and bounces off the bed towards the bathroom.

Max makes his way downstairs and back to the scene of the earlier argument, where Joan is in the process of laying out frozen Yorkshire puddings on a baking tray.

'I'm sorry, Mum. You were right. It wasn't nothing and I shouldn't have flown off the handle at you. But I've had a good chat with her and I think she'll be fine now.'

'Good, I'm glad. You know I don't like it when we have words. Now, are you sure you don't want to stay for lunch? There's plenty here.'

'Thanks, but not today. I think Ellie and I need some time alone and, anyway, I've promised her an afternoon of ice cream and movies now.'

'Right you are. But I haven't had a chance to ask – did you have a nice time last night? You look as though you didn't get much sleep.'

Max blushes and I feel the jealousy beginning to creep back in.

'Yeah, it was a really good night, thanks. Lots of fun.'

'So was it the same young lady you've seen before? Or a new one altogether?'

'You make it sound like I've got a whole harem of women at my disposal. Yes, it was the same one I've seen a few times lately. Her name's Eve. I think you'd like her.'

Please stop there, Max. We don't need your mum to like her. We don't need your mum even to be thinking about her just yet. It's still early days, remember?

'Eve. What a pretty name. And what does she do?'

'She's a head teacher, in a state school up in Finsbury Park. She's pretty impressive, actually.'

I hear the tone of faux-nonchalance in his voice and can tell he's trying to minimize the pride in his words, but it's too potent for him to conceal it entirely.

A toxic air of rivalry blows in my direction again, not just the emotional rivalry and the sexual jealousy, but the professional envy too; the inescapable feeling that Eve's precocious success eclipses my own achievements and the painful awareness that I'll now never have the chance to accomplish all that I hoped.

'A teacher? So you two must have a lot in common? She sounds perfect, Max. When might we get to meet her? Why don't you bring her over for dinner one night?'

A meet-the-parents dinner already? Isn't that just a little premature? I don't remember such a great hurry for me to meet Max's parents when we were first dating. In fact, if I remember correctly – which I'm pretty certain I do – it was over six months before that introduction took place. Why the rush now to envelop Eve into the Myerson family fold?

'It's a bit early for that, Mum. And, anyway, there's Ellie to think about. I haven't said anything to her about Eve and I don't want to yet.'

'I wasn't suggesting you bring Ellie too. We could have a grown-up dinner, just the four of us. How about next time Ellie's at Celia's for the weekend? What's that – in about a fortnight's time?'

It's hard not to find Joan's proposal galling; the suggestion that my mum babysit our daughter in order that my husband is free to bring his new girlfriend round to meet the possible future in-laws. As tactless proposals go, it ranks pretty highly.

'It's in three weeks. I don't know, Mum. Don't you think it's a bit weird, bringing her round to meet you so soon?'

'Not at all. We're all adults. No one's suggesting you're going to marry the girl. It would just be nice to meet her. She sounds very interesting.'

So now she's interesting as well as perfect. I wish Joan would have the decency at least to try and disguise her obvious excitement at the prospect of Max's new girlfriend.

'I'll think about it. I'm not making any promises.'

That's not really the reassurance I was hoping for. Last time Max told his mum he wasn't making any promises, he was out on an internet date a month later.

Ellie skips into the room, her face now dry of tears and free of blotches.

'Can we go and watch a movie now, Daddy? I'm ready for ice cream.'

Before I find out the answer to Ellie's almost certainly rhetorical question, the clouds begin to gather beneath me and I know it's only a matter of seconds before they'll separate me from the living world once more. I'm not sure I mind too much today. I'm exhausted and confused and right now I can't seem to make up my mind whether to be grateful to Max for being such a wonderful father, for dealing so sensitively with Ellie and for telling her such beautiful stories about our life together, or whether to be angry with him for even contemplating the possibility of another woman usurping my place in our family.

I always thought that life dealt us a convoluted hand of conflicting emotions to play with. Who knew that death was going to be this complicated too?

# CHAPTER 14

My lonely world gives way to the living, revealing that I'm back in Joan and Ralph's house and that I've returned just in time to gatecrash the cosiest of dinner parties. It's a scene that's painfully familiar to me, one in which I've participated a hundred, two hundred times before, and yet today the fourth chair, the one positioned with its back to the door and its outlook on to the garden because, Joan says, the guest should always be afforded the best view, is taken not by me but by the woman who appears to be slipping into my shoes with disconcerting ease.

Eve congratulates Joan on the fish pie they're all tucking in to, a dish which was always my favourite too, and I see Max slip a hand under the tablecloth – the antique lace tablecloth that only ever made an appearance in my presence on Christmas Day – and, I'm guessing by her smile, squeeze Eve's thigh underneath.

'You must be very clever, petal, to be a head teacher at your age. In my day, you had to be on the verge of retirement before they'd give you that honour.'

Petal. That was always Ralph's name for me. Now he's calling her it instead. I look at Eve's face, radiant in the candlelight that I've never seen used in Joan and Ralph's house before, and I can't deny that she's infinitely more suited to the epithet than I ever was.

'Well, I suppose things have changed quite a bit, particularly in the last ten years or so. Teaching had such a bad reputation for a while that I think they were crying out for people who genuinely want to contribute something to the profession.'

'Discipline. That's the problem in schools these days. And that's why they have trouble recruiting people who want to work in them. Young people have been allowed to run amok. We see it, every day, at the bus stop at the end of the road, don't we Ralph?'

Max rolls his eyes at Eve who responds with a conspiratorial smile. It's so early on in their relationship – what must it be, a couple of months? – and yet already they seem to have perfected the art of silent communication; those surreptitious looks in collective gatherings employed to strengthen the pair bond, secure its boundaries and protect it from invaders.

It's what I used to have with Max. Except now I'm the one facing the most dangerous of intruders and I'm completely devoid of any defences at all.

'You must be ever so good with children, Eve. I bet you have a really natural flair with them. You've got that air about you, I can just tell.'

Joan's loaded declaration is concluded with an encouraging smile in search of affirmation, as though eager for confirmation that Eve lives up to the already elevated image Joan has of her.

'I do love being around young people, it's true. I find them really energizing, even the troublesome ones. I suppose it helps to remember that we were all their age once.'

Joan laughs, approbation radiating from her face, and I can see that Eve's won herself a fan before they've even finished the main course.

'Well, you know, sometimes I do find it funny that Max ended up in teaching after all the trouble he gave his teachers when he was younger.'

Eve's eyes light up with playful curiosity.

'Oh, really? Was he a bit of a handful then?'

'A handful? I'll say. He seemed to think school rules were put in place for nothing more than him to break them. When I think of all the times we had the school on the phone to complain about his latest antics. Honestly, there was a time when I used to dread the phone ringing in case it was one of his teachers on the other end again. I know you wouldn't believe it to look at him now but he was a proper little tearaway.'

Eve grins at Max who shrugs his shoulders with amused resignation. He's played this part before, at least once.

'So what kind of things did he get up to?'

'What didn't he might be a better question. Ralph, tell Eve the story about the swimming pool.'

'Which story? The one with the dye or the one where he ended up naked?'

'Really, Dad. I'm sure Eve doesn't want to hear any of this.'

'Are you kidding? I want to hear all of it.'

Of course she does. Why wouldn't she? I remember when I heard these stories for the first time too, almost certainly on one of my early visits to the Myerson household as well; I remember my surprise at Max's misspent youth and, more than that, the sense of familial inclusion that accompanied the telling of such tales.

'Well, there was the time he managed to get his hands on a couple of cans of red water dye – I don't think we know to this day where he got it from, do we, Joan? – and decided it would be a good idea to empty the lot into the school swimming pool.'

'You're joking? What happened?'

'What happened was that the pool looked liked someone had been murdered in it. When the caretaker turned up on Monday morning, he assumed some God-awful crime had been committed over the weekend and called the police. You were lucky not to be expelled over that one, Max.'

'I know, Dad. You've been telling me that for the past twenty-five years.'

Max is feigning fatigue at having these stories relayed yet again but I can see in the wryness of his smile that he's enjoying this opportunity to be teased in front of Eve, for her to be privy to another dimension of his past, for his parents to share these private histories with her.

'So weren't you punished at all?'

'He got a one-day suspension and a fortnight of after-school litter duty. You thought he should have got more, didn't you, Ralph? But he was bright, you see, and it was just before they were doing their mock exams and the school needed him to boost their overall grades. That's the only way you got away with it, Max – by the skin of your teeth.'

Joan raises her eyebrows with an air of maternal forbearance, as though Max is still a teenager and she's just hung up the phone to the school yet again.

'And what about the naked incident? That one sounds intriguing.'

'You don't want to know. Thanks, Mum – I think we can leave the school anecdotes there for today. Plenty of opportunity for Eve to hear the horror stories another time.'

Max rubs an affectionate hand up and down Eve's arm and for a second their eyes lock in mutual mischief. I see Joan clock the gesture and proffer a surreptitious, sideways smile to Ralph, who beams conspicuously back at her.

This is all disarmingly cosy.

'The funny thing is, Eve, although Max had a bit of a naughty streak throughout his teens, he was never a problem at home. He's always had such a strong sense of family, right since he was little. What was it you used to say when you were growing up, Max? That when you got married you wanted to have five sons so that you could manage your own five-a-side football team. Five sons. Can you imagine it?'

And there, without even knowing it, Joan provokes my guilt all over again. Five sons. His very own mini football team. By the time we actually got married, of course, that childhood fantasy had long since disappeared into the youthful ether. But one son. He'd have loved just one. And the thought that it won't be me, that it may be someone else, that it may even be Eve who one day gives him what he always wanted is a possible future I'm not yet ready to consider.

'Five sons, really? And do you still have ambitions to spawn your own football team?'

My heart would skip a beat if it had any left to miss. Max looks slightly taken aback as though this isn't a conversation he expected to be having with Eve in front of his parents, but he manages to camouflage any sense of embarrassment with a self-deprecating chuckle.

'I think with the benefit of rational adult thought, five's probably a few too many. I don't know, to be honest. I'm just very grateful to have Ellie. Even having one child feels like a blessing.'

A heavy silence falls on the group and as I look around the room I notice a strange expression on Eve's face; it's a complex, confused look, a mask of social conviviality behind which is something strained, something uncomfortable, something sad even. I wonder whether Max's half-hearted response is a disappointment to her, whether her expectations have been tempered, whether she was hoping for greater confirmation that Max might envisage a future that included more than a single child.

I wonder just how far ahead into this relationship Eve is thinking.

It's Ralph who breaks the silence.

'I bet you never gave your mum and dad any trouble, did you, petal? Not like our Max did?'

Eve emerges from the privacy of whatever thoughts she was musing on, a residue of preoccupation still lingering behind her eyes, and turns to smile diffidently at Ralph.

'Oh, I don't know about that. I'm sure all teenagers are a worry to their parents in one way or another.'

'But your mum and dad must be so proud of you now. Look at you. You're young, beautiful, clever, talented, you've got a smashing career. I know if you were my little girl I wouldn't be able to stop bragging about you to anyone who'd listen.'

Ralph's words sting me like the swarm of a thousand bees. I hadn't prepared myself for this. I've only ever contemplated how I might feel about Max and Ellie having someone new in their lives. I haven't really thought about the prospect of another woman taking up residence with my wider family. But hearing Ralph speak to Eve with such admiration, such esteem, such warmth, I'm pierced by a new instrument of loss. Ralph's been the closest person I've had to a father for the past decade, the only paternal presence in my life since my own dad died, and I don't think I can bear him transferring his affections to her. Not to her. Not yet.

Not for the first time since Eve entered our lives, I'm overcome by a woeful sense of professional inadequacy. I spent fifteen years of my life doing a job that I enjoyed, that I believed had some merit, that I think I did well, but now all that seems insignificant in comparison to Eve's meteoric rise and precocious success. Now all I can think about is all that I didn't achieve, all that I didn't have time to achieve, all that I assumed, somewhere in my mind, I'd be able to achieve in the decades I trusted were still ahead of me.

Physically beautiful, professionally successful, kind, calm and charming; there's no denying the fact that Eve outclasses me in every conceivable category. And, in truth, she'd be everything I'd wish for Max if only I were ready to wish for anything beyond a little more time in remembrance of marriages past.

Right now, Max's previous marriage is clearly the last thing on his mind. He's grinning with pride. But Eve's smile is less convincing, tentative even.

'I'm not sure about that. I'm just lucky that I really love what I do, I think.'

'Oh, come on, petal. There's no need to be so modest. I bet your parents were over the moon when you told them you were going to be a head teacher. I know how proud we were when Max got his deputy headship.'

There's a lengthy silence which edges just a fraction too far over the line of social acceptability and I can sense the collective awkwardness from up here.

'I . . . I don't really see my parents.'

Eve's faltering response concludes with downcast eyes, as though there's a danger inherent in meeting anyone's gaze. It's the first time I've seen even the tiniest crack in her self-assured demeanour.

'What, you mean you don't see them at all? Ever?'

It's clear from Max's reaction that this is the first he's heard of any family rift. There's the tightening of his cheeks and the slight narrowing of his eyes that only someone who knows every nuance of Max's expressions would immediately detect.

Eve turns to face Max, composure fully restored.

'It's just one of those things. We had a silly falling out a few years ago that somehow never got resolved. You know how it is.'

There's another weighty silence in which I'm sure I'm not the only one thinking that they don't, in fact, know how it is at all.

'I'm just . . . I'm just surprised you hadn't mentioned it before. That's all.'

There's a hint of accusation in Max's voice that he's unable to conceal in spite of his parents' presence.

It's Eve's turn now to place a reassuring hand on Max's leg.

'That's because it's not a big deal. Really. Can we just drop it?'

She's smiling appeasingly, but there's an imploring undertone in her voice. Max holds her gaze for a few seconds, and I can see him negotiate his way through a minefield of emotions before Joan decides it's her responsibility to break the tension.

'Well, I'm sure they'd be terribly proud of you, if they knew. I think it's just lovely, Eve, you doing so well in your job. And it's lovely to have you here, too, really it is. You're a real tonic.'

With those words of treachery, Joan places a hand on top of Eve's, squeezing it with maternal approval. Eve may be estranged from her own mum but it would appear that Joan's more than willing to fill the vacancy.

The two women smile at one another, as if two long-lost friends freshly discovering the soul mate they've been searching for.

Joan's not quite done yet though.

'You will come back soon, won't you? Come back whenever you like, the door's always open. You're welcome any time.'

And with that invitation the transition's complete. They've not even reached dessert yet and Eve's already usurped my place in Joan's affections.

I can't remember the last time I felt this hopeless. Or sad. Or angry. Watching the four of them confiding and smiling and admiring one another in the candlelight, I feel more excluded from Max's world than I've ever done before. Because with every confidence shared, even the difficult ones, and every anecdote revealed, however embarrassing, I can see that my life – the life I had with Max and Ellie – is disappearing from view.

Life as I knew it is ceasing to exist.

I close my eyes, suddenly dizzy with an anger that emerges from the shadows of my own grief, and keep them shut tight to stop the fear of falling, even though I know that there's nowhere for me to fall from, nowhere for me to fall to.

For the first time since I died I realize that there is something worse than being stuck here on my own; it's watching the world revolve without me and understanding that I'm no longer a part of it. It's the painful acknowledgement that the role I had to play during the short time I was alive now seems so very insignificant. I didn't have an important job or change anyone's life or earn an impressive amount of money. I didn't make a name for myself, not even a small name, didn't reach the top of any pole, greasy or not, didn't leave behind anything substantial by which to be remembered. I didn't achieve fame or notoriety, didn't accomplish any particular goals, did nothing at all out of the ordinary.

I didn't, in short, consummate my life.

Instead, I loved a man who seems to be in the process of replacing me already and I gave birth to a daughter who'll probably barely remember me by the time she's my age.

It's not much to feel proud of, is it?

I promised myself, when I first got here, that I wouldn't become bitter, that I wouldn't resent the lives of the living, that I'd be grateful for the small mercy of the sporadic access I'd been afforded. I promised myself that I wouldn't become consumed by a catalogue of accumulated regrets for all that I'd been unable to achieve in my too-short life. But that was then, when I still felt a part of everyone's lives, if only for the purposes of mourning. Now they're pushing me to the periphery and who knows where that will take me or where, in the end, it will leave me.

I catch myself suddenly, ranting like a madwoman in life's attic, venting my frustrations to the empty void and open my eyes to discover that I'm back alone in the whiteness. It is, I admit, probably the best place for me right now. I'm not sure I could have tolerated another moment impotently watching over that domestic cosiness and being so painfully aware of my exclusion from it. Because there's nothing more lonely than passing by a party to which you're not invited, is there?

# CHAPTER 15

Bright yellow light begins to puncture the clouds beneath me in determined bursts, giving way to mottled patches of blue sky, the stark white monotony dispersing with a sense of relief.

The trees at the end of Mum's garden are semi-naked, the few remaining leaves a resigned shade of brown as if in acknowledgement of their own impending retirement. Underneath are Mum and Ellie, wrapped snugly in knitted scarves and woolly hats, collecting piles of redundant leaves and coaxing them into the wheelbarrow that's been on the earth for longer than I was.

It's the first time I've been home since I died. Home to Mum's, that is. I don't know — and have given up speculating — why it's taken so long for this particular homecoming to occur. But it's paradoxically both reassuring and unnerving to revisit somewhere so rich in memories for me, memories from when I was Ellie's age and even younger, memories of standing exactly where Ellie is now but in clothes from a different time and with the experiences of a different era and next to a woman whose face didn't yet bear the evidence of compound grief.

'Every time I put some in, Nanna, they just keep blowing out again.'

Mum laughs.

'I know, darling. It's getting a bit full, isn't it? Shall we take it over to the compost heap and empty it? It's probably about time.'

Mum picks up the handles and begins wheeling the barrow to the other side of the garden, Ellie holding on to one side in pretence of helping to bear the weight.

'You're not too cold are you, Ellie? Is that hat keeping you nice and warm?'

'I'm not cold at all, Nanna. I love this hat. It's really snuggly.'

Mum looks at Ellie, a nostalgic smile lighting her eyes.

'Your mummy always loved that hat. She used to say it made her feel cocooned, as if the wind couldn't touch her. I didn't know I still had it until today. Lucky I did or else you wouldn't have been able to help me out here, would you?'

Of course. That's my hat Ellie's got on. The red-and-white striped one I insisted on wearing even after it was too tight and didn't fit properly over my ears any more. And now it's protecting Ellie from the elements, just as it used to protect me.

'Did Mummy like gardening too? It's much more fun gardening here than at home. Our garden at home is tiny.'

Ellie screws up her nose in mock disdain.

'Oh, Ellie, you are funny with your silly faces. It's not a bad size for a London garden, you know. But I can't pretend I don't love you gardening here with me. And, yes, Mummy was a very keen gardener too. Right from when she was little. She always used to help me clear the leaves, just like you're doing now.'

Ellie beams, pride dancing in her eyes.

'What else did Mummy like doing in the garden?'

They're back under the tree now, Ellie scooping hand-fuls of uncooperative leaves into the barrow, as many escaping from her tiny gloved hands as willingly accepting their fate.

'Well, her favourite time of year was about now, when we'd clear the leaves and plant the bulbs that would come up in early spring. She loved daffodils best. And tulips. She always got so excited when the first buds would emerge and we'd both try and guess what colour the first flower would be. Her favourites were the deep purple ones.'

'Can I help you plant the bulbs too, Nanna?'

'Of course you can, darling. We may not have time today as Daddy will be here soon to pick you up, but I'll make sure I save some for you to do next time you come. Maybe we could buy some special tubs just for you that you can look after whenever you're here. How does that sound?'

Ellie wraps her arms around Mum's hips. Mum pulls Ellie tight towards her as if she'd be content never to let her go.

'Look at the time, Ellie. If we're going to have that hot chocolate before Daddy gets here we should leave the rest of this gardening and head on inside.'

'But we haven't finished yet. I don't want you to have to do all of this all by yourself.'

'That's very thoughtful of you, darling, but you've been extra specially helpful today and there's really not much more for me to do. Come on, you've earned that last piece of cake too, I think.'

Mum takes Ellie's mittened hand in her own, as my little girl skips through the back door and into the kitchen.

'Nanna, do you think I should be allowed to have a puppy?'

Mum closes the fridge door, milk in hand, and eyes Ellie with a look I know all too well; the wry smile that indicates she knows exactly where this conversation is heading and has every intention of treading so incredibly carefully that not a single eggshell is so much as cracked let alone broken.

'Why do you ask that?'

'Well, I really, really want one but Daddy says I can't have one.'

'And why does he say that?'

'He has this whole, stupid list of reasons. Like, he says that having a dog is a big responsibility and he hasn't got time to walk it every day even though I said I'd walk it and he wouldn't have to do anything.'

Mum adopts her mock serious face, the one that I recognize so well from my own childhood.

'To be fair to Daddy, I don't think you'd really be able to go out and walk a dog on your own, would you? You're still a bit young for that, don't you think?'

Ellie looks stumped for a second. But only a second.

'Well, it's not as if Daddy would have to walk it all by himself. I'd go with him. And that would be exercise for me which would be good because Daddy's always saying that children in London don't get enough exercise. And he says it's not fair to leave a dog at home all by itself all day even though it wouldn't be all day because me and Granny and Grandpa could go and get it and take it back to their house after school. And he says that puppies grow into dogs and that I'm too young to have a dog and that the novelty would wear off and then he'd have to look after it all the time, but he's wrong, I wouldn't get bored of it and I would look after it and I am going to be eight next year and that's not too young to have a puppy, is it?'

Mum begins to let out a laugh which she tries – and fails – to bury inside a kiss on top of Ellie's head. Ellie pulls away from her, a scowl corrugating her forehead.

'What are you laughing at, Nanna? It's not funny that I'm not allowed a dog.'

'I'm not laughing at you, Ellie. I'm laughing because you sound so much like Mummy. Hearing you takes me right back to when she had exactly the same conversation with your grandad all those years ago.'

'Did Mummy want a puppy too?'

'Almost as much as you do, I think. I remember her trying all sorts of things to try and persuade us.'

'What sort of things?'

Ellie's ears have pricked up and there's an unmistakeable pique of curiosity in her eyes.

Mum hesitates for a second, perhaps wondering whether full disclosure is unfair to Max. She starts chuckling to herself in a moment of private reminiscence that clearly isn't going to do much to assuage Ellie's interest.

'What, Nanna? What is it? Tell me.'

'Okay then, but you're not to tell your daddy I told you.'

Mum's laughing now, in memory or in mischief I'm not sure, but I'm as intrigued as Ellie by what's tickled her so much.

'I remember Mummy making a huge collage of all the things we could do if we had a dog. She must have cut out hundreds of pictures from magazines. There were pictures of dogs on beaches and dogs in parks and wet dogs in rivers and warm dogs sleeping in front of fires. It must have taken her hours. Your grandad said it was like a photographic shrine and Mummy insisted that we have it up on the wall here in the kitchen for weeks.'

Mum's nostalgic pleasure is infectious now and Ellie catches the bug; she starts giggling too and I watch on, relishing this rare opportunity to see the woman and the child I love most in the world conjoined by laughter.

'And did that make you let her have a puppy?'

'I'm sorry to say it didn't, darling. But that didn't stop Mummy coming up with lots of other ideas to try and convince us.'

'What ideas? Go on, tell me, Nanna.'

Mum smiles at Ellie with a look of playful complicity.

'Only if you promise not to use them with Daddy. Promise?'

Ellie narrows her eyes in contemplation of the solemn vow she's about to make.

'I promise to try.'

'Well I suppose that'll have to do. I remember Mummy making lots of promises about all the things she'd do around the house if we got her a dog. She said she'd always do all the washing-up and regularly clean the car and tidy her bedroom without ever being asked. But we knew all those were too good to be true. And then I remember her persuading a friend to bring her dog to our house in the hope it would show Grandad how nice it would be if we had our own.'

'And did Grandad like it?'

Mum's laughing so much now she can't answer Ellie straight away.

'Well, not really. You see, it was quite a wet day and suddenly this enormous, damp Irish setter was lolloping through our house, leaving muddy footprints all over the carpet. Grandad was chasing it and trying to grab hold of its collar but he wasn't very experienced with dogs and he just couldn't get hold of it. I'll never forget the sight of him chasing after that dog, the pair of them bounding around this kitchen. It was one of the funniest things I've ever seen.'

'So what happened? Did Grandad catch it?'

'Well, as it rampaged back through the hallway its tail was wagging so fast that it knocked over the hall table with your Grandad's precious collection of National Trust magazines on it. The look on his face as they all clattered to the floor. Your Grandad didn't get cross very often but he was definitely quite cross that day.'

I'd forgotten about that little escapade with my friend's dog. Charlotte, she was called. My friend, that is, not the dog. I can't remember the dog's name. But I do remember the telling-off Dad gave me after Charlotte and her dog had finally been escorted from the house, and the gloomy realization that my plan had well and truly backfired.

'So did Grandad not let Mummy have a puppy either? Why are daddies so mean?'

'Oh, your daddy's not mean, darling. You're very lucky to have such a lovely daddy. And your Grandad wasn't mean either. Your daddy's right, dogs are a lot of work. Maybe once you're a bit older Daddy will change his mind.'

'Did Grandad change his mind?'

A fleeting shadow of sadness darkens the happiness in Mum's eyes, too brief and too well-camouflaged for Ellie to notice, but not discreet enough to be hidden from me.

'Let's go into the sitting room to eat your cake, darling. I'll bring in your hot chocolate. It's much cosier in there with the fire on.'

Ellie scampers out of the room carrying her slab of heavily iced cake on a plate large enough for dinner. Mum clearly hasn't stopped fretting about crumbs on the sofa in the last thirty years.

'So did Mummy ever have a puppy?'

Consternation settles on Mum's face. I don't know how she's going to answer Ellie truthfully without upsetting her. It looks like she doesn't either.

Mum draws Ellie towards her on the sofa, wrapping her arms around my little girl's innocent shoulders.

'She didn't, no. She stopped being quite so keen for one after a little while. And then she got interested in other things and well – you know – she grew up and a puppy wasn't at the top of her wish list any more.'

The best fibs are often concealed with a peppering of the truth. It's true that I grew up – too fast, overnight almost – but it wasn't that I became interested in other things. It was that I became distracted by aspects of life that really ought to have been beyond my single-digit years; by funerals and grief and possessively guarding my one remaining parent. So the prospect of a puppy really did seem like the last thing any of us needed. And yet we'd come so close. My tenth birthday, Dad had said, when my badgering and cajoling and persistence had finally got the better of him. It was a promise I'm sure he wouldn't have broken.

'Well, I'm not going to stop wanting a puppy, however old I get and however long I have to wait. Even if I have to wait till I'm grown up and have a house of my own.'

Ellie chomps into her cake with determined gusto while still encased in Mum's arms, leaving the two of them in silence for a few seconds.

'So when she really wanted a puppy and was doing all those things, how old was Mummy then?'

'Well, she'd have been about your age, I think. Maybe a little bit older, but not much.'

Ellie looks thoughtful, munching away in her own little world for a few seconds.

'Nanna? What was Mummy like when she was my age?'

Mum releases Ellie to face her on the sofa, studying her intently as if seeing something there for the first time.

'She was a gorgeous little girl. Just like you are.'

'Can we have a look at some of the photo albums again? Are there any of when she's exactly the same age as me?'

'Of course we can. Let me root them out. They're in the sideboard in the dining room.'

Less than a minute later Mum has returned with two well-thumbed photo albums, both a shade of brown that was the height of fashion three decades ago.

'Here we go. I think these two are about right. Yes, this one's from 1981 and this one's . . . wait, let me put my glasses on . . . yes, this one's '81 too. Perfect.'

Mum opens the first album across both their laps and I hover above to see for myself what photographic memories lie in store.

'Look at Mummy's funny top. Those sleeves are so puffy. She looks really funny.'

I look over her shoulder to see what's provoked such amusement. It's a picture of me standing in this very sitting room, hands slung on hips in imitation of the older girls I'd watch walking home from secondary school across the field at the bottom of our garden. I'm wearing a faux-satin, candy-pink top complete with sleeves engineered to look like a surge of wind has just billowed inside of them. I can see why Ellie thinks I look faintly ridiculous.

'You may think it looks silly but it was the height of fashion in those days. It was Princess Diana's dress that did it. Big sleeves like that were everywhere after her wedding.'

Of course. It was royal wedding inspired, that top. I'd been desperate for some item of clothing to evoke that seemingly fairytale event and I remember Mum traipsing round the shops with me one Saturday morning a few weeks later, patiently pulling out blouse after blouse from cluttered rails, and me refusing every item until she finally picked out that one, its synthetic material shimmering under artificial lights. I barely took that blouse off all summer holiday.

'Well, I still think it looks silly. Is that Mummy with Grandad?'

'Yes, that's right. You've seen lots of pictures of Grandad before, haven't you? I think I'm right in saying that was right at the end of the school holidays, the bank holiday weekend if my memory serves me correctly. Mummy persuaded us to take her to Brighton for the day.'

'Daddy keeps saying he's going to take me to Brighton but he hasn't yet. Is it nice?'

'It's lovely. Although we didn't get to see much of it on that particular trip. The traffic had been appalling, just as your grandad had feared, and we'd had to turn around for home almost as soon as we'd arrived. Your grandad always did find it difficult to refuse Mummy on things like that. A bit like your daddy and you.'

'Except when it comes to dogs. Then he's really good at saying no.'

Mum and I smile in unison.

I remember that trip to Brighton. The days leading up to the bank holiday had been fiercely hot and I'd been taunted by too much footage on the evening news of children playing on beaches and splashing in water and I remember feeling as if every other child in the UK was at the seaside except me. Dad had been deeply ambivalent about driving all the way to Brighton just for a day trip and he'd been right; not only had the traffic been terrible but the weather that day had turned so instead of a sea breeze cooling sun-kissed skin, we found ourselves shivering on an overcast promenade. On the interminable car journey home, I remember vowing to myself never to wear shorts on long day trips ever again.

'Look, there's Mummy in my hat.'

I peer over Ellie's shoulder and she's right. There I am, standing in an unidentified forest, wellies on feet and that stripy hat on my head.

'So she is. Can you see how tightly she's got it pulled over her ears? You can barely see her eyes. It's a wonder she could see where she was going.'

Ellie giggles and starts Mum off too.

'Oh, I do love to hear you giggling, Ellie. You've got the most infectious laugh of anyone I know, do you know that? It reminds me of Mummy's laugh. Hers was catching too.'

Ellie smiles, almost shyly, and huddles further under Mum's protective arm.

'Who's that old lady there, Nanna? The one holding Mummy's hand?'

'That's your mummy's nanna. My mummy. Your great-grandmother.'

'She's in loads of these pictures. Mummy must have liked her a lot.'

'Yes, they had a lovely relationship. They – your mummy's nanna and grandad – lived just on the other side of town so Mummy used to see them nearly every day.'

'A bit like me with Granny and Grandpa?'

A pained look passes over Mum's face fleetingly before she steels herself to answer.

'Yes, darling. A bit like that.'

I can see the hurt in Mum's eyes and it's enough to unleash the guilt in me all over again. If only I'd never moved away, if only I hadn't settled so far from home, if only I hadn't chosen to raise my family miles from Mum, perhaps then she'd be able to have the same relationship with Ellie now as I did with my grandparents then. As Ellie does with Joan and Ralph. It's only now, now that I'm separated from Ellie permanently, that I can understand how much it must have hurt Mum when I moved to London. How much she must hate being two hours away from Ellie when Joan and Ralph are just a few minutes. How the simplest, seemingly pragmatic decisions we make can have ramifications we can't comprehend until it's too late.

Perhaps if only I'd never moved away I wouldn't be here now. Perhaps I'd be there, looking at photograph albums with Mum and laughing at gaudy blouses and stripy hats and reminiscing about ill-fated trips to the seaside. Perhaps I'd still have the rest of my life ahead of me instead of nothing more than the impotent imaginings of what might have been.

I stop myself in my own regretful tracks. I've been down this path before and I know that all that awaits me at the end of this bitter cul-de-sac is a form of temporary insanity. If I hadn't moved away I'd never have met Max and there'd be no Ellie and the question of proximity to grandchildren may well have been purely academic.

'You know what, Nanna? You should just move in with Daddy and me and then I'd get to see you every day like I do with Granny and Grandpa. We've got a spare room and everything.'

Mum looks taken aback. Perhaps she's wondering how Ellie's managed to articulate her own private wish. Perhaps she's gratified that such a thought should even cross Ellie's mind. Perhaps she's imagining an alternative life in which Max had agreed to let her do just that.

'That would be wonderful, wouldn't it, darling? But you and Daddy have such a cosy time together and I'm all settled here, aren't I? You know that I'm always, always here for you, though, Ellie. You're the most precious thing in the world to me and I so love our weekends together. You can come here as often as you like. You know that, don't you?'

Ellie smiles and nods and I feel a surge of relief wash over me that Ellie still has my mum to look out for her.

The doorbell rings and Ellie jumps up to answer it. Mum stays in the sitting room, seemingly lost in her own thoughts, until Ellie returns with Max in tow, forcing Mum to snap out of her reverie.

'Hi Celia. How's the weekend been?'

'Oh, lovely thanks, Max. We've had a super time, haven't we, Ellie?'

Ellie nods enthusiastically.

'Nanna and I baked a cake and went for a long walk and did a jigsaw puzzle that was really hard and had hundreds of pieces in it and I've been helping out in the garden, haven't I?'

'You certainly have. You've been a marvellous little helper.'

'And you know what else, Daddy? Mummy really wanted a puppy when she was my age and Grandad wouldn't let her have one either. Nanna thinks you should let me, don't you Nanna?'

Mum raises a knowing eyebrow at Max before turning to Ellie in mock reproach.

'Now, you cheeky monkey. I said no such thing, as well you know. Max, would you like a cup of tea before you head off? I'm afraid your daughter's just devoured the last of the cake.'

'No, I'm fine thanks, Celia. We really need to hit the road – I've got a ton of marking to do when we get back. Munchkin, do you want to run up and get your things and we'll get going?'

Ellie does as she's told and I wonder whether she's always this well-behaved at Mum's these days. I remember countless times when the three of us were on the verge of leaving and Ellie would kick up a fuss, necessitating arduous patient cajoling to get her into the car without a full-scale tantrum. Perhaps she's simply grown up a bit. Or perhaps she's just happier now to be returned to the parental fold.

'So what have you been up to this weekend, Max? Anything exciting?'

I wonder how much Mum knows, whether she's even aware of Eve's existence. I can't help hoping she isn't. Not just for my sake, not simply because her knowing would somehow make their relationship all the more real, all the more threatening, but for Mum's sake too. She's still too fragile. Surely Max must realize that?

'Oh, you know, not much. Got some jobs done around the house – all the things Ellie won't usually let me get on with at weekends. Saw my mum and dad. Nothing wildly exciting. Even had a lie-in this morning – I'd almost forgotten what they were like.'

'That's lovely. You of all people deserve a restful weekend.'

So she doesn't know. I'm glad. I wouldn't want Mum having to imagine what I'm imagining now: the lie-in *à deux*. In my bed, no doubt. Mine and Max's bed. I feel a wave of anger with Max for the likelihood that he's allowed Eve to invade our most sacred of marital spaces.

'I'm ready, Daddy.'

'Excellent. Say goodbye to Nanna then.'

'Bye, Nanna. Thank you for a lovely weekend. The cake was yummy.'

'You're very welcome, darling. I'll see you in a few weeks' time. And make sure you get Daddy to scan that project you were telling me about, the one about rainforests – I'd love to see it.'

'Okay.'

Mum walks them to the front door where she embraces Ellie with an ardour that reveals how little she wants to say goodbye. But seconds later they're gone and Mum returns to the sitting room. I go with her, delighted to have Mum all to myself for the first time since I died.

She sits on the sofa and pulls the open photograph album on to her lap, where she begins to study the images, her fingers running over the protective plastic film securing them in place, her eyes darting from one picture to the next as though there's too much to take in, too much to focus on, too much to remember. I watch her, looking at the photographs, and want so much to be sitting by her side, to hold her hand and hear her breath and smell the distinctive face powder that she's worn every day, ever since I was a child. I want to be a flesh-and-blood daughter for her again, the daughter to whom she gave so much and who now has nothing to give in return.

Mum slumps back into the sofa, her hands holding on tightly to the book of remembrance on her lap as if to let it go would be to allow all the memories it contains to disperse into the ether, never to return. Her head rests on the cushion behind her, her eyes staring impassively into the empty room beyond, only the sound of her slow, lonely breaths punctuating the silence.

And it's at this moment, just when I want to stay with Mum even if only in spirit, just to keep an eye on her, just to feel that I'm by her side even if she can never know it, that the scene before me begins to mist and then cloud over and within seconds Mum has disappeared. With her go the photograph albums and the sitting room in which I spent so many years, watching TV and playing games and opening Christmas presents and feeling as safe and as happy as all young children deserve to.

Instead I'm alone again, with only my anger for company. Anger that Mum's having to endure this repeated grief when she's already suffered so much. Anger at Joan and Ralph's daily contact with Ellie, in contrast to Mum's monthly visits. Anger that Max is allowing another woman into my bed without a second thought. Anger that Ellie has nothing but photographs to remind her of the mother she may one day barely remember.

Anger that life is going on without me.

It's a year and a half since I was prematurely evicted from life and yet I feel no closer to understanding where I am or what I'm doing here.

All I do know is that I have more time than I want or need to think about all that I wish I'd achieved with my life, and an eternity stretched out before me to regret all that I didn't.

# Bargaining

# CHAPTER 16

Just as I'm convinced that the clouds are beginning to dissolve, I wonder if I've made a mistake, if access isn't being restored after all, if there's some trick of the light that's fooled me into thinking I'm about to take up my place on life's viewing balcony when in fact I'm going nowhere. Because although I'm sure I can detect movement and identify vaguely familiar shapes and hear the gentle babble of collective conversation, what I'm looking down on appears to be as white as the world I inhabit.

The clouds clear a little further allowing nebulous forms to morph into focus and I see that I'm in a restaurant – a stark, austere restaurant – in which everything, from the floor to the ceiling, from the crockery to the table cloths, from the art to the uniformed staff, is glaringly, uninterruptedly white. It's exactly like my world except with food, company and almost certainly extortionate bills.

In the corner of the white room is a long, rectangular table and gathered around it are Harriet, Max, Ellie, Connor and about twenty of Harriet's friends. This, I realize, must be Harriet's birthday lunch. She always hosts her own party, always at whichever restaurant happens to be the most coveted venue of the hour, the place where most people couldn't get a table for two in six months' time let alone a table for two dozen at a week's notice, always at her own, vast expense, not an eyelid batted at the free-flowing Dom Pérignon or the guests ordering whole lobsters and filet mignon.

And she always invites Ellie. Ever since Ellie was just old enough to sit in a high chair at the head of the table, banging her rattle disruptively to the beat of Max's and my embarrassment, Ellie's been a permanent fixture of this annual gathering. They've got a funny relationship, those two; Harriet's always treated Ellie more like a minia-ture grown-up than a child and Ellie's response has been to behave with greater maturity in Harriet's company, almost as if she's trying on the costume of the adult she hopes one day to become.

It suddenly dawns on me, with simultaneous disap-pointment and frustration, that if this is Harriet's birthday lunch it must be mid January already. Which means that I've missed Christmas and New Year. Again. That's two consecutive Christmases that have been cele-brated without me present in any form, living or dead, tangible or invisible. Two years that I've missed Ellie waking up at the crack of dawn and finding her gift-filled pillowcase outside her bedroom door, two years of missing her dragging the bulging sack into our bed-room and Max helping her lift it on to the bed, two years of watching her open her presents and delighting in what's she's received and her excitement that, at five o'clock or six o'clock or whatever ungodly hour she's woken up, this is only the beginning of a day overflow-ing with gifts.

The thought strikes me, like an unexpected slap across the face, that perhaps my absence coincided with Eve's presence. Perhaps Ellie has met Eve and the three of them spent Christmas together. Perhaps, buoyed by the successful introduction to Joan and Ralph, they decided to expedite their burgeoning romance. Perhaps they all spent New Year together too. Perhaps Eve's at home right now awaiting their return.

A new sense of possessiveness overwhelms me. I want to be with Ellie, to be still – and always – the woman taking primary care of her.

It's at times like this that I most fear my absences, these voids of time and space, the duration of which I have no way of calculating until I return. The times when all I can do is imagine what's taken place while I've been gone and then, finally, when I'm eventually allowed back, try to piece together the fragments of information I manage to accumulate, like an incomplete jigsaw puzzle of someone else's life.

I look at Ellie now, seated on Harriet's lap in the middle of the table, and remind myself how lucky I am to be seeing her at all.

'How old are you today, Hetty?'

'Too old to be telling anyone, you little rotter. One day, in a very very long time, you'll be my age too and then you'll know why I'd rather keep that magic number to myself.'

'But it's not like you're *really* old. Like a hundred or something.'

Harriet laughs.

'No, indeed, I'm not a hundred. Thank you for that vote of confidence.'

Ellie beams as though in receipt of unmitigated praise.

'You're still really pretty, though. You've hardly got any wrinkles. And I like your sparkly earrings.'

Harriet pulls Ellie in for an even tighter squeeze.

'And you, young lady, know how to say all the right things to a woman on her birthday. That's why you're my favourite person around this whole table. That and your impeccable taste, of course. These earrings were a birthday gift to myself. I figure who needs a man to buy me diamonds, when I can afford to buy them for myself?'

Ellie fiddles with the cluster of gems dangling from Harriet's ears for a few seconds, an inquisitive expression on her face.

'Hetty? Why don't you have a husband?'

Harriet eyes my little girl with amused intrigue. If there's one person who can handle Ellie's irrepressible questions, it's Harriet.

'Well, grown-up girl, I just haven't met anyone I want to marry.'

'So is that why you don't have any children of your own?'

Harriet hesitates for a second and I detect a rare faltering disquiet on her face before she settles into a reassuring smile.

'Why do I need children of my own when I've got you to ask me awkward questions and admire my jewellery?'

Ellie pulls free of Harriet's embrace, her nose wrinkled with the warning that her queries haven't yet been fully answered.

'No, but really. Don't you get lonely all on your own?'

Harriet's face softens, a momentary lapse in her customary self-assurance.

'I think everyone gets lonely sometimes, Ellie. Even people with families of their own.'

It's the first time I've ever heard Harriet admit to loneliness, even obliquely. Perhaps it's symptomatic of the reflectiveness that often accompanies birthdays, however loudly they're celebrated.

'So do you think you'll ever have babies? Because if you did they'd sort of be like my cousins, wouldn't they? Because you're sort of like my aunt. And I don't have any cousins so that would be really cool.'

Harriet considers Ellie's question for a beat longer than I'd imagine she needs to.

'Oh, I don't know, gorgeous girl. I think I'm probably a bit too old now, don't you? That's why I'm so nice to you, little lady, so I'll have someone to come and visit me in the geriatrics' home when I really am old and wrinkly and talking nonsense. That's what goddaughters have to do, you know? It's all part of the deal.'

Ellie smiles as if not entirely certain whether Harriet's joking or not. I'm not really sure, either.

Connor saunters over and whisks Ellie away to the other end of the table where he involves her in a game with two of our university friends, which appears to involve identifying the less salubrious eating habits of other diners. I watch Ellie interacting so confidently with this group of adults and can't help but feel proud of her. I don't know where she gets that confidence from. Both Max and I were painfully shy as children. But that's another revelation about childrearing that I didn't know until I had my own; that children can be so much more than the sum of their inherited parts, so much more accomplished, in so many ways, than both of their parents.

I notice, out of the corner of my distracted eye, that Max and Harriet are now standing apart from the rest of the group, huddled in the corner, engaged in what looks like a heated discussion. I leave Ellie in Connor's capable hands to listen in.

'What the hell are you talking about, she's "special"? You weren't supposed to meet someone "special". You were just supposed to go out and have a bit of fun.'

I think I can probably guess who Harriet's talking about and it sounds as though this may be the first she's heard of her.

'Harriet, I don't get it. You badgered me for weeks, telling me I had to go and meet new people and, now that I have, you – of all people – seem to be surprised by this turn of events. What on earth did you think was going to happen?'

'I expected you to go on a few dates, flirt a little, get a bit drunk now and again. Have some fun. Stop moping around the house. I certainly didn't expect you to present me with a formal announcement that you're now in possession of a girlfriend. A girlfriend, Max? For god's sake, what about Rach?'

At last. I had wondered when – if at all – amidst all the excitement about Max's rejuvenated love life, someone might do me the courtesy of remembering that I did once exist. Not even that long ago. Not in the grand scheme of things, anyway.

'Oh come on, Harriet, you can't have it both ways. I don't remember you evoking Rachel's memory a few months back when you unilaterally set up a dating profile for me. And please don't insult me by suggesting that just because I'm seeing someone new I've somehow forgotten about Rachel. You've no idea how much I miss her still.'

He's right, I don't. It's reassuring, in all honesty, to hear him say that. I was beginning to feel that the only place I hold in Max's mind these days is a repository of memories to be bequeathed to Ellie when the time is right.

'Don't you dare put the responsibility for your actions on my shoulders, Max. I don't remember saying you had to go and fall in love with someone, for god's sake.'

As soon as the words leave Harriet's lips, a strawberry rash erupts on Max's neck before travelling north to invade the rest of his face. His eyes betray a surprise at his own unease. But he's not quite as astonished, I think, as I am.

He's in love with her. Max has actually fallen in love with someone else. And, if his reaction is anything to go by, he hadn't even been aware of it himself until a few seconds ago.

I feel like the non-existent ground beneath me has begun to shake, that whatever's holding me up is about to let me down, that every part of my ethereal being has destabilized in an instant. It's as though whatever quasi existence I'm still in possession of has rapidly, in one dramatic purge, drained out of me, leaving a vast, gaping chasm into which an invisible wind is now sweeping through, battering me from every conceivable angle.

'Oh my god. You actually think you're in love with her, don't you? God, you idiot, Max. It's too soon, can't you see that?'

I can, yes, of course I can. I just wish you'd seen that, Harriet, when you set up that profile without so much as Max's consent. I wish that sometimes you didn't charge headlong into conducting situations that simply aren't yours to orchestrate.

'Don't be ridiculous. You're jumping to silly conclusions. It's only been a few months. There's no need to get ahead of ourselves.'

'I don't think I'm the one getting ahead of myself, Max. God, if you could have seen your reaction to the mere mention of the L word. It was written all over your face. If you don't want to admit it to me, fine, but I know what I saw.'

She's right. There is no denying it. Max's reaction was greater confirmation than a thousand words.

Harriet and Max fall into an uncomfortable silence, as if suddenly aware that there are twenty or so guests sitting at the table, getting drunk on Harriet's champagne and enjoying the birthday she's supposed to be celebrating.

'So, what does Ellie make of her new stepmum-in-waiting? I imagine she's completely freaked out, isn't she?'

'She doesn't know yet. I haven't told her. So I'd be grateful if we didn't make a big deal of it today.'

'Well, I suppose I should be grateful for the small mercies of common sense.'

Max takes a deep breath and I exhale a sigh of relief. I don't think I'd dared acknowledge to myself quite how unprepared I was for the prospect of Ellie having met Eve in my absence. At least I know now they didn't spend a pseudo-family Christmas together.

'Well, actually, I'm planning to tell her pretty soon. We – Eve and I – have agreed that she should meet Ellie at half term.'

Please, Max, no. Not Ellie. Not yet. She's not ready. It's too great a risk; a risk of reigniting her fears that nothing's stable in her life, that she can't rely on anything to remain the same, even for a matter of months. And a danger that she'll think you're deserting her too, that she's being abandoned in favour of another woman's attentions. Don't do it to her, not yet. She's just not ready.

And neither am I.

'You can't, Max. Don't be stupid. What you get up to with this Eve woman is your business, but it's not fair to drag Ellie into it. It's much too soon.'

'Sorry, Harriet, but I disagree. By February, Eve and I will have been seeing each other for six months and Rachel will have been gone for nearly two years. I don't think it's too soon on either count.'

It's that incomprehensible timeline again. The timeline with which every living person seems to be intimately familiar and yet which no one ever bothered to tell me about before I died. Where is it written that nearly two years is an acceptable interval after your wife's untimely exit for the introduction of your new girlfriend to your motherless daughter?

'Max, I know I can't tell you what to do. Who am I, after all, but your wife's bolshie best friend? All I can say is that I think it's a mistake. As Ellie's godmother, as someone who made a promise to both you and Rach that I'd always look out for her, I'm telling you – categorically and unequivocally – that I think it's too soon. And on that note, I'm going to go and get pissed because it's my birthday and it's a bloody outrage that I'm the only person here – apart from you and Ellie – who's still sober.'

With that, Harriet strides over to the table where she positions herself on the lap of one of her devastatingly handsome male friends, sweeps the glass out of his hand and decisively downs its contents.

I hate seeing them argue, my husband and my best friend. I hate being the cause of their conflict. I hate not being able to mediate a resolution.

I turn my attention back towards Max but as I do the whiteness of the restaurant begins to blur, the tables, chairs, floors and walls merging into one amorphous, homogeneous mass, and I know that my access is rapidly receding. I catch one last, hazy glimpse of Max's face before my view disappears altogether. He looks sad, the expression of a man acutely aware of his isolation in a room full of people. I wish I could have stayed with him just a little longer, just to see that he recovered without Ellie being any the wiser, just to ensure his and Harriet's reconciliation.

I wish, in all honesty, that I could have seen Harriet convince Max that he was wrong and she was right, that I could have borne witness to Max's change of heart, that I could have been reassured that Harriet had been able to unpick the mess that she is, after all, responsible for creating.

Now all I can do is sit and wait and hope that during the course of however long my absence, someone manages to convince Max that introducing Ellie to Eve isn't in anyone's best interests.

# CHAPTER 17

I've arrived to find Max and Ellie sitting on the sofa watching one of Ellie's favourite television programmes, a clips show of funny home movies which always has her in fits of giggles. This edition seems to be an animal special which is probably about as close to televisual heaven as Ellie can get.

'Awww, Daddy, look at that puppy. He's getting sprayed by that hose and is all wet. Silly dog.'

Ellie's giggling uncontrollably, fidgeting with delight.

'See, what did I tell you, munchkin? Dogs really aren't all that clever.'

Ellie eyes Max suspiciously.

'Daddy, that's a puppy. Of course puppies are silly. But then they grow up into lovely, clever, cuddly dogs.'

'Oh, do they now? I can't think why you haven't mentioned that before.'

Max smiles teasingly at Ellie who scrunches up her forehead to manufacture an unamused frown but she can't help herself grinning.

As the end credits begin to roll, Max hits the mute button on the remote control.

'Oh, Daddy, why did you do that? I love that music.'

'Sorry, munchkin, but there's something I want to talk to you about.'

Max sounds serious. Ellie looks annoyed. I feel preemptively anxious.

'You know how sometimes you make new friends at school and you want me to meet them and sometimes you bring them home for tea?'

Ellie looks at him curiously. Rightly so.

'Well, I've made a new friend who I think you'll really like and I'd like you and her to get to know one another.'

So he's going ahead with it. In spite of Harriet's objections, in spite of common sense, in spite of the voice there must surely be in his head urging caution, he's going to introduce my little girl to the woman who's currently stealing a march on his heart. I'd had a horrible feeling that Max's mind was going to be unchangeable on this subject.

Ellie squints at Max and it's almost as if I can see the cogs of her nimble, hyperactive mind revolving behind the whites of her eyes.

'What kind of friend? What's her name?'

'Her name's Eve and she's a special friend, someone I've been spending a lot of time with lately. I've told her so much about you that she's dying to meet you. Do you think you might like to meet her too?'

That's not really fair, Max. We both know that Ellie's going to want to do whatever she thinks will please you. That's what well-behaved, thoughtful seven-year-old daughters do.

'What's she like? Will I like her?'

'Well, I hope you'll like her. I'm sure she'll like you. She's a teacher, like me, and she's very calm and kind and she's lots of fun too. And you know those cupcakes we had the other day, the ones with the stars sprinkled on the top? Eve made those.'

'I thought Granny made them?'

'I know you did. But she didn't, it was Eve. They were delicious, weren't they? Eve's a great cook. And she likes reading books and watching films and going for long walks in the country – all the things we like, really. She's really easy to talk to, as well.'

I listen to this roll call of Eve's attributes and interests and it's hard not to feel that Max hasn't merely replaced me but has managed to secure himself a free upgrade in the process.

'Daddy?'

'Yes, sweetheart?'

'Is Eve your *girl*friend?'

Max's face is full of surprise. He'd clearly underestimated our seven-year-old daughter's astuteness. I have to admit, I had too.

A few seconds pass, during which I'm guessing Max is contemplating the potential ramifications of the two possible, opposing responses. Should he tell the truth and risk Ellie's rejection of Eve before they've even met, or should he kick the difficult query into the future's long grass and hope that, by the time the question emerges again, the answer won't have quite the same impact?

I feel for Max right now, honestly I do. In spite of the jealousy and the frustrations and the categorical conviction that it's an error of judgement to be introducing Eve into Ellie's life at this premature moment in time, he's still the man I love, still the man I married, still the man I vowed I'd always support, for better or worse, in sickness and in health. Till death do us part, which it hasn't yet, not quite, not entirely.

'Well, I suppose she is, yes, munchkin. How do you feel about that? Is it strange thinking of Daddy having a girl-friend?'

Ellie contemplates her response, clearly in no hurry to make a rash decision on such a critical question. I'd give anything to know what's going on in her head right now, to be able to guess what she's thinking. If there was a sin-gle superpower I wish the afterworld had afforded me, it would be to read the thoughts of the little girl I never wanted to leave behind.

'Is she pretty?'

'Well, I think so, yes. She has long blonde hair and blue eyes and a lovely smile.'

'Is she as pretty as Mummy?'

Max's response is oppressively hesitant. I'm not sure I'm ready to hear the answer.

'They're both pretty in different ways, angel. Mummy was beautiful – just like you – and Eve is pretty in a differ-ent way.'

That wasn't quite the clear victory I was hoping for. Couldn't he have brought himself to tell the whitest of lies, on this of all topics, just to Ellie?

'So why is she your girlfriend? Is she your girlfriend just because she's pretty?'

'No, not just that, angel. There are lots of reasons. A girlfriend is just a really special friend who you like spend-ing time with more than your other friends. Don't any of your friends at school have boyfriends?'

Ellie's nose curls up into a horrified grimace.

'Ugh, no. Boys are disgusting.'

Max allows himself a wry smile while Ellie fiddles distractedly with the stitching on the arm of the sofa. Max is forever telling her to stop picking at it but today he leaves her to play with it uninterrupted.

'Daddy. Is Eve going to be my new mummy?'

Ellie looks up at Max, her eyes suffused with emotions I doubt she yet fully understands.

Of all the reactions in either of our worlds, I wasn't expecting that one. I feel heartbroken for Ellie, for the multitude of questions that must be weaving chaotically through her mind and for the harsh reality that has placed her so unfairly in this bewildering position. For her having to grow up so much faster than either Max or I would ever have wished.

I feel heartbroken for Max, too, for the lone parenthood he's unexpectedly found himself practising, for the difficult conversations he's striving to manage and for the catalogue of decisions he never anticipated having to make.

And I feel heartbroken for myself, too, fully aware of the possibility that one day the answer to Ellie's question may be yes.

Max strokes Ellie's hair with that gentle touch of his, tucking a stray curl behind her tiny ear and running his fingers over the smooth skin of her cheek. He looks sad, fearful almost, as though a future he hadn't begun to contemplate is rushing forward to greet him and he's just not ready to play host to it yet.

'No, my angel. Eve's not going to be your new mummy. She's just a special friend of mine who I'd like to be a special friend to you too.'

Ellie looks at Max doubtfully, as if not quite convinced she's being told the truth. Her head drops back down to the arm of the sofa and she begins fiddling again as though that loose thread is the only thing in the world she dare focus on.

'But if you like her more than all your other friends, does that mean you like her more than me too?'

Her voice is barely more than a whisper and she hesitates before lifting her eyes to await Max's answer. I'd give anything right now to be able wrap her body in my arms and restore the security she so needs and deserves.

Max instead fulfils that desire for me, Ellie half-heartedly allowing herself to be pulled on to his lap.

'Don't be silly, sweetheart. There's no one in the world I love more than you. Not now, not ever. We're a special two-person team, me and you. And no one will ever, ever change that.'

Ellie allows her body to relax into the reassurance of Max's arms but her face still betrays the confusion of a thousand unanswered questions.

'Sit tight a second, sweetheart. I've got something I want to give you. I was going to save it for your birthday but I think you should have it now.'

Max goes to the wooden cabinet at the far end of the sitting room from which he retrieves a small red velvet box and hands it to Ellie.

She opens it to reveal an exquisite heart-shaped silver locket engraved with tiny flowers. It couldn't be more perfect for Ellie. Max couldn't have chosen any better.

'Let me open it for you, munchkin. I want to show you what's inside.'

Max prises open the delicate heart. Inside are two photographs, one on either side. The first is of Max, a portrait I took of him in Greece on that final holiday, the columns of the Parthenon just visible behind his head. The other is of me, taken shortly before I died, on a long walk the three of us had made over the South Downs at Easter. That was almost two years ago now.

'What I thought, you see sweetheart, is that whenever you wear this, you'll have the two people who love you most right next to your heart. Because you're the most special person in the whole world to me and one thing I know for sure is that you were always, always right in the centre of Mummy's heart, too. And so even when you and I aren't together during the day, and even though Mummy's not here any more, I want you to remember just how much we both love you.'

As he says this, Max places the locket around Ellie's neck, adjusting the clasp until he's sure it's secure. Ellie holds back her hair for him and I hold back my tears.

'I know how much you like looking at photos of Mummy and I thought this way you can always have Mummy with you, wherever you are.'

Ellie is gazing inside the locket that's now hanging around her beautiful, graceful neck. She looks up at Max and smiles before climbing back on to his lap and resting her head on his chest.

'I love it, Daddy. Thank you. It's really, really pretty.'

Max and Ellie remain huddled on the sofa together and I long to be with them, to hold them both tightly and never let them go. I'd give everything else I ever treasured when I was alive, every material possession I ever owned, for a single day now with Ellie and Max.

Just one more day. It doesn't seem much to ask, does it?

The air beneath me begins to billow gently and I know what that means. I issue a silent, unknowable goodbye to Max and Ellie before they disappear from sight, still holding on to one another tightly in the world below.

# CHAPTER 18

'Why are you acting so strange, Daddy? Stop pulling my arm. Are you cross?'

Max and Ellie are hand in hand, hurrying around the outer circle of Regent's Park. It's a grey, overcast day and there must be a chill in the air because Ellie's wrapped up tightly in her winter coat and purple, fake-fur-lined boots, complete with woolly hat, gloves and scarf. Max seems to be in a bit of a panic, charging along at a pace that Ellie can't hope to keep up with; he's dragging her along as though his sheer momentum can make a seven-year-old's legs move faster than they were ever designed to.

'Of course I'm not cross, sweetheart. I'm just worried we're going to be late. We said we'd meet Eve by two-thirty and it's past that already.'

So that's the reason. I bet this is The First Meeting. No wonder he's nervous. I'm nervous all of a sudden and I'm not even invited.

I've thought about this meeting almost constantly during the solitary hours of what must have been the past four weeks or so. I'd felt so certain at first that I wanted it to be an abject disaster, that nothing would please me more than for it to become swiftly apparent that Harriet and I had been right all along. But then it began to dawn on me that if Eve and Ellie don't get on there are only two possible outcomes; either Max feels he has to end his affair with Eve, making him unhappy, or Max continues his relationship with Eve, despite Ellie's objections, making Ellie unhappy. And there's no version of either Max or Ellie being unhappy that would ever make me anything other than miserable too, with or without Eve's involvement.

Max and Ellie arrive at the entrance to London Zoo and there she is, waiting for them, in the most stylish casual attire I think I've ever seen: chocolate-brown Hunter wellies over light brown jeans, a dark green semi-fitted three-quarter-length coat and a fawn cashmere scarf tied so beautifully around her elegant neck that she really ought to be giving master classes.

'I'm so sorry we're late. You haven't been waiting ages have you? Anyway, Ellie this is Eve. Eve meet Ellie.'

Ellie looks at Eve shyly as if she can't quite believe that someone this pretty is actually about to talk to her.

'Hello.'

'Hello, Ellie. It's really nice to meet you. I've heard so much about you from your dad. He never stops talking about you.'

A bashful smile graces Ellie's lips as she leans her body in closer to Max.

The three of them enter the zoo, Max shooting Eve a reassuring nod over the top of Ellie's head. Eve responds with a deep breath and an apprehensive raising of her perfectly plucked eyebrows.

She's nervous. She's really nervous.

I haven't, in all honesty, spared too many thoughts over the past month for how Eve might manage this meeting but now we're all here I can see that it isn't going to be easy for her either. There's clearly more riding on today's events than probably any of us have truly dared to consider.

The three of them wander slightly aimlessly around the zoo for the first half an hour or so, Max cautiously driving the conversation, taking care to steer it towards uncontroversial topics: how parrots learn to talk, why flamingoes are pink and whether spiders can run faster than ants. It's not until they reach the monkey enclosure that Ellie seems a bit more relaxed and the interrogation begins.

'What's your favourite colour, Eve?'

'Green probably. Why, what's yours?'

'Mine's pink. Daddy's is blue. Mummy's was purple. And what's your favourite food?'

'Oh, that's a hard one. I like so many different types of food.'

Ellie's eyes narrow with the impatience of someone who thinks procrastination is overrated.

'But if you had to choose one? What would you choose?'

'Probably roast beef. What about you?'

'My favourite food of all time is ice cream. Do you know what Daddy likes best?'

'No, I don't think I do. What is it?'

'Shall I tell her, Daddy?'

It's an unconscious move on Ellie's part, I'm sure, but nonetheless a definitive establishment of the group's hierarchy.

Max nods.

'Daddy likes a big, juicy steak best. With fat chips and a salad with avocado in it. Which I think is disgusting. I hate avocado. It's so slippery in your mouth. Eww.'

Max and Eve both laugh at Ellie. She grins sheepishly but I can tell she's relishing the attention.

'And what's your favourite film? Not a grown-up film but a children's film?'

'Gosh, that's a tricky one too. My favourite film when I was your age was *Mary Poppins* but that's probably a bit old-fashioned for you, isn't it?'

'I love *Mary Poppins*. Mummy and I watched it hundreds of times together. I know all the words to "Supercalifragilisticexpialidocious". I can sing it for you now if you like?'

Max puts an arm round Ellie's shoulders and pulls her towards him tenderly.

'Maybe later, munchkin. We don't want to frighten the monkeys now, do we?'

Ellie produces the faux-offended frown she's perfected over the past couple of years, a look which immediately reduces Max and Eve to giggles. She's adorable when she pulls that face. Eve's lucky to have witnessed it on their first meeting.

'And . . . what about your favourite, um, outfit? Do you like trousers best or dresses?'

'I suppose it depends on where I'm going. Like, today, I wouldn't have been comfortable in a dress – I'm much happier in jeans. But when I'm going to work or out in the evening I definitely prefer wearing dresses or skirts. I think us ladies look prettiest in dresses.'

Ellie nods in earnest agreement.

'Mummy liked dressing up too. She wore dresses to work every day, usually black ones or purple ones and usually those ones you wrap round you like a dressing gown. They sound silly but she looked really nice in them.'

Eve smiles and I can't read whether it's a smile of genuine encouragement or polite tolerance. I'm gratified, I can't deny, by Ellie's frequent references to me. What mother wouldn't feel reassured that today, of all days, they haven't been forgotten? But I find myself feeling unexpectedly awkward, too. Because I can't really imagine what it must be like for Eve right now, full of hope that this four-foot bundle of energy should have neither the power nor the desire to disrupt her burgeoning relationship with my husband and yet fully aware that the success of the day's outing is in her hands. It's confusing for all of us. If you'd told me, just a matter of weeks ago, that I'd be empathizing with Eve's position today, and half-willing Ellie to stop mentioning me quite so often, I'd simply never have believed you.

'And what do you like better, animals or children? I think that's a really hard one because I really like my friends but I also really like dogs.'

Max and Eve exchange one of those knowing glances and I suspect this isn't the first time that Eve's heard about Ellie's puppy obsession.

'Oh, definitely children for me. I love dogs too but I really like being around young people. That's why I'm a teacher.'

Ellie allows herself a few moments to contemplate Eve's response.

'So what do you think's nicer – being a mummy or a teacher? 'Cos Daddy says that being a teacher is a bit like being a parent and that's why it's such an important job.'

Eve hesitates for a moment and there's that flicker of disquiet again, the same look I noticed on her face at Joan and Ralph's during that first dinner party.

There's a discomfort in Ellie's eyes too, the impatience of a query desperately in search of an answer. I can't help wondering what's going on in that active little imagination of hers, whether her mind is already racing ahead to fantasies and fears of a time when Eve might prefer parenting to teaching.

'Munchkin, do you think that might be enough questions for now? Perhaps Eve would like to hear more about you. Why don't you tell her about the school trip you went on last week, the one to the Science Museum, while we go and find the lions?'

The three of them head towards the big cats, Ellie chattering away, holding on tightly to Max's arm in a clear demarcation of territory. To any passerby, however, I'm sure they look like the perfect, happy, nuclear family.

It reminds me of the day, four years ago, when I was the woman walking by Ellie's side at the zoo, when she'd skipped in between Max and me, imploring us, again and again, to swing her into the air. She'd giggled infectiously each time we raised her off the ground, her bare legs swaying high ahead of her, the adrenaline rush like a drug she simply couldn't get enough of. That day had been so lovely, witnessing Ellie's wonder at seeing so many animals that for her – until then – had been the preserve of picture books and television shows, watching her astonishment as previously fictional creatures came to life before her eyes. It had been the apes in Gorilla Kingdom that had mesmerized her the most, though. She'd been bewitched by the primates' humanoid mannerisms, laughing whenever one of the animals scratched himself, or picked something up with his hand, initially disbelieving

Max when he informed her that they were, in fact, our closest relatives, then joking that she was pleased she didn't have a gorilla for a daddy.

It feels both like only yesterday and, paradoxically, light years ago. I remember how Max and I had agreed on the way home that it had been our favourite family outing to date, how it had been one of those rare, perfect days that make you forget, temporarily, all the fears and insecurities and anxieties you have about your ability to parent this little person you've been given the inexplicable privilege of taking care of and instead purely enjoy the pleasure of their company. It was a day I'll never forget. I wonder if Ellie remembers it at all though. I suspect not. I suspect she was too young.

As the three of them head towards the lions' den, Max and Eve exchange a surreptitious glance over Ellie's head. It's a look of mutual reassurance, of mutual relief, of tentative confidence. It's a look that communicates they can't quite believe how well this is going.

I can't quite believe it either.

Because as proud as I am of how well Ellie's behaving, I can't silence the uneasy voice in my head that's reminding me just how hard, how unnerving, how destabilizing this situation must be for her. The voice that says perhaps Ellie's on her best behaviour because she's fearful that if she doesn't ingratiate herself with Eve, she risks losing the certainty of her father's devotion. The voice that's warning me no seven-year-old can keep that up indefinitely.

'Can we go and see my cousins now, Daddy?'

Max looks at Ellie quizzically.

'What cousins, sweetheart? You don't have any cousins.'

'The gorillas, silly. They were so funny last time we were here. I want to go and say hello to them again or they'll think we don't like them.'

She remembers. I really didn't think she would. Perhaps she doesn't remember all of it, perhaps she only remembers the gorillas and nothing else, but her remembering anything at all about that day is more than I dared hope for.

'Of course we can, sweetheart. But do you fancy a break at the adventure playground first?'

'Okay, Daddy. Race you there.'

As Ellie runs on ahead, Max slides his hand into Eve's and kisses her gently on the cheek before whispering something in her ear. Whatever he says makes her smile in gratitude, her face radiant with happiness.

A few metres ahead now, Ellie glances over her shoulder to ensure they're still following her, just in time to catch Max take Eve's head in his hands and kiss her fully on the lips. The brightness in Ellie's eyes darkens immediately. A cloud of confusion, hurt and rejection shadows her face, the pleasure of the day evaporating in a single, disconcerting instant. Oblivious to Ellie watching them, Max and Eve rest their foreheads together, their fingers entwined, immersed in a moment of mutual infatuation so clearly to the exclusion of all others.

I shift my glance rapidly from Ellie to Max and back again, waiting to see what Ellie will do next. For what seems like minutes but is probably, in reality, no more than a few seconds, she watches them stealthily in a haze of bewilderment and embarrassment. Whatever expectations Ellie had before today's introduction, she evidently wasn't prepared to witness this.

Suddenly she screws her eyes tightly shut, turns her body in the opposite direction and, safe now in the knowledge that she's managed to obliterate the sight that's so perturbed her, opens her eyes and runs at full speed towards the playground. A split second later, Max finally prises himself away from Eve's embrace and looks around, only to see Ellie running on ahead. He's infinitesimally too late to know what she's seen.

What on earth was Max thinking? Has it not occurred to him – or to Eve, for that matter – that they have one shot at this, they have just one opportunity to make a good first impression on Ellie, to prove themselves a couple who aren't destined to exclude her? Did he not imagine that she might see their embrace and that, if she did, she'd be heartbroken? Is his intoxication so inebriating that he can't keep in mind just how hard this must be for Ellie?

Max and Eve, ignorant still as to the cause of Ellie's marathon sprint towards the playground, hurry on behind her, laughing to one another about a joke I'm not privy to.

When they finally catch up with her, she's already on the swings, motioning herself back and forth with a mechanical rhythm suggestive of someone lost in the depths of their own dark thoughts. Max calls over to her, catches her attention, and points to some benches at the far end of the playground, where he and Eve settle themselves, his arm around her shoulder, her hand on his thigh.

Keeping one eye firmly on Ellie, I join Max and Eve at the bench.

'Well, I think it's fair to say that this is going better than either of us expected. Are you okay?'

Max runs his fingers through the ends of Eve's immaculate hair.

'I think so. I can't believe how nervous I was before you both arrived. I think it was worse than waiting to go for a job interview.'

'I'm so sorry we were late. Totally my fault. Even after all this time I forget how long it takes to leave the house when you've got a child in tow.'

'It's fine, I didn't mind at all. It might have been a blessing, actually. Gave me a few moments to take some deep breaths and stop my legs shaking quite so much.'

They exchange a mutually supportive smile, while I take a moment to check on Ellie. She's still on the swing, still lost in her own thoughts.

'As I've been trying to tell you for weeks now, you didn't have anything to be worried about. There was never any chance that Ellie wasn't going to like you. I can't imagine how anyone could find anything to dislike about you. They'd have to be mad, or stupid, or both. And Ellie's neither.'

Eve strokes Max's thigh and my stomach churns at the sight of a gesture which seems so natural to them and yet now so alien to me.

'It's not really about whether Ellie likes me at this stage, though, is it? It's about how she feels about you bringing anyone into her life. It must be so hard for her, even contemplating the thought of sharing you with someone else, even just for an afternoon.'

'Eve, I really don't want you to worry. Ellie knows how much I love her. And she's a lot tougher than she looks.'

'I'm sure you're right. I just really feel for her. I can't imagine what it must be like to lose your mum so young. It must be so unbearably hard on her. And I've no doubt there are going to be times when it's even harder. Adolescence without her mum around isn't going to be easy.'

I know she's just trying to be sympathetic but I don't feel that either Max or I really need Eve to point this out for us.

'You being sensitive to that is one of the many reasons you're so amazing and why I just know you two are going to get along fine. She really likes you. I can tell.'

'Really? Do you think so? I wasn't sure when she was grilling me earlier whether I was giving her the right answers.'

'Oh, don't worry about that. It may sound like she's conducting the Spanish Inquisition, but she only ever bombards people with questions like that if she's actually interested in them. I think it's fair to say that you're a bit of a hit.'

'She's completely adorable, Max. You must be so proud. She's such a credit to you.'

'Without wanting to sound like a boastful dad, I do think she's pretty wonderful. But the fact that today is going so well is credit to you, too. I know how concerned you've been about this first meeting but you're doing brilliantly.'

Eve thanks Max with a lingering kiss into which Max allows himself to be lost, appearing to have little intention of finding himself again in the immediate future.

I look up to check on Ellie – someone's got to – and, with a stab of panic, see that she's halfway up a climbing frame that's much, much too high for her, a piece of equipment that's clearly meant for much older children. She's glued to the spot, her eyes fixed firmly on the sight of her father embracing this interloper, the look on her face one of upset, betrayal, anger, revenge. I've never seen a look like it on her before. It's as though she's entered an entirely new emotional sphere, with a frame of reference she's having to learn in record time, and which she's still such a long way from understanding.

I turn back towards Max and Eve, willing them with every fibre of my defunct being to tear themselves apart, to look up, to notice the danger Ellie's in. But they're too engrossed in one another, too infatuated with their romance, too self-congratulatory about the day's supposed success, their eyes focussed exclusively and hypnotically on one another.

I return my gaze to Ellie to find her continuing her ascent now, wilfully and fearlessly climbing to a height she knows is beyond her, that she knows is beyond the realm of safety, that she knows, by rights, someone should stop her from reaching. But there's no one to prevent her, no one to ensure her safety, no one to give her a reason not to continue.

I'm shouting now, shouting desperately with every ineffectual decibel I have, shouting at Ellie to stop climbing, imploring her to come back down, beseeching her to return to safety. And I'm shouting at Max, too, begging him to cast his eyes away from Eve, just for a second, pleading with him to register where Ellie is and what's she's doing, urging him to remember he has a seven-year-old daughter whose welfare he's in sole charge of and who's in the throes of testing his love for her in the most immediate way she can.

Ellie's nearly at the top now and she glances towards Max and Eve once more, giving them one final opportunity to acknowledge her, affording them one last chance to redeem themselves, issuing them with the clearest of challenges – if only they'd notice it – to choose her over one other.

I look to where Ellie's gaze is directed and am frantic to see that her silent entreaty is as futile as mine. Max and Eve are still locked in a prolonged embrace, still unaware of Ellie's threat, still terrifyingly oblivious to the impending danger just a few feet away from them.

As I turn back to Ellie, my eyes reach her just in time to see her left foot slip, her hands thrash above her in a belated attempt to make contact with the iron bars, and her flailing body fall through the air.

I hear her scream before she hits the ground.

And then everything goes white.

I close my eyes, hoping it's just a trick of the light, willing it to be nothing other than sheer panic that's caused me to lose sight of her at this most critical moment. But when I open them again, there's no Ellie to be seen, no playground in view, no sign at all as to what fate may have befallen my daughter. Just this hateful, barren, bleak void, all around.

I don't know what to do. I feel like I can't think, like I can't move but I can't stay still, that I have to get back to her even though I know there's no way I can.

Whether I close my eyes or open them, all I can see is image upon horrific image, gruesome scenes taking up squatting rights in my mind, refusing to move, however hard I try to evict them.

What if she's really badly hurt? What if she's broken something? What if the something she's broken is life-threatening? What if her head hit the ground first? What then? What if the thing that's happened is the thing I really can't bear to contemplate?

There's never been a moment I've been more ready to strike a deal – if striking deals is something I can do from here. I'll do anything, anything at all, I promise, as long as Ellie's okay. I'll stop hoping Max's relationship stalls, I'll stop wishing Ellie puts the brakes on it for him, I'll stop bemoaning the brevity of my life. I'll stop asking for anything more, ever again.

Whatever you want, whatever I have to give, just take it, please, and make sure Ellie's okay.

# CHAPTER 19

It's been hours. Long, painful, interminable hours. Hours of worry and anxiety, of frantic plea bargaining with something or someone I'm not sure I even believe in, let alone can see or hear or confirm actually exists.

I've still no news yet. I'm not sure there's anything worse than waiting for potentially bad news alone, is there? This suspension of time, this absence of knowledge, this anxious isolation are all far less bearable than any physical pain I've ever known, even that which brought me here in the first place.

I don't think my inscrutable, white world has ever felt so stark before. Or so severe. Or so solitary. It's never felt so vast, so empty, so far from everyone I know and love. They're an eternity away and although I've known, deep down, since I arrived that what separates us is not just the unpredictable white mist clouding my view, but the division between the active and the passive, between the living and the netherworld, between life and death, it's only now that I really feel it – painfully, viscerally – as though the knowledge has seared itself on to my broken heart and is burning through whatever solace, whatever consolation, whatever misguided sense of involvement I had left.

Right now, I'm not sure I even trust that I'll ever be able to see them again.

I keep picturing Ellie on top of that climber, the moment of her fall reduced to super-slow motion, every individual frame a horror story in its own right, every sequence taunting me for my failure to have intervened, to have stopped her, to have saved her. Every second a cruel reminder of my impotence.

What's the point of a place in this netherworld if it doesn't come complete with the powers of a guardian angel? If I can't prevent tragedy? If I can't do a single thing to protect my little girl from harm?

Please let her be okay. Please. I'll never ask for anything again. I promise.

Something flutters beneath me and, not for first time during recent hours, I allow my hopes to be raised that perhaps this is it, perhaps the clouds are going to clear, perhaps I'm going to be allowed to see her, to see how she is.

I strain my eyes, determined to focus on what lies beneath, to pierce my way through the white mist, to bring the world into view through sheer force of will and desperation and maternal tenacity, to find my way back to the daughter who needs me.

And for once the clouds comply and I'm there, I'm back, only the place I've arrived is the last place I'd hoped to find her. I'm in a cubicle, a hospital cubicle where Max and Eve are sitting on chairs next to a bed on which my baby girl is lying with her arm in a sling and a face almost as pale as the austere white sheets underneath her.

'How's your arm feeling now, angel?'

'A bit sore still, especially if I try and move it.'

'Well, you know what the answer to that is, then? Just don't move it! I'm sure it's going to feel a lot better in the morning, sweetheart. We're lucky it was only a little sprain and a very minor concussion. I was convinced there for a second, when you were out cold, that something much worse had happened. As that nice doctor said, you're a very lucky girl not to have done more serious damage. Honestly, I don't know what you were thinking, going up to the top of such a big climbing frame.'

Only a sprain and very minor concussion. Thank god. Thank whoever or whatever needs thanking. The relief is exquisite and I want to savour it.

But she'd been out cold, my little angel. She'd been lying there, on the ground, motionless. Poor Max. I can only imagine the anguish he must have being going through.

'I'm sorry, Daddy.'

Max strokes Ellie's forehead and kisses each of her unslung fingers in turn.

'There's nothing at all to be sorry for, sweetheart. I'm just so relieved you're okay. You gave us such a fright there, munchkin. When I think about how far you fell . . .'

Max's unfinished sentence trails off into a parallel world of possibilities none of us dare to articulate. There's an unsteadiness in his voice to accompany the film of salt water that he manages to blink away before Ellie has a chance to notice. I catch Eve watching him, though, and wonder whether any woman could help but fall for a man who weeps for the fate that chose not to befall his daughter today.

'When can we go home, Daddy? It's really boring here.'

'Hospitals are always boring, I'm afraid, angel. We can leave just as soon as the doctor comes and gives you the all-clear. It shouldn't be too long now.'

Max smiles apologetically at Eve. I can't imagine this was how either of them wanted to spend their inaugural outing together. Ellie notices their silent exchange and I watch her face shift emotional season from boredom to angst.

'Daddy, are you cross with me?'

Ellie's voice is hesitant as though not quite convinced it was ready to come out of hiding.

'Why on earth would anyone be cross with you, angel?'

Ellie hangs her head, whether through embarrassment or fear or guilt it's impossible to tell.

'For climbing up too high and falling off and ruining the day.'

Max holds her hand and smiles at her questioningly as though unsure what's provoked this momentary anxiety.

'Don't be silly, sweetheart. Of course we're not cross with you. It was a nasty accident and no one blames you at all. We were just worried about you, that's all. But you're going to be just fine, aren't you?'

Ellie nods her head haltingly, seemingly unconvinced by Max's reassurance.

'You promise you're not angry?'

Max smiles at her with that patient, gentle, paternal smile reserved exclusively for Ellie.

'Shall I tell you something, sweetheart? It's something Mummy used to say after you were born. She said that when you have a child, all of your priorities shift, so that instead of worrying about yourself any more, you spend all your time worrying about this little person instead. And it's amazing how one little person – like you – can totally take over your whole universe. But you did and you still do. Because as soon as Mummy and I became parents, what we wanted most in the world is for you to be happy and healthy and safe. So if anything bad happens to you, whatever it is, whatever the cause, the only thing I care about is that you get better and that you're okay. Do you understand?'

Ellie gazes at Max intently before her face breaks into a tentative smile, as if perhaps only partially understanding Max's explanation but seemingly in possession of the comfort she was seeking.

'Ellie, what do you think about me going in search of some chocolate? I think we're all probably in need of a sugar hit. That's okay, isn't it, Max?'

Max nods and smiles in assent, and Eve slips behind the patterned blue polyester curtain, leaving Max and Ellie alone for the first time today that I've seen.

Max looks over his shoulder, as if checking the coast is clear.

'So, what do you think of Eve, then? I know it's been a strange day but earlier, before your accident, we were having a nice time, weren't we?'

Ellie looks contemplative, as though remembering afresh events from just a few hours ago that she'd already persuaded herself to forget.

'She's okay.'

The disappointment is legible on Max's face.

'But she's been really kind to you, hasn't she? When she sat with you in the back of the car on the way here – she looked after you really nicely then, didn't she?'

I'm not sure what's more uncomfortable: to witness Max's desperation that Ellie afford Eve some approbation or to imagine Eve cradling my little girl in her arms en route to the hospital.

'I suppose so.'

'And she's been fun while we've been stuck here, hasn't she? Telling us all those funny stories about some of the naughty things students at her school have done.'

Ellie nods impassively.

'Daddy? Will Eve always come with us on days out now?'

Max looks slightly surprised, as though the thought hadn't even occurred to him.

'Of course not, sweetheart. I just wanted you to meet her, that's all. I mean, it would be nice if sometimes we invited her to do things with us, don't you think? Because I'd enjoy it and I think she'd enjoy it too. She really likes you, Ellie. She told me earlier. She said you were adorable – her words, not mine.'

Ellie smiles shyly but I think it's going to take more than a single compliment to win her over.

'I was thinking actually, munchkin, whether we might ask Eve if she wants to come to your birthday party?'

Max looks suitably ambivalent about whether or not this is a good idea. I can't believe he's even suggesting it. Not so soon, not right now, not after all that's happened today.

'But she won't know anyone.'

'That's true. She could get to know people, though, couldn't she? There are lots of nice people coming, aren't there?'

Ellie withdraws into a temporary introspection. I wish I could let her know that she's allowed to feel wary about this, that she doesn't have to agree if she doesn't want to, that Max is still going to love her even if she doesn't want his new girlfriend gatecrashing her birthday party.

'But, Daddy, you said we already had a full house for my birthday party and that's why I was only allowed to invite ten friends.'

There's a mischievous sparkle in Ellie's eyes, discernible only to those who've seen it before. Max tightens his lips to hold back the knowing smile.

'You're right, Ellie, I did. Ten friends is quite a lot, isn't it?'

'But if you're allowed to have an extra friend to my party then shouldn't I be allowed an extra friend too?'

Ellie looks up at Max, her dark eyes wide with faux-innocence. Max meets her gaze with mock seriousness, befitting the negotiations at play.

'Okay, Ellie. That seems fair to me. If Eve comes to your party then you can bring another friend too. Who will you invite?'

Ellie's eyes narrow with contemplation.

'Well, the thing is, I want to invite Lottie but I want to invite Emily too. And 'cos they're best friends they'll be sad if they can't both come.'

Max is smiling now, complicit in just how deftly he's being wound around our little girl's finger.

'So what do you suggest then, munchkin?'

'Well, you always tell me it's important to play nicely at school and not leave people out. So really I think I should invite Lottie and Emily. Just to be fair.'

Max can't hold back the laughter any longer.

'You drive a hard bargain, Ellie Myerson, but you have yourself a deal. Lottie and Emily and Eve are now all duly

263

invited to your birthday party. I just hope we can find a cake big enough for all those guests.'

I can't believe it. Of all the people in the world, Eve's the last person who should be going to Ellie's birthday party. Even I wasn't allowed to be there last year. I don't know how I'm going to cope if the same thing happens this year, if my access doesn't materialize that day, if I know that Eve is sharing my daughter's birthday with her while I'm not even allowed to view it silently from afar.

Ellie celebrates her triumph by sliding off the bed and hugging Max with the one working arm still at her shrewd disposal. As she does so, the blue curtain is pulled back and Eve reappears, bumper-sized block of Dairy Milk in hand and a young female doctor in tow.

'Now, young lady, I don't remember saying you were ready to get out of bed yet, did I? And you know you have to follow the doctor's orders when you're in here, don't you?'

Ellie giggles sheepishly and clambers back on to the starched white linen with Max's help.

'Well, I think you're all good to go, if you can bear to leave us. Mum and Dad, I suggest an early night and just keep an eye on her for twenty-four hours. Any signs of nausea or dizziness – and certainly if she vomits at all – bring her straight back in. Other than that, Ellie, I suggest you give climbing frames a wide berth for a little while.'

Mum and Dad. An easy enough mistake to make. But not such an easy one to witness.

And not, it seems, one that's raised so much as a flushed cheek on the faces of either my husband or his new girl-friend. Not even Ellie bothers to contradict her.

As the doctor exits the cubicle, sweeping the curtain closed behind her, my access disappears instantaneously, without so much as the lightest fluctuation of air to warn me that my time here today is up.

It's been a torturous few hours, in so many ways, and although I'm unspeakably grateful for the chance to find out that my little girl's okay, I also can't help feeling relieved that the day is finally over.

# CHAPTER 20

'Come on, munchkin. Let's get you up to bed.'

I'm in the hallway of my house, where Max, Eve and Ellie are walking through the front door, all three of them in the same clothes I left them in earlier, Ellie's arm still in a sling and the darkness outside telling me that we've entered the day's final chapter.

Three times in one day. It's unprecedented.

'Awww, can't I stay up for a bit? It's not even that late.'

'Not tonight, sweetheart, sorry. It's already past your bedtime and you need to get some rest after the adventurous day you've had.'

'But the doctor said you had to keep an eye on me and you can't do that if I'm in bed. Can't I stay up just a little bit longer? I'm not even tired.'

'You're over-tired, angel. That's why we need to get you to bed. Say goodnight to Eve and I'll come up with you and tuck you in.'

Ellie exudes a theatrical sigh and says a cursory goodnight to Eve. As Max accompanies her up the stairs I see him turn back and shrug his shoulders apologetically at Eve, although I can't be sure whether he's apologizing for Ellie's behaviour or for the temporary interruption to their evening.

As Max pushes Ellie gently up to her room, I loiter downstairs with Eve, watching her as she wanders around my former sitting room, surveying what's on display. I wonder how many times she's been here before and what she makes of my former home, with its photographic shrine to a life she's never been part of. There's a framed picture of Max and me on our wedding day and another of the two of us in a safari jeep on honeymoon; there's the three of us in hospital the day Ellie was born, and again huddling around her cake at her first birthday party; there are large framed montages of our holiday in Italy and another one from Greece. There's noticeably little space left for any new additions.

Eve's studying all the photographs now, as I'm sure any new girlfriend would, and I'm wondering what she thinks of them, whether they make her sad that this is a family she's not a part of or threatened that here is a happiness she can't hope to compete with or irritated that Max isn't yet ready to give up the ghosts of the past in spite of her offering him such an undeniably attractive present. Or perhaps she's imagining the day when she might take them all down and replace them with photos of herself.

Max comes back into the room, looking less relaxed than he'd like to be.

'Is everything okay? Is Ellie still not too keen on going to bed?'

'Oh, it's not that. She's just really out of sorts. She's usually great about bedtime. Today's just been a lot for her to take in.'

I don't know whether it's intentional or not but there's a hint of blame in Max's voice as he flops down on the sofa and gestures for Eve to join him, throwing his arm loosely around her shoulder with neither the conviction nor commitment she might have come to expect.

'Well, it must have been a horrible shock, falling from that great height. And it was her first time in A&E, you said. That's never nice for anyone.'

'It's more than that. Oh, I don't know. Perhaps we shouldn't have rushed things. Perhaps it was all too soon, her meeting you today. Maybe we should have waited after all.'

I see Eve's body tighten as if bracing herself for an unspecified attack and a tautness settle on her face that I haven't seen before.

'To be fair, I did say I thought it might be a bit premature.'

'Yeah, well, I wish now you'd tried a bit harder to talk me out of it.'

The tautness evolves into annoyance as Eve pulls away from Max's perfunctory embrace.

'Max, it was your idea. You're the one who's been pushing for this while I've been tiptoeing around on eggshells trying to support whatever you thought was for the best. It's really not okay to blame me because it didn't quite go to plan.'

'I'm not blaming you. I just think, on reflection, we might have been better to wait, that's all. She's clearly more sensitive about it than we thought.'

Eve jolts off the sofa and begins scrabbling for her shoes from under it in what looks suspiciously like an intention to leave.

'Than *we* thought? I don't remember my reservations being that important to you during all those conversations when I told you I didn't think we should rush Ellie. God, I don't know why I ever thought this was going to work.'

Max is staring at her, open-mouthed, clearly bemused as to how a couple of casual remarks have precipitated this outburst.

'You're not thinking of leaving, are you? I'm sorry. I didn't mean to take it out on you. It's just been a tough day.'

'I know, Max. I was there. It was tough for me too. Although you seem to have conveniently forgotten that in your haste to blame me for everything.'

'I'm not blaming you for anything. I'm sorry if it came across like that. Hey, what's going on?'

Max tries to rub a conciliatory hand on Eve's arm but she shakes him off with a force I don't think any of us – including her – were expecting.

'I was stupid to think this could ever possibly work. It won't. I should have known that from the beginning.'

'What are you talking about? Ellie will be fine, it's just a temporary wobble. I haven't had a chance to tell you yet but she's even invited you to her birthday party next month. I'm not sure we could have hoped for a better outcome today, could we?'

They're both standing now, on either side of the fireplace, Max looking imploringly at Eve, desperate to make amends for whatever misdemeanour he's inadvertently committed. Eve swings her head round to look at him, her expression a contortion of upset and disappointment and something else I can't quite put my finger on.

'What, so we can play happy families? It's just not that easy, Max. I'm sorry, we should never have let it get this far. I'm going to go now, it's for the best.'

'Please don't go. I don't understand what's going on. I want you to stay.'

'There's no point. You don't get it. There's just no point.'

There's a desperation and a despondency in her voice that seem disproportionate to the conversation they're having. I feel as perplexed as Max as to what's going on.

'What do you mean there's no point? There's every point. We're fantastic together, you and I. You know it as well as I do.'

'But sometimes that's just not enough, Max. Really, please don't make this any harder than it is.'

'Eve, whatever's going on, whatever I've done to upset you, I'm sorry. Whatever it is, we can work it out, I promise. And the reason I can make that promise is because I love you.'

Three tiny words, those three words that expend so little energy to say and yet everything to mean. They're the words I knew would sear my already broken heart if I ever heard him utter them to anyone else. And now he has, and they are, the hot, burning sensation coursing through my veins and threatening to scorch me from the inside out.

'Don't say that, Max. Don't waste that on me. I'm not the person you should waste that on.'

'It's not wasted. It's the truth. I've known it for ages and now I've said it I can't imagine what on earth has kept me from telling you for so long. I love you and I want to be with you. So please tell me what's going on.'

Max puts his arms around her and as he pulls her towards him she bursts into deep, visceral tears. She allows

Max to guide her back to the sofa, his shoulders relaxing with the relief of a crisis postponed if not averted.

'I can't. I'm sorry, Max. I just can't. Telling you wouldn't make any difference. It won't make anything better. It'll only make things worse. Trust me, please.'

'Tell me what? What's so bad you can't tell me? It can't be any worse than some of the stuff I've told you.'

Eve raises her eyes and I see in them the weight of a burden too heavy to bear alone.

'It is, Max. It is worse. And I'm so, so sorry I haven't told you before. You don't know how many times over the past six months I've wanted to confide in you, and I know it sounds like the weakest of excuses, but there's just never been the right moment. I didn't want to risk ruining what I knew was such a good thing. Because I don't think connections like this come along very often and I desperately didn't want to jeopardize it. That's the only reason I haven't said anything before. Can you at least believe that?'

Max nods, all the reassurance and confidence drained from his face and replaced with a terror in his eyes about whatever truth is on the verge of emerging. The momentary silence between them now is deafening, a silence which may transpire to be the catalyst for a myriad of disappointments.

Eve takes a deep breath and closes her eyes, stemming the tide of her own tears. When she opens them again she turns to face Max and begins to talk.

'When I was growing up, my parents' best friends were a couple called Duncan and Julie. They were the kind of foursome who did everything together – weekends away, Sunday barbecues, taking care of each other's children.

They were like a second family, really. But when I was fifteen, Duncan and Julie separated and for some reason – I never found out why – my mum and dad took Duncan's side and I never saw Julie again.

'I'd known Duncan all my life and I suppose, looking back, I was a little bit in awe of him; he was funny and charming and it was around this time that I first started noticing he was quite handsome too. I don't really remember being aware of that before he and Julie broke up. He was spending a lot of time at our house and often he and I would spend hours talking on our own and gradually he started confiding in me about the separation, spinning me all the tired, clichéd lines about why and how they'd grown apart. Except I was fifteen and I didn't know what tired clichés they were then. I was just flattered by the attention and by the fact that an adult was talking to me as though I were an equal. You know how it is when you're fifteen and all you want is for people to treat you like a grown-up and it never dawns on you that your desperation to be seen as an adult is precisely what marks you out as a child still.

'Anyway, to cut a painfully long story short, one thing led to another and before I really had time to stop and contemplate what was happening, I found myself having an affair with Duncan. Although affair is probably too grand a term for it. It was more of a six-week-long mistake. I'd only ever kissed two boys before and neither of those encounters had exactly set the world alight. I suppose Duncan made me feel like the woman I wanted to be but didn't yet realize I wasn't ready to become. He should never have encouraged that kind of trust from me in the first place, should never have submitted to his own pathetically weak-willed desires, should never have got involved with someone so young, not least given the deception of my parents it involved. He was a complete bastard, really, although it took me quite some time to understand it.'

'A bastard, Eve? The man took advantage of you, he betrayed your parents' trust, he broke the law, for god's sake. He should be behind bars.'

Max is incandescent with rage and it takes Eve's firm, calming hand on his shoulder just to keep him on the sofa with her.

'Max, I know it's hard but you promised you'd let me get to the end. I'm so sorry; that's really only the pro-logue.'

Max raises his eyes to meet Eve's imploring gaze, his own face contorted with disbelief and disappointment and the fear of someone who can see the past rushing from the shadows to confront him and a future he'd hoped for slipping uncontrollably from his grasp.

I look at Eve and can see the apprehension in her eyes too. Her face has taken on a complexity and a history that until now her beauty had successfully concealed. Of all the possible secrets in Eve's otherwise perfect closet, I doubt Max would have imagined this one any more than I have.

Eve's hand drops from Max's shoulder and into her own lap, where she begins twisting the ring on her right middle finger with agitated preoccupation. She takes a long, deep breath as if hoping to inhale the fortitude she needs to continue.

'The reason it only lasted a few weeks — it may well have gone on much longer otherwise — was because I got pregnant. We hadn't exactly been taking precautions which, looking back, astounds me; not that it should have occurred to me because every fifteen-year-old assumes they're impervious to trouble, but it still amazes me that Duncan took that risk.'

Eve was pregnant? At fifteen? I'm not sure I can think of any adult less likely to be the bearer of this particular secret. I'm flabbergasted. Although not as stunned as Max is, judging by the look of disbelief on his face as he stares at Eve unblinkingly, as though in need of every available second to reassess his girlfriend anew.

'Suddenly the unimaginable was terrifyingly real. I was fifteen and pregnant by a forty-two-year-old friend of my parents. It was like my worst nightmare had come true. You've no idea how strict and conventional my mum and dad were – I just knew it would destroy them. So I did what you do when you're fifteen and realize too late that you've made a terrible mistake: I kept it a secret. All I told Duncan was that I didn't want the affair to continue and that if he didn't leave me alone I'd tell my parents what had happened which, unsurprisingly, was enough for him to retreat immediately. And then I buried my head in the sand and hoped that somehow, miraculously, it would go away. I don't really know what I was thinking. I suppose I wasn't thinking much at all. I suppose I was just panicking. I just pretended it wasn't happening and allowed months to go by in a state of complete denial.

'It wasn't until I was over four months pregnant that my mum noticed I'd put on weight, despite the fact that I'd barely been eating anything other than toast for weeks by that point. After a single trip to the GP she knew the reason why. Even then, even when we went to the doctor, I thought that somehow it wasn't going to be true, that he'd find something else wrong with me, that the baby would have inexplicably disappeared. I suppose I hoped that my fear might have taken care of it for me.

'My parents were mortified, as I knew they would be, as any parent would be. But the perverse thing was that they weren't angry with Duncan in the slightest. They never so much as threatened to tell the police. All their fury landed at my feet; I was a disgrace to them, they hadn't brought me up to be so immoral, I'd thrown my life away, they couldn't bear to look at me, I disgusted them – it was a fairly extreme litany of disappointments. They insisted I should have an abortion and that no one else should ever know about it. And I agreed because I didn't know what else to do. I think by that stage I was almost relieved that someone else was taking control of the situation. I just wanted everything to go back to normal. It didn't dawn on me then that nothing was ever going to be normal again.

'By the time I had the abortion I was already twenty-two weeks pregnant, so I had to be induced and give birth to the baby. I can barely remember any of the details now. I think I've blocked most of it from memory. But there were some complications and I haemorrhaged and so they had to operate on me. I remember my fear as I was wheeled into the operating theatre but it wasn't until afterwards that they told me that the only way they could save my life was to remove my uterus. So when I came round from the anaesthetic, I woke to the discovery that not only did I no longer have a baby, I no longer had the means to have any other children in the future.'

Max emits a tormented sigh and instinctively takes both of her hands in his as though, all these years later, he may yet be able to protect her.

My own head is dizzy with the rush of revelation. It's too much to take in. Of all the adversities in all the world, having that choice taken away from you is the last affliction I'd wish on anyone. Anyone at all.

Max opens his mouth as if to respond, but Eve shakes her head and it's clear that there's yet more to come.

'I'm sorry, Max. I know how hard this must be, but I'm nearly done, I promise.

'After it was all over, my parents could barely look me in the eye any more. I'd been their perfect child, their only child, the girl who could do no wrong and they just couldn't get beyond what had happened. And then one evening a few weeks later, just before I was starting my GCSEs, my parents announced over dinner that as soon as my exams were done they wanted me to leave home. It was so extreme, absurd almost, that I just assumed they were punishing me with an empty threat, that it was simply their anger talking. It genuinely didn't occur to me, not then, that they might actually mean it. But three weeks later, I came home from my final exam to find two suitcases in the hall and my bedroom cleared of everything else I'd ever owned. It was as if I'd never existed, as if they'd wiped all evidence of my life from the house. My mum was in the kitchen and I asked her what she'd done with the rest of my things but she wouldn't tell me. I'll never forget the look on her face. She didn't cry or look upset or even disappointed. I think I could have borne it more easily if she had. Her face was so cold, so hard, as if all the feelings she'd ever had for me had turned to stone and she was facing nothing more than a stranger. She handed me an envelope, in silence; inside there was £200 and a piece of paper on which she'd scribbled the name of a hostel on the other side of town. I pleaded with her not to do it, begged her to let me stay. I don't think I've ever known such panic before or since. But there wasn't so much as a flicker of doubt on her face. She simply told me that I shouldn't still be there when my dad got home. I tried to hug her but she wouldn't – or couldn't – reciprocate. And so I left.'

Eve stops talking abruptly, an almost imperceptible twitching of her forehead the only indication of a mind quietly humming with the memory of its own past tragedy.

I think about my mum and about Ellie and about the perversion of parental responsibility Eve has described. I just don't know how any parent could do that. Or how any child would survive it.

Eve's still staring straight ahead, her eyes seemingly fixed on nothing at all in the present. She emits a breath heavy with the burden of confession and continues to speak.

'I went to the hostel and got myself a room – I remember it so clearly, as if it were yesterday, that stark, bare, brown room – and I remember thinking that it wasn't humanly possible to feel more lonely than I did right then. Hardly anyone had mobile phones so it wasn't as though I could text my friends for support and school had finished so I didn't even have that for comfort. I spent a couple of days on my own, locked in that room, in a sheer state of panic about what I was going to do. Then it finally dawned on me that I had two choices: to give up or to take care of myself. So I started looking for work and that's when I really landed on my feet. I got a job in a café run by a gay couple and, looking back, it was Russell and Nick who really saved me. They kept me employed full-time all summer, helped me find and furnish a bedsit, made sure I always had enough to eat – I'm sure I ate double my wages in café food alone – and let me carry on working there part-time when I went back to school in the autumn to start my A levels. I can't see that I'd have survived without them. When I went to university I did the same thing: got myself a job waitressing five nights a week and all day Saturday and supported myself for three years. And the rest you sort of know.'

Max strokes Eve's hand. She looks exhausted. So does he.

I feel overcome with guilt. And a powerful need to apologize to someone who doesn't even know I still exist.

'I can't believe you had to go through all that. I can't imagine how resilient you must be to have supported yourself like that.'

'Oh, I don't know. I think it's just that you find out what you're capable of when there aren't any other options. It's such a binary choice: either you find a way to survive or you don't. And I don't think the latter was ever really an option for me.'

Eve has recited all this matter-of-factly, as though it's the script to someone else's life, but I can see from her face how much the revelation has cost her.

'And what about your parents now? Are they sorry for what they did, can they see now how terrible that was?'

'I've no idea. I haven't seen or spoken to them for fifteen years. The last time I saw my mum was in the kitchen that day she told me to leave. I can't bring myself to contact them – not after what they did – and they've never tried to find me as far as I know, so I can't see how or why that's ever going to change.'

Max takes a deep breath as if to inhale the full emotional impact of Eve's confession.

All this time, for all these months, I've been desperate for Eve's fatal flaw to be revealed, to discover the imperfection that would make me feel just a little less inadequate in her virtual presence. But I hadn't counted on her having a secret quite so profound, quite so critical, a secret that would bring any woman unimaginable pain. A secret with an impact that may yet alter the course of Max and Ellie's lives in ways they haven't begun to envisage.

'Eve, I'm so sorry. I can't imagine what that must be like. I can't imagine my parents ever doing that to me, or me to Ellie. No wonder you never want to talk about them. I'm so sorry about those times I've pushed you to tell me about them. If only I'd known . . .'

'I haven't wanted to keep secrets from you, Max. I've just never been able to trust that other people wouldn't react the same way my parents did. It's why I've never told anyone any of this before.'

'You've never told *anyone* at all?'

'No. It sounds crazy, doesn't it? Other than Russell and Nick I've never told a soul. I think I've always felt too humiliated, not just about what I did, actually not really about that at all – I've managed to forgive my fifteen-year-old self for those mistakes now. But I feel so ashamed of what my parents did to me. What does it say about me, after all, to have descended from people who can behave like that?'

'It says that you're remarkable to have dealt with it and to have become the amazing person that you are. God, I can't believe you've been carrying this on your own for fifteen years.'

'I suppose I just haven't been ready to face it all. It's why I've never wanted anyone getting too close because I know that somewhere down the line this has to come out and that's always felt like a sacrifice too far. I wasn't being coy when we first . . . you know . . . got together. I really don't make a habit of having people stay over.'

Max looks at Eve as though seeing something new in her for the first time.

'I never thought you were being coy. I found it pretty endearing, actually. And it wasn't as if I was in possession of my Casanova credentials either, was it?'

Eve's half-smile and her gently reassuring squeeze of Max's hand tell me more than I want to know about the private events I've been spared from witnessing these past few months.

'You know this doesn't change a thing, don't you? Except I'm possibly even more in awe of you than I was before. You are incredible, Eve. To have accomplished everything you have, under those circumstances, is nothing short of extraordinary. I really want you and me to make a go of this, to make a go of us. I honestly think it can work.'

I look at Eve expecting to see the relief of someone who's just been issued with the reprieve she was seeking. But Eve's face shows no signs of a woman who's just been reassured by a man she might be in love with that he's definitely still in love with her.

'It's not that simple, though, is it? It's not just about you and me. It's about the children we could never have together even if we wanted to, even if you thought that's where we might be heading before I told you all of this. It's a huge sacrifice for anyone and it's not one I want you to have to make.'

Eve drops her head and she can't hold back the fifteen years of tears breaking through her barrier of self-protection. I watch her cry and hear her pain and I can't imagine that she'll ever be able to stop.

Max takes her in his arms and rocks her gently back and forth.

'Hey, it's okay. It's going to be okay, I promise. It's heart-wrenching for you, I know, but it doesn't affect my feelings for you in the least. Really.'

'But I know that's not true. Your mum told me, that first time I met her, about how you'd always wanted lots of children. You've already lost one person you thought you could have a big family with. It wouldn't be fair of me to deny you that again.'

Max laughs, kindly but loudly, and I suspect it's not the response that either Eve or I were anticipating.

'That was when I was eleven. I'm all for consistency of beliefs but I don't think I should have to honour the childish fantasies I had before I'd even hit puberty. I had no idea what I was talking about, much less clue about what was involved in actually having children. God, the thought of having five kids now freaks the hell out of me. It's utter madness.'

Eve manages a wistful smile and wipes her face free of tears.

'But you did want more than one?'

'Yes. If we're being totally honest, I did. But after all that's happened I've learnt to be grateful for what I do have, and I couldn't be more inordinately grateful for Ellie.'

My mind is racing with stories of lives the three of them may never lead. The siblings Ellie may never play with. The son Max may never take cycling. The child Eve will never give birth to. Of all the futures we think may lie before us, the one we end up with is invariably not the one we ever imagined.

'Ellie's wonderful. I've loved getting to know her a little bit today. But I suppose she's part of the reason I panicked tonight. I'm not sure I've got the strength to immerse myself in another family only to be rejected again.'

'You're not going to be rejected, Eve. I don't know how to convince you other than to tell you again and again that I love you and that I can see us having a future together.'

Max pulls Eve towards him and kisses her with such tenderness that I can't imagine her emerging from his embrace with a single doubt still in place.

'I can't believe you're being so calm about this. I honestly thought you'd send me packing. It's quite a lot to deal with. I'm not sure it's baggage anyone should have to take on board, really.'

'And you haven't had a lot of my baggage to deal with? Eve, everyone brings baggage to a relationship. Everyone.'

'I know they do. But I think mine's heavier than most.'

'Heavier than mine? Do you really think so?'

'At least yours wasn't of your own making.'

'Neither was yours, Eve. Not in the slightest.'

Max looks intently at Eve and I can see a decision stealthily working its way across his face.

'Okay, you've confided your deepest secret to me so it's only fair I do likewise. When Rachel first died I genuinely thought about ending it all. Not just an ambient flirtation with an idea that seemed easier than the reality I was having to deal with. But bleak, dark thoughts, coming from places I hadn't even known existed. And it really scared me because I never believed that was something I'd even think about, let alone seriously contemplate. It scares me even now, just remembering it, to be honest. It's pretty frightening when you discover something about yourself that you really wish you hadn't.'

It's frightening, too, to discover something about the person you love that you really wish they hadn't endured. I'd known Max had been depressed in those early months, but I hadn't known how severely. I can't bear the thought of him having gone through that alone.

'I'm so sorry, Max. It must have been such a terrible time. I can't really imagine what you must have suffered or how you came through it.'

'To be honest, when I look back on that period, I'm not sure how I got through it either. But like you said, you just do. Something else kicks in and you've no idea from where or how but it does and it saves you from yourself, however much you might not want it to at the time.'

They both fall silent and I suspect I'm not the only one to be reflecting upon the ways in which each of us have — and haven't — been saved from ourselves.

'So what pulled you through? Or don't you know?'

'That's easy. It was Ellie. Having a young child makes the decision for you. Well, it did for me anyway. I needed to find something or someone to fill the gap that grief had left behind and Ellie was there, the whole time, waiting patiently and perfectly in the wings.'

There's another silence, more loaded than the last, and I wonder to what extent Max's confession has exacerbated Eve's sadness.

'I think I know what you mean. I'm not suggesting they're comparable, but I think the grief of losing my fertility has been filled to some extent for me by teaching. I remember when I first became aware, in my early twenties, that I needed something to fill the maternal void. I felt that I'd been robbed of the one consolation, the one comfort shared by every parent on the planet; that when they die, their lives will carry on through their children. It's the ultimate immortality project, isn't it, having children? And it's been the one thing I knew I'd never have for almost as long as I can remember. So I had to find another way of trying to achieve that, another way to make sure I left something behind, another way of exerting an influence which might outlive me.'

'And that's what you get from teaching?'

'I think so, yes; it gives me the proximity to young people that I'll never otherwise have and it allows me to have some impact — however small — on their lives. Sometimes

I'll be talking to a student and I imagine that one day they might share whatever it is I've taught them with their children or with their nieces and nephews or with students of their own. And that seems pretty remarkable to me, that fragments of knowledge I pass on now might find their way unexpectedly to people I don't even know, through however many degrees of separation, at some unknown point in the future. I like to think of it as ripples of influence and experience pulsating from one generation to the next and I think if I could manage that just a handful of times, with just a handful of students, then it will have been worth it. Does that sound really stupid?'

I can't remember when I last heard something that sounded less stupid.

'It doesn't sound stupid at all. In fact, it might be one of the wisest things I've ever heard. Do you know, I've never really sat down and thought about why I chose teaching over every other profession on offer, but what you said makes total sense. Maybe that's what all jobs are, in one way or another; some attempt to leave an imprint on the world, however small.'

'I think that's right. And I suppose, for me, in the absence of having children of my own, teaching's become my personal immortality project. Although I've yet to see quite how effective it might be.'

Eve laughs and Max does too and in their laughter is the catharsis of collective confessions.

'So now we've shared our darkest secrets, you know there's no way out? You're stuck with me for the foreseeable future whether you like it or not.'

'Really, Max? Are you sure? I don't think this is a decision you should rush. I want you to sleep on it and mull it over and we can talk in a few days.'

Max shakes his head, smiling with confident reassurance.

'I don't need a few days. It's simple. I love you and I want us to make a go of this.'

'You love me in spite of everything I've told you?'

'I love you in spite of and because of everything you've told me. I'll make a deal with you, Eve: if you have the courage to jump into this relationship with me, I promise always to be honest with you and never to spring any nasty emotional surprises on you. Deal?'

Eve smiles and pulls Max's face towards her.

'Given that I love you too, Max Myerson, I don't see how I could possibly refuse.'

They both laugh and then they're kissing and I know that my time here, today, needs to come to an end.

I close my eyes firmly and count to a hundred and when I finally open them again, Max and Eve have disappeared, replaced by the empty white world that once was a cause for fear and loneliness but which is increasingly a source of solitary comfort.

I think about the declarations they've made to one another today and I'm reminded of the time Max first said those three decisive words to me, on that long, deserted beach in Norfolk, the wind blowing a near gale, his declaration being swept out to sea so that I wasn't sure whether I'd heard him correctly. The words I had to ask him to repeat and when he did I reciprocated, surprised by my own certainty there and then that I'd never need

286

any other man to say them to me again. The words that I've spent over a decade believing would only ever be spoken romantically by Max to me. Words for which I'd give anything to hear Max or Ellie say to me one last time.

I think about Ellie, my own perfect little immortality project, and about the fact that all I want, all I'll hope for from here on in, is that she's as happy and safe and loved as she deserves to be. Because as imprints on the world go, she's about as good as it gets.

# Depression

# CHAPTER 21

I hear the hubbub of overexcited children before I see anything, and as the chatter becomes gradually louder and the clouds dissipate I see that I'm here, I'm exactly where I want to be, for the first time since I died.

Ellie is wearing a calf-length, short-sleeved lilac dress, the delicate netting of its full skirt covered with sequins, the sweetheart neckline perfectly framing her cherubic face. Her hair is bouncing effusively below her shoulders, just a small strand either side clipped to her head with purple, fairy-shaped grips, giving her the appearance of a woodland nymph. She looks beautiful. I'd say that even if she weren't my daughter. The party appears to be in full swing, a game of musical statues currently entertaining Ellie and a dozen of her friends, with Connor in charge of iPod proceedings.

I take stock of my old sitting room to see who else is here. In the far corner, by the kitchen door, are Harriet and my mum, whispering collusively like naughty school-girls, failing – if, indeed, they're even trying – to conceal the evident topic of their conversation, given that every few seconds one or other of them looks over to the oppo-site end of the sitting room, where Eve is standing chatting to Joan and Ralph. I'm grateful for their loyalty, but I don't want anything to sour Ellie's day.

Eve, of course, looks stunning. She's wearing a floral-print bias-cut silk dress, the kind of dress I might have seen hanging up in a shop window and, in a moment's self-delusion, taken to the changing room to try on under a spell of naive optimism, until I'd look in the mirror and remember, again, for the umpteenth time, that curvy hips and bias-cut dresses were never going to be the best of sartorial friends. She's accessorized with nude kitten heels and a simple diamond solitaire necklace, the soft waves of her hair flowing serenely across her shoulders. To be fair, if I was in Mum or Harriet's position, I'd probably find it hard not to skulk in a corner and gossip about her too.

There are other people I know here too, a couple of other parents from school and a few friends of mine and Max's from way back, most of whom have children of their own now, all of whom are used to the weekend birthday party drill. Max is standing just behind Eve, talking to one of his old university friends and her husband, and I see him interrupt Eve's conversation with his parents to introduce her to Rebecca and Mark. I'm unable to resist a pang of envy, knowing that this is their first public outing together, their first joint hosting, clearly Eve's first encounter with many of the people who populate Max's life. The people who used to populate my life too.

I know I should be grateful just for being here. It's what I've wanted more than anything else during the past few weeks, after all. But I can't deny it's hard, watching Eve and Max in the midst of the social and familial group that less than two years ago was mine and his, not his and hers.

Ellie and her friends have moved on to Pass the Parcel now, the children sitting in a watchful circle bound by hope. With Mum and Harriet still chatting surreptitiously in the corner, I decide to eavesdrop on them first.

'I was as surprised as you were to find her here, Celia. I knew things had got serious but . . . Ellie's birthday party?'

'Well, it's nice to know I wasn't the only one to have been kept in the dark about her coming today. It was rather a shock when I arrived, I have to admit.'

'How long have you known about her?'

'Clearly not as long as everyone else. He told me on the telephone a couple of weeks ago. But I'd guessed something must be going on from a few things Ellie's said.'

Mum glances over at her granddaughter just as the music stops and she unwraps the final layer of wrapping paper to discover a set of fluffy pens inside. Trust Connor to ensure that she wins the prize.

'So what do you make of her? She's not what I was expecting. She's looks so . . . young.'

'Everyone looks young to me, Harriet. She seemed perfectly friendly in our very brief introduction earlier. I barely got time to form an opinion. It's just so strange, seeing her here, in Rachel's house, with Max.'

So this must be the first time either of them have met her. I can't say I'm impressed by Max's timing. Doesn't Ellie have enough to contend with without her birthday party playing host to myriad adult complications too?

'It feels strange to me so I can't imagine how odd it must feel for you. What's Ellie said?'

'Not much, and I haven't wanted to push her on it, not least since I've only spoken to her on the phone for the past two months. Max cancelled her last visit ostensibly because it was half term but Ellie let slip it was then that she'd met Eve. At the zoo.'

'Ouch. That's rough. I'm sorry, Celia. This must be so hard for you. God, Rach would be furious if she knew how insensitive Max was being.'

Not furious, no. Just sad that Max is being so much less thoughtful than I've come to expect him to be.

'It's not that I mind him having someone new in his life per se. I do think it's far too soon, obviously, but Max made his feelings about that quite clear to me before. I just worry about what might happen in the future.'

'What do you mean?'

'Well, none of us know quite what this woman's intentions are. Or how serious they are about each other. And I'm well aware how precarious my position will be if Max has a new partner on the scene permanently.'

'What, you think they'll try and freeze you out?'

'It wouldn't be entirely surprising, would it? Why on earth would she or Max want his ex-mother-in-law hanging around? I couldn't bear it, Harriet, if I didn't get to see Ellie very often. It would break my heart.'

It would break my heart too. In all my anxieties about Eve stealing my life, I hadn't contemplated the prospect of her excluding Mum from theirs too.

'I wouldn't go jumping the gun, Celia. It's very early days yet.'

'You wouldn't guess it from the way Joan's behaving. You'd think Eve was already a permanent fixture here.'

Mum and Harriet look over to where Eve is laughing with Joan and Ralph, just as Joan takes Eve's hand in hers and rewards it with an approving pat. Mum's right. The adoration on Joan's face is undeniable.

'Joan does seem to have taken a bit of a shine to Eve, but who knows how long that will last?'

'It's mortifying. She's behaving as though Rachel never existed. It's disrespectful as much as anything else.'

Before Harriet has a chance to respond, Ellie bounds over and grabs her hand.

'Come and judge the dancing competition, Hetty. I want you to judge the girls and I'm going to get Eve to judge the boys. Come on.'

Ellie drags a less-than-thrilled Harriet to the other side of the sitting room where the sofas have been pushed back to create a temporary dance floor. Harriet and Eve stand awkwardly side by side, on opposing sides of so much more than a child's competition.

Mum is left standing alone in a crowded room. It's a scenario she hates, I know, although it's possibly preferable to the alternative winding her way towards Mum now in the shape of Joan.

'Celia. It's nice to see you. I wasn't sure if you'd make it this year.'

I sense Mum's hackles rise from a whole world away.

'Of course I'd make it. Why on earth wouldn't I?'

If Mum's cemented smile is an attempt to hide her irritation under a veneer of social niceties I fear she hasn't been altogether successful.

'Well, you know, what with it being such a long way for you to come. It's so good of you to make the journey just for a couple of hours.'

'It's really not that far, Joan. And I'm hardly likely to miss my own granddaughter's birthday party, am I?'

'No, no of course you're not. I just wish you could have seen Ellie this morning when we were getting everything ready for the party. She was so excited.'

This is, of course, the last thing Joan wishes and all three of us know it.

'So what did you get Ellie for her birthday? I don't think I saw her open it.'

'No, we gave our present to her earlier, before everyone else arrived. We got her some roller skates. Well, they're more like boots really. It's what she asked for. She was thrilled with them.'

There's an expectant pause in the conversation while Mum waits for Joan to return the question. When it doesn't materialize, Mum's left with little option but to fill the conversational hiatus.

'I'm sure they're very nice. I'm going to save my present for Ellie until later. One last present when she thinks they're all done for another year. It's a little surprise, a special trip I've got planned for the two of us. I can't wait to see her face when I tell her.'

Mum smiles and I suspect she's not even trying to keep the note of triumph from her voice. I wonder if the 'little surprise' is the trip to Venice that Mum's been promising Ellie ever since she was a toddler, ever since she saw footage of it on the television and couldn't believe there was a real city where people travelled by boat rather than by car.

Joan is spared the necessary ingenuity of an appropriate response by Max, who has lowered the volume on the music and is standing in the middle of the room with his arm around Ellie's shoulders.

'If I can just have everyone's attention for a minute, please. Now Ellie made me promise that I wouldn't embarrass her by making one of my – what did you call it? – "silly soppy speeches" so I'll try not to make it silly but I can't promise it won't be soppy. I can barely believe it was eight years ago that I first held this little lady in my arms and brought her home here to this house. I know it's a cliché but it really does feel like only yesterday. It seems astonishing that such a tiny bundle of a baby has become the lovely, thoughtful, kind young lady standing here now who I can see is getting more embarrassed by the second – sorry, munchkin, I'm nearly done. I'm so very, very proud of you, angel, and I love you very, very much. So, everyone, please raise your glasses and join me in saying "Happy Birthday, Ellie".'

As everyone toasts my little girl, Max hugs her and I can see she's trying to conceal the delight on her face as though she's not sure whether it's socially acceptable to look as pleased as she does by all the attention she's getting.

Suddenly the lights are dimmed and the room goes quiet, and I detect the flicker of candlelight emerging from the kitchen. As the cake comes into view I can barely believe my eyes.

The cake bearer isn't any of the obvious candidates: not Max, nor Mum, nor Joan, nor Harriet or Ralph or Connor.

The cake is being carried in by Eve.

Eve is presenting my daughter with her birthday cake. I can't believe Max could be so insensitive.

As Eve goes to place the cake on the table where Ellie and her friends are crowded round expectantly, I catch a glimpse of it and all at once my chest tightens and I feel like I can't breathe all over again except this time I know it's not the mechanics of my heart at fault. I glance over at Mum and she's seen it too and she's looking at Harriet, both of them exhibiting the panic I'm feeling, and I look up at Max standing next to Eve, assuming he'll display some sign of concern too, but he's grinning proudly at Eve as though there's a triumph to be celebrated, and she rewards him with a smile filled to the brim with pre-emptive success.

And then Eve puts the cake down on the table and Ellie looks at it and then she looks at Max and then she looks back at the cake again, and then her bottom lip just begins to tremble.

And then she bursts into tears.

'What, munchkin? What on earth's the matter?'

Max endeavours to part the sea of children blocking his path to Ellie but Celia gets there first and swoops Ellie into her arms.

'Max, what on earth were you thinking?'

'What? Ellie, what's wrong? Come and have a cuddle with Daddy.'

Ellie tightens her grip around Mum's neck, sobbing effusively.

'The cake, Max. How could you?'

'What's wrong with it? I think it was really kind of Eve to make it. I can't see what the problem is.'

Can't he? Can he really have forgotten?

Mum turns her back on Max to exit the circle of bemused children whose only preoccupation is when they might be allowed their long-promised sugar rush. She keeps hold of Ellie in the corner of the room, trying to rock her out of her distress, leaving Harriet to take up the aggrieved mantle. And it's Eve whom Harriet turns to face.

'You should have checked with one of us first.'

Eve looks slightly shell-shocked as though she's come under attack without so much as a warning that there's even a battle to be fought.

'I'm . . . I'm sorry. We just thought it would be nice if Ellie had a home-made cake. I didn't mean to offend anyone. And I certainly didn't want to upset Ellie.'

'Of course she's upset. Did you think she wouldn't remember, Max?'

'Remember what?'

Max's annoyance very slowly begins to dissipate, the first tremors of a disquieting memory unsettling his earlier confidence.

'The cake, Max. The purple butterfly cake. The cake Rach made for Ellie's sixth birthday. The cake that's almost identical to the one your girlfriend has just presented her with two years later. You didn't think that might be a problem?'

Harriet has hissed the words at Max so as to be audible only to those in her immediate vicinity.

Max's face turns the colour of fire-grate ash. Eve intakes a sharp, shocked breath and covers her mouth with her hand as though to ensure she doesn't let escape whatever it is she's feeling.

'Oh my god. I totally forgot. It's not Eve's fault, it's mine. It was my idea. It's totally my mistake.'

Max joins Mum and Ellie in the corner of the room where my little girl is still sobbing quietly on Mum's shoulder. He rubs her back slowly, rhythmically and eventually she allows herself to be slid into his arms.

Harriet remains in the circle of children, glowering at Eve – whose face is now flushed with the self-consciousness of unwelcome attention. The room is quiet save for Ellie's whimpering, all eyes on the two women now at the centre of the storm, the children bewildered and impatient, the adults intrigued and apprehensive.

Eve picks up the cake from the table, the candles still flickering uncertainly, and carries it towards the kitchen, blowing out the eight fading flames on the way. As the candles go out so, in an instant, does my access.

The disappointment churns deep in the pit of my stomach. It's too soon for me to be excluded today, before I can be sure that Ellie recovers, before I can know that she's able to enjoy the rest of her party, before I can determine that adult conflicts aren't going to spoil her day further. Before I can discover how on earth Max could possibly have forgotten a single detail of a day I'll always remember.

Alone in the whiteness, I think back on the last birthday I shared with Ellie. Her sixth birthday, with the other, inaugural butterfly cake and the garden swing we'd given her as a present and the chaotic party we'd foolishly held at home rather than in the local church hall, against the better judgement of our wisest friends. I'd give anything to turn back the clock, to relive that day, to share one of life's milestones with my daughter again. Or, if not to relive it, then at least to have known at the time that it was going to be my last.

I begin to think about all those lasts of everything that I'd not known were to be finalities; not just Ellie's last birthday but Max's too, and the last Christmas and the last summer holiday. The last time I put Ellie to bed and tucked her in and read her a story and kissed her goodnight. The last time I cooked dinner for the three of us and we sat around the kitchen table, sharing stories of our separate days, ingesting so much more sustenance than just the food on our plates. The last time Ellie crawled into our bed when she'd had a bad dream and spent the night sprawled between us, taking up more room than any six-year-old feasibly should. The last time Max and I made love, that final Sunday night, both of us too tired really but incentivized by the dates in my diary signalling the imminent closure of our fertile window for another month, neither of us knowing then that such a hungry and determined sexual encounter was to be the culmination of countless acts of intimacy. The last time, on that final, fateful morning, that I awoke with Max still sleeping beside me, feeling overcome as I did every morning, as I had felt every single day since we first moved in together, overcome with gratitude and happiness and love that this was the man I was lucky enough to be sharing my life with. The last time Max kissed me, that night in the restaurant, so surprising and romantic, as though he'd known somehow, deep down, that the evening had to be special for reasons greater than his promotion. If only I'd known, if only there'd been some forewarning that such an unexpected public display of affection was to be the conclusion of every kiss, every touch, every physical moment we'd ever shared, then I'd have known to savour it, to treasure it, to commit it indelibly to memory so that it could never be eroded.

If only I'd known that each of those events was to be the last, that I should hold on to every one of them as though my afterlife depended on it, perhaps now I'd be able to take more solace in my memories. Memories which so often hide their finer emotional details from me as if taunting me with my inability to locate them.

I think about the people who hope to die suddenly, to be saved from the anguish of a long, drawn-out illness, the people who claim to covet my form of death more than any other, and I think about how misguided they are. I think about how much more grateful I'd have been for knowledge of what was to come – however difficult, however distressing, however upsetting that may have been – if it had meant I'd been able to savour my lasts and to say my goodbyes. If it had prevented me from taking so many precious, final moments for granted. If I'd been spared the hours I now spend scouring my mind for fragments of memory which were fragile to begin with and now seem to weaken with every day that passes.

And if it had meant, too, that Ellie and Max hadn't been robbed of those lasts, that they'd been able to savour those never-to-be-repeated moments, that they weren't also denied the opportunity to say goodbye.

Because perhaps if we'd been able to relish those finalities, perhaps if we'd been gifted our goodbyes, perhaps now we'd all find it easier to resign ourselves to life continuing without me.

Or maybe I'm deluding myself. Maybe there's nothing in the world – not in this world or theirs – that could take away the longing. Because there's nothing that can change the fact that I'm dead and that they're alive, or that all the hope in the world won't allow me to relive a single day with them. No way of me knowing what they still remember and what they've already forgotten. Nothing to take away the fear that every one of those experiences the three of us shared, every memory that currently binds the three of us together, may simply dissolve in the end into the ether, like ashes scattered on an ocean.

# CHAPTER 22

'I'm surprised you came. I assumed Eve would be arch-enemy number one.'

Connor is sitting with Harriet at a wooden table in a pub that's almost as familiar to me as my own kitchen. It's the pub around the corner from our house, a pub which, when we first moved there, was full of old men sporting faces permanently flushed from decades of daytime drinking, but was soon bought out by an ambitious young chef who turned it into a gastropub and began charging fourteen pounds for fish and chips without any of the area's newest residents batting an eyelid. Max and I used to eat there almost every weekend before Ellie was born, and not infrequently after she came along. It's where she had her first meal out, in fact, sitting in a plastic high chair, banging her spoon on the table and eating home-made vegetable purée while we laughed at the fun of having her dine out in public with us. Today there's no sign of Ellie but I can see Max and Eve standing over the other side of the room, surveying the specials board.

'Well, you know what they say: keep your friends close and your enemies closer. I've barely met the woman so I figured it was time I got the lowdown on her.'

'And there was me thinking you'd agreed to come to make up for being such a bully to her at Ellie's birthday party.'

Harriet pokes an indignant finger into Connor's shoulder.

'I wasn't a bully. I was merely protecting Ellie's feelings. Someone had to. I didn't see you leaping to her defence.'

'Yeah, well, there was barely room to move with all that angry oestrogen circling the room. Anyway, now you're here, play nicely, will you? Max was bricking it about today so go easy on the pair of them. It's not exactly a picnic for anyone, this situation.'

Harriet raises a sceptical eyebrow as she glances over to where Max and Eve are holding hands and giggling by the chalkboard menu.

'They don't exactly seem to be struggling. Look, it's just weird for me, okay? I love Max, you know I do, but Rach was my best friend and it's pretty tough to see him with anyone other than her.'

Connor makes the risky move of placing a placatory hand on Harriet's arm. She doesn't immediately shake it off with her customary defensiveness.

'No one expects you not to feel weird about it. I loved Rachel too. She was like the more grown-up younger sister I never had. Remember all those nights the four of us would go out and get totally hammered? They were awesome. She was awesome. But if Max isn't allowed to move on with his life now that she's gone then he might as well be dead too. Sorry – it's harsh but true. So do you think you might be able to cut them just a bit of slack? Even if only to get the four of us through three courses and a couple of bottles of wine?'

I'm expecting Harriet to baulk at Connor's gentle reprimand but instead she raises a pair of non-committal eyebrows at him as Max and Eve rejoin them at the table.

'So, what looks good up there? Have you decided what you're having, Eve?'

'I'm going for the scallops and pancetta to start and then the rack of lamb to follow. Completely gluttonous, I know, but I'm starving.'

'That sounds like a good choice. I think I might join you.'

As Harriet closes her menu, Connor catches her eye and smiles approvingly. She grins sardonically in response.

'What about you, Max?'

'I can't make up my mind between the rib-eye and the sirloin. I'll decide by the time they come to take our order.'

'And there was me thinking it was women who had trouble making up their minds.'

'I don't think any sensible woman has any trouble making up their mind about you, Connor. Anyway, Max, how's Ellie been since her birthday party? Is she okay about the cake debacle now?'

Connor turns exasperatedly to Harriet, boring his eyes into the side of her head where she's seated next to him to try and attract her attention, but she stares straight ahead at Max, awaiting his answer.

'She's fine, Harriet. As you'd expect, given that she was fine five minutes after it all happened.'

'I wouldn't have said she was fine, exactly. I'd say she put on a brave face in difficult circumstances.'

Eve's face flushes to match her crimson scarf as she buries her nose into a very large glass of white wine. I know Harriet's only trying to defend me and it's not that I don't appreciate it but even I don't blame Eve for a mistake she could never have known she was making.

'Kids, huh? So damn fickle. That's why I'm happy to stick with being an uncle, albeit a bloody great one at that – dive in, give presents, get love, hand back. Seems like the perfect contribution to childrearing, if you ask me.'

Connor raises his glass and the other three toast him, laughing, conflict diffused. It's strange watching Connor play the diplomatic role; in our foursome he was invariably the joker, mocking the three of us mercilessly and rarely refraining from confronting our faults.

'I think we all know that the reason you haven't had children, Connor, is because you're congenitally unable to get up before noon most weekends. You might find that a bit of a challenge if you ever had a baby in the house.'

Max laughs playfully at his brother and it's nice to see the teasing reversed for a change.

'I hold my hands up. I'm too selfish to have kids. I don't see anything wrong with admitting that. Some of us just have the self-awareness to know we're better off on our own, don't we Harriet?'

A shard of discomfort pierces Harriet's eyes and I can't tell whether it's due to unease or irritation.

'Oh, I don't know. I'm sure most people are in possession of enough narcissism to want to have children, whether or not they resist it. And narcissism's not something you're generally short of, is it Connor?'

'Touché. Although I could never see you giving up your freedom to gurgle at babies and wipe up their sick and change their stinking nappies, Harriet. Let alone give up your job or your social life or that crazy shoe collection you've got going on.'

'Well, maybe it's not the dark ages any more and women don't have to give up everything for the sake of motherhood. God, Connor, someone has let you know that we're in the twenty-first century now, haven't they?'

Harriet empties her wine glass in one defiant mouthful while Max and Eve watch on, wryly entertained, apparently viewing the argument as a conversational amuse-bouche.

'Look, I'm just telling it how it is. Women can delude themselves all they like that parenthood is now some happy-clappy world of libertarian equality but the fact is it's women who have the kids and women who stay home to look after them when they're small. You can't argue with biology, however many feminist books you read. I'm right, aren't I, Eve?'

Eve suddenly pulls herself to attention as though she hadn't expected to play a part in this particular pantomime.

'No, Connor, you're playing devil's advocate, as well you know. If you say that women's choices haven't changed in the past fifty years then you're clearly talking nonsense and you're just trying to wind us both up.'

There's a moment's silence and I wonder if Connor's going to take offence at being put in his place. But he looks at Eve and bursts out laughing.

'Well, that told me. Although I'm not being deliberately contrary. I do think that women's choices are a lot less free than we all like to pretend they are. I'm a feminist – I'm on your side.'

Harriet practically explodes next to him.

'A feminist? You? Ha! I don't think someone who picks up a different woman every Saturday night only never to see her again after Sunday morning can legitimately describe himself as a feminist.'

'What are you talking about? That's the sexual revolution for you. We've got your lot to thank for that.'

'God, if feminism's got you in its corner then it really is a lost cause.'

'Very funny. Anyway, I don't know why you're getting so hot under the collar. You're the standard-bearer for a woman's right to choose, aren't you, Harriet?'

'I'd like to choose not to be having this conversation with you, if that were possible.'

Eve laughs, and she and Harriet share a complicit smile. I'm not sure how I feel about my best friend and my husband's new girlfriend forming an allegiance, even if it is a one-off in opposition to Connor at his most irritating.

'You love our little disagreements, Harriet – don't even bother denying it. Anyway, all this is an academic argument for you. How old were you last birthday? Thirty-eight? Your biological clock would be in need of some serious winding if you suddenly had a change of heart now.'

Connor laughs obstreperously at his own joke. Max allows him a half-smile of social support but both Harriet and Eve avert their eyes, Harriet out of the window and Eve on to the dessert menu enclosed in a perspex stand on the table. I know why Eve might be finding this conversation awkward but I'm not sure what's rankled Harriet so much. It must be the reference to her age that's riled her; she's always had a certain vanity about each accumulated year so perhaps she doesn't appreciate the reminder, not least in the presence of a woman nearly a decade younger.

'Right, before you manage to offend both women at the table, I suggest we go to the bar and sort food since it doesn't look like anyone's coming to take our orders.'

'Offend anyone? Moi? I don't know what you mean. Excuse us, ladies. Back in a tick.'

As Max and Connor head off to the bar, I see Harriet get up and walk towards the toilet. Perhaps she's not quite ready for a one-on-one with Eve just yet. I join Max and Connor, where they're both ordering rib-eye and chips for themselves.

'She's a knockout, Max. I thought so at Ellie's party but she seems a lot more relaxed today. I've no idea how you managed to pull someone so far above your station, but well done, mate. She's a keeper.'

'Thanks for the backhanded compliment. But seriously, that means a lot. She is pretty amazing, isn't she?'

'I think you mean she's pretty *and* amazing. God, I can't believe you're going to end up with someone who looks like a bloody model. I thought that was my prerogative.'

Connor laughs at his own joke again but Max shifts uncomfortably from one foot to the other while the colour of his cheeks suggest that someone's suddenly turned up the heating very high.

'What? What did I say now?'

'It just feels weird, you talking about me "ending up" with someone. I always thought that someone was going to be Rachel.'

Connor settles a fraternal arm around Max's shoulder, a rare gesture of genuine affection rather than the play-fighting that typically substitutes for it.

'I know, mate. But life moves on. And I think you're doing a bloody brilliant job of that at the moment, so don't start beating yourself up.'

Max inhales a deep breath that he lets out very slowly, as if to expel a whole head of thoughts he doesn't want in his possession.

'I know it's probably stupid, but I just can't stop feeling guilty.'

'Guilty about what? It's not like you're being unfaithful, for god's sake.'

'Well you say that but it feels like I am. I still spend so much time thinking about Rachel, even when I'm with Eve; in a way it does feel like a kind of infidelity.'

I know it's probably wrong of me, but I can't help indulging a small flutter of gratification; I'd thought I was as far out of Max's mind as I am out of sight. It's a surprise — a rare, nice surprise — to know that my presence in Max's thoughts hasn't been entirely eclipsed by Eve.

'Max, if we start facing charges of infidelity because of what we think rather than what we do then every man on the planet is going to find himself condemned.'

Connor smiles mischievously but his attempt to introduce a note of levity bypasses Max.

'I'm just so used to Rachel being the person I discuss everything with. It's like there's a part of my brain reserved for the question "What would Rachel think or do or say?" I even find myself asking her opinion of Eve. How wrong is that?'

Connor opens his mouth and I can sense that there's a flippant comment on the verge of escaping but then he thinks better of it and I see on his face a decisive and deliberate shift towards solemnity.

'Yeah, okay, that is pretty wrong. But it's still early days with Eve. What is it? Six months? Give it a bit more time and you'll stop thinking about Rachel so much, I'm sure.'

'Seven. But that's just it. I'm not sure I want to. I kind of like the fact that she's somehow still alive in my head, that I can still talk to her about stuff. I don't actually want to lose that.'

And I don't want you to lose it either, Max. Because as long as I'm alive in your head it's like I never really left you. And leaving you is the last thing I ever wanted to do.

'So let me get this straight. You feel bad because you're thinking about Rachel all the time but you don't actually want to stop thinking about Rachel. But you do want to be with Eve even though you're thinking about Rachel all the time. God, this is precisely the reason I steer clear of relationships – they're so bloody complicated.'

'Yeah, of course I want to be with Eve. It's just that I feel guilty to Rachel for falling for Eve and guilty to Eve for thinking about Rachel as much as I do. It's not that complicated, is it?'

'Max, it's pretty confusing from where I'm standing. Seems to me you feel guilty for being happy and guilty for grieving. That sounds like a lose–lose situation to me.'

'I never said it was logical. But what do you think I should do?'

'Well I know what you shouldn't do. Don't tell Eve that you're still thinking about Rachel all the time, however much that overactive conscience of yours says you should.

I know what you're like. But trust me, she won't want to hear it.'

'So I just carry on with Eve as though there's nothing going on?'

'Max, there *is* nothing going on. Like I said, you can't be held accountable for thoughts out of your control.'

'I don't know. It just feels a bit . . . dishonest.'

'Yeah, well, sometimes dishonesty is the best policy. Now, I suggest you get back over to the table where that stunningly beautiful woman who you've somehow managed to dupe into being your girlfriend is sitting all on her own. God knows what Harriet's been doing in the ladies' all this time. I'll get the drinks in and bring them over.'

Max obediently complies with his brother's instructions, passing Harriet on her way back from the toilets, who makes a detour to join Connor at the bar.

'What have you been doing in there all that time? Whoa – what did you do to your face?'

'Ever the charmer, Connor. I put on some lipstick, that's all.'

'No, it's great. Smoking, in fact. You should wear lipstick more often.'

Harriet lets the compliment hang in the air, whether to allow it to linger or to encourage it to dissolve I'm not quite sure.

'So, how am I doing on the playing nicely front? I feel like I'm on my best bloody behaviour.'

'A shaky start but you're warming up. It's not so hard to be nice now, Harriet, is it?'

Harriet delivers one of her withering looks, a look which to most people is a clear sign to shut up but which to Connor is usually little more than a challenge. She jumps in before Connor has the chance to continue.

'Listen, while I've got you on your own there's something I wanted to talk to you about. It's about Celia. I don't know if you can have a subtle word with Max – and I mean, subtle, Connor, none of your usual bull-in-china-shop clumsiness – but she's feeling really vulnerable at the moment and I think she could do with a bit of TLC.'

'Vulnerable about what?'

'You know – Max and Eve, her relationship with Ellie, whether she's going to be pushed out if Eve plants her feet firmly under the table. She's really down about it.'

'But that's ridiculous. Max would never stop her seeing Ellie.'

'Well, that's easy for you to say. You're on the right side of the family. She's not. I don't think it's totally irrational of her to worry about her place in the family if the configuration starts to take on a new shape, do you?'

Connor's face is full of scepticism but I'm grateful to Harriet for watching Mum's back. There's no one else to keep an eye on her now, after all.

'Are you sure this is about Celia? Sounds like there might be someone else who's feeling a little bit left out.'

Harriet visibly bristles. I don't suspect either of us is used to competent levels of emotional literacy from Connor.

'Yes, thanks for that, Dr Freud, but we're talking about Celia. So, will you talk to Max or not?'

'Okay, okay. I'll have a word with him. Now, can you take the glasses over to the table and I'll bring the bucket?'

'You ordered champagne? What are we celebrating?'

'I dunno. The weekend? Freedom? Saturday lunch with two beautiful women?'

Harriet shoves Connor playfully on the arm and as the two of them head back to the table a shaft of precocious spring sunlight streams confidently through the window and blinds my view temporarily. It takes a few seconds to pass and, when it does, I find it's taken my access with it.

I think about the four of them having lunch together and feel a potent, querulous envy that I'm no longer a member of the quartet that was such a substantial part of my life for a decade.

I think about the fact that it's been almost two years since I had a conversation with anyone, since I was in the same room as someone else, since I stood face-to-face with another human being and looked them in the eye, and had them look back at me. It's only now, observing an event so familiar and yet now so remote, that I'm reminded of what that feels like. And how much I miss it.

I think about Max's confession and wonder whether Connor's right, whether Max's memory of me will fade as the days since I died accumulate until he's not able to recall my voice in his head even if he wanted to. Because if that happened I think it would be a death worse than the one that I've already known.

# CHAPTER 23

I'm in a bedroom I don't recognize and the reason I'm sure I don't recognize it is because it's nicer than any bedroom I've ever been in before, dead or alive.

The bed is a carved mahogany four-poster and the room is all polished wooden floorboards and open fireplaces and a roll-top bath sitting proudly in the corner as though someone forgot to tell it it's supposed to have a room of its own. It's the kind of hotel room I've only been able to fantasize about since Ellie was born, that decisive moment when dirty weekends at country house hotels gave way to playgrounds and parks and gratitude to the organizers of family activity days at London galleries.

In the bed, under a purple damask bedspread and dazzling white duvet lie Max and Eve, their sleeping bodies entwined, each facing the majestic Georgian windows hung with heavy silk curtains, her back to him, his chest and arms enveloping her, the outline of their plaited legs indistinguishable from one another.

I know I shouldn't be here. I know there are lines – private lines, moral lines – that even the dead should endeavour not to cross. I know I should try to will myself away, that I should try even if I fail, that it's the intention that matters more than the outcome. But I can't. Because the knowledge that I should leave is overpowered by my desire, however masochistic, to stay.

I try to recall the sensation of being where Eve is now, of feeling the heat of Max's body warm the small of my back, of slumbering under the heavy weight of his arm draped protectively across my shoulder, the only occasional chill in the air when he'd stir, disrupting the duvet that encased our sleeping limbs, allowing the briefest blast of the world outside to penetrate our privacy. Those moments under the covers in the dark were, I used to think, some of the most peaceful any couple could ever know.

Suddenly there's movement below and I hear a familiar sound, a sound I haven't heard for many months now, the sound of Max snuffling his way towards wakefulness. I panic, acutely aware of how wrong it is for me to be here, fearful that they'll find me, hovering over their bed, watching them while they sleep, and the terror of them discovering that I've been spying on them, not just today but for months now, and them despising me forever for it.

But then I remember that they can't see me, that I'm as invisible to them as I am dead, that I could be perched on the end of the bed or sitting naked in the bathtub and they'd be none the wiser. For a second I wonder which I'd prefer: to be discovered, right here, right now, and for my voyeuristic secret to be exposed or to remain invisible to Max forever more.

I look down to see Eve stir now, too, and turn her body to face Max. He opens his eyes, smiles as though he can't quite believe his luck to have discovered he's woken, yet again, next to her naked body, and kisses her tenderly on the lips.

'Good morning, beautiful.'

'Good morning, my darling.'

And that short exchange alone is the very reason I should have tried to leave when I had the chance, before it was too late to witness a scene which was only ever bound to haunt me.

That's our morning greeting, mine and Max's. It was our wake-up call, each and every day of the three-thousand-odd nights we spent together. It was one of the things that had made me fall in love with Max in the first place, that inaugural morning after the night before, when we'd woken up in bed together, neither of us yet sure whether this was to be the first of many or the one and only, when he'd kissed me on the lips and uttered those three affectionate words. He was the only man I'd ever known who'd welcomed me into the day with such tenderness, and I'd been certain then that Max was different, special, worth so much more than a single night.

And now those words, like all his other terms of endearment, belong to Eve rather than to me. It's worse, somehow, witnessing this intimate morning ritual than it was hearing him proclaim his love to her for the first time. That's a declaration that can, if necessary, be faked. This is an intimacy that cannot.

'Thank you for this.'

Max strokes a strand of Eve's hair from her cheek across her shoulder.

'For which bit of it?'

'For all of it. For booking this. For arranging for Ellie to stay at Mum and Dad's. For being so thoughtful. You were right – this is just what we needed. A couple of days alone and away from it all.'

Eve grins and nibbles his ear. I wonder whether she's discovered that proclivity for herself or whether Max had to tell her about it, like he did me.

'You're very welcome. It's not like it was entirely altruistic. Eight months in and this is the first time I've had you all to myself for seventy-two glorious hours. And I intend to make the most of every second.'

Eve pounces on Max and kisses his neck in a way that somehow reminds me of a lion flooring a gazelle in a natural history documentary. Max gives in for a few seconds before pulling away distractedly.

'I know it's been hard, only getting whole nights together when Ellie's at Celia's. I do appreciate how patient you're being. It's not as if I wouldn't love to spend every weekend with you if we could.'

Max pulls Eve back into his arms but it's her turn now to extricate herself from their embrace.

'Funnily enough, I've been thinking about that.'

'About what?'

Max doesn't seem particularly interested in what Eve's been thinking about. He's kissing each of her fingers in turn and it's making me wonder what I've managed to do on other occasions to will myself away. Whatever it is doesn't seem to be working now.

'About our overnight dilemma. I was wondering whether it might be time for us to think about me staying at yours when Ellie is there?'

The inflection at the end of Eve's sentence allows it to masquerade as a question even though both she and I know it's anything but.

Max returns Eve's hand to her, the light-heartedness on his face suddenly shifting down a couple of gears.

'I . . . I thought you were okay with us taking it slowly. Easing Ellie gently into the idea of it.'

'I am. I was. I just think there'll come a time when we'll want to have a bit more freedom about when I sleep over. And I wonder whether that time might be sooner rather than later?'

That inflection again. The statement disguised as a question.

Max sits up and spends a few seconds fussily arranging the pillows behind him before leaning back on them and pulling the duvet high up over his bare chest.

'I don't know. I'd love to. Of course I would. I just think it might be too soon for Ellie.'

Eve strokes her elegant fingers along Max's naked arm.

'Baby, I think Ellie's probably a lot more robust than you give her credit for. I know you want to protect her and that's one of the many reasons I love you but things have been going really well between the three of us lately, haven't they?'

The three of them. She says it as though they're a permanent triad.

Max nods half-heartedly in unconvinced agreement, leaving Eve to continue presenting him with the evidence.

'Just think of the last few weekends we've had together, and all those days over the Easter break. She had a lovely time at the food festival and she was on great form at the water park. We've had — what? — about a dozen days together now. I think she's dealing brilliantly with it all.'

A dozen days? Eve's spent about a dozen days with my baby girl and I've only seen – or even known about – two of them. If there's anything to fuel the frustration of maternal absence, it's the awareness that you have no idea what your child's doing, who she's meeting, with whom she's spending time without your knowledge let alone your consent.

'I know. It's fantastic how relaxed she's become with you in the space of just a couple of months. You're amazing with her. But I still think single days are a different kettle of fish to sleepovers. I really don't want to provoke any setbacks. Last autumn I managed to nip things in the bud and I really don't want to go there again.'

'I completely understand and that's the last thing I want too. But it was a completely different situation then – we'd barely started dating and it was only that one time she wet the bed. Things have moved on considerably since then and I honestly think she might be ready.'

She honestly thinks? What does she know? She doesn't know my little girl or what she wants or needs or how sensitive she is to change. Come on, Max – I'm relying on you to do the right thing here.

'I'm not sure. You know how much I'd love us to be together every weekend but I'd hate for us to rush it and screw things up, just as Ellie's getting used to the idea of having you around.'

Eve leans forward on her elbows, the duvet slipping provocatively from her shoulders, and kisses Max's nose.

'I don't think we're in danger of that. We're pretty invincible, me and you.'

Eve laughs and I'm struck by how much more confident and assured she is compared to the woman who only a couple of months ago was baring her darkest secrets, almost catatonic with the fear of rejection. I'm struck, too, by how much their relationship has changed since I last saw them alone together.

Max pulls her into his arms, allowing him to hold her close while avoiding her gaze.

'It's not just Ellie. I don't want it to seem too soon to other people either. Like my mum and dad. Or Celia. I think we'd be the recipients of a raised eyebrow or two if you started sleeping over, don't you?'

'Oh baby, you know your mum and dad will be delighted for any indication that things are going well between us. They just want you to be happy. And as for Celia – well, it's not like we have to formally announce it to her so it could be weeks before that's a bridge we have to cross. Surely it's something we can deal with when the time comes?'

My blood would be boiling if it was still somehow on the move. Surely Max is going to defend my position, my mum's position, his own right to feel uncomfortable about this?

'I suppose you're right. You really don't think other people might think it's too soon, though? I don't want to be . . . well, disrespectful, I suppose.'

Eve props her head up on Max's chest and gazes at him with her Disney princess blue eyes.

'Max, next week it's going to be two years since Rachel died. I know you just want to do the right thing and I couldn't love you more for being so honourable and considerate to her memory, but you are allowed to move on with your life. And if anyone seriously doubts your integrity just because your new girlfriend sleeps over occasionally I really think that's their problem, don't you?'

With every persuasive word spoken I can feel Max slipping further away from me, yet another metaphorical mile stretching out between us.

'I guess you're right. It is only Ellie I should worry about really.'

'So why don't you ask her? It is her house after all and it wouldn't be fair for me to come and stay without her agreement. Why don't we let her decide for herself?'

Max looks contemplative but I know what his answer's going to be before he utters a word.

'You're right. Of course that's the right thing to do. And if she's uncomfortable about it, you'll be fine waiting a bit longer?'

'Of course. I'll wait as long as you need, as long as Ellie needs. I just think it's worth testing the water.'

Max smiles gratefully at Eve as though she's just solved a problem for him rather than creating one for all of us.

'You are good at all this stuff, Eve. I'll talk to Ellie next weekend.'

Another woman sleeping in my bed. With my husband. In my house. With my daughter asleep in the room next door. It's my very own Goldilocks moment.

'Now, what do you want to do today? There's that stately home not far away or we could find a nice pub and settle down with lunch and the papers.'

Eve pulls Max back under the duvet before answering him.

'Really? You want to go out? I can think of activities right here in the hotel that I'd much rather spend the day doing, unless you have any particular objections?'

I close my eyes as tightly as I can and try to think about anything that's not my husband and his beautiful girlfriend about to make love just a few feet below me. I begin to hear noises that all but the most committed voyeur would seek to avoid and start humming to myself the first song that comes to mind, one of the songs I used to sing to Ellie when she couldn't get to sleep.

A few seconds later and the only sound I can hear is my own voice. I don't dare open my eyes just yet, though, for fear that the silence may indicate not the lack of access I'm hoping for but simply a different, quieter form of activity.

Eventually, cautiously, I peek out of the corner of one eye, determined not to assail myself with the full spectacle on display if I can possibly help it.

There's nothing but whiteness. With growing confidence, I open my other eye and discover with overwhelming relief that I've been saved from becoming an invisible and inadvertent spectator of my husband's sex life.

I mentally review everything I've just witnessed in forensic detail – the affection, the endearments, the intention for Eve to embed herself ever more deeply into my daughter's life – and I realize that instead of the shock and denial or the fury and frustration I've felt before, there's a sense of emptiness, of passivity, of inertia. The feeling that comes with having witnessed the undeniable intimacy between the man who used to be my husband and the woman who may one day want to be his wife.

There's a single thought going round in my head and I cannot escape it: this feels like the beginning of the end of my presence in the centre of Max's life.

# CHAPTER 24

'I think you might need to stir the sauce a bit more, Daddy, or else it's going to go all lumpy. And I hope you're keeping an eye on the clock. You've only got five minutes left and the pressure's on.'

Max obediently stirs the sauce before returning to the chopping board, where he attacks a courgette with a paring knife.

'I hope you haven't forgotten about the dessert, Daddy. Time is running out, you know.'

Max throws her a mock-terrified look before launching open the fridge door and providing evidence that dessert – chocolate mousse by the look of it – is ready and waiting for her delectation.

I've appeared in my kitchen to find Max and Ellie playing *MasterChef*. It's one of Ellie's favourite games and she, of course, is the judge. It's a role she's perfected over the years, amalgamating the most extreme characteristics of different adjudicators from various television reality shows into one, caricatured parody. She calls herself Miss Teri Judge – a name she came up with all by herself – and, when I was alive, barely a weekend went by without the preparation of at least one meal being subjected to Ellie's playfully critical eye. It's reassuring to see that nothing much has changed.

'Be careful how thickly you're slicing those courgettes, Daddy. You know it's horrid if they're too fat. And I wouldn't want to have to mark you down for a last-minute error, would I?'

'Sorry, boss. You're absolutely right. I was going to make an avocado salad but I remembered at the last minute that it's not your favourite.'

'I *hate* avocado. I've told you that a hundred times. And you still put it in my sandwich a few weeks ago.'

Max laughs.

'That was months ago. But admittedly it was after you'd already warned me once or twice that you weren't keen. It's quite hard, you know, keeping tabs on everything you do and don't like.'

'It's not that hard, Daddy. I like everything except avocado. And liver. And black pudding. That's disgusting.'

Max pokes his tongue out at Ellie by way of a response, which she returns enthusiastically.

'I was very careful today to select only the finest ingredients that I know are favoured by Miss Teri.'

'I think that's sensible. You've been ahead all series and you wouldn't want to lose points when you're so close to the title now, would you?'

Ellie hops off the chair she's perched on and heads for the hob, where she sniffs the sauce bubbling away in a saucepan.

'It's smelling good. I just hope it's not as tangy as last time. You had way too much lemon in it then.'

'I have, of course, taken heed of your comments from the last time I cooked this dish, and I can assure you there's only the lightest splash of lemon in it this time.'

Ellie giggles.

'Three minutes, Daddy. Come on. You've still got to dress the courgette salad, drain the gnocchi, mix the sauce in, heat the plates and cut up the garlic bread.'

'Don't you worry, I have this all under control. Sort of.'

'Well, I think I'll be the judge of that in a little while.'

Ellie's loved cooking ever since I can remember. I have recollections of her as a toddler, only just able to stand independently, begging to be lifted on to a chair so she could 'help' me beat a cake mix or whisk a dressing or stir a sauce. She'd watch me sample dishes in progress and demand to emulate me, her taste buds perceptive and sophisticated long before her palate should by rights have been ready. As she got older, she became a genuine asset in the kitchen, the perfect little sous-chef. Back then it was me who did most of the cooking, not Max, but now it's him who is, by necessity, in control. And it's impressive how he's mastered the art of our family's culinary repertoire and even added a few new recipes of his own.

'It's countdown time, Daddy. Five, four, three, two, one. Finish cooking!'

As Ellie seats herself at the kitchen table, Max places the last dish on to its oak surface – a brown wicker basket heaped with garlic bread – and sits down himself with a dramatic sigh and a theatrical wiping of his brow.

'So, what are you presenting us with tonight, Daddy?'

'Well, Miss Teri Judge, tonight I've prepared gnocchi with a mushroom, lemon, onion, garlic and cream sauce, drizzled with truffle oil and served with Parmesan shavings. To accompany it we have a courgette, lemon and mint salad and, just because I know you love it, garlic ciabatta bread.'

'That sounds marvellous. But let's see how it tastes, shall we?'

Ellie dives into her first mouthful of gnocchi, adopting an exaggeratedly contemplative look on her face as she savours it. She follows it up with a couple of forkfuls of salad and concludes with a hunk of garlic bread.

'Delicious, Daddy. If your dessert is as good as your main course, then I can safely say that you're going through to the final.'

Max laughs.

'Why, thank you very much. I'm honoured, young lady.'

They fall quiet for a minute or so, while food takes precedence over conversation. It's Max who eventually breaks the silence of consumption.

'Ellie? You like Eve, don't you?'

'Yes, she's nice. She has lots of pretty clothes too.'

'She does, doesn't she. Well, I was just wondering how you might feel if sometimes – not often, just occasionally – Eve stayed here for the night, with us.'

Ellie puts her fork down and eyes Max inquisitively. I know it's wrong of me, but I can't help hoping she objects, if only to prolong the stay of emotional execution.

'Why? Does she get scared in her own house, all by herself?'

'Not really, no. I just thought it might be nice if sometimes, when she and I have been out locally for the evening, she didn't have to drive all the way home. A bit like when you have your friends here for sleepovers. Sometimes it's just more fun to have someone stay the night, isn't it?'

Ellie pauses for more thought. I'm sure she senses that Eve staying the night isn't quite the same as an eight-year-old's sleepover, but whether or not she understands precisely what the difference is it's impossible to tell.

'But where would she sleep? When my friends come over they sleep on the blow-up Barbie bed in my room but that would be much too small for Eve.'

Max looks uncomfortable, as though he hadn't contemplated the prospect of quite so many questions.

'Well, I expect she'd sleep in my room, with me.'

Ellie's face takes on a slightly bewildered air as though this wasn't a possibility that had crossed her mind until this moment and, now that it has, she'd rather it hadn't.

Max seems unnerved by the silence.

'Sweetheart, she'd only stay over if you felt okay about it. This is our house – yours and mine – and we both have to be happy about everything that happens here, don't we?'

Ellie remains quiet. I can only imagine that her silence is indicative of the fact that she's not comfortable with the prospect or else why the long hesitation?

'But don't you like it just being me and you here?'

Max places a paternal hand on top of Ellie's pale bare arm.

'Of course I do, angel. I love this being our house and us hanging out on our own together. Don't you think, though, that sometimes it might be nice to share it too?'

Ellie does as Max suggested and has a think.

'But if Eve was here you might not tuck me up in bed at night any more.'

Max risks a smile of pre-emptive relief.

'Of course I would. You know that tucking you up in bed is one of my favourite times of the whole day.'

'But you might be too busy with Eve to read me stories.'

'Sweetheart, I would never be too busy to read you stories. Our story time is the best. Three chapters a night, every night, without fail, for as long as you still want them. I promise.'

Ellie takes a strategic pause for some more thinking, her head resting thoughtfully on her hands.

'But how often would she stay? Would we still have nights here on our own, just me and you?'

'Absolutely, angel. I doubt Eve would stay over more than once or twice a week, at the most. And only really at weekends. It'll still be just me and you the majority of the time.'

'But what about my morning snuggle? I like getting into bed with you in the morning.'

Max hesitates momentarily as though he's imagining the possible alternatives and endeavouring to conclude the most appropriate response. I can see it's a minefield for him, this brave new world of single-parent relationships and, I've got to be honest, as much as I hate the subject of this particular conversation, I don't think he could be handling it any better.

'No one's ever going to stop me having my morning cuddle with my little munchkin. Maybe I'll even come and snuggle in your bed instead.'

Max tickles Ellie along her ribs and she squirms out of his reach before taking another mouthful of gnocchi, chewing it slowly, methodically, her face full of dutiful decision-making.

'Okay, Daddy. If you promise you'll still tuck me up and read books with me and we can still have our morning snuggle, I don't mind if Eve stays sometimes. But not all the time. Just a few times.'

Max leans over to kiss the top of her head and I realise that I hadn't, in truth, been expecting any other decision from her. They fall into a mutually agreeable silence, Ellie finishing the last of her supper and Max pouring himself a second glass of wine. The first, I'm guessing, was absorbed all too quickly as Dutch courage.

'Daddy?'

'Yes, munchkin.'

'Are you going to stop wearing your wedding ring?'

Max lifts his head to meet Ellie's inquisitive gaze, her question clearly the last place he expected this dinner-time chat to lead.

All of time – even my time, even the borrowed time I'm using now – seems to halt in its tracks while we both wait for Max's answer.

'What makes you ask that, sweetheart?'

'Don't know. I just wondered.'

Max hesitates, and in that deafening, loaded, unbearable silence are a multitude of possibilities I'm not yet ready to face.

He slides Ellie's chair across the wooden floorboards so that the two of them are facing one another, knees touching.

'Are you worried about me taking my wedding ring off, angel?'

Ellie shrugs, focussing intently on the floor.

'Sweetheart, I'm not planning to take my wedding ring off any time soon, I promise.'

Ellie raises her face towards Max, eyeing him with only partial reassurance.

'Ellie, do you know exactly what a wedding ring is?'

She shrugs her shoulders again, possibly because she doesn't know and doesn't want to admit it or possibly because she's not fully committed to finding out.

'When two people get married, they give each other rings because they want to let the rest of the world know that they've made a commitment to one special person. It's a symbol, a bit like the badge you have on your Brownie uniform to show everyone that you're a member of the Brownies. A wedding ring is like that; it shows everyone that you've joined a really special club with just one other person, who you love more than anyone else.'

Ellie takes a second to consider the analogy.

'So, does that mean that if you took it off one day, for good . . . would that mean you were telling everyone in the world that you don't love Mummy any more?'

'No, not at all, sweetheart. Because people can love each other without having rings to prove it. I love you, don't I, and we don't have rings?'

'That's different. You're my daddy.'

'Yes, you're right, it is different. But there are lots of people who love each other like Mummy and I did who don't have rings. What about your friend Susannah's parents? They're not married and they don't wear rings, but they still love one another, don't they? So even if I did take my ring off one day, it wouldn't mean that I didn't love Mummy still, would it?'

Ellie contemplates Max's argument for a moment before compressing her forehead into a thoughtful frown; where one answer leads, yet more questions follow.

'Does that mean you're still married to Mummy, right now, even though she's not here any more?'

It's the perfect question and one that I'd ask Max, too, if only I could. Although now that it's out there, I'm not sure I'm ready to hear the answer.

Max strokes Ellie's hair and the wait for his reply feels interminable.

'There'll always be a part of me that's married to Mummy, for as long as I live. Not just because there'll always be a part of me that loves her but because she gave me you and you're the most precious thing in the whole world to me.'

He kisses the top of her head and she grins with a mixture of pride and self-consciousness before climbing on to his lap. It's the reassurance both of us wanted and needed.

'So, Daddy, how did you know you wanted to be married to Mummy in the first place?'

'That's a very good question, sweetheart. I fell in love with Mummy at a friend's wedding. I'm sure Mummy's told you this story before but my version's a little different to hers. She was sitting opposite me on a big round table and I thought she was really, really beautiful. I couldn't help myself staring at her, but then I got worried that she'd think I was a bit odd, so I tried to stop staring but I just couldn't.'

Ellie giggles.

'So did Mummy think you were weird, then?'

No, I didn't. I thought he was wonderful. I don't think any stranger had ever paid me so much attention before, and that silent, drawn-out flirtation had been nothing short of thrilling.

'I hope not. But I was really keen to impress her and get her attention and so, in front of all the other people at our table, I started telling jokes and trying to be really funny in the hope that she'd notice me.'

'And did she think you were funny? 'Cos some of your jokes can be really bad, Daddy.'

Ellie is engrossed in the story now. She's always loved stories about our time together before she was born. Lots of children can't bear them, they can't tolerate the notion that there was life before they lived it, but Ellie's always been fascinated by her own pre-history.

'Well, I think she must have done because as soon as the meal ended and we were free to leave the table I asked her if she wanted to get a drink at the bar and she said yes. Now, she wouldn't have done that, would she, if she thought I was a weirdo?'

'She might have done if she was really bored!'

Ellie laughs at her own joke, and I watch her, proudly, marvelling at how sweet and endearing she is in spite of everything she's had to contend with.

'And then what happened?'

'Well, then we spent the rest of the evening together and I stopped being so nervous and we just had a really lovely chat. And I knew, even based on just that one conversation, that Mummy was the funniest, kindest, cleverest, loveliest, most beautiful woman I'd ever met.'

Ellie beams with the pleasure of being invited into an adult confidence, burrowing herself under Max's arm and into the crux of his shoulder.

'Was that when you started loving Mummy?'

'I suppose it was, sweetheart, yes.'

Ellie snuggles down further, then frowns, then sits upright, abruptly, as though something very important has just occurred to her.

'Daddy? Do you love Eve?'

The unearthly silence in my world is echoed in the kitchen below me, as Max allows himself a few brief seconds to contemplate his response. Even though I know the answer, I'm not sure I can bear to hear it again, or bear witness to Ellie hearing it at all.

'Yes, angel, I do. But not in the same way that I loved Mummy.'

'Why? What's the difference?'

'Well, Mummy was the first big love of my life and you can only ever have one of those.'

'Why can you only have one?'

'You can love lots of people during the course of your life but your first big love is something special. Before I met Mummy, I'd had other girlfriends and some of those I even thought I loved, but after I met Mummy I knew that it hadn't been real love before. With Mummy it was different, right from the beginning. It's magical, when you realize for the first time what it's like to love someone in a romantic way. And that first time can only happen once.'

Ellie looks thoughtful as though Max has provoked more questions than he's answered.

'But you love other people too, don't you? Like Granny and Grandpa? And Connor? And me?'

Max holds Ellie tight to his chest and rests his head on top of hers.

'Of course I do, angel. But there are different kinds of love. The way I love you is different from the way I love anyone else in the world.'

'How's it different?'

'Because you're my daughter, you're a part of me, and that makes my love for you completely unique. It's what's called unconditional love. It means I'd do anything for you, anything at all, without you even asking, if it would keep you safe and make you happy.'

Ellie ponders this for a few seconds, as if wondering how best to put it to the test.

'Anything at all, Daddy?'

'Yes, my angel. Anything.'

'In that case, please can we have dessert now because I really want some chocolate mousse.'

Max laughs and pulls himself out of his chair with Ellie still clinging to him.

'You, little one, are incorrigible. But your wish is my command. And, anyway, you can't give me my final score until we've finished the whole meal.'

As Max and Ellie head for the fridge, I feel the familiar shift of air beneath me and as Max opens the fridge door, I lose both of them completely.

I'm left alone with the bittersweet recollection of today's events. Because even the comfort of Max's paternal care can't detract from the evening's critical resolution: Eve is going to be sleeping in my bed. She's going to sleep in my bed and wake up with my husband and in no time at all it will be her – not me, not Max even – tucking Ellie in at night and reading her a bedtime story. I just know it. Eve is stepping into a ready-made family – my family – and beginning to live my life instead of me. And there's nothing I can do to stop it.

I thought my broken heart was already full with grief for the life I've lost. Now I discover there's a whole new realm of sadness waiting for me in the wings, waiting to make its entrance when I least expected it, without so much as a formal cue – grief for the life that I'll now never lead. For all the possibilities I'll now never know. For the date nights I'll never have with Max and the family holidays the three of us will never go on together. For the friends of Ellie's I'll never meet, the boyfriends I'll never disapprove of, the future husband I'll never get to know, the wedding I'll never attend. The successes I'll never share with my little girl and the failures from which I'll never help her recover. The birthdays of family and friends I'll now never celebrate, the parties and picnics I'll miss, the Christmases and Easters and Bonfire Nights I won't attend. All the countries, cities, towns, villages, islands and oceans I'll never visit, the miles of planned road trips I'll never drive, the wonders of nature that have stood for millennia that I'll now never see with my own eyes. The books I'll never read, films I'll never see, music I'll never listen to, pictures I'll never paint, piano playing I'll never properly master. The work I'll never start or finish, the jobs I'll never apply for, the professional milestones I'll never achieve. The mornings – all those thousands of expectant mornings – that I'll not wake up with Max beside me and Ellie clambering over me and know what it is to be truly grateful for the familial hand life has dealt you.

All of life, from every momentous event to every microcosmic detail, every day I hadn't yet lived and now never will. It's grief for the life I might have led. For the life that someone else is about to embark upon in my place. For the life I so desperately want back but know, deep down, I can never have.

# CHAPTER 25

'I've schlepped all the way across bloody town to check on you, at nine o'clock in the bloody evening, and now you're telling me you couldn't even be bothered to go?'

The living world has come into view – and earshot – to reveal that Harriet is shouting and angry, which isn't, in and of itself, unusual for Harriet. What is unusual is that the place where she's shouting is my kitchen and the person she's shouting at is Max.

'It's not that I couldn't be bothered. I don't know why you have to put it so scathingly. Ellie had drama club after school and I didn't want her to have to miss it.'

'That's the lamest excuse I've ever heard. Why can't you just admit that you didn't want to go?'

Harriet isn't just angry. She's upset. And getting upset isn't something Harriet does very often.

'I don't know why you're attacking me like this, Harriet. Why's it such a big deal to you what day I go?'

'You don't know? Really? You don't think I should care about the fact that my best friend's husband can't be bothered to make the fifteen-minute trip to the cemetery on the second anniversary of her death? You don't think I should give a shit about that?'

It's my two-year anniversary. I had no idea. There are no calendars up here for me to know what day of the week it is, much less which date in the year, and I gave up

340

long ago trying to keep methodical track of time passing.

Two years that I've been dead. It's strange – it feels both aeons longer and yet, at the same time, like it was only yesterday that I found myself here and wondered whether this was a version of heaven or hell or something altogether different in between.

And today Max didn't take Ellie to the cemetery to visit my headstone. Today he's chosen not to commemorate the moment I left them. Today he is, perhaps, allowing Ellie to forget. And if that's the case I don't know how to feel anything other than desolate at the prospect.

'Harriet, I don't need you to tell me how to remember my wife. And I don't appreciate you coming here and shouting at me in my own house, not least while Ellie's asleep upstairs.'

'Well, you clearly do need to be told given that ever since Blondie came into your life you've been acting as though Rach never even existed.'

Max grips the wooden work surface and I can see that it's taking all his self-control not to rise to Harriet's bait.

Is she wrong, though? Because the only explanation I can think of as to why he's chosen not to take Ellie today is that his preoccupation with Eve has relegated me to little more than an afterthought in his life, even today of all days.

'Harriet, I think it's best if you don't bring Eve into this, if for nothing else than for the sake of our friendship. Ellie's coming with me to the cemetery on Saturday. It's not getting the date right that's important for Ellie. It's about ensuring the act of remembrance. And we'll be doing that at the weekend.'

Harriet seems apoplectic now.

'That's not good enough, Max. It is about the date. It's everything about the date. Can you imagine, for a second, that if the tables were turned Rach wouldn't have taken Ellie to visit your headstone today?'

No, I can't. I can't imagine that. I like to think that I would have gone to visit him on every anniversary, for the rest of time, and ensured that Ellie was by my side on each and every occasion.

'Really, Max, this isn't about you. It's about Ellie, and it's obvious that the reason you're getting so defensive is because you know I'm right. You know it's a dereliction of paternal duty not to have stood before that headstone with her and honoured Rach's memory today.'

Max has been staring intently out of the kitchen window, his back towards Harriet, as if evading her gaze will ensure the avoidance of conflict, but suddenly he swerves towards her, his eyes betraying a fury I've never seen in him before.

'A dereliction of duty? I'm supposed to take this from *you* of all people, someone who doesn't even have children, someone who thinks that money and status and having their name mentioned in some stupid lawyer's journal once in a while is an adequate substitute for real human relationships? Don't you dare lecture me about how to raise my daughter when you haven't got a maternal bone in your body.'

The room erupts into a deafening silence. I've never known emptiness so palpable before. Max is hunched over the kitchen sink, spent, depleted, almost certainly reviling himself already for the outburst. Harriet is static, her face rigid with shock, seemingly unsure whether she's incapable of moving or simply unwilling. A few seconds pass, neither of them speaking, not even the sound of their breath disrupting the atmosphere.

Suddenly Harriet rushes to grab her bag from the table and all but stumbles out of the kitchen. The front door slams behind her a couple of seconds later.

Max grabs a cup from the draining board and hurls it into the sink, shattering it on impact. The crash creates a turbulence both in his world and mine; my access disappears in an explosive instant. No gradually assembling clouds this time, no faint tremor of air, no tentative mist to forewarn me of my impending exit. Just an abrupt ending, as though a light had been switched on, bathing the conflict beneath me in unbearable brightness.

I keep seeing that look of rage on Max's face, and I fear for whether their relationship will recover. I think about Harriet and where she might have gone – to a bar? back to the office? home alone? – and about how Max's words seemed to sting her with a sharpness against which she'd normally be able to anaesthetize herself. I think about that decisive ending, about Harriet's incensed departure, and I can't imagine what external force will persuade her to come back through that door again.

I think about how painful it is to watch them argue, how frustrating it is to be impotent to intervene, to mediate a resolution, to ensure that this isn't a permanent fracture.

But Harriet's right. Of course the date matters. And Max's decision not to commemorate the day with Ellie is his most definitive declaration yet that he's consigning me to a distant corner of their lives, to the most secluded recess in the ancestral attic, to the final resting place in familial history.

Since the very beginning, from the moment I arrived here and realized that life, for me, was no longer to be lived but merely to be viewed silently and invisibly, my greatest fear has been not the netherworld's isolation, nor the possibility of never returning, nor the fantasies about what, if anything, may come after this place. My greatest fear has been to discover one day that I've been forgotten. To watch on painfully, powerless, as I view my own demise in the memories of the people I love. To observe the little life I have left, the vestiges of remembrance, gradually disperse like vapour rising from a lake on the coldest of days.

It's not the mortality of the body that's the real tragedy of the dead. It's the dissolution of memory. For the dead, to be forgotten is as if never to have lived at all.

But maybe that's the fate we all face in the end. Not if we'll be forgotten but, simply, when.

# Testing

# CHAPTER 26

I don't understand. I've surfaced in Max's bedroom – our bedroom – to the discovery that I'm as alone here as I am in my own world. This has never happened before. I always arrive to people, to Max and Ellie and whomever they're with and wherever they are. I've never descended upon an empty room before.

I haven't been in this room for ages, not for about a year I think. In spite of the quietness there's a nostalgic reassurance to be back here. It's all pretty much as I remember it: the white painted iron bedstead enveloped by a now slightly off-white duvet cover and the tattered brown leather armchair which was only ever used to house discarded clothes we were too lazy to hang up in the wardrobe. There's the chest of drawers we bought from a second-hand shop, the one Max thought I was crazy parting with cash for, until I sanded and varnished it and even he had to concede that it had been a bargain. And there's the Braque print above the bed, a wedding present from my mum, the two blue birds that greeted me every morning for all those years.

But there, by my side of the bed, is the only unfamiliar object on display. It's a brown leather holdall, suspiciously consistent with the kind of bag someone might use for an overnight stay. And there's only one person I can think of who'd be leaving an overnight bag by my side of the bed.

I hear voices coming from the kitchen and head downstairs with the weight of a thousand rocks sinking in my stomach, painfully cognizant of who I'm going to find before I even get there.

Eating chocolate ice cream in the kitchen are Max, Ellie and, of course, Eve. She has, quite literally, got her feet under my table.

'So was it today that you had to hand in your art project, munchkin?'

'No.'

'So, when is it?'

'Dunno.'

'But you've worked so hard on it, you must know when it is?'

Ellie shrugs her shoulders, her eyes fixed doggedly on the dessert in front of her. Max looks at Ellie, frowning, and then at Eve, embarrassed. He seems a bit bemused, leaving Eve to take up the conversational reins.

'Did you find out any more about your end-of-year school trip, Ellie? Have they decided on the seaside or an adventure park yet?'

'Dunno.'

'Which one do you hope they're going to pick?'

'Don't care.'

Max and Eve trade a look of concern. It's a silent, collusive exchange, one that firmly establishes them as the adult group from which Ellie's excluded. I feel sad on her behalf, for the little girl who, for whatever reason, just doesn't feel like being chatty with her dad and his new girlfriend tonight.

They finish their ice cream in silence, Ellie barely raising her head and steadfastly refusing to meet anyone's gaze.

'Eve?'

Ellie fiddles with the cuff on her cardigan, her eyes focussed intently on a loose thread at which she's gently tugging.

'Where do you live?'

'You know where she lives, Ellie. Stoke Newington. Why are you asking?'

Max's interjection is abrupt, impatient. I don't understand what's occurring between the three of them this evening, but whatever game they're playing it doesn't appear to be Happy Families.

'I just wondered. Do you like your house, Eve?'

Eve smiles at Ellie – an open, trusting smile – and I don't think she detects any danger in Ellie's tone yet. But I can see the agitation behind her eyes.

'Yes, I love my house, Ellie. It's really cosy. It has a lovely fireplace in the sitting room, where I can have real log fires in the winter, just like you can here, and the bathroom has a gorgeous old Victorian bath in it. And I think you'd like my bedroom – I decorated it with floral wallpaper which is really pretty. You should come and see it sometime.'

I watch Ellie's face as Eve talks and see an ominously familiar cloud cast a shadow over her innocence. She's weighing up the pros and cons, assessing the risks, deciding whether the action she's considering is worthy of the potential ramifications.

'So, if you like your own house so much, why do you have to come and sleep at our house tonight?'

'Ellie. Stop that now. I won't have you being rude to Eve like that.'

Max is frustrated but he's yet to give way to anger. I can see the petulance and defiance radiating from Ellie's eyes. In siding with Eve instead of her, Max has thrown down the gauntlet and it looks like a challenge Ellie's more than ready to accept.

'I wasn't being rude. I was only asking a question. If Eve doesn't like it that's not my fault.'

Eve opens her mouth to respond, but Max dives in first.

'You're being rude and you know full well that you are. If you can't sit with us nicely and be polite then perhaps you should go to your room.'

'Perhaps *you* should go to *your* room. With Eve. Isn't that what you'd rather do?'

There's a shocked silence while we all absorb the impact of Ellie's fury. She's blinking, fast and frequently, a sign I know all too well as the harbinger of tears.

'That's enough, Ellie. I want you to apologize to Eve, right now.'

Ellie jumps out of her chair, as though standing to deliver her next round of ammunition will lend credibility to her argument.

'Why are you being so mean to me? Eve's suddenly allowed to just turn up at our house and stay the night and do whatever she wants and I'm not even allowed to ask a question about it. Why are you being so unfair?'

Ellie stands staring at Max, her fists clenched and her breath heavy, waiting to see what he'll do next. Now's the moment for Max to prove the point that Ellie so desperately needs validating, to pass the test she's so clearly setting; that he's watching her back, that he'll take her side, that he'll forgive her her trespasses as she'll forgive Eve for trespassing against her. For trespassing all over her house, no less.

'I'm not going to ask you again, Ellie. I want you to apologize to Eve.'

Ellie's face is crimson with rage now, her bottom lip quivering with restrained anguish, and I want Max to stop, I want him to think, I want him to bury his embarrassment, just for a second, and put our daughter's needs first. I want to hold him by the shoulders and look him in the eye and remind him that our little girl's never rude to anyone, that she hardly ever misbehaves, that for her to act out like this tonight she must be unsettled by something. And that it's more than likely – it's obvious, isn't it? – that what she's upset about is Eve sleeping over. I want to be able to haul Ellie on to my lap and settle her emotional storm and hold Max's hand and put an end to this rarest of conflicts between the two people I love most in the world.

But it's not me, in the end, who's afforded the opportunity to defuse the situation.

'Really, Max, it's okay. We've all had a long week and we're all a bit over-tired. Let's just have a nice evening and forget about it.'

For once, for the first time ever, I find myself willing Max to listen to Eve's advice. But the look of determination on his face, so perfectly and ironically mirroring that of his opponent, tells me that he has no intention of backing down.

'It's not okay. Now, Ellie, for the last time, will you please apologize to both of us for being so rude?'

Ellie's face disintegrates. Hot tears erupt like lava from the angriest of volcanoes, burning her cheeks with righteous protest, her eyes scorched with humiliation. She has little option but to storm out of the room and up the stairs, where she slams her bedroom door with a thud of fury.

Neither Max nor Eve speak. I watch the anger drain from Max's face as the first, tentative signs of guilt dare to make themselves known in the lines on his forehead. Eve fiddles with the pendant hanging around her neck, watching him earnestly as though awaiting an indication of what's supposed to happen next. Max appears to be in no hurry to break the silence.

'I'm sorry, Max. It looks like you were right. I honestly thought she'd be okay with it. I'd never have suggested it if I didn't.'

Max turns towards her with a momentary look of confusion, as though he'd forgotten she was still in the room.

'Well, I don't take any pleasure in being right on this one.'

He averts his gaze again and I detect a fleeting disturbance on Eve's face – whether hurt or irritation or fear or indignation I can't tell – as Max leaves her stranded in another loaded silence.

After what seems like ages to me, and probably even longer to Eve, Max leans across and takes Eve's hand in his.

'I'm sorry. It's not your fault. It was my call at the end of the day. I should have listened to my instincts on it rather than be swayed by the fact that Ellie seemed fine when I asked her about it.'

Eve puts her hand on top of Max's, her face awash with contrition.

'I'm sorry too. It's really disappointing. I so wanted tonight to go well.'

'I know you did. I did too. But maybe we were just a bit naive on this one.'

He's gallantly used the plural even though all three of us know there's a singular cause for tonight's emotional fiasco.

'I have to go and check on Ellie now.'

They finally look one another in the eye and there's a heartbeat of tension before Eve replies.

'I know you do. It's fine. Really. I'll clear up down here.'

Max makes his way up the stairs and into Ellie's room where he finds her, face down, sobbing unremittingly into her fluffy dog pillow. He sits on the bed next to her and places a placatory hand on her shoulder. Ellie shrugs him off with a violent rejection that I've no doubt surprises us all.

'Don't touch me! I don't want you to touch me! Leave me alone.'

Max looks perplexed. I don't think he'd allowed himself to see before quite how upset she was.

'Hey, sweetheart. What's going on? I'm sorry I got cross with you. I just didn't like you being rude like that. It's not like you. Do you want to tell me what's wrong?'

He ventures a second attempt at physical contact, this time stroking her back, gently, tentatively, an action Ellie is usually unable to resist.

'Get off me! I don't want you to hug me. I don't want you to touch me. I want Mummy. I just want my mummy.'

She's hysterical now, tears streaming down her face, her voice choking on angry sobs. I've never seen her like this before, never seen her so distressed, never heard her so distraught. And I've never wanted anything so much as to take her in my arms, to stroke her hair and kiss her forehead and give her back the security she so desperately craves. It's the only expectation a child has of their mother, the unconditional love and care and reassurance that should be every child's birthright, and it's the one thing I'm failing to give her when she needs it most.

Max, I can see, is fighting back the tears too. He's been hit by a tsunami of grief for which he was, today, completely unprepared. His only hope this evening had been the cosy domesticity of sleeping, for the first time, under the same roof as the daughter he adores and the woman he's now in love with.

'Hey there, munchkin. Can you try and take a deep breath and let it out really slowly for me? I know you miss Mummy, and I know lots of things are really, really hard for you, but please try and remember that I'm here for you and so is Eve and we're both going to look after you.'

Ellie suddenly sits bolt upright as if physically assaulted by Max's words and she struggles to articulate herself amidst the crying.

'I don't want her to look after me. I don't even want her here. I hate her. She doesn't know how to look after children. She doesn't even have any children of her own.'

She's shouting now and there's not even a sliver of doubt that Eve would be able to hear her outburst downstairs.

'Ellie, sweetheart, you have to try and calm down. I know you're upset, I can see you're angry, but I can only help make it better if you let me.'

'I don't want you to make anything better. I hate you. I wish Mummy was here. I wish Mummy was here and you weren't. I just want Mummy back.'

Ellie's crying so hard now I'm worried she's going to make herself sick. I'm desperate to be with her, to be the mother she needs, to be able to hold her and kiss her and let her know just how much I love her.

I thought there was nothing worse than to watch your child suffer and be powerless to intervene, to help, to remedy. Now I understand that it's immeasurably worse to know you're the cause of the very pain you're unable to relieve.

Max takes decisive action, pulling Ellie into his arms and holding her so tightly, so securely, that she couldn't escape the love of his embrace even if she tried. He begins to hum, ever so gently, one of the lullabies I used to sing to Ellie at bedtime when she was small. Over and over he repeats the same few lines until slowly, gradually, her defences soften and, sobbing still, she allows her body to relax into Max's arms. Eventually, amidst heartbreaking whimpers and the last remnants of tears, she lifts her head from where it's buried in his chest.

'That's Mummy's song.'

'I know, angel. But I don't think she'll mind me borrowing it just this once, do you?'

Ellie's short, shallow breaths begin to relax as she looks up thoughtfully at Max, her face still stained with the tears and temporary blemishes of her breakdown.

Max continues singing my favourite bedtime song, 'Goodnite, Sweetheart, Goodnite,' rocking Ellie back and forth in his arms where she's still curled up in his lap. After a few bars, Ellie joins in and I'm amazed she can still remember the words. It's been over two years since I last sang it to her.

The two of them sit together, singing the song that's reminiscent of so many nights with Ellie huddled in my own arms, of evenings bathing her before bed, of reading to her in her pyjamas, of singing to her until she slept. Invisible, inaudible, I hover above them and begin to sing too, the three of us joined together by the same tune from opposite sides of the life divide.

We sing the chorus over and over, the only few lines that any of us know, the song which spoke to Ellie back then of a night's separation but whose resonance now is so much more profound, so much more poignant.

'Daddy, I'm sorry I was horrible to you earlier.'

'There's absolutely no need to apologize, angel. I'm sorry I made you so sad.'

Ellie takes Max's hand in hers and fiddles absent-mindedly with the ring on his fourth finger.

'It's just . . . this is our family and I like it just being me and you.'

Ellie's whispered the words as though there may be danger attached to voicing them too loudly.

Max strokes her forehead and holds her even tighter.

'Angel, our family will always be me and you at heart. And Mummy. Other people may come and go, some of them may even stay – one day I hope you'll get married and have children of your own – but the three of us will always be special to each other. Because this is the first family you ever knew and no one can ever change that.'

'Not even if someone else starts sleeping here a lot?'

'Not even once you're big and grown-up and want to go and live somewhere without your daddy hanging around any more. Sweetheart, you're always going to be my number one priority. No one will ever, ever be more important to me.'

Ellie allows a pulse of silence to pass.

'Not even Eve?'

Max holds Ellie's face in his hands and looks at her with the intensity of someone determined to communicate the strength of their feeling.

'No one, angel. I promise. Eve wants to be friends with you because she knows how much I love you and she'd like to know for herself just how special you are. That's all.'

Ellie yawns and rubs her eyes and Max helps her into her pyjamas, before she summons the energy to haul her limbs under the duvet and into bed.

'Daddy, will you stay with me till I fall asleep?'

'Of course I will, munchkin.'

'You promise not to leave? Even though Eve's downstairs, all by herself?'

'Sweetheart, I'm not going anywhere, I promise you.'

Ellie holds his hand in hers and closes her eyes. It's less than a minute before the depth of her breathing indicates that she is, already, fast asleep. Max extricates himself from her embrace and tiptoes silently from the room.

I stay with her, watching over my slumbering angel in wonderment. It's two years since I witnessed this and it remains, unequivocally, the most beautiful sight in the world. Her eyelids flutter with dreams I hope are happy, and her nose occasionally twitches as it always has done in the early stages of sleep. She's so peaceful now it's hard to imagine that just minutes ago she was so distraught. Hard to imagine, too, all that she's had to endure and all she has yet to contend with.

I'm full of love for her, but it's a love of regret and longing and absence. The bittersweet love of a mother unable to perform that most instinctive, that most primordial, that most critical of tasks: to protect their child from all of life's harm through the sheer power of maternal presence.

I could watch Ellie sleep all night, but the netherworld has alternative plans. I feel myself being drawn away from her bedroom, lifted high up above it as the clouds gather beneath me until Ellie disappears from view and there's nothing left for me to see but empty space.

# CHAPTER 27

'You look tired.'

Max rubs a hand up and down Eve's back where they're both standing, in their pyjamas, in my kitchen.

'I didn't sleep that well. I just couldn't stop worrying about last night. I know you said Ellie was okay by the time she went to sleep but it was a pretty horrible evening all round, Max.'

So it's the morning after the night before.

'I know. But we can't undo what happened yesterday. We've just got to try and hope that things are a bit better this morning.'

Eve retrieves the stove pot from the cupboard next to the oven and starts making coffee with a familiarity I instinctively baulk at. This may have been her first time sleeping over with Ellie in the house but it's clearly not her first breakfast here.

'I know you're trying to be optimistic and I know I should do the same but I can't help feeling a bit helpless about it all. Why should Ellie want another woman in her house after all? I wouldn't if I were her. I can't blame her for wanting you all to herself.'

Max smiles and pulls Eve into his arms.

'Now that, Eve Abraham, is the truest thing you've said all morning.'

Eve laughs while nonetheless pulling free from his embrace.

'But seriously, Max. What are we going to do? Perhaps I shouldn't see Ellie at all for a while? Give her a bit of space with you, that's probably what she needs, isn't it?'

'I don't think we should be making any rash decisions about anything right now. Let's allow the dust to settle this weekend and then take a view. Okay?'

Before Eve has time to answer, Ellie bounds into the room with her customary morning effervescence.

'I'm starving. What's for breakfast?'

Ellie flops into one of the kitchen chairs, her fluffy white-and-purple polka dot dressing gown tied snugly around her waist, her dog-slippered feet swinging energetically under the table.

Max and Eve exchange a tentatively optimistic glance by the hob before Eve turns to answer.

'I thought I might make some French toast. If you fancy it, that is.'

'Yum. French toast is my favourite.'

'I know, a little bird told me. Have you ever tried it with maple syrup before?'

'No. That sounds weird but kind of nice. Is that what we're having this morning?'

'Well, I thought we might, if you'd like to try it?'

Eve starts beating eggs and milk, while Max and Ellie sit at the kitchen table, Ellie at the laptop playing games, Max on his tablet reading out snippets of news to Eve. It's nothing short of domestic bliss, the calm after the storm, a hint of how harmoniously this new composition may yet play out after last night's discord.

It takes me back to all those hundreds of mornings when I was the woman preparing Ellie's favourite breakfast for her. It was a weekend ritual between us from the time she was old enough to express her own mealtime preferences, a ritual that I'd assumed would continue for many years to come, interrupted only perhaps by the customary years of teenage withdrawal, resumed again when a family breakfast was once more to be enjoyed rather than endured. I'd always imagined that one day I'd be sitting with Ellie and her own children around the kitchen table – perhaps not that exact table, perhaps not this precise kitchen, but with the same enthusiasm for French toast, the same cosy domesticity, the same feeling of complete happiness that accompanies a day begun with the people we love the most.

'Here we go, Ellie. There's one slice to get you started, and there's more going in the pan now. Don't forget the maple syrup.'

Ellie slathers the warm, crisp toast with maple syrup and takes a comically oversized mouthful.

'Mmm. This is delicious. This is definitely my favourite breakfast of all. Mummy used to make me French toast nearly every weekend.'

'Well, I'm sure this isn't as good as your mummy's. No one's cooking is ever as good as your mum's.'

Ellie takes another mouthful, responding before she's quite swallowed it all.

'Mummy's French toast was the best. But this is really good too. Daddy, can we start having this for breakfast every weekend again?'

'Well, I don't know about every weekend, sweetheart. But we can definitely have it more often, if you'd like.'

Ellie grins with the delight of a child in possession of a promise. As Eve returns to the hob to embark on the second batch, Ellie follows her and, apropos of nothing in particular beyond culinary gratitude, wraps her arms around Eve's body in what is unmistakably an unsolicited, spontaneous hug.

'Thank you, Eve. The breakfast is really nice.'

Eve turns around to face her, glancing with shy pleasure at Max on the way. He's grinning with pride – whether for Eve or Ellie, I'm not sure – as Eve lifts Ellie into her arms.

'You're quite welcome, little one. I'm glad you're enjoying it.'

Ellie rests her head next to Eve's neck, her legs wrapped round the perfect waist of this ready-made maternal substitute, her arms draped over blonde shoulders. As she absent-mindedly strokes Eve's back I wonder whether it's possible to die twice from a broken heart.

I want nothing more in the world than for Ellie to be happy, settled, comforted, cared for. Nothing could be worse than witnessing her distress last night. But I'd always assumed that the fiercest of my netherworldian heartbreaks would be to watch Max fall in love with another woman. Now I discover it is, in fact, to see Ellie do the falling.

The doorbell rings and I'm guessing from the looks of surprise around the kitchen table that they're not expecting anyone.

Ellie jumps down from Eve's arms with the anticipation of an excitable puppy.

'Can I answer the door, Daddy. *Please*. I am eight now, after all.'

Max laughs and tilts his head by way of a sanction, prompting Ellie to scamper out of the room before he changes his mind.

In the absence of his daughter's vigilant eyes, I watch as Max walks over to Eve and embraces her from behind, brushing the hair clear of one shoulder and talking quietly into her ear.

'You're amazing with her. We can do this, you know. It's going to be fine.'

He rewards the top of her shoulder with multiple, rhythmic kisses, his breath no doubt warm on her neck, his hands on her arms no doubt offering the gentlest of reassuring embraces.

'Look who's here!'

Ellie bolts back into the room tailed by none other than my mum, who's arrived just in time to catch the last vestiges of her son-in-law, in his pyjamas, kissing the bare neck of his new girlfriend, also in her pyjamas, in the kitchen of her daughter's house first thing on a Saturday morning.

In the few seconds of heavily pregnant silence that follow, I watch my mum's eyes dart shrewdly around the room, absorbing each individual fragment of information in order to reach the irrefutable conclusion.

You'd need an axe to cut through the atmosphere in here.

'Do you want some French toast, Nanna? Eve made it with maple syrup and it's really yummy.'

Mum turns to Ellie, a rictus grin fixed on to her face.

'No thank you, darling. I've had breakfast already.'

The temporary respite from silence over, it's a few more seconds before Max regains sufficient composure to find his voice.

'Well, it's nice to see you, Celia. What are you doing in town this weekend? You hadn't said you might pop by?'

It's intoned as a question but he's failed to keep the hint of accusation from his voice. I feel desperately sorry for Mum. This is a scene no grieving mother needs to witness.

'I'm just on my way to stay with some friends in Highgate for the weekend so I thought I'd pop in and say hello en route. I'm sorry – I thought you'd be up and dressed by now. It is nearly ten. I didn't realize I'd be interrupting anything.'

Her tone is of contrition, though I sense it's herself she's feeling most sorry for and, quite honestly, I don't blame her.

'Don't be silly. You're not interrupting. Can I at least get you a cup of tea?'

There's an effort to sound casual in his voice but I doubt anyone bar Ellie will be duped by it.

'I'm fine, thank you, Max. I wonder if I might just have a quick word? In the sitting room? In private?'

Max nods, sheepishly, and follows her out of the kitchen. The door's barely closed behind them before Mum starts speaking in an anguished, indignant whisper.

'How could you, Max? How could you be so insensitive?'

'Celia, I didn't know you were coming today. I don't think it's fair to accuse me of being insensitive when I didn't even know we'd be seeing you this morning.'

'I don't mean me being here and seeing that. I mean *her* being here, today of all days.'

'I don't understand. Why today of all days?'

'You mean it really hasn't occurred to you? You don't think it's a little inconsiderate to have her ensconced in my daughter's house this weekend? You didn't think Harriet would have told me that you didn't take Ellie to the cemetery on Thursday? And that you're supposed to be taking her today? Although I don't suppose even that's happening now if she's here.'

Max emits the sigh of a man who knows that he has to upset some of the people most of the time.

'Of course I'm still taking Ellie to the cemetery today.'

'Please don't tell me she's going with you?'

'Her name's Eve, and no, of course she's not. Ellie and I are going on our own.'

Mum seems almost disappointed by this, as though her anger would have been better served by a different response. She lowers herself on to the sofa, the sting removed from the confrontational tail.

'I still think it's wrong, her being here this week of all weeks. I know you want to move on with your life, and I'm trying to be supportive of that, really I am, but don't you think there are some times that are sacred, that should be preserved just for family?'

Max sits down next to Mum, his face full of the placation I know so well.

365

'Honestly, Celia? Yes and no. Of course I think it's important to take Ellie to the cemetery and for us to mark the anniversary, though I disagree with you and Harriet that it has to be on the exact day. Not at Ellie's age, anyway. And on the subject of me moving on, I know this is hard for you, and I'm trying to sympathize with your position too, but I honestly think that two years isn't a bad time for me to be making these kinds of transitions.'

Mum's face resumes her look of annoyance and I can see that Max has, inadvertently, riled her all over again.

'Two years is nothing, Max. It's the blink of an eye in the course of a lifetime. I just wish you could have waited a little longer. Would it really have been impossible for you to have given it a bit more time, to have allowed the dust of Rachel's memory to settle, before you brought another woman into her home? This was Rachel's home, Max. How do you think she'd feel knowing there was another woman staying here now?'

It's a rhetorical question, not simply because I'm not there to respond, but because Mum's tone has already made it clear what the answer is.

'I honestly don't know, Celia. I can only try and do what feels right, here and now. It's taken all this time but I think I'm only just beginning to understand how much shock I was in after Rachel died. I think the abruptness made it almost impossible to comprehend that she really had gone. It's been the most difficult thing I've ever had to acknowledge, that my day-to-day life with her is over. But I think I finally have, and so in a way I suppose it does feel like this is the right time to start moving on. Because however much I wish it weren't the case, Rachel's not here for me to share my life with any more, and it feels like either I accept that or I spend the next forty-odd years in a permanent state of denial.'

Max's tone is gentle, imploring, patiently indisputable. It's why so many of our conflicts – mine and his – ended so quickly, so calmly. It's a tone that's difficult to argue against, a tone that's difficult to resist. And it's a tone he maintains as he continues talking.

'Look, I know it must have been a bit of a shock, walking in to find Eve here this morning. But she really is very nice and she's great with Ellie. I think she's great for Ellie. I'm not suggesting for a second that it won't be hard for you, but I'd really like you to get to know her and to be able to spend time with all three of us in the future.'

It's the most heartfelt of entreaties and it seems to me almost perverse that so much can be said in two short speeches.

Because this is the first time I've heard Max so clearly express an intention to build a life without me. A life in which he loves another woman. A life in which he'll allow – encourage, even – someone else to mother my child. I feel like I'm watching the death of my marriage, a marriage I have no desire to dissolve and yet one which I'm powerless to save. As though Max has handed me a decree absolute for a divorce I never agreed to.

'Do you really mean that, Max?'

'Mean what?'

'That you want me involved in your life with Eve? That you'd like us all to spend time together?'

'Of course I do. Why wouldn't I?'

Mum's shoulders relax with the relief of receding anxieties.

'I've just been so worried, Max. I didn't know how you'd feel about having your ex-mother-in-law around while you're . . . while you're starting a new relationship. To be honest, I've felt like little more than a glorified babysitter for the past few months.'

Max places a sympathetic hand on Mum's arm.

'I'm so sorry if I've made you feel like that. Of course you're always going to be part of our lives. Ellie's only got two grandmothers and I don't think she'd ever give up either of you without a damn good fight.'

All three of us smile at the thought of Ellie's tenacity.

'Thank you, Max. That means so much, more than you could possibly know. And I know I don't tell you often enough, but I do think you're doing a marvellous job with Ellie. I'm really very proud of you. And Rachel would be proud of you too.'

She's right, I am. I didn't realize until after Ellie was born that choosing the person with whom you'll have children is probably the most important decision you'll ever make in life. And it wasn't until I died that I realized the full extent of my gratitude towards the person with whom I'd been lucky enough to make that choice.

'I hope she would. All I'm doing really is carrying on the work she started, that she and I started together. I've no doubt that the reason Ellie's so amazing and resilient is because of everything that Rachel gave her in those first six years, all the love and patience and affection and encouragement. Ellie's the person she is because of

Rachel, there's no doubt at all in my mind about that. So I guess Rachel and I are proud of each other.'

There's a calmness wrapped up in the warmth of Max's voice that I don't think I've heard before.

'Well, I'm certainly proud of both of you. And I know I've got to let you move on, at a pace that feels right for you. It's just different for me, I suppose. I'm not sure there's much for me to move on to.'

'Don't be silly. You've got Ellie and me and I think you've got more friends than the two of us put together. I'm often exhausted just hearing about your social life.'

'I keep busy because I have to, Max. Because if I didn't I'd think about Rachel even more than I do now. I know it's terrible for you, losing your wife at such a young age. I know how I felt when Robert died. But losing a child is something else entirely. It's the cruellest abomination of nature. When you think about all that love you put into raising them, all that time you invest in their happiness, all the hopes you have for their future, you never imagine for a second that they might not have the chance to fulfil everything you dreamed for them. When Robert died I was distraught, of course I was. But when Rachel was taken from me I felt as though the natural order of things had been turned upside down. As though the world had gone mad. The one thing you expect when you have a child is that they'll outlive you. That's how it's supposed to be, isn't it? So I don't expect there'll ever be a time for me when anything feels quite right again.'

Mum's voice is quiet and measured, as though resigned to the iniquitous hand fate has dealt her. And it's somehow all the more upsetting for her sober acknowledgement of it.

Max puts an arm around her shoulders and, as I watch my husband comfort my mum, I can't hold back the miniature wells of loneliness forming in the corners of my eyes. My tears drop sedately on to the gathering clouds below and I know that my access, for today, is at the beginning of its end.

Seconds later, back in the empty void I now think of as home, my mind begins wandering to places it probably shouldn't visit, to thoughts of the new trinity – of Max, Ellie and Eve – and the possible life they'll have together, without me. All this time I've been so preoccupied with my guilt about abandoning them that I haven't prepared myself – not really, not deep down – for what it would feel like the day they began abandoning me. And now that they are I really don't know what to feel about it. Because how does one possibly square the circle of desire that your husband and daughter should be loved with the sadness and regret that you're not the person able to provide it?

# CHAPTER 28

White gradually gives way to blue before the sun emerges too, revealing the clearest and brightest of days. There's a wide gravel pathway flanked on either side by sculpted gardens dotted with immaculately pruned miniature conifers. Ahead is a majestic, red-brick palace, sunlight bathing the walls in tangible warmth giving it the aura of a building contentedly on fire. The leaves on the trees in the near distance are burnt orange, golden, defiantly crimson; it's the perfect autumnal day.

If autumn, it must be over four months since I was last here. I've missed the whole summer. Four months of Ellie's life that have elapsed without me. A third of a year is a lifetime in an eight-year-old's development. Who knows how much she might have changed in my absence, how much taller, broader, happier or sadder she might be?

Four months of Max's relationship developing without my knowledge, too. Now I'm here I'm not sure I dare contemplate the possible evolution of his love affair, even though I've speculated about little else in my time apart.

I've been to this place before. Last time Ellie was in a buggy, wearing a red-and-pink polka dot dress and a white cotton sun hat that I was forever putting back on her head after she'd yanked it off with irritation. The sun that day was higher, hotter, less forgiving. Max had pushed the buggy, his well-defined cyclist's calves emerging from khaki shorts, his eyes protected from the glare by comically over-sized sunglasses he insisted were fashionable. I remember sweat trickling down my back and my fear that the loose cotton sundress I was wearing would fail to conceal the evidence. We spent most of that visit taking refuge in the coolness of the house, regretting having left the shaded sanctuary of our garden on such an unrelenting day.

Today it's a much more grown-up Ellie who's walking towards the visitor entrance of Hampton Court Palace, hand in hand with her daddy, her clothes today very much her own choice, I'm sure – dark blue skinny jeans, green Converse shoes and a pistachio-coloured mac complete with butterfly-shaped toggles. She hasn't, I'm relieved to see, altered all that much; her hair's been cut since I last saw her but it's still long and beautiful, still bouncing happily below her shoulders. She's carrying a small purple handbag, the strap swung over her shoulder in imitation of the grown woman she'll one day become, the only indication that she's got just that little bit older, just that little bit more mature, in my absence.

There's no sign of Eve today and I'm grateful; grateful I can spend some time with Max and Ellie on their own. Grateful they're spending time alone together too.

Tickets procured, they begin their self-guided tour of the house, Max in his element, passing historical knowledge to Ellie as if it were as critical for her personal development as the DNA he bequeathed her nine years ago.

They're wandering through the first room, Max regaling Ellie with the soap opera of the Tudor dynasty, when he suddenly interrupts his own train of speech.

'Sweetheart, you like Eve, don't you? You and she get on really well, don't you think?'

My ears tune in immediately to what sounds like the beginnings of a conversation I don't want to miss.

'Yeah, she's fun. And I really like it when she helps me with my homework. Especially Maths. I hate Maths.'

Max squeezes Ellie playfully on the shoulder and she pretends to wriggle free of his grasp.

'I think you made that perfectly clear last weekend when you announced you couldn't see the point of it when you could do sums much more easily on the computer.'

Ellie giggles.

'But it's true.'

Max issues Ellie with one of his mock-disapproving frowns.

'Outside of Maths, though, you like the three of us spending time together, don't you? We've had a lovely summer, haven't we?'

'I love the summer holidays. I wish school hadn't started again so soon. When can we go camping again?'

They went camping? I just can't picture Eve in a sleeping bag, somehow.

'We could go at half term, if you like, if the weather's not too bad. It wasn't much fun that night it rained, was it?'

They both start laughing in recollection of a memory I'm unable to share.

'Eve was so silly when the tent started leaking and she thought there was an animal in her hair. That was funny.'

I try to imagine the three of them hunkering down in a tent together, a true test of familial authenticity, but something stops the picture forming in my mind.

'It's really nice that Eve enjoys so many of the things we like, isn't it? Like our Sunday country walks. And our cooking contests. And our Saturday morning swimming.'

'Dad, it was awesome when Eve was trying to teach you how to dive and you kept landing on your belly. I wish we could have filmed it and put it on YouTube 'cos I bet loads of people would have watched it.'

Dad. That's the first time I've ever heard Ellie call Max that. It seems that my little girl may have grown up more in my months of absence than I first realized.

Ellie stretches out her arms, mimicking what I'm guessing were Max's attempts at diving. There appears to be a whole world of new experiences the three of them are undertaking together. A whole new family life in the making.

'And you like her sleeping over now as well, don't you?'

Max is continuing to walk as they talk, feigning distracted interest in the Renaissance paintings on the wall, but his mask of composure is an insufficient disguise. He seems nervous. I just don't understand what about.

'I like it when she stays over on Saturdays. The other nights are fine too. But it's best on Saturdays because you two are rubbish at guessing who's going to go through on *X Factor* and I always beat you.'

Max attempts a smile but fails to conceal his palpable anxiety.

'You see, I was wondering how you might feel if, perhaps, rather than just staying at our house at the weekends, maybe Eve stayed with us all the time? If she lived with us?'

Eve move in? So soon? They've barely been dating a year.

Eve meeting Ellie, Eve attending family events, Eve sleeping over occasionally – each of those milestones felt like they could, if necessary, be reversed. But Eve moving in, with all her possessions, redirecting her post to my house, sharing in the payment of bills, taking over my half of the wardrobe. I'm just not sure I'm ready for that. Not now. Not yet.

'What, you mean, like, lived with us all the time?'

'Yes, angel, that's exactly what I mean. How do you think you might feel if that were to happen?'

Ellie's face is quizzical, as if assessing the various responses available and attempting to distinguish her real feelings from those which she knows would make Max happy.

'But what about her house in Stoke Newington? Doesn't she want to live there any more?'

They wander into the Great Hall, the vastness of the space an appropriate backdrop for the scale of their conversation.

'It's not that she doesn't want to live in her house, sweetheart. It's just that she likes being with us – with me and you – so much that she'd like to be with us all the time. And I'd like that too. I think we'd have a lot of fun, the three of us together. But the most important thing for me is how you feel about it, because if you don't like the idea, then we won't even consider it. I promise.'

When he puts it like that it sounds so fair, so reasonable, so considerate. And yet I can't seem to stop my whole body from shaking.

Ellie isn't saying anything. I'm worried this is too much for her to process, too big a decision for her to take part in, too soon for such a disruption to her last remaining haven of security and stability.

'But I don't want to share you with someone else. Not all the time. I like it just being me and you.'

Her voice is mumbled, her tone tentative, the intonation of someone who needs to be heard but is fearful of the consequences. I want to scoop her up in my arms and tell her not to worry, to reassure her that Max is never going to do anything to make her unhappy.

'Sweetheart, I love all the time we spend together too. And nobody will ever get in the way of that, I promise. If I thought Eve moving in would mean you and I would be together less I wouldn't want that either. It would just mean that Eve would be around for more of the time that we do spend together.'

Max looks expectantly at Ellie. I don't blame him for having this conversation with her if that's what he and Eve are planning. I just wish they weren't planning it so soon and that Ellie wasn't faced with such a difficult dilemma; to please her daddy and go against her own wishes, or to please herself and risk paternal disappointment. How does any eight-year-old square that invidious circle?

It's the inevitable burden of the single-parent child, I know, the precocious responsibility for adult dilemmas. Parenting your parents: it happens to us all in the end, but so much sooner – much too soon – for the likes of Ellie and me. I never wanted Ellie to have to be like me in that regard. I never wanted her to have to know how it feels, worrying about your parents and sharing in their problems at an age when you should be innocent of everything outside your own pleasurable exploration of the world.

Perhaps Eve's presence in their lives might provide precisely the mitigation they need to avoid a repetition of history. Perhaps the decision Ellie faces now is the price she has to pay for a normal adolescence. Perhaps all of us need Eve more than we'd care to admit. More than I'd care to admit.

'I don't think Mummy would like it. It's her house, not Eve's.'

Ellie looks up at Max, a frown of contemplation furrowing her brow. I wish I could thank her for her thoughtfulness, for keeping me in mind, for considering my feelings even after such a long absence. I wish I could reverse time, could give Ellie back the family she so deserves, the family that doesn't expect her involvement in decisions that should be light years beyond the reach of any eight-year-old.

'Do you know what I think, munchkin? I think Mummy would just want us to be happy, whatever that involved.'

Would that it were that easy. Sometimes I think I'd give anything to be able to wish them happiness without a shoal of conflicting emotions clouding the waters. But that seems so elusive when I'm still in mourning for the life I've lost.

'But if Eve moved in, it wouldn't feel like Mummy's house any more. It would feel like Eve's. And what would we do with all of Mummy's things?'

'Our house will always be Mummy's house, sweetheart, because it's home to so many memories of her, so many memories the three of us share. If Eve moved in, it would be like us starting a new chapter in a book, but that wouldn't mean we'd forget the chapters that had gone before, would it?'

Ellie pauses for thought while they wander, hand in hand, out of the Great Hall.

'Why are you so sure that Mummy wouldn't mind?'

'Well, angel, it's just a feeling I have but you see, Mummy taught me so much about relationships and love and family. In fact, she taught me almost everything I know. It was Mummy who taught me how to be a good husband and how to be a good dad. So I suppose I feel that since it was Mummy who helped me learn all of that, she wouldn't want it to go to waste forever. And Eve moving in with us would be a way to make sure that didn't happen.'

I'm struck by a tempest of shame. I feel like a chastened schoolgirl who's just been awarded a prize after a morning's misbehaviour. I had no idea Max imbued me with credit for something I feel in no way worthy of, especially not now, especially not since I've been gone.

'So what do you think, sweetheart? Have you got other worries about what might happen if Eve moved in?'

Ellie nods her head slowly, the vivacity of her bouncing curls at odds with the consternation on her face.

'What is it? Can you tell me?'

Ellie seems unsure of her answer to the question, as though she's contemplating the advantages of disclosure over concealment.

'It's what you said a minute ago about all the memories of Mummy at home. Everyone's always telling me that I have all the nice times with Mummy to remember her by. But sometimes I don't. Sometimes I can hardly remember anything at all. And then I get scared in case one day I totally forget her. So what if Eve moves in and brings all her memories with her and makes loads of new memories and they rub out all the memories that I do have left of Mummy?'

Ellie is clenching and releasing both her fists repeatedly, as though voicing her confession out loud somehow makes it all the more distressing.

Max crouches down to her level and takes her left hand in his right.

'Oh, sweetheart. I think you'll be surprised, as time goes by, just how many memories of Mummy come back to you when you least expect it. That's the thing about remembering; it doesn't always happen to order, but I promise you that there is so much more stored away up there than you realize right now.'

He pulls Ellie into his arms, kissing the top of her head as though to magic her memories back to life.

'Do you know, the other day I was having a shower and I suddenly remembered the time that Mummy and I went on holiday to South America – it was years ago, before you were even born. I remembered that we'd been on a beach when all of a sudden it had started to rain, not cold rain like here but hot, tropical rain. I remembered us running around the beach getting all wet, laughing at how silly we were being. I hadn't thought about that afternoon for ages, and I have no idea why it popped into my head last week, but those unexpected memories will find their way to you too, in just the same way. I promise.'

I smile to myself. I haven't thought about that South American downpour for years either. Funny, those events that at the time feel like they'll stay in the forefront of your memory forever, so special and unique they are and yet, like the millions of experiences we amass in however long or short our lives, they disappear into hiding for years, decades even, to be remembered at the most unlikely and unpredictable moments. It was a magical afternoon, on that beach in Brazil. We were the only people there. What Max has rightly neglected to relate is that we stripped naked and ran around on the sand, laughing at our own unexpected childishness. I remember us drinking rain directly from the sky as we stood in the ocean with water up to our waists, splashing one another's bare skin before having rushed, impetuous sex, right there on the beach. It was so out of character for both of us, that almost-public display of private affection, and all the more special for its rarity.

'It's funny, Dad, 'cos earlier on when we were walking in here, I thought I remembered being here before when I was little but then I wasn't sure if it was a real memory or whether I was just making it up in my head.'

It was real, my darling girl, I promise you it was real. And nothing could make me happier than knowing there's a fragment of it in your mind still, waiting to be mined, sifted and polished, ready to radiate multiple reminiscences whenever you need it.

'That's not just in your head, munchkin. We came here when you were about a year old and it was one of the most humid London days I can ever remember. You got very cross because you were hot and sticky and so Mummy bought a bottle of water and we sat in the shade and she dabbed cold water all around your face and neck to cool you down. And shall I tell you something else about that day?'

'What?'

'Just after Mummy had managed to calm you, we were sitting on the grass under a tree in the gardens and we were trying to teach you how to kiss. Mummy kept saying, "Can you give me a kiss, Ellie?" and then she and I would kiss each other to show you how it was done. And on about the fifteenth time of Mummy asking you, all of a sudden you crawled over to her and planted the biggest, wettest kiss on her lips. It was the first time you'd ever done it. We were so happy, we kept asking you to do it again and again, and you were so pleased with yourself for learning something new and making us laugh so much that you carried on, kissing each of us in turn, for about five wonderful minutes. It was one of the sweetest things you'd ever done and Mummy and I were so excited.'

He's right. I'd forgotten but that's exactly the story of Ellie's first kisses. She was adorable that day. Every time she succeeded in another kiss we'd clap and she'd giggle infectiously and there was nothing but delight in that repetition for any of us. It made the whole humid trip worthwhile.

Ellie is smiling now, her anxiety evaporating in the recounting of a single memory.

'Is that true, Dad? Is that really what happened?'

'As true as you and I standing here right now, making very little progress on seeing this humongous big palace.'

Ellie giggles and the two of them resume their tour with a renewed sense of purpose.

They're in a dark, oak-panelled room now, where Max puts a hand on our daughter's shoulder and stops her, literally, in her tracks.

'Do you know the best method I have for remembering Mummy when I most want to?'

'What?'

'Whenever I want to think about Mummy, all I have to do is look at you.'

Max ushers Ellie over to the far side of the room where a large, ancient, gilt-framed mirror is hanging on the wall. He positions her in front of it and stands behind her, his hands on her shoulders, the two of them studying the pair of reflections staring back at them. I think of the centuries' worth of people who've stood exactly there, examining their own image, and wonder what stories that mirror must hold.

'Whenever you want to get a sense of Mummy in the world, all you have to do is look in the mirror, sweetheart. You're the spitting image of her; you've got the same curly hair that bounces happily even when you're sad, the same dark brown eyes that hold the promise of all the secrets of the world, the same warm smile that makes everyone want to be friends with you. You look just like her. And it's more than that, it's not just your looks. You have lots of her mannerisms too, and I don't know if you learnt them from her when you were little or whether you've inherited them, but they always make me smile. Like the way you roll your eyes – without even being aware of it – when someone says something you think is silly. Or the way you flap your hands in the air when you're really excited. And the frown your face gives off when you're angry is exactly like Mummy's, which is why I sometimes can't help laughing when you're cross.'

I gaze at Ellie's reflection and I see for the first time that Max is right. I don't understand how I hadn't noticed it before. Maybe it's because she's grown up so much over the past couple of years or perhaps it's because we see ourselves so differently from how others see us. But studying Ellie's face right now is like looking at a photograph of myself at that age. He's right about the mannerisms too. Max used to laugh at my 'flappy hand syndrome' and was forever warning me to be careful of my uncontrollable eye-rolling for fear it would get me in trouble one day. I'd never recognized either trait in Ellie until this moment.

Ellie is giggling at herself in the mirror now, possibly embarrassed by the scrutiny under which she's been placed, possibly from the pleasure of this latest discovery.

'Am I really like her, Dad?'

'I promise you, munchkin. You're like two very pretty peas in a pod.'

Ellie's grin widens, creating the faintest of dimples in her flushed cheeks.

'What other ways am I like Mummy?'

'Okay, let me think. There's the fact that you're both incredibly impatient and can't understand why you ever have to wait for anything. There's the way you both walk – I always loved Mummy's walk, the way she sort of jiggled her hips as she moved, and you do exactly the same thing. Even the way you scoop all the icing off the top of a cupcake and eat that first before devouring the rest – that's exactly what Mummy used to do too. And there are loads of other similarities as well. You love cooking, just like

Mummy, but you hate Maths and so did she. You like lakes and mountains and big open spaces which Mummy always loved too. And you're really interested in talking to people and they like talking to you as well, which is a very special quality that you definitely get from Mummy. Honestly, angel, there are a million ways you're like her.'

Ellie slips her hand into Max's as they continue their immersive tour of the past.

It's funny how I'd never seen those parts of myself in Ellie before. I'd thought the imprint I left on Ellie was purely genetic, an invisible code which, when mixed with Max's, would produce an entirely unique formula. I'd thought that mannerisms couldn't be inherited and that she and I hadn't been given long enough together for anything like that to be learnt. I'd thought that tastes and aversions were individual, not preferences to be bestowed through the generations. I'd thought that there was no trace of me left, not of my personality nor my idiosyncrasies nor even my foibles. But now I can see that there are vestiges of me alive in Ellie and perhaps they'll be alive in her children too and perhaps that, after all, is one of the great gifts of parenthood.

Max and Ellie have moved into the Tudor kitchens now, Ellie marvelling at the enormous fireplace and the antiquated utensils.

'Dad, if Eve moved in wouldn't it mean that you and her would be together all the time and I'd be on my own?'

Max gazes at her intently as though he can't imagine why she'd ever even suggest it.

'Angel, I'll never leave you by yourself – not even for an evening – unless you're okay with it. The only change that would happen if Eve moved in is that she'd be there to help with your Maths homework every night and the three of us could watch TV together whenever we wanted and you really could have French toast for breakfast every weekend. I think it might be quite cosy, don't you?'

Ellie's eyes narrow in contemplation.

'But you and I would still get to play *MasterChef* and we'd still sometimes just snuggle on the sofa on our own with a movie and you'd still let me stay up late at the week-ends, wouldn't you?'

'Absolutely, angel. Nothing at all between you and I would change.'

Ellie looks up at Max with an intensity that seems to contain so much of her own turbulent history.

'Okay, Dad. I don't think I mind if Eve wants to come and live with us, as long as you promise we can still do stuff on our own together, just the two of us.'

Max raises Ellie into his arms and kisses the top of her nose.

'Sweetheart, there'll always be time for you and I to have fun on our own together. You're my super-special girl and I wouldn't want anything or anyone to come in between us, ever.'

They hug one another, as oblivious to the other visitors wandering around them as those strangers are to the momentous decision that's just been made.

'So when will she move in? Will it be next weekend?'

'No, not quite so soon I don't think, angel. I thought it would be nice for you and me to have a bit more time by ourselves first and Eve will have lots to organize at her own house. So how about we ask her if she wants to come in a couple of months' time, at the beginning of December? That way we could all be together for Christmas, if you think you might like that?'

'Okay, Dad. 'Cos we wouldn't want her to be all by herself at Christmas, would we?'

My husband and daughter embrace one another in a centuries-old kitchen, and as I watch them I think about the decision Max and Ellie have reached today and the conversation by which they've journeyed there. I wonder whether the greatest test going forward is not whether I can bear the torment of Eve taking my place at home but whether the existing memories, the inherited characteristics, the shared experiences of a different cast can survive such a fundamental change in personnel.

As Max and Ellie leave the ancient kitchens and head down a passageway to wherever their odyssey will take them next, a door swings shut behind them and the clouds rapidly accumulate underneath me. In a matter of seconds, both the present and the past have vanished and I'm back alone in the whiteness.

I'm not lonely though. I'm not distraught or depressed or indignant as I so often am when my access ends. Today I think of Ellie and her flapping hands and her rolling eyes and her fingers swiping the chocolate icing from the top of a cupcake and I know, for the first time, that even though I'm here a little part of me remains down there, with her.

# CHAPTER 29

Pulp's 'Disco 2000' is blasting from oversized speakers. The room – a plain, 1960s, square brick hall – is decorated with balloons and streamers and banners. People are dancing but there's no one I recognize. For a second I fear there's been a mistake in my access, that I've been delivered to the wrong event, that I'm gatecrashing a stranger's party from beyond the grave. I spin round, hoping to see at least one familiar face, but this group looks significantly younger than my peers.

I'm about to take myself off to hover in the corner in the hope that something or someone will clock the mistake and get me out of here when I notice the banner above the door: 'Happy 40th Max'.

This is Max's fortieth birthday party? But Max doesn't even like parties. At least, the Max I was married to didn't. And who are all these people who look like they've yet to reach their fourth decade let alone their fifth? Old friends of Max or young friends of Eve?

It's a reminder, as if I needed one, of just how much has changed in my absence. I remember Max and I discussing our fortieth birthdays when they still felt sufficiently distant to joke about. He had said he'd like us to return to New York for his, to take Ellie back to the city in which she first came into being. I'd wanted to head to Iceland for mine, to explore somewhere new together, to discover it from the very beginning with Ellie. It looks like Max may have changed his mind about a lot of things since I've been gone.

I finally spy Max, Eve and Ellie in one corner of the room, where Ellie is arranging presents on a table and Max is chatting to Eve, his arm protectively encasing her tiny waist. She looks amazing. She's wearing a gold sequinned shift dress and satin three-inch heels, a combination which should, if there were any justice in the world, make her look like she's walked straight out of the WAGs' enclosure at a premiership football match. Instead she looks elegant and stylish, her golden hair luminescent next to the sequins, her slender frame proving the perfect hanger for the simplest cut of dress.

I make my way over to them, arriving just in time to witness, up close and much too personally, Max kiss Eve passionately and lingeringly on the lips.

'Thank you, baby – it's a fantastic party. I love it. Although I can't imagine how you managed to organize all of this, and invite all these people, without me suspecting a thing. I clearly need to watch out for your devious streak.'

So this was all Eve's doing. I might have guessed. I can't imagine Max arranging something like this for himself.

'Well, I did have a lot of help from my fabulous party co-planner, didn't I, Ellie?'

'Dad, you have no idea how hard it's been to keep this a secret. I had to go through the entire address book on your mobile phone while you were in the shower every day for about a week to find all the phone numbers for your friends. Then, do you remember the other week when I said I really needed my old PE kit from the loft for a fancy dress thing at school? Well, that was a total fib – sorry. I wanted to get on your computer and find all those old songs you like, from the 1990s and everything, so Eve could give a list to the DJ. And this morning, when you went out for your bike ride, me and Eve and Granny and Grandpa sneaked over here and decorated the whole place.'

Ellie's eyes sparkle with the pleasure of being released from a secret that's been a challenge to keep.

'Clearly I'm going to need to be careful of your scheming side too, young lady. I can't believe you managed to snoop through all my things without me knowing.'

'Eve said it was for your own good. And it wasn't like I did it without permission.'

Ellie and Eve nod at one another in mutual acknowledgement of their success.

'And when on earth were you having all these surreptitious conversations? I can't think when you've had the opportunity without me being around.'

'Oh, Ellie and I can be very efficient party planners when we need to be. There were the Saturday morning planning sessions in the changing room at the swimming pool and the two nights you were out at parents' evenings. And you don't really think that Ellie and I have been shopping three consecutive Saturdays while you've been at the football, do you? Honestly, Ellie, what does your dad take us for?'

Ellie giggles while I try to absorb the extensive inventory of the life that Eve now shares with my daughter.

'Well, you should both be very proud. You did brilliantly at keeping it all a secret and this party – well, I think it's the best party I've ever been to.'

Eve and Ellie share a mutually congratulatory hug and I can almost feel the warmth emanating from their embrace. They seem genuinely fond of one another, I can't deny it. Children are no good at faking that kind of attachment. I can't deny, either, the sheer pleasure of seeing Ellie happy, contented, relaxed. And, by the look of it, loved.

'Max, I'm going to pop to the kitchen and get the last of the food out. I think people are going to need to start soaking up alcohol soon.'

'I'll come with you and give you a hand. Ellie, why don't you go over and talk to Grandpa – it looks like he'd appreciate the company.'

I look over to where Max is pointing and see Ralph sitting on his own by a depleted tray of sandwiches. I spy Joan now, too, following Max and Eve into the hall's small kitchenette, where Eve busies herself unwrapping mini bagels and focaccias on to large china plates, and decanting bumper bags of crisps into mahogany bowls.

'It's such a lovely party, you two. The music's a bit loud but I suspect that's just me showing my age. You are clever, Eve, arranging all this without him ever guessing.'

'You're not wrong there, Mum. It's a fantastic surprise. To be fair, Eve, you probably knew I'd never have agreed if you'd asked me, didn't you?'

Eve bows her head and arches an eyebrow in mock guilty fashion, before they erupt into an explosion of laughter and he kisses her in a way I'm sure he never kissed me in front of his mum.

Joan is laughing too, her back against the open kitchen door, where I can see Mum and Harriet approaching.

I hoped they'd be here too, but I hadn't dared assume it after some of the conflict I've witnessed recently. I just wish Mum wasn't about to enter the kitchen at the very moment Max and Eve are engaged in yet another public display of affection. I don't know what it is about the combination of my husband, his new girlfriend, my mum and kitchens, but it seems to be the perfect recipe for emotional upset.

'So have you two settled on a date for Eve to move in yet?'

As Joan waits expectantly for an answer, Mum and Harriet stop in their tracks, out of Joan's sight but within earshot, and exchange a mutually perplexed look. Max and Eve, with a view behind Joan that Joan can't see, stand mute, their mouths slightly ajar, as if on the verge of replying but having lost the words somewhere between their brains and their mouths.

'There's no need to look at me like that, with your mouths open like a couple of gawping fish. It's a perfectly sensible question isn't it? I was wondering if your dad and I could help in any way, maybe picking up your things, Eve, or are you getting removal men for that?'

Max and Eve remained glued to the spot, each wearing the expression of a teenager caught smoking behind the bike shed. It's Mum, eventually, who finds a voice for all of them.

'So, were you going to tell me yourselves, or were you just going to let me find out next time I come to collect Ellie for the weekend?'

Joan spins round like a startled bird that's just discovered someone else has been pecking at her nest. Instead, she finds my mum and my best friend standing inches behind her, Mum glaring with humiliated rage and Harriet fixed with the look of someone who knows they're about to bear witness to an unmissable showdown.

'I'm really sorry, Celia. We only decided very recently and I just haven't had a chance to tell you.'

'Well, you can tell me now.'

'Perhaps now's not the best time to talk about it. Maybe Max can tell you tomorrow? We don't want to spoil the party after all, do we?'

It's Joan's attempt at diplomacy, but a true diplomat would have recognized that of the five people squeezed into a kitchen well beyond capacity, she's the least suited to staging an intervention.

'That's all very well for you to say, Joan. You're not the one who's been kept in the dark, are you?'

'We weren't keeping you in the dark, honestly, Celia. We're actually very excited about it. Eve's coming to live with us in about six weeks' time, at the beginning of December, so the three of us can be settled for Christmas.'

Max delivers a placatory smile, but I'm not sure he's going to be able to charm his way out of this one.

'It's just seems rather soon. Why the rush?'

'There's no rush, Celia. We just felt that the time was right. For us.'

Mum frowns in the face of Max's phlegmatic response. Harriet, meanwhile, is uncommonly quiet, for reasons I don't understand. I'd expect her to be leaping to my defence in a situation like this.

'Is there something you're not telling us?'

Mum sounds combative now, a tonal outfit she's not used to wearing. Max and Eve glance at one another, either in confusion or complicity, I'm not quite sure. Mum takes it as her cue to continue.

'The only reason I can possibly imagine as to why you'd be wanting to live together so soon is if Eve's planning to get pregnant. Or maybe she is already?'

Joan takes in a theatrical breath, Harriet raises a shocked eyebrow, Max hangs his head in resignation and Eve looks calmly ahead. Mum, meanwhile, attempts to hide her own surprise that such an indiscreet accusation could have emanated publicly from her lips.

'I think that's quite unnecessary, Celia, if you'll forgive me for saying it. Max and Eve's private life is just that – private.'

'For goodness sake, there's no privacy to be discussed. Is there any chance everyone can stop jumping to conclusions and accept the fact that there's no ulterior motive, that Eve and I simply want to live together?'

Eve places a calming hand on Max's arm.

'It's okay, Max. To be honest I think it's time we told them anyway.'

'Told us what?'

Now it's Joan's curiosity that's got the better of her.

'Don't, baby. There's no need. Just leave it.'

Eve shakes her head, and turns to meet the trio of expectant faces, their inquisitiveness suddenly delivering her a room bursting with undivided attention.

Max's expression is pained, agitated, the face of a man who's desperate to keep the worms in the can after it's

393

already been opened, but who knows it's a struggle he's destined not to win.

I can't believe she's going to tell them all, here and now. I feel strangely protective of her, aligned with Max's desire to prevent a revelation she may later come to regret.

Eve seems to be the only person in the room who's retained her composure throughout the whole messy conversation.

'The truth is, if Max and I stay together, which I sincerely hope we will, we won't be having any children together for the simple reason that I can't. I had an operation when I was younger and there were some complications – I'd rather not go into the details, if you don't mind – so childbearing's not an option for me. Or for us. But that's fine because Ellie's amazing and she's all any family needs. This move is what all three of us want, and it would be great to be doing it with your blessing – with blessings from all of you – if we could.'

No one speaks. Joan looks annoyed and I wonder whether she's irked at having been invited late to the confidence party or whether she's preoccupied with the sudden prospect of only ever having one grandchild. Mum's face betrays a combination of shame and relief, while Harriet I'm unable to read; if I didn't know her better I'd say hers was an expression of sympathy, but I know that's unlikely. Perhaps I'm misreading sympathy for boredom.

It strikes me that this is a decisive moment in the lives of the five people inadvertently trapped together in the cabin-sized kitchen, with Madonna's 'Like a Virgin' providing a suitably inappropriate soundtrack to their silence. This is the moment they can choose to embrace Eve's adversities and welcome her into the fold, in spite of their own insecurities and anxieties. Or it could be the perfect opportunity to beat Eve with the confessional stick she's just handed them and reject her conclusively.

Against every bet I'd have made had I been offered one before arriving here this evening, I find myself championing the former.

It's Mum who finally breaks the silence, in a voice that's been transformed from accusation to atonement.

'I'm really very sorry to hear that, Eve. That must be dreadful for you. If I'd known, of course, I'd never have been so tactless.'

Before Eve has to respond, Joan jumps in, determined not to be outdone in the sympathy stakes.

'That's so awful for you, love. I wish you'd confided in me earlier. It's a terrible thing, infertility, but you're obviously coping with it very well.'

Joan cocks her head to one side and squeezes Eve's hand as though reacting to news of a terminal illness rather than an inability to procreate.

'It's fine, really, both of you. I just didn't want there to be any misconceptions as to why I'm moving in with Max, or about our future together for that matter.'

Before anyone has a chance to share whatever's on their mind, Connor saunters in, helps himself to a handful of crisps and bites into a smoked salmon bagel before he clocks that he's walked into a crowded room in which the tension is almost as resounding as the music outside.

'What have I missed? Bloody hell, what's wrong with you lot? Did someone die? I thought this was supposed to be a party.'

Connor throws a slightly drunken arm around Harriet's shoulder.

'Max and Eve were just telling us about their plans. To live together.'

There's an edge to Harriet's voice, as if she's passing the argumentative baton to Connor in the expectation that he'll produce the appropriate indignation for all of them.

'Yeah, I know. It's great, isn't it? I'm made up for them. It's what – only a few weeks away now?'

Harriet shakes Connor's arm from her shoulder, firing a look of disbelief in his direction at the same time.

'You knew? And you didn't tell me?'

'It's not my news, is it? Anyway, you know now. What's the problem?'

Harriet glares at him as though the answer to his question should be self-evident.

'And what about Ellie? Does she get a say in all of this?'

There's the slightest tremble in Mum's voice and it's clear that she hasn't yet recovered from the unexpected news.

'Boo.'

Mum jumps and turns to find the subject of her question standing behind her, grinning, a piece of chocolate cake in one hand and Ralph in the other.

'Why is everyone standing in here like party poopers? Come out and dance with me. Some of this music isn't as rubbish as I thought it was going to be.'

'We were just hearing the news about Eve moving in with you and Daddy.'

Mum's tried to keep the pointedness out of her voice, I can tell, but she's never really mastered the art of neutrality.

Perhaps she's hoping that Ellie will do her obstructive bidding for her.

Instead, Ellie strides over to Eve and wraps her arms around Eve's slender hips.

'Yep, it's going to be great. We're going to redecorate the whole downstairs and I'm allowed to help choose the colours and Eve's going to teach me how to make loads of different types of cakes and we might actually remember what days I need to take my PE kit to school. It's going to be really cool.'

The silence is articulated by faces that speak a thousand words. There's victorious satisfaction from Joan, astonishment from Mum and what looks like sadness in the eyes of Harriet. Only Connor presents an expression with no axe to grind.

'You're right, princess. It's fantastic news. I can't imagine for a second why someone as gorgeous and fantastic as you, Eve, would want to move in with my degenerate brother, but he's certainly one lucky man.'

'Don't say that, Uncle Connor, or you'll put Eve off and then she really might not want to come.'

Eve laughs and lifts Ellie into her arms, the tension broken finally by the enthusiasm of an eight-year-old girl.

'Don't you worry about that, little one. Nothing could put me off moving in with you and Dad. We're going to have a lovely time.'

As Ellie throws her arms around Eve's neck, Mum watches on, bewildered by her granddaughter's affection for this woman she barely knows, and it suddenly dawns on me that I've probably spent more time in Eve's company than Mum has.

'You know, I think Ellie's right. We've been kitchen bores for far too long this evening and, given that it's my party, I think we need to get back out there and enjoy it. Now, my two favourite ladies, who wants to dance with an old man on his fortieth birthday?'

'Yay. Let's go, Dad.'

Max, Eve and Ellie dance out of the room, with Joan and Ralph hot on their heels, Joan looking over her shoulder to present Mum with her infamous 'I hope you're pleased with yourself' face as a parting gift.

'Bloody hell. That was all a bit heavy for a Saturday night.'

Harriet punches Connor on his arm, not entirely playfully.

'Yes, well, it could have been avoided if you'd had the common sense to tell me what was going on.'

'It wasn't my news to tell. Look, I know it's probably a bit weird for you both – for you, especially, Celia – but can't you cut Max some slack? He's had a pretty rough ride these past couple of years and I for one think it's great to see him so happy.'

Mum looks at Connor wearily, and I suspect the tiredness in her eyes has little to do with the late hour.

'I don't begrudge him happiness, Connor. But you must understand that all these . . . developments are more difficult for some of us than others to take on board.'

'I know. I understand. It's difficult for everyone. But tonight's probably not the best time or place to think about it, is it? Now, who wants to come and dance? Come on, Harriet. I haven't seen you set foot on the dance floor all evening.'

'You go on. I want to have a quick chat with Celia.'

Connor raises a wry smile that suggests it doesn't take a genius to guess what she wants to discuss, and leaves them to it.

'Well, I didn't see that coming.'

'Oh, Harriet. Me neither. It's all a bit of a shock. I hadn't realized quite how fond Ellie is of Eve.'

'I know. Ellie seems to adore her. I always thought that after you and Joan, I was the next favourite woman in her life, but I can see that's not the case any more.'

Mum squeezes Harriet's hand sympathetically but I can see her mind is elsewhere.

'You know, it's probably terrible of me to admit this, but it's a bit of a relief, knowing that Max probably won't have any more children. Ever since Rachel died it's been gnawing away in the back of my mind: what if Max has more children with someone else, where would that leave Ellie? It wouldn't be easy for her. I wouldn't wish Eve's plight on anyone, but I do think it's probably the best outcome for Ellie, don't you?'

Harriet's face adopts a look I don't think I've ever seen before, a discomfort that's out of character for someone who's rarely phased by any conversation, whatever the topic.

'So you don't worry about Ellie being an only child, then? Aren't only children supposed to grow into awful, self-regarding, sociopathic adults?'

'Oh, I think that's all a myth. Rachel was an only child, after all, and she couldn't have been more thoughtful and loving.'

'Whereas I've got a brother and I'm notoriously selfish. You're probably right. If you don't mind me asking, why did you only ever have one child? Did you not want any more?'

Only Harriet would have the gumption to ask my mum that question. I asked it, of course, plenty of times, but then that was my prerogative.

'I didn't feel the need for another after Rachel came along. Robert and I loved her so much it felt almost greedy to want more. We were happy, just the three of us. I do remember my mum encouraging me to try for a second. She said we ought to in case anything ever happened to Rachel, as though another child would be a sort of insurance policy.'

'You mean like "an heir and a spare"?'

Mum smiles ruefully at Harriet's remark and I know that however long I'm here I'll never stop feeling guilty for having left her.

'So do you wish now you'd had more than one?'

'I don't really think about it. There's no point in dwelling on things, is there? We can't change the past, after all, and wishing that we could only makes us unhappy.'

Harriet puts an arm around Mum's shoulders and I'm grateful to her for performing the gesture I'd so love to fulfil myself.

'Come on. Let's go back out, shall we? There's probably not much more of this party left.'

I follow them into the main room and there, in the middle of the dance floor, is Max, one hand in Ellie's and the other around Eve's waist, the three of them dancing together as if it's the most natural act in the world.

The sight awakens a memory in me, something I haven't thought about for ages. It's the recollection of Max and me dancing with Ellie in our arms when she was a baby, our nightly post-bath, pre-bed ritual. We'd put Ella Fitzgerald or Billie Holiday on the iPod and hold Ellie's naked body between us, swaying in time to the music, her newly washed skin the softest, smoothest sensation in the world, that pliable flesh which sprang back in surprise every time you squeezed it, irresistible to touch, to stroke, to kiss.

I remember how happy the three of us were during those cosiest of evenings and, as painful as it is to see myself replaced in the group by its newest member, I'm grateful to them for restoring the memory to me. There's nothing I'd trade for that precious time, as the day ended in collective affection, when Ellie would often be at her happiest. If it was a choice between living again now and never having had that, I'd take naked baby Ellie in my arms every time.

I wonder whether this evening is a test for the dead as much as it is for the living. Is there a decision for me, too, as I watch friends and relatives accept Eve into the family fold, a decision about where I'm going to pitch my virtual tent? Am I going to stay out in the cold, bitter and resentful, as excluded emotionally as I am physically, consigning myself to yet more isolation, loneliness and regret? Or do I follow the lead of the living, accept the irreversibility of my absence and appreciate Eve for all that she brings? Because what more could I hope for, after all, than to share Max and Ellie with someone who loves them, cares for them and wants to restore happiness to their lives?

A song blasting from the speakers summons me from my reverie. It's one of Max's unexpected favourites: 'Never

Forget' by Take That. The room erupts into collective celebration, fifty or so guests shouting rather than singing the chorus in unison, arms waving drunkenly in the air, the odd lighter swung above dizzy heads for nostalgic effect. Even Connor and Harriet are joining in, dancing and laughing together with the euphoria of an evening spent in the company of decade-old friends. I've never listened to the lyrics properly before, but now that I do it feels as though the song was written for me, for me right here, right now.

I hover alone in the corner, watching in isolation as the living enjoy the life that's still theirs to lead, seeing Max and Eve and Ellie jumping together in time to the chorus, knowing for sure now that this is all someone else's dream.

# CHAPTER 30

The last remaining guests have just left, nudged gently and tipsily through the door by Max and Eve, who've been trying to clear the room for the best part of half an hour. The clock on the wall tells me it's twenty past one. It's been a long night already.

It's been a strange night too, lingering in the shadows, an invisible gatecrasher to my husband's landmark birthday party. I should be used to it by now, being suspended on the outside looking in; it's all I've done for the past two and a half years and I'm well acquainted with the heartache and loneliness and envy that accompany the role. But tonight was different. Tonight felt different.

Ever since I died I've witnessed conflict and upset and grief as the people I've left behind find their own pace at which to adapt to the changes effected by my absence. But tonight I looked on as secrets were shared and confessions entrusted, and in place of the implosion I'd anticipated there was, instead, a quiet cooperation.

I watched Harriet and Eve dancing together to Girls Aloud, heard Mum chatting with Max as though nothing out of the ordinary had taken place, saw Ellie flitting among the guests, the prettiest of social butterflies.

If this was the night when everyone's love for Max and Ellie was put to the test then they all seem to have passed with flying colours. It feels like there's only one person remaining who's yet to prove themselves.

I take myself into the kitchenette where Harriet and Eve are washing plates and glasses. Max is standing aside, Ellie asleep in his arms.

'Max, why don't you go and sit down with Ellie? You're not much use here anyway with Ellie asleep on you. Harriet and I can clear up – if you don't mind, Harriet?'

'Not at all. God knows when my cab might deign to make an appearance. Go on, you might as well make the most of it being your birthday, Max – there aren't many days I'd offer to do your washing up for you.'

Max kisses Eve and leaves with Ellie slumbering in his arms. Harriet and Eve work silently for a few minutes, Harriet washing and Eve drying, and I wonder whether this is the first time the two of them have ever been in a room on their own together.

'So, it turns out you and I may have more in common than we imagined.'

It's Harriet who's broken the silence.

'Oh, really? What's that?'

I'm intrigued. There aren't many women I know who seemingly have less in common than my best friend and the new love of my husband's life.

'I'm sure Max told you about the row he and I had a few months back. The one on Rach's second anniversary?'

Eve blushes lightly but just enough to confirm Harriet's presumption.

'He didn't go into detail but I got the gist, yes.'

'Well, it clarified something I'd been mulling over for a while. Since Rach died, actually. It got me thinking that

404

perhaps Max was right and my life has been a bit self-absorbed. And that maybe it was worth thinking about the whole procreation thing before it's too late.'

I'm amazed. Harriet never expressed even the slightest inclination towards motherhood to me before, not once in the twenty years we knew one another.

'Wow, that's a big decision. I know we haven't known each other long but I got the impression you didn't want children.'

'I never have before. But when your best friend dies of a heart attack in their mid-thirties it does tend to focus the mind a bit. And it got me thinking about what I'd leave behind whenever I die. I looked at Ellie and thought about her growing up and having kids of her own and them seeing in the next century and suddenly a few articles in law journals didn't seem like the sum total of the legacy I wanted to leave behind. Don't get me wrong – I love my job and I wouldn't swap it for anything. But I don't know – perhaps it was as simple as hearing the biological clock ticking loudly in my ear.'

I can't help smiling up here. It's so typically Harriet, to do whatever you least expect of her. Some people react to their approaching forties by having affairs, getting divorced and hoping to find their younger selves in new relationships. Others go in search of youthful solace in a fast new car or a trim, surgically enhanced body. A few hope to find comfort at the bottom of a wine bottle or in nightclubs frequented by their sons and daughters. But my best friend discovers in her impending mid-life crisis a sudden desire for the motherhood she's always professed to repudiate.

Who knows how it might have affected me if I'd ever got there?

'So . . . well . . . what's your plan?'

'Therein lies the sixty-four million dollar question. I had an appointment at a fertility clinic – a good one, obviously, I did my research – to find out about the possibility of donor insemination. After all, it's not like I'm expecting Prince Charming to rock up on a white horse any time soon and impregnate me.'

'God, that's a big step. So how did it go?'

'Not all that well, as it turns out. They seemed to think I've already used up practically my entire lifetime's consignment of eggs and that the menopause is knocking impatiently at my door.'

'Oh, I'm really sorry, Harriet. That must have been incredibly tough to find out.'

'It wasn't the best hour of my life, I'll be honest. I'd pretty much given up on the whole idea but then I read about another clinic with success rates that put the rest of the IVF world to shame so I'm thinking about making an appointment there. We'll see. It's ironic, really. After a lifetime of certainty that I didn't want children, now it feels like motherhood's all I ever think about. Maybe it's as simple as wanting what it seems you can't have. I've never been very good at not getting my own way.'

Harriet smiles self-deprecatingly and I can't imagine how she must be feeling because I can't really imagine the Harriet I know wanting children in the first place. Her tone right now is stoical, matter-of-fact, but that's just her barriers of self-protection at work. That much I do know.

'I know that feeling all too well. It's unnerving how quickly it can become an obsession. I remember when I began actively wishing that I could have children – probably about five years ago now – and suddenly it seemed like every woman I passed on the street was pushing a pram. And then four of my colleagues went on maternity leave at the same time and three of my old university friends got pregnant within six months of one another. It starts sending you slightly crazy, doesn't it?'

I think about all those months Max and I were trying to give Ellie a sibling and how all-consuming and emotional and obsessive it was. And I was already fortunate enough to have one child.

'Yes, but I never thought I'd become one of those women. I'm not sure it suits me, although there doesn't seem to be a lot I can do to stop myself. It's just a bit of a nasty surprise to discover at the age of thirty-eight that I've inadvertently made decisions about the rest of my life that I never – not consciously, anyway – intended to make. I guess I was seduced by the fantasy that women really could have it all, without appreciating that there's a pretty harsh sell-by date attached to that particular offer. I'm sure everyone thinks they've got all the time in the world. But we haven't, have we?'

She's right, we haven't. I thought I was the only one who felt it so keenly, but I can see that it's as true for the living as it is for the dead. I don't suspect anyone ever feels like they've had enough time. I'm sure most of us postpone decisions every day, whether the casual or the critical, as if there'll always be a tomorrow.

'Well, it sounds like this other clinic might be promising. When do you think you might start the ball rolling there?'

'I'm not sure. I've only just started email contact with them so I don't know yet whether they think they'll be able to help.'

'Look, I know you've probably thought of every option, but if this clinic doesn't work out have you considered adoption or even fostering? I'm sure agencies would be crying out for someone like you.'

'Yep, I've considered those – for about a nanosecond – and dismissed them already. I'm far too narcissistic to want to look after someone else's baby. If it hasn't got my genes, I don't think I could muster the inclination to devote my energy to it. Funnily enough, I did wonder whether adoption's something you and Max had thought about though?'

Adoption? It's not something that's even crossed my mind. But now that it has I feel instinctively unnerved by the prospect.

'We did talk about it once but we don't think it's for us. Not least because of how unsettling it could be for Ellie. Like I said earlier, Ellie's wonderful and she should be blessing enough for any family.'

She is. It's true. It makes me wonder now why Max and I ever got so preoccupied with having another child.

'Well, if science can't sort me out I'll just have to accept that it wasn't meant to be. I'm still not a hundred per cent convinced it would be the right move, anyway. There's a part of me that's unsure whether I want to give up my life in its current incarnation, whether having a child I'd only ever really see at weekends, a child who would know the nanny better than they knew me, would be right for either of us. So if it doesn't work out for whatever reason, I'll just have to be content with godmothering Ellie and hope that I'm nice enough to her over the next forty-odd years that she deigns to come and visit me in the nursing home once in a while.'

Harriet laughs but there's a sadness behind her smile.

'Ellie adores you, you know that. She's the most devoted goddaughter I've ever known.'

'I'm lucky, I know. I'll always have Max and Rach to thank for that. But the thing is, and I'm sure I'll regret admitting this the second I walk out of the door and I probably wouldn't be confessing it at all if I wasn't still a bit drunk, I felt envious of you tonight. Because of all the kids in the world, Ellie's the one I'd most like to be a surrogate mum to. But now that you're moving in, I'll no doubt be displaced one rung further down the pecking order of her affections.'

So that's why Harriet was quiet. I knew something was wrong with her. I'd just never have guessed in a million years exactly what.

'Harriet, with Rachel gone, I don't think there can ever be too many women trying to fill the maternal role for Ellie, do you? It's certainly not a job any one woman can hope to accomplish alone, that much I'm well aware of.'

'Well, you're clearly doing a great job with her so far. Seriously. However jealous I am to acknowledge it, I can't deny that she's mad for you.'

My old best friend and my husband's new girlfriend exchange tentatively sympathetic smiles.

'Thanks for confiding in me, Harriet. I'm sure it can't have been easy.'

409

'Well, it seemed like the right thing to do after you confided in all of us earlier. That was one of the things Rach taught me, about relationships being built on mutual honesty and self-disclosure. It's not something I've ever been particularly good at, but Rach was one of the few people patient enough to wait for me to reveal my hand. Most people never get past what my mum kindly describes as my brittle exterior. But I think if you and I are going to be in Ellie's life for the foreseeable future, then I'd rather us be friends if we can.'

'I'd really like that too.'

The lightest breeze of envy blows my way but following swiftly behind is a much warmer air, an unexpected flurry of reassurance at the prospect of a burgeoning friendship between Harriet and Eve. I don't think I'd realized until now quite how guilty I feel about leaving my best friend. Perhaps there simply wasn't room in my remorse-ridden war chest for any more regret, no space to accommodate yet another person I'd inadvertently abandoned. It's only now, hearing her confide in Eve, that I realize how much Harriet lost when our friendship died with me.

It's only now, too, that I realize quite how much I miss Harriet as well; I miss being able to tell her anything, miss knowing that her pragmatism and common sense are always at the end of a telephone. I miss her being the person I turn to when I want sensible advice, when I know the practical solution to a dilemma and just need someone to drive it home. It's the kind of counsel I've often been in dire need of here.

I think about my relationship with Harriet, about the decisive moment we went from being casual acquaintances to lifelong friends. I can recall that twenty-year-old conversation as if it were yesterday, the two of us sitting wrapped up in gloves and scarves on a cold autumnal day in our first term, huddled together on a bench outside the university refectory, smoking cigarettes when it was still cool to smoke and drinking coffee that neither of us had yet developed a taste for. I remember telling her about the day my dad was killed, about how it was the first time I'd ever felt murderous feelings towards another human being, towards the drunk who'd carelessly knocked Dad down and how, ever since, I'd felt the heaviest burden of responsibility for my mum, a responsibility I couldn't imagine ever being lifted from my shoulders. I remember Harriet's reticence and my sense that she had something she wanted to say but that she couldn't find the words or perhaps the courage to say it, and me cajoling her into telling me what was on her mind, but discovering that the more I pressed her the further she retreated.

And I remember delivering that self-disclosure speech, a monologue full of the self-assured certainty that accompanies late adolescence, about how friendships evolve from the risk of shared confidences, how the failure to do so could only lead to estrangement, how the exposure of my own vulnerable hand should have made it easier for her to reciprocate, all the time fearing that, at the end of it, she'd tell me I was being stupid or, worse still, pretentious. But instead she'd looked me straight in the eye, as if weighing up the likelihood of betrayal, and then looked down at the floor again and begun reciting her story as if entrusting it to the empty air rather than to me.

That was the time she first told me about the day her mum collected her from school with a tear-stained face and unkempt hair, and how Harriet knew immediately that something really bad had happened, something she didn't want to ask about for fear of being told the truth. She described arriving home with her mum and her brother to the news that their dad had gone away and that he wasn't going to be living with them any more. She talked of how she'd known, even at that age, that such a disappearance wasn't normal, and of her certainty that one day she'd be told the rest of the story to which this was only the prologue. She said it was over a year before her mum revealed the truth; how one day over dinner, without any warning, her mum had announced to her and her brother that their father had moved to France to live with a woman he planned to marry and that she didn't expect he'd ever come back, didn't even know exactly where he was living. She'd told them they needed more money, that she was going to have to take an extra job in the evenings in a local pub, that Harriet would need to look after her brother to avoid the services of a babysitter they couldn't afford.

Harriet said she remembered all too clearly the determination not to let her mum down, on those nights when she tucked herself under the duvet wanting nothing more than for her mum to be there to put her to bed, or those evenings she had bad dreams and awoke to the realization that there was no one to comfort her. She understood exactly, she said, those feelings of filial responsibility, feelings that don't leave you even long after you've left home yourself.

That was the conversation, we both admitted later, when we knew we'd be friends for life.

It's a conversation I never imagined Harriet would still be referencing nearly two decades later.

I'd thought the only reverberation I'd conferred upon the world was Ellie, but now I see I've left fragments of myself in the most unexpected places, with people who are only now beginning to reveal the cast of imprints I hadn't previously detected. I'd assumed I'd brought all of myself here with me, but now I'm discovering that there are multiple traces I've left behind.

I can see that my friends and family are in the process of forming fresh allegiances, putting both old loyalties and new relationships to the test. It's a test that involves accepting I've gone, that their lives go on without me, that they'll need to find new people to love and to laugh with and with whom to share life's adventures. My test is, in many ways, both greater and lonelier: to acknowledge my own absence, to resign myself to the bittersweet recognition that the people I love most can be happy without me, and for that acknowledgement not to destroy the significance of the life that I shared with them.

With Harriet and Eve finishing the tidying up below, I will myself away with an ease I haven't experienced before. Not for the first time, but new enough to be surprising still, I find myself appreciating the solace that my isolation affords me, and the space it allows to reflect on all that's taken place tonight.

It occurs to me that the greatest test of unconditional love may be allowing the people we care most about to love and be loved by others. The only question remaining, for me at least, is whether I have the capacity to pass that test.

# Acceptance

Acceptance

# CHAPTER 31

The void around me opens up to reveal that my former hallway is stacked with bulging black plastic bags. They're piled on top of one another, like mistreated prisoners in need of escape. One bag hasn't been tied properly, leaving its contents visible to anyone squeezing – or hovering – by. I peer into it and there, lying forlornly on top, is my favourite brown cardigan, the one I practically lived in on winter weekends when we were too cold, or just too cosy, to leave the house. Underneath I spy the belt of my red 1950s-style dress, the one with the scoop neck and the pencil skirt that Max always said was his favourite, the one he proclaimed he'd be happy to see me wear every day, forever more. The dress he once told me he'd have been happy to marry me in had I not opted for a traditional, unjustifiably expensive ivory number.

Now it seems he can live without both me and the dress.

I wonder if there could be any clearer indication that the people you've left behind are ready to embrace a life without you than the sight of your worldly possessions stuffed into the inanimate objects' equivalent of a coffin? Seeing these two dozen or so bin liners piled up, inertly awaiting their fate, it's as though another little part of me is preparing to depart the earth for good.

I hear the murmur of voices upstairs. With the all-too-familiar fear of what I might find when I go to investigate, I make my way to the first floor.

'Dad, can I keep this?'

Ellie calls out her question to Max, whose feet I can see protruding from the loft, balanced precariously on the rickety ladder we were always meaning to replace. Moving across the landing I see that Ellie is sitting on my bed – or what used to be my bed – with Eve. They're surrounded by clothes, shoes, handbags, jewellery, make-up: the remains of a life no longer in use.

Ellie is holding a silver teardrop pendant, nothing particularly special, not even the original Tiffany's version that was so ubiquitous in the late 1990s but an imitation I'd bought for myself as a present after securing my first proper job as a marketing assistant for the London Tourist Board. I'd been so proud of that job and a few years later was still wearing the necklace that to me symbolized my first foray into adulthood. Ellie's always loved it too. When she was a toddler in my arms, she'd fiddle with it, fascinated, attracted perhaps by its shape of sadness or perhaps by the weight under her tiny fingers or perhaps, simply, by the sheen of polished silver reflecting a distorted miniature version of the world around her. I remember how I'd chastise her for pulling it too hard, fearing she'd break the chain, irritated sometimes that I couldn't wear jewellery she wasn't compelled to grab. Now I'd give anything for her to grasp whatever she liked from around my neck.

'As Dad said before, you can keep whatever you want. If there are things you'd like to have in your bedroom right now, you should put them in one pile. And if there are things you think you might want later, then Dad can easily put them in the loft for you. The important thing is that we don't say goodbye to any of your mummy's things that you might want one day.'

Eve's answer sounds perfectly reasonable. Rationally I can hear that. It's just hard to be rational when you're watching your life being prepared for an eternity at the rubbish tip.

Max emerges from the loft with a framed drawing of a mother suckling a child, a Picasso pastiche I produced when I was pregnant with Ellie.

'You know who drew that, don't you, munchkin?'

'No, who?'

'It was Mummy. I think it was around the time you were born. She said that you inspired her.'

Ellie stares at the drawing as if hoping to find something of me in it that she hadn't known before.

'It's really pretty. Mummy was clever at drawing, wasn't she? Can we put this up on the wall in my room?'

'Of course we can, sweetheart. Why don't you pop it in there now so it doesn't get mixed up with the things we're taking to the charity shop?'

So that's where those black plastic bags are heading. I suppose it's preferable to the dump, at least.

Ellie doesn't move. She's wearing her thoughtful face, the one that indicates she's mulling over a possible question or, at least, the viable prospect of asking it.

'Do you think the people who buy Mummy's things from the charity shop will look after them? What if they buy them and then just throw them away?'

Max and Eve exchange a loaded glance, silently debating whom they feel is better placed to answer.

'You know what, Ellie? When people buy things second hand, whether from a charity shop or an antiques market or even a car boot sale, they tend to treat them better than if they'd bought something new. I know I always do. There's something really special about second-hand items; you know they've had a history – a whole life – before you owned them and it makes you treat them with even more respect precisely because they've belonged to someone else before you. So I honestly think all your mummy's things will find very nice homes to go to.'

Eve's right, but it's a truth sadder than fiction. Because however much my belongings might be appreciated by whomever ends up owning them, those people will never know the history of those objects, will never know the stories attached to them, will never know why they were special to me. I'm the sole proprietor of those memories.

They won't know that those pink slingbacks with the slightly loose clasp that Eve has just taken out of the wardrobe were the ones I was wearing in New York the day Max and I ran in search of an empty doorway to shield ourselves from a torrential downpour that appeared out of nowhere and then refused to depart for the rest of the afternoon. They won't know that the blue belted vintage dress draped over the side of the armchair is the one I was wearing in the wedding marquee that day I first met Max and that I've kept, sentimentally, ever since. They won't know that the handbag Ellie is currently rooting through, where she's found nothing more than an old lipstick and a couple of crumpled tissues, is the one I bought with my first annual bonus, a bag that cost more than was reasonable to spend on a repository for keys, wallet and a travel card. They won't know that the wooden box lying on the bed awaiting bagging was a purchase from the Marrakech souk where I'd bargained my way down to twenty per cent of the original price, with Harriet egging me on. They won't know that the red glass bowl Max is covering with bubble wrap, the bowl that has been sitting on my dressing table for the past decade playing host to an array of assorted earrings, was actually my grandparents', one of the few items I'd rescued from their three-bedroom cottage in Wiltshire before the house clearers had moved in and offered us a derisory price for the lot. Whoever ends up owning all of these things won't know any of that.

'But do you think Mummy would be sad that her things won't be here any more? That we won't be looking after them for her?'

She's directing the question to Max. Perhaps only he can reassure her that her participation today is legitimate.

'I think Mummy would be pleased that her things are going to find new homes, to be useful to other people and give them pleasure. I think that would make her happier than them being stuck in wardrobes and cupboards forever, not being used by anyone.'

I'm honestly not sure whether that's true. There's something comforting about all my things still being housed in my former home. Maybe it's the desire for them to be retained under one roof, the fear of them being scattered too far and wide, in unknown locations with unknown proprietors, never again being able to track their fate. Maybe it's simply the fear of yet more change.

Ellie is hauling an opaque plastic trunk from under the bed and, as she lifts the lid, I realize with debilitating panic that it's the box containing everything I don't yet want her to see: my diaries, letters, notes I've sent and received, scribbles of thoughts and feelings, a compendium of my inner life dating back to before I was Ellie's age. I'm not ready for her to read any of that. Not yet. It's too soon and she's too young.

Max glances across at her just in time, a momentary frown of alarm on his face.

'I don't think we need to look through that box today, sweetheart. That's one I'm going to put in the loft and we can go through it together some time in the future.'

Ellie looks suspicious, as if aware that she's being denied the most coveted of prizes. I thank Max silently for answering my unknowable entreaties as he carries the box to the bottom of the loft ladder.

'Dad, I'm thirsty. Can I go and make some hot chocolate?'

'Of course, angel. Make that three and we'll come down and join you in a few minutes.'

Ellie hops off the bed and clatters noisily down the stairs.

Eve looks out in the direction of Ellie's departure and waits until she hears the kitchen door close behind her.

'There are another two bags here for the spare room. I didn't want to mention them in front of Ellie, obviously.'

Eve's reference to the spare room sounds suspiciously euphemistic, except that we do have a spare room and that's where Eve and Max are heading right now, each with a bag of my life in their hands.

The spare room, once home to little more than a sofa bed, a desk and a few bookshelves, now appears to be the vault for a dozen cardboard boxes and about the same number of plastic bags. I'm guessing it's all mine. Who knew it was possible to accumulate quite so much baggage in a relatively short lifetime?

As Max and Eve pile the two most recent additions on top of existing mounds, Eve surveys the room with a sigh.

'When do you think you'll get time to deal with all of this?'

'Well, the dump is open till ten tonight so I figured I'd head off after Ellie goes to bed, if you don't mind staying with her on your own till I get back? I shouldn't be too late. I'm hoping to be able to get it done in two runs.'

So all of this does belong to me. Or at least it did. It's not going to belong to anyone for much longer.

'I really don't want Ellie to see that I'm throwing away so much of Rachel's stuff. But I don't know what else to do with it. I feel guilty about getting rid of it, but then I feel guilty at the thought of keeping it all as well. I know it doesn't make any sense to hold on to every single thing she ever owned, and I know it wouldn't be fair on you if I did. When you move in next week, I want this to feel like your home. And that's never going to happen if every drawer you open contains some sort of reminder of Rachel.'

So this is all in aid of Eve's imminent occupancy. I suppose I should have guessed.

'Max, I've said it already but I'll say it again. There's no rush for any of this, not on my account.'

'No, I'm ready. It's not just for you. It's for me too, and for Ellie. For all of us. We can't realistically move on when this house is full of so many tangible shadows. It's irrational, anyway, holding on to all these things – all her schoolbooks and her work files and old painting equipment that wouldn't be of any use to anyone now anyway. No one's ever going to look at any of this stuff so it doesn't make any sense to keep it. I know that.'

All those personal effects of mine: the artefacts of my childhood, my adolescence, my working life, my private passions. All of that being dumped into a landfill site, like a common grave for anonymous possessions. It's like a second funeral, for the last remnants of my corporeal life, only this time there'll be no hymns, no eulogies, no family or friends in attendance to ensure a safe send-off.

I feel like crying.

It's not me who breaks down, though. It's Max who sits on the sofa bed and suddenly begins to sob – slow, muffled cries, the sounds of a man desperate to restrain himself but at the mercy of feelings beyond his control.

Eve sits down next to him, placing one arm around his shoulders and the other on his leg, saying nothing, allowing him to mourn in silence.

'I'm sorry, Eve. I don't know what's come over me. It's just a lot harder than I imagined. I've been telling myself that I can be pragmatic about this, that it's just a job I have to do, that it's the next necessary, logical step, but it's so much more complicated than that. Every single item we're packing up reminds me of something, something to do with Rachel. I feel like I'm doing a lifetime's memorializing in a single day. I've been trying to keep it together, for you and for Ellie, but I just feel overwhelmed.'

Now it's my turn to feel guilty, to be swathed in the selfishness of someone who's neglected to remember that I'm not the only person for whom this is a day of finalities.

'I really didn't want to lose it in front of you today, Eve. I don't want you to think that this has any bearing on us or that I'm not ready for you to move in because I am. I can't wait for you to be living here full time. I suppose there's just always going to be a part of me that still misses Rachel, that's still angry with the world for taking her away from me and Ellie so bloody early. A part of me, if I'm honest, that will always love her. But that's completely separate from the love I have for you. I need you to know that. It doesn't diminish my feelings about you, about us, in any way at all.'

I wipe away my own tears that have greeted this unexpected revelation. I've watched over the past year as Max has fallen in love with another woman, begun to build a life with her, invited her into our home and allowed her to mother our daughter. I've watched as my presence has receded from his life, as he's cleared space for her to step into my role while I've been powerless to intervene. I've assumed that I'd been dismissed from our home, from his memory, from his heart even. But now I discover that there's still a place for me in Max's life, even as he builds a new one with Eve.

I look around the room at the boxes and bags of belongings destined for the dump. Max is right. These aren't my life. They're inanimate remnants of a life so much richer, a life so much fuller and a marriage that can't be obliterated however far it's buried underground, whatever new relationships live above it, however long Max survives me.

I wish I could tell him not to worry, tell him that I understand, tell him that he need not feel guilty about this removal of material possessions. Tell him that they could bury the lot six miles under and it wouldn't diminish the relationship we had. I wish I could hold him and look him in the eye one last time and tell him that it's okay.

It's Eve, instead, who holds Max's face in her hands.

'I don't want you ever to feel that you can't talk to me about Rachel. Of course I know how much you still miss her and that a part of you will always love her. I know that she'll always be special to you if for no other reason than she's the mother of your daughter. And I don't imagine for a second that I could ever replace her, for you or for Ellie, and neither would I want to. We're starting something new, you and I, and that's a continuation of the past, not an eradication of it. All I ask is that you promise never to shut me out, never to keep those feelings to yourself. I want to be able to share it all with you, even the painful parts, to be involved in remembering Rachel with you and Ellie. After all, who knows whether you and I would have fallen in love if you hadn't already lived with and loved someone else so successfully. Not all men have learnt how to do that, you know. We've both got a lot to thank Rachel for, when you think about it.'

Max wraps Eve inside his arms in an envelopment of love and gratitude. As I watch them hold on to one another, Eve's words repeat over and over in my mind with all the reassurance that I hadn't realized until now I needed from her.

I feel absent from Max's life but not, for the first time, excluded. It's as though I exist, somewhere, in the folds of their embrace and the knowledge of that provides the impetus I need to tear myself away, to leave them to the disposal of objects I no longer require. It's a moment to allow them their privacy and to retreat, for the time being, back into the world to which I now belong.

# CHAPTER 32

There's a white transit van parked outside our house, its back doors swung open, revealing its contents to any passerby with a tendency towards curiosity. There's not much to see, just a couple of boxes and a lone oversized Selfridges bag. I wonder whether I've been absent only a matter of hours, whether this is the van that will transport my worldly possessions to charity shops and rubbish dumps and recycling centres. If it is, I think I'd rather not be here to witness it.

While I'm contemplating whether to try and will myself away before I see things I may wish I hadn't, Ellie, Eve and Max emerge from the front door, empty-handed. Max climbs into the back of the van, hands Ellie the Selfridges bag, Eve one of the boxes and carries the final package out himself, closing the van doors behind him with a decisive thrust of his hips. The three of them walk into the house and close the door behind them. I join them inside a second later.

The hall is again filled with boxes, bags and suitcases, but the luggage is not any I recognize. This, I'm guessing, is a day for moving in rather than moving out.

'Right, that's the last load and I, for one, am exhausted. I vote for a tea-and-biscuit break. Do you ladies agree?'

'Dad, why would I ever say no to a biscuit? I'll make the tea.'

While Ellie runs into the kitchen, I follow Max and Eve into the sitting room and am greeted by changes that signal, once and for all, as if I needed any further proof, that this is no longer my home.

The photographic shrine to my life with Max and Ellie has been removed, a solitary six-by-four framed picture of the three of us together in Greece nestling cosily among the books. The walls are now adorned with art they haven't housed before; nice art, good art, expensive contemporary art by the look of it. Just not art that Max and I ever owned together. The mantelpiece is now the proud exhibitor of a single eight-by-ten framed photograph of Max and Eve together on a summer's day at what appears to be a wedding or a garden party. Their arms are draped affectionately around each other's waists, both of them laughing – not just smiling, but laughing – into the camera. They look happy. Really happy. I wonder whose party it was, or whose wedding. Whether I knew the hosts or whether the event was part of Max's new social life, a life I know so little about.

I notice that the tatty green armchair, the chair I'd been imploring Max to dispose of since we first moved in together, the chair he'd acquired when he was a second-year student from somewhere I suspected wasn't a shop but rather a street corner, the chair he'd refused to part company with for the duration of our cohabitation, has finally disappeared, replaced by a small, smart, brown leather sofa. I see that a stripped pine desk has taken up residence adjacent to the French doors at the far end of the sitting room and a new bookcase is waiting patiently in one of the alcoves to be filled with whatever tomes Eve's brought with her.

It's strange, witnessing my old house undergo these changes. A bit like going into a neighbour's home, familiar in shape and size but disconcertingly different in colour, style and furnishings. Or like a memory that contrasts sharply with another's recollection of the same event, with no clear barometer for which version – if either – is the truth.

Ellie walks in carefully, precariously carrying a tray too weighty for her little arms. She manages to deposit it safely on to the wooden trunk in the middle of the room before edging herself between Max and Eve to settle down on the sofa with them. Max responds with an amused grin and shifts himself to make room for her.

'Seriously, ladies, I'm pooped. Do you think we've done enough for today?'

'Are you joking, Dad? There's still loads to do. We haven't even started unpacking yet. Didn't you see all those boxes in the hall?'

Max laughs and hugs her towards him.

'You're a hard taskmaster, Ellie Myerson, do you know that?'

'Mmm . . . well, I wonder where she can possibly get that from? Weren't you up marking essays until well past midnight last night? And on a Friday night too.'

'Ah, but that, you see, was only with a view to freeing up the whole weekend to help you move in, wasn't it?'

'I don't know, Ellie. Your dad – he's the last of the great charmers, isn't he?'

Ellie and Eve exchange a conspiratorial glance before the two of them pounce on Max and begin tickling him relentlessly.

'I surrender, I surrender. I admit I'm as much of a task-master as my crack-the-whip eight-year-old daughter.'

'Too little, too late, Max, don't you think, Ellie? Get him just below the ribs, that'll teach him.'

Ellie is giggling wildly and Max can barely breathe he's laughing so hard.

'It's . . . not . . . fair. You . . . have . . . to stop . . . if someone . . . surrenders. That's the . . . deal.'

'What do you think, Ellie? Shall we let him go?'

'Only if he promises that as soon as he's finished his tea we'll unpack the rest of your things until it's time for pizza and *The X Factor.*'

'I promise . . . I promise. Anything to get . . . you two . . . harridans . . . off me.'

Ellie clambers down from her vantage point on Max's chest and Eve flops back on to the far side of the sofa, the three of them still trying to catch their breath.

I look at Max and I notice for the first time how much his face has changed. It's free from the gloom that's furrowed his brow and darkened the light behind his eyes for the past two and a half years. It's the face of a man who's happy, who's contented with his given lot, who has, at last, found the peace he's been in search of for far too long. The face of a man restored to well-being after a painful period of emotional ill health. It's heart-warming to be reacquainted with the exuberance of the man I married, consoling to witness these qualities returned to him, even if I can't be there to share them. And I have Ellie and Eve to thank for bringing Max back to himself. He couldn't have done it without them. Without both of them. I know that.

I look at Ellie, at the uninhibited grin animating her face, and there's nothing but pleasure lighting her eyes. Whatever anxieties she may have harboured about Eve's permanent involvement in their lives have clearly long since evaporated.

I scan the room again and instead of regret for the objects of mine that are no longer present, I feel unexpectedly relieved by their absence. Seeing Eve's belongings in what used to be my home doesn't feel like the usurpation I was anticipating but rather a liberation from the debris of the past. I feel suddenly unencumbered, as though all those material possessions had been tying me to the living world by a cord that's now been cut, releasing me from the burden of my own grief.

Surveying the house now, the house that was once the location of so many happy times with Max and Ellie, what I unearth are strangeness and familiarity housed under the same roof. It's not, I know, my home any more. It's finally letting go of me, as I am of it.

Max slurps the last of his tea ostentatiously and, proving that he's as good as his word, leaps off the sofa and pulls Ellie to her feet in the process.

As the trio troop upstairs in crocodile fashion, I remain in the sitting room with no inclination to follow, keen to allow them the privacy they've so often been denied, uneasy about the intrusion that I've inflicted upon their lives. It's time I left them to unpack alone.

# CHAPTER 33

Laughter penetrates the clouds and when they finally clear I find myself in the kitchen at home with Ellie and Eve. They're in the midst of a baking session, the intended outcome of which is, judging by the ingredients laid out and the festive songs emerging from the iPod dock, a Christmas pudding.

They're both singing along to the music, Ellie's nose covered in flour and her hand dipping into the cup of raisins at frequent enough intervals to prompt Eve to reweigh them before adding them to the mixing bowl. They look like a proper team. A proper family. A mother and daughter if you didn't know better.

'What do we have to do now?'

'It's really simple, although don't tell anyone I said so because they'll be really impressed that we made this from scratch. Once all the ingredients are nicely mixed together, we cover the bowl and secure it with string and then boil it in water for about five hours.'

'*Five* hours? That's ages. And then is it ready?'

'Pretty much. We should have made it about three weeks ago really. A week isn't long enough because ideally we'd feed it some brandy every few days for about a month before Christmas Day to make sure it's really tasty.'

'Brandy? So will it make me drunk?'

Eve laughs and dabs some more flour playfully on to Ellie's nose.

'Possibly, yes. But we won't have time to do that this year anyway so I think you'll be fine.'

Eve places the mixing bowl in a large saucepan and adds boiling water before the pair of them begin clearing up the happy mess they've made.

'Eve? You know how everyone says that Christmas is the time of the year when you're supposed to be most happy? Well, the thing is, sometimes I'm not. Sometimes it's when I'm most sad.'

Eve stops wiping down the work surface and turns to face my little girl, a crease of concern between her eyes. There's a solemnity in Ellie's expression that's all the more poignant for its contrast to her playfulness just moments ago.

'Why do you feel sad, pumpkin? Aren't you looking forward to Christmas? We're going to have a super time, with Granny and Grandpa and Uncle Connor on Christmas Day and then down in Salisbury with Nanna on Boxing Day. You can't feel sad about any of that, can you?'

Ellie seems momentarily swayed by Eve's enthusiasm, but then her own reservations resurface and her eyes begin to moisten before the saddest, solitary tear trickles down her cheek.

'What is it, Ellie? What's made you so sad all of a sudden?'

Eve takes Ellie's hand and guides her towards the kitchen table, where she sits down and lifts Ellie on to her lap. It's the most natural of maternal instincts and I can't fault Eve's actions. It's as if she's been doing it all her life.

'It's just that when I feel happy at Christmas it makes me feel bad at the same time because Mummy really loved Christmas and I know how sad she'd be that she's missing out on all the fun.'

Her confession concludes with a plaintive sob as Ellie loses the battle to hold back the troupe of tears intent on seeing the light of day. Amidst the yearning to take her in my arms and soothe her distress, there's a deep pride in her too. I wonder whether many children her age could be so thoughtful, so sensitive, whether she was predetermined to be so caring or whether my death has made her more perceptive than she would otherwise have been.

Eve holds Ellie in her arms and gently strokes her cheek.

'I'm sure you and your mummy had some lovely Christmases together. And even though she's not here any more, you'll always have the memories of those Christmases with her, won't you?'

Ellie responds with an almost imperceptible nodding of her head. When she begins to speak, her voice is hesitant, barely more than a whisper.

'I think Christmas is the time I miss Mummy the most.'

And Christmas is the time I miss you most too, my angel, if that's even possible when every day I miss you with a ferocity I'd have thought unbearable had someone warned me of its magnitude before I got here. I wish you could know just how much, Ellie, how much you're loved and missed and how incredibly proud I am of you.

435

Eve wipes Ellie's damp face with soft strokes of her fingers.

'Why don't you tell me about some of the best memories you have of Christmas with Mummy?'

Ellie takes a few deep breaths, as much to stem the tide of tears as to consider her answer.

'I liked it when I'd wake up and find the sack of presents Father Christmas had left outside my bedroom door and I'd take it into Mummy and Daddy's room and I'd get into their bed and they'd watch me open all my presents. That's my best bit of the whole day, I think.'

I think that was always my best bit too.

I remember her very first Christmas, Ellie not yet a year old and more eager to practise her new crawling and climbing skills on our bed than to sit patiently between us, Max and I taking it in turns to open presents for her, laughing at her fascination with the wrapping paper and her almost complete disinterest in the toys inside. And then, year by year, that fascination gradually reversing, until her third Christmas when she finally understood that tearing off the sparkly, coloured paper was just a means to an end to reveal the real prize underneath.

That third Christmas was truly magical. Ellie was giddy with excitement about Santa's impending visit and she'd followed me round the kitchen, her anticipation reaching fever pitch as I prepared a glass of milk and a mince pie for him and a carrot for Rudolph, full of the speculations evoked by the idea of a man on a sleigh flying through the air to deliver gifts right into her home. She made us laugh with her endless queries and her concern for Santa's wellbeing: 'Won't he get cold out all night?' 'Won't he be tired

436

not getting any sleep?' 'What if the reindeers crash in the dark and he gets hurt?' 'What if he forgets to visit our house?' The last one, I assured her confidently, would never ever happen.

'And what's been your favourite Christmas present of all time?'

Ellie barely needs time to think before bouncing on Eve's lap with the urgency of a newly made decision.

'I know! It was my last Christmas with Mummy and after I'd finished opening all the presents in my sack, Dad said that Santa had left something downstairs for me because it was too heavy for him to carry up to my bedroom. So we all went down into the sitting room and there was a brand new bike with a big red ribbon tied around the handlebars. That was definitely my best Christmas surprise ever.'

'That sounds like a fantastic Christmas Day, Ellie. I'm sure you'll never, ever forget it. You know, I've just had a thought about what we could do this afternoon. Why don't we make a memory map about Mummy, to help you keep all your best memories in one place?'

Eve's voice is bright and encouraging and, whatever a memory map is, I'm grateful to her for endeavouring to keep Ellie's sadness at bay.

'What's a memory map?'

'It's a big collage of photos, mementoes, souvenirs — anything you have to remind you of your best times with Mummy. We'll collect together all your favourite things and glue them on to one big piece of card and then we can hang it on the wall in your bedroom so that you can see it every night before you go to sleep and every morning when you wake up. We could make it while Dad's still out at football. How does that sound?'

That sounds wonderful.

Ellie leaps off Eve's lap, her energy levels restored by such a heart-warming suggestion, and heads for the sitting room.

'I love it. Can we do it now? There's a big box of photos in the cupboard under the TV and I'll get my special treasures box from my bedroom too. That's got loads of things in it from days out with Mummy.'

As Ellie rushes off in search of tangible memories, I watch Eve watching Ellie, a smile of warmth on her face, a smile of gratitude on mine. It can't be easy, can it, coming late to this familial party and negotiating her way through the minefield of bereavement etiquette? I've spent so much time being envious of her stepping into my role, being jealous of her living my life even though it's not mine to live any more, I think I may have been blinded to some of her admirable qualities: her kindness to Ellie, her compassion and love for Max and her generosity towards me, the woman who's done little more than complain about her since that very first date sixteen months ago.

Perhaps it's time for the dead to be as generous towards the living as the living are to the dead.

Ellie's back at the kitchen table now, rummaging through two big boxes and pulling out various ephemera to show Eve, who's stuck four sheets of white A4 paper on to a piece of cardboard and is sitting waiting, scissors and glue at the ready.

'What's this Ellie?'

'That's my ticket for the Parthenon. Mummy and Daddy took me to Greece and it was the best holiday ever. There was this restaurant we went to nearly every night in Athens 'cos they had the best grilled prawns in the world. And then we went to an island – I can't remember its name – and the sea was so clear that even when you were in really deep you could still see your toes. And sometimes it was so hot in the middle of the day that we had to go back to our apartment, but we had this really comfy hammock and Mummy or Daddy would lay in it with me and we'd read books together. I want to go back there one day.'

Ellie concludes her elaborate description of a holiday I hadn't even dared imagine she'd remember as she rummages around in one of the boxes for more treasures.

'Well, in that case, I definitely think the ticket should go on the memory map, don't you? And maybe we can find a photo of that holiday too?'

'Yep, definitely. I think I want to be an archaeologist when I grow up. It's really cool. You get to dig up things from thousands of years ago and then work out who they belonged to. It's like a jigsaw puzzle but without the picture on the box to show you what it's supposed to look like. I think that would be an awesome job.'

She really is special, my little girl. I've no doubt her career plans will change countless times over the coming decade, but right now there's pleasure enough in the knowledge that her current ambitions are inextricably linked with experiences she shared with both Max and me.

'Is that you in this photo, Ellie?'

Ellie looks at it and giggles.

'Yep, that's me as the Ladybird when we did *James and the Giant Peach* at school. Dad has a video of it somewhere and it's really embarrassing. I was only about five and everyone kept forgetting their lines so the teacher kept having to shout them out for us. But Mummy made my costume for me and it was definitely the best costume in the whole play.'

I remember that costume. It took hours to make. Ellie was the world's most impatient model during fittings – she'd fidget every time I started making adjustments – but when I finally showed it to her in the mirror, she'd gazed at her own reflection with such wonderment that the hours spent at the sewing machine seemed immaterial. I can still see, so vividly, that look on her face now – the look of someone enthralled by their own transformation.

'There's loads of other things I still want to find for the memory map, Eve. I want to find a picture of Mummy and me at the piano – I know there's one somewhere – because she used to teach me tunes like 'Twinkle Twinkle'. And I want to find my first swimming badge because Mummy and Daddy taught me how to swim. And I've got the ticket here somewhere from when Mummy took me to see *Mary Poppins* at the theatre. Oh, and when we went to the ballet too, *The Nutcracker* at the Opera House. I want to add those. I was just thinking as well, what about sticking on a page from one of my exercise books when I got a gold star for spelling homework? Because Mummy always helped me with my homework. That would be okay, wouldn't it?'

'That would be just fine. I think all those sound like lovely things to put on your memory map. You know,

Ellie, I know it's really, really sad that you lost your mummy when you were so young, but it sounds like you had some really lovely times together. In fact, I think you probably had more lovely times with your mummy in those few years than some people have with mummies who are around for much, much longer.'

Eve's right. We did have lovely times, Ellie and I. I'd look at her sometimes, when we'd be out on one of our trips together to the theatre or to the cinema or just to wander around parks or galleries, and I'd think how lucky I was to have a daughter who was so much fun to be with. I had friends who complained about husbands disappearing off to various sporting activities at the weekend, but to me it always seemed like rather a special gift. All those afternoons with Ellie, just the two of us, milling around town together – I wouldn't have swapped them for anything.

Ellie looks at the photo she's holding now – of her, Max and me ice skating at Somerset House – and suddenly seems less convinced by Eve's positive analysis.

'But I still miss her. Sometimes remembering nice times with Mummy just makes me miss her even more.'

Eve retrieves a stray curl from Ellie's forehead and pops it back inside her red hair clip.

'Of course you still miss her, Ellie. You'll probably always miss her. But think about all the ways in which your mummy's still with you, like all the things you've told me about this afternoon. Swimming and playing tunes on the piano and doing your homework well; they're all things Mummy gave you and they're all things you'll have with you forever. And I'm sure there are lots of other things too. What about Mummy's roast potatoes – think how many people are going to enjoy those because she taught you the recipe. You might still be making those potatoes in fifty years' time, maybe even for your own children, maybe even your own grandchildren, and all because Mummy showed you how to make them. That's pretty special, isn't it?'

Ellie giggles, perhaps at the idea of a potato being special or perhaps at the thought of one day having children of her own.

'So would that be like Mummy teaching me how to do funny voices in storybooks 'cos now I do them to all my friends at school during reading time and everyone really laughs? Or like when she taught me how to draw a dog's face really easily and everyone in my class thinks it's really clever?'

'That's exactly right, Ellie. They're both very good examples. And it's true of how memories work too. I never met your mummy but I feel like I know her because of all the lovely memories that you and Dad share with me. So there's lots that I know about things the three of you did together, and the kind of person she was, even though I never had the opportunity to meet her myself.'

I'm shocked and not a little humbled. All this time I've imagined that it must be difficult, painful, irritating even, for Eve joining a family with the memory of her predecessor so potent in the air. But now Eve's telling me I've got it all wrong, that these are conversations she not only tolerates but embraces, that she'll go out of her way to make room for me in her life with Max and Ellie.

'Look how many people you've already got on your memory map, Ellie. Not just you and Mummy and Dad but Granny, Grandpa, Nanna, Harriet, Connor . . . and is that a photo of you with Mummy's friends at work? You know, even though she died very young, your mummy touched the lives of lots of people and they all have their own memories of her, so in that way she's still very much here with all of us.'

Ellie surveys the map she's made of our life together, and for the first time I feel secure in the belief that Max and Ellie – with a little help from Eve – will be devoted guardians of our collective memories.

'My mummy really was special. She always knew when I wanted my head stroked, and could always make me feel better, however sad I was. At night, when she tucked me up in bed, we'd play this game where I'd tell her I loved her up the sky and round the world and then she'd tell me she loved me up the sky and round the world and back again, and then I'd add on round the moon and then she'd add on one of the planets and sometimes we'd carry on doing it for ages, until we'd gone round the whole solar system. And Mummy would always end by saying she loved me to infinity and beyond, like Buzz Lightyear in *Toy Story*, and that's when she'd kiss me goodnight and turn out the light. Sometimes I just want to be tucked up by her again and tell her I love her.'

Ellie's staring down at the memory map, fiddling self-consciously with the stick of glue, but the image I'm immersed in now is of Ellie aged five, giggling in bed as we declared our love for one another via a whistle-stop tour of the universe. I loved that bedtime ritual of ours. And I love, too, that she still remembers it so well.

'Why don't you then, Ellie? There's nothing to stop you telling your mummy that you love her. Look, here's a really nice photo of her the day she married your dad. You could say it to her now.'

Ellie looks unsure.

'Would that be a bit like Mummy talking to me before I was born?'

'What do you mean?'

'Dad told me that when I was still in Mummy's tummy, she used to talk to me lots and tell me about everything that was going on in the world before I could see it for myself. Would me talking to Mummy now be a bit like that?'

'Yes, I think it'd be just like that. Because Mummy couldn't see you then, just as you can't see her now, but it didn't stop her wanting to tell you things, did it, just as you want to tell her things too?'

Ellie picks up the photograph Eve has handed her. It's a portrait of me just moments after the registrar pronounced us husband and wife. I'm beaming, my smile directed away from the camera and upwards, towards something out of frame. That something was Max and I think it was, after the birth of Ellie, the happiest moment of my life.

Ellie looks at the photo and then at Eve for reassurance, who provides it by way of an encouraging smile and a coaxing nod.

'Mummy, I just wanted to tell you that I miss you and I hope you're okay and I hope you're not missing us too much. And I wanted to tell you that I'm going to miss you especially over Christmas and I hope that whatever you're doing you have a nice time. And what I really wanted to tell you is that I still think about you all the time even though you're not here any more and I love you lots and lots.'

I try to dry my cheeks but there's a steady stream of tears to replace those I wipe away. I never thought I'd hear anyone say that again. And of all the people in the world, there's no one I'd want to hear it from more than my precious little girl.

Because I love you too, angel, more than you could ever possibly know. More than I ever knew possible. To infinity and beyond.

Ellie puts the photograph on to the table, face down, and dabs glue on its reverse before fixing it to the top right hand corner of her memory map.

'Do you think that was okay?'

'I think that was just perfect, Ellie.'

Ellie looks up, her face calm, her declaration perhaps providing the catharsis she needed.

'I think I'm almost done. Oh, there's one more thing I want to put on.'

Ellie rummages around in her special treasures box and eventually extricates a thick pile of yellow Post-it notes.

'What are they?'

'They're drawings Mummy did for me. When I was little I sometimes used to have bad dreams and I'd find it really hard to get to sleep because I was scared about what I'd dream. So every night when Mummy put me to bed, she'd draw me something nice – like an angel or a fairy or a big, smiling sunshine face – and she'd stick it above my bed and tell me it would watch over me while I was sleeping to make sure I didn't have any nightmares.'

I had no idea she'd kept all of those. I remember trying to devise a new amiable icon for her every night for about a month until the nightmares disappeared as suddenly and inexplicably as they'd arrived.

'Okay, I'm finished.'

'Right, shall we go and put it up in your room then?'

Ellie nods and together they carry the collage upstairs and into Ellie's bedroom.

'What do you think? Shall we prop it up on the mantelpiece and then you'll be able to see it when you're lying in bed? Look.'

They sit on the bed together and Eve puts an arm around Ellie's shoulders.

'I think your mummy would be proud of that, don't you? There are some really lovely memories up there.'

Ellie nods, the half-smile not quite detracting from the sadness in her eyes.

'I know you miss her, Ellie; it's only natural that you do. And you know that's fine, don't you? Because people only have one mummy and that's what makes someone's mummy so very special.'

Eve tries to look into Ellie's eyes but her face remains downcast.

'You know I'm not here to try and replace her, don't you? No one can ever do that because your mummy was unique to you. But I do hope that you and I can become very good friends and that you'll keep telling me lots of things about her because she sounds really special and I know she must have been because she made you and you're very special indeed.'

Ellie surrenders herself into Eve's arms and their embrace seems to disable time, securing them both in an orbit of hope for the future.

'Thank you for making that with me, Eve. I really like having you around, a lot.'

Eve laughs and kisses the top of Ellie's head.

'I can assure you that the feeling's mutual, pumpkin. Now, do you think we ought to go downstairs and see if the water needs topping up on that Christmas pudding?'

Ellie hops off the bed and the two of them leave the room, hand in hand.

I remain in Ellie's bedroom and take another look at the memory map sitting in pride of place on the mantelpiece. It really is a lovely thing. Ellie's written captions above some of the items, others she's left blank, assuming they're self-explanatory. I spot a photo of the three of us that day we went to the zoo – we must have got a passerby to take it for us, I don't quite recall – and another – one of my all-time favourites – of Mum, Ellie and me in the garden at Mum's in Salisbury: three generations of women lined up in the sunshine, beaming against a backdrop of roses in full bloom.

I feel like I've spent so long regretting the brevity of my life, convinced it was too short to be anything other than inconsequential, mourning the ambitions I was never able to fulfil and the successes that were never achieved, but I realize now that's just one interpretation. It's the judgement of someone who was bitter and angry and perceiving their glass to be half-empty, deprived of the elixir of life they felt to be rightfully theirs. But there's another perspective, one that's just emerging into view through the mist and fog of early mourning. It's an altogether brighter landscape of a life filled with enduring love and accomplished work and events – both the momentous and the ordinary – that the living will remember until the day they die.

I look at a photo of Ellie sitting in front of the Christmas tree with Max and me at his parents' house that last year we had together. She looks so content and carefree and, for the first time since I died, the thought occurs to me that there's only one obstacle standing in between Ellie and a happy family life, only one thing that needs to be done to ensure she can have the future she needs and deserves. I just don't know whether I'm ready to do that yet. I don't know if I'm even capable of it, whether it's not a maternal sacrifice too far. But if Eve's able to offer such considerable generosity to me and such great kindness to my daughter and so much love to my husband, I must surely try and find it within myself to reciprocate.

# CHAPTER 34

I'm astonished. Happily astonished, but astonished none-theless. I've fantasized that I might be allowed here today but I never really expected it. It's as if all my Christmases have come at once this year: first Ellie's birthday, then Max's and now this – Christmas itself. Well, Harriet's Christmas Eve drinks, anyway.

Harriet's Night Before Christmas party has been an annual event for over a decade. Ever since I moved in with Max, in fact, and she bought her first flat. The guest list is invariably eclectic or random, depending on your point of view; there's always a smattering of our friends from university, numerous colleagues, a couple of devas-tatingly handsome men Harriet's toying with the idea of seducing, her close family and then the people she's always very sweetly described as her extended family: me, Max, Ellie, Connor, my mum, even Joan and Ralph. She always invites them all. This year I'm the only one of them who's not present. Not visibly, anyway.

She's done herself proud with the decorations this year. The Georgian town house in Islington she bought the year I died is designed as if with Christmas parties in mind: majestic ceilings, full-height windows, polished wooden floorboards and restored fireplaces in every room. Tonight the first-floor sitting room is illuminated with transparent fairy lights across the bookshelves, while a department store-sized tree sparkling with gold and silver baubles dominates one corner of the room. The table is glittering with tea lights in frosted glass holders, highlighting the vast platters of food that Harriet has, almost certainly, had delivered from the local deli this afternoon: stuffed vine leaves, mini filo tarts with sun-dried tomatoes, sea bass ceviche, beef carpaccio, plump kalamata olives and a range of cheeses you'd usually only savour in a five-star restaurant or specialized delicatessen. The far end of the table is lined with four separate champagne buckets, each displaying its own bottle of Pol Roger, for which I've no doubt there are sufficient replenishments in the fridge. One thing you can never accuse Harriet of is not knowing how to throw a party in style.

Surveying the room, I see Ellie standing by the window playing a game with Connor, which appears to involve him encouraging her to punch him on the arm as hard as she can without him so much as flinching. I suspect there's a woman he's got his eye on somewhere and that this dual display of machismo and avuncularity is all part of the seduction strategy. My mum is over by the bookcase, chatting to the person I'd least expect her to be with – Eve. And the hostess herself is seated on a pale grey Conran sofa, deep in conversation with my husband. I haven't seen Harriet since her revelation after Max's birthday so I join them first.

As Max steadies a plate of food on his lap with one hand while drinking from a glass of champagne with the other, I notice that there's something missing, something that I wasn't expecting to have been removed so soon, something for which I don't feel adequately prepared.

The third finger of his left hand is emphatically bare. I can just about make out the very faint circle of paler skin where the thick, platinum band had sat confidently for almost a decade, never imagining that it wouldn't remain there until the day he died.

A sting of rejection pierces me from the inside out, an attack by the twin forces of envy and betrayal. I very nearly capitulate to them before the ghost of Max's voice comes back to me, the words with which he reassured Ellie all those months ago repeating themselves gently in my head like a calm, persistent mantra, gradually restoring me to the safe ground of rationality. It's not about love, that ring, but about commitment, a commitment of which Max was robbed as much as I was the day I inadvertently left him.

'I'm sorry, I really am. I still don't know what came over me that day. I hope you know me well enough to know that I'm generally not that insensitive. But those things I said were totally out of order and I've felt terrible ever since.'

As Max puts his glass on the floor, I try not to look at – or think about – that empty finger.

'It's okay, Max. Really. You've apologized, like, a hundred times over the past seven months and it really is forgotten, I promise.'

'I know, I know. It's just that it was the last thing you deserved, not least when you've been so good to me since Rachel died. It was just really tough, that second anniversary; I felt like there was no way I wasn't going to upset someone and so I ended up going the whole hog and managing to upset everyone all at the same time.'

Max smiles at the recollection as if it's already a distant memory. I suppose, for him at least, a lot has happened since.

'Look, you and I both know that tact and conversational discretion aren't exactly my forte. I know full well I blundered into that conversation like someone suffering from diplomacy Tourette's. It was never my place to lecture you like that. I just don't know when to keep my mouth shut sometimes.'

Harriet raises a playful eyebrow, as if waiting for Max to contradict her. He declines, with a mischievous smile.

'You had every right to be upset. She was your best friend and you didn't feel I was honouring her memory sufficiently. Neither of us was on top form that day, I think it's fair to say.'

They collude in a moment's silence, a tacit mutual agreement that this concludes the incident, once and for all.

'To change the subject completely, I'm guessing Eve told you about my failed jaunts to the fertility clinic?'

Max hesitates for a second before appearing to decide that, after the conflicts and misunderstandings of the past year, the truth is almost certainly better than fiction.

'She did, yes. She was worried about you. I was really sorry to hear it, Harriet. Infertility's not something I'd ever thought about much before I met Eve. Have there been any developments? Eve said there was one other clinic you were looking into.'

'Funnily enough I got an email from them yesterday. They've had a look at my medical records and seem to think the doctor I went to before was unnecessarily pessimistic. I don't know. The cynic in me says I'm being an idiot and they're simply speaking to the colour of my money – you'd think I was asking to put down a deposit on a flat the amount they charge. It's hard not to feel a bit optimistic, though.'

Harriet smiles drolly and takes a long sip of champagne.

'But that's great news. Seriously, Harriet, I'm delighted for you.'

'Well, we'll see. At the end of the day, if it doesn't work out, it's not like I don't have a great job and a pretty nice life to keep me occupied. It just feels like something I want to try, at least, and if it works out that would be fantastic but if it doesn't . . . well, I'll cross that bridge when I come to it.'

'Any support you need – anything at all – I'm here for you. You know that, don't you? To be honest, I've always thought you were a bit hasty in closing the door on motherhood altogether. I think you'd be a great mum if your relationship with Ellie is anything to go by.'

'Let's not go jumping the fertility gun just yet. It's still early days. But I am grateful to you and Rach. I'm not sure I'd have come close to this conclusion if I weren't so involved in Ellie's life. And if Rach . . . well, if what happened to Rach hadn't made me reassess my priorities. Of course, there's also you to thank for that final argumentative kick up the butt I needed.'

'I thought we weren't going to mention that again?'

'Last time, I promise. Now, I probably shouldn't have taken so long to tell you this, Max, but I do think Eve's great. Truly. I can see how happy she makes you – I think you'd have to be blind not to – and there's no disputing the fact that she's fantastic with Ellie. Just as soon as I've got over my rivalry with her in that respect I think she and I are going to be good friends.'

I can't help laughing. Harriet and me both on that front.

'Thanks, Harriet. That means a lot. I'd really like us all to be able to hang out together, with or without Ellie. Might we even be making up a grown-up foursome some-day soon?'

Harriet emits a loud, exaggerated groan.

'Fat chance of that, I'm afraid.'

'So you're not seeing anyone at the moment?'

'Nope, there's not so much as a glimmer of light on that horizon. I barely meet anyone outside of work these days and much as I love my job there's no way I'd ever date another lawyer – I couldn't cope with another worka-holic in my life. And I don't know if you've noticed, but the pool of eligible men over thirty-five isn't just dried up and empty, it's full of last year's leaves and a couple of dead birds to boot.'

Max laughs before a mischievous expression lights up his eyes.

'This might be a bit left field, but you know who's always had the hots for you? Connor. Seriously. He's always really liked you. I don't really understand why he's never asked you out. Perhaps he thinks it's all a bit too close to home. But you could do a lot worse, couldn't you? You might even help calm him down a bit.'

'Connor? You're joking, right? I mean, no disrespect or anything and I know I've been single a long time but I can't imagine a worse recipe for dating disaster.'

'Oh, come on. He's not that bad. Some people would even think he's a bit of a catch. And at least you've known him long enough to know where all the skeletons are buried. What's so wrong with him?'

'You mean other than the fact that he's never committed to anyone for longer than a month and even that's been a struggle on the monogamy front. He's even more vain than I am and I can't remember the last time he dated someone who wasn't just about young enough to be his daughter. No, Max, you're way off beam with that piece of matchmaking.'

It takes a few seconds for Max's laughter to subside sufficiently for him to respond.

'I can't really argue with any of that. But I do think he's ready to settle down now. Seriously. He just needs the love of a good woman, Harriet.'

'I think he's had the love of plenty of good women in his time. Anyway, given where I am on the childbearing front at the moment, I can't think of anyone less suitable to have a relationship with. I may try to have an actual baby, Max – I don't need an oversized one in my life too. If I was going to start dating anyone it certainly wouldn't be someone who's even more terrified of parenting than I am.'

'I think you might be wrong on that score too, Harriet. I know Connor talks the bachelor talk but I wouldn't be surprised if he didn't wake up to the alarming sound of his own biological clock one day soon. Just look at how fantastic he is with Ellie. As if he wouldn't make a great dad.'

All three of us look over to the Christmas tree where Connor is lifting Ellie up to reach the chocolates at the very top.

'Yes, well there's a very good reason for that. It's because he's on the same wavelength as an eight-year-old child.'

'Fine, Harriet. Whatever you say. I just thought I'd put it out there. But it sounds to me like the lady doth protest too much.'

Max smiles playfully, provoking an ironic, conversation-terminating glare from Harriet.

I have to say, I agree with Max; I don't think it's such a left-field idea at all. It was something Max and I talked about the very first night we introduced Harriet and Connor to one another, at that dinner party over a decade ago where the four of us played at being sophisticates before we really knew the rules. Harriet and Connor had spent the entire evening arguing about anything and everything with a passion which – in Hollywood movies, at least – has only one possible conclusion. All that combative flirtation may never have amounted to anything but I'm not sure I'd rule it out entirely, even all these years later.

Joan and Ralph are approaching the sofa and I find myself tensing with the anticipation of conflict. It's very generous of Harriet to invite them to this party every year, but I can't help thinking that it's also just a little masochistic; I can't remember a single occasion when my best friend and my mother-in-law have inhabited the same space without finding myself dragged into a corner by Harriet to placate her fury after Joan's issued the latest in a string of barbed criticisms. Why she'd keep opening herself up to the inevitability of verbal attack – especially without me there to calm her down afterwards – is beyond me.

Joan's smiling. Ralph looks a little nervous.

'Such a lovely party, Harriet. Your best yet, I think. I've met such a lot of interesting people – I even got talking to a judge earlier and he was very charming. I mean, what a fascinating job that must be. It's so kind of you to invite us, we do appreciate it.'

It happens very rarely, but Harriet is stumped for words. She exchanges a bewildered glance with Max, who returns it with a look of amusement. Ralph is beaming – if I'm not mistaken – a little triumphantly.

'Well . . . er . . . that's very nice of you, Joan. I'm glad you're having a good time.'

'Oh, we're having a lovely time. All this food and champagne too. I think I've had four glasses already. It's gone straight to my head.'

'Well, there's plenty more where that came from. Speaking of which, if you'll excuse me, I'd just better check that supplies don't need stocking up.'

Harriet makes a tactful exit and Max invites his mum and dad to join him on the sofa.

'That was nice of you, Mum. I think Harriet really appreciated that.'

'Yes, well, Max, it is a lovely party. Credit where it's due, that's what I always say.'

Max raises a wry smile but manages to curb the multiple responses I've no doubt are keen to escape his lips.

'Why don't you sit there for a minute, Mum, while Dad gets you a glass of water. I'm just popping to the bathroom and then I'm going to check on Eve quickly.'

As Max slips out of the door, I head over to where Mum and Eve are still chatting intently in the corner.

'Please don't apologize and please don't think any more of it. I do understand how difficult this must be for you, Celia, and I'm sorry if we haven't been as sensitive to that as we might have been. The last thing any of us want is for you to feel uncomfortable, least of all around Ellie.'

'That's very kind of you. I'm not going to deny it's been hard, but that's not Max's fault and it's certainly not yours, Eve. It's just that losing a daughter . . . well, there's nothing that can ever prepare you for it.'

'I can't imagine how terrible it must be. It's hard enough having been estranged from my parents all these years – I know Max told you I haven't seen them for a while – but I'm not pretending for a second that's anything close to what you've been through.'

'I don't want to be morbid – not tonight of all nights – but I don't think you ever really acclimatize to your child not being there any more. I suspect there'll always be moments when I forget and pick up the phone to ring Rachel. Maybe it's because it was so unexpected, so sudden, that there are so many unsaid thoughts still mulling around in my mind. I think Rachel knew how proud of her I was, I'm sure she did, but I do wish I'd had one last opportunity to tell her.'

You just did, Mum.

'What's going on here, then?'

Max joins Mum and Eve, a champagne bottle in his hand, from which he refills both their glasses. Mum looks slightly sheepish.

'I've just been apologizing to Eve for some of the misunderstandings we've had recently. I know this isn't an easy situation for anyone, not least for you two, starting a new relationship with such a lot of emotional baggage in tow, and I really am very sorry if I've created any additional tension. It's just taken some getting used to, that's all. I hope you can both forgive me.'

There's an insecurity in Mum's tone and it pains me to hear it. I hate seeing her so vulnerable, especially at a party like this. In spite of her resolution to remain on her own after Dad died, I know that she's always found family gatherings particularly difficult.

Max throws a generous arm around Mum's shoulders and squeezes her affectionately.

'There's absolutely nothing to forgive, Celia. It's been a strange year for all of us and the important thing is that we've got through it with our relationships intact. I'm not sure the same could be said for many other families.'

Mum smiles at him, gratefully and with palpable relief, as he kisses her on the cheek.

'Well, I'm really looking forward to having the three of you over on Boxing Day. Are you still okay to bring dessert, Eve? Ellie tells me that the Christmas pudding is looking splendid. And that you've made a cake as well. You really shouldn't have but it's very good of you.'

'It's no trouble at all. We're all really looking forward to it too. Here's to a lovely Christmas.'

Eve, Max and Mum clink conciliatory glasses. It would seem that this is a night for reparations all round.

Max was right. Not every family would have survived the tragedies, the transitions, the emotional upheavals that my family's endured over the past two and a half years. I suddenly realize that this is the first time I've seen my loved ones harmonious since I died. And instead of making me feel excluded, it brings me an unexpected sense of peace.

Ellie bounces over to the corner of the room, dragging Connor behind her.

'Guess what, Dad? Connor says he's bought me the best Christmas present ever this year. I can't wait to find out what it is.'

Max looks at his watch.

'Well, you're not going to have to wait too much longer, munchkin. It's only an hour and a half until Christmas Day so we'd better get you home to bed or else Santa might have to give our house a miss this year.'

As Max, Ellie and Eve say their goodbyes, the netherworld decides it's time for me to leave this particular party too.

It's been an evening of unpredictable atonements. The social accord which I'd once assumed would upset me with its promise of lives lived contentedly without me has, instead, brought me unexpected tranquillity. I suppose that just goes to show that we never stop surprising ourselves, even long after we're dead.

As the vision and then the sound of a party still in full swing are swallowed by the gathering clouds, I'm left hoping this isn't the last of Ellie I'm going to see this Christmas.

# CHAPTER 35

The bright clouds disperse but underneath is complete darkness. I'm disoriented for a few seconds, my eyes needing time to adjust to the dramatic change in light. Eventually I begin to discern outlines of shaded objects in the world beneath me.

I'm inside a building and I can see a small figure walking down a hallway, dragging what must be a heavy load behind them. They reach a door and stop, tentatively, halting for a few seconds, the deep self-conscious breaths betraying the concentration of their producer. I see a hand raised and placed gently on the door, pushing it open slowly, cautiously, until the pathway is clear and they're free to enter whatever room it was they were searching for.

Suddenly a light snaps on, startling me and temporarily disabling my vision.

'Happy Christmas, Dad! Happy Christmas, Eve!'

I open my eyes to discover that we're in my bedroom – what used to be my bedroom – where Max is now emerging from underneath the duvet, rubbing his eyes in an attempt to rouse himself towards wakefulness. Eve is lying next to him, beginning to stir but not quite yet in the land of the conscious. And in the doorway is Ellie, dressed in red pyjamas adorned with miniature snowmen, her face bright with excitement and her hands clasped tightly around the neck of the bulging pink pillowcase waiting patiently beside her.

I'm here. I'm here with them for the first Christmas since I died. I don't know who or what I'm supposed to thank for letting me be here today, but thank you, who-ever or whatever you are.

'Happy Christmas, munchkin. You do know it's only quarter to six, don't you?'

'I know. I've been awake for ages already and I've been really good and stayed in my room till now. I'm only fif-teen minutes earlier than when you said I could come in. But look what a big sack of presents I've got.'

Ellie summons all her energy and, in one melodramatic heave, hauls the bloated pillowcase in front of her. Eve sits up and kisses Max good morning.

'Happy Christmas, Ellie. So, are you getting in then?'

Without the need for any further encouragement, Ellie drags her sack of presents round to Max's side of the bed, scrambles over him as if his body were simply an obstacle to be traversed, locates the almost imperceptible gap between her dad and his girlfriend and slips, feet first, under the duvet. Max smiles and hoists her bounty on to the bed for her.

I watch the three of them under the covers together, Ellie beginning to unwrap one present after another, stocking fillers dominating the top half of the sack as has always been the tradition, Max and Eve both feigning suf-ficient surprise to suggest they've never seen any of the items before, taking it in turns to marvel at novelty bars of soap and TV character-adorned stationery. I find my mind wandering back to the time when I was under that duvet, when Ellie was opening presents next to me, when I could lean over and touch Max's bare chest and know that this was just how I'd always hoped domestic life would be.

I'm drawn to thoughts of that last Christmas the three of us spent together, and find that the memories start flooding back without me even having to invoke them, memories that must have been in hiding for the past two and a half years and are only now deeming it sufficiently safe to make an appearance.

I remember Ellie creeping into that very same room, clambering silently on to our bed and awakening us to the realization that it was still only five-fifteen in the morning. I remember us stalling the opening of presents with the suggestion that Max go downstairs first to make coffee for us and hot chocolate for her. I remember Ellie and I snuggling under the duvet together to ward off the cold air yet to be heated by radiators that weren't due to warm up for another half an hour, entertaining one another with lists of the things we were most looking forward to about the day ahead, hers being the opening of presents and mine the infamous lunch we'd have later at Joan and Ralph's, a lunch which invariably left everyone vowing not to eat again until the year was officially over. I remember Max coming back upstairs, carrying three steaming mugs on a tray and telling us to get up and look out of the window, and Ellie and me refusing, saying it was too cold, diving further under the duvet and giggling at our own rebelliousness. I remember Max coaxing us, saying we'd regret it if we didn't, and us finally relenting, hurrying out of bed to brave the frosty air, and opening the curtains to be greeted by nothing but whiteness, everywhere, as far as we could see, a blanket of purity illuminating the darkness. I remember Ellie's unadulterated joy as she surveyed that magical winter wonderland, the world as she knew it enveloped by a never-ending carpet of snow and her asking if we could go out, there and then, to build a snowman. I remember Max turning on the radio and us hearing the announcer proclaim it to be an historic snowfall, the deepest settling in a single night on record and the first white Christmas in London for three generations, and us reiterating to Ellie how lucky she was to have witnessed at such a young age what we'd had to wait all this time to see for ourselves. I remember retreating back under the duvet, leaving the curtains open so we could see the blanketed branches of the trees from where we huddled under the warmth of goose down, and Ellie opening her presents, all three of us knowing in our own way that this really was the most special of mornings. I remember the excited glances that Max and I shared as Ellie worked her way through her sack of gifts, knowing that the best was yet to come, and the expression of contagious delight on her face when we finally carried her downstairs to discover the present we hadn't been able to fit into a pillowcase.

I remember it all as if it were happening right now, as if these feelings belong to the present rather than the past, and it makes me realize how divorced I've been from so many of my recollections to date, how I've replayed events as if watching a home movie of someone else's life. But these memories are different. They're the memories of someone who's no longer afraid of the emotions that accompany them, however bittersweet those feelings may be.

All this time I've been fearful that Eve's presence in my family's life would slowly begin to erode not just Max and Ellie's memories but mine also. Instead her occupancy seems to be reacquainting me with memories I hadn't even known I'd lost.

Ellie is halfway through her presents now. Abruptly she stops unwrapping a parcel and places a hand on Max's arm in an incongruously mature gesture.

'Do you know what would make this morning perfect, Dad? If Mummy was here too and all four of us could be together for Christmas.'

Ellie's words begin to reverberate insistently in my ears and something shifts in me, something intangible and unknowable, something that emerges from the sleepiest hollow to lift a barrier between myself and my past, a barrier of my own making, of my own mourning. It's the realization, final and unequivocal, that my part to play in life really is over.

I think about that final Christmas Day again and discover that it's followed by wave after gentle wave of memories that feel real and visceral and joyful in a way I haven't experienced since I got here: the memory of Ellie giggling with wonderment on the beach at Hope Cove the first time we showed her the sea, Max and I running in and out of the too-cold water with her in our arms, her chubby knees spilling out of the yellow wetsuit we'd squeezed her fleshy limbs into; the memory of Ellie laughing infectiously as Max pushed her on the playground swing, demanding that he send her higher and higher, proclaiming triumphantly that she could touch the sky; the memory of Max and me boarding a plane with

Ellie for the very first time and her disbelief when we took off that such a cumbersome object really could fly.

I remember the day Harriet and I graduated, the high heels and lipstick we wore to customize those drab gowns, and the pride on my mum's face when the head of department congratulated me on my First as we drank Pimm's on the lawn outside college, the sun beaming as if to welcome us to our adult lives. I remember my first day at work, the anxiety I woke to that morning that I might not be up to the job and the quiet confidence by the time I went to bed that it was going to be okay, that it might even be more than okay, that I might actually have found my niche. I remember the campaign I'd been working on in the months before I died, the campaign that had been the hardest I'd worked on any project since university and which I'd known, long before it was celebrated with an award Max collected in my absence, was the best work I'd ever done.

I remember the Saturday morning Max and I first visited our house, me four months pregnant and still the victim of day-long nausea, us both knowing immediately that this was the home in which we wanted to raise our child, with its butler sink in the kitchen and low autumn sun peeking through the south-facing patio doors and a fire burning with welcoming warmth in the sitting room's wrought iron grate. I remember the first night we brought Ellie home, and laid her in the middle of our bed between us, marvelling at the miracle of having created something so undeniably perfect. I remember that morning in Aguas Calientes two years earlier, waking up with Max in the dark on the double mattress of our cheap hostel room, joining our guide and his other foreign wards for the dawn ascent to Machu Picchu, arriving at the top in time to watch the sun rise over the ancient monuments and Max asking me if I wanted to spend the rest of my life with him.

I remember them all and they're all indubitably mine. They're no longer distant memories, no longer scenes from a life that I have neither the ability nor the courage to watch without an accompanying soundtrack of bitterness, regret and loss. Instead they play out now to a light euphoria at the recognition of a life well lived. Like long-lost relatives returned from lengthy travels overseas, their reappearance is the catalyst for an appreciation of how much they've been missed.

They're memories that have finally found their way back to me, to embrace me, console me, and provide me with the greatest comfort I've known since I died. Perhaps only by accepting that the present is no longer mine to live am I able, finally, to engage with the past.

It suddenly occurs to me that maybe my being here today isn't a simple coincidence. Perhaps the reason I've been absent from so many family events, from the anniversaries and the birthdays and the annual festivities, isn't due to my exclusion by an external force beyond my comprehension or control. Perhaps I simply wasn't ready. Perhaps it would have been too painful. Perhaps only now am I able to watch these domestic milestones as an observer rather than a participant without feeling that my world – whatever that is – is falling apart.

Perhaps the only person who's been controlling my access all along is, in fact, me.

Ellie pulls her final present from the sack. It's a large, oblong-shaped gift wrapped in the prettiest paper, glittering gold stars on a silver backdrop that I'm guessing was Eve's discovery.

'Before you open this one, munchkin, we wanted you to know that it's from Eve and me. We asked Father Christmas if he minded us giving you your big present this year, so we left it out for him to put in your sack with all the others.'

Ellie returns her gaze to the present, handling it now even more carefully than before. She painstakingly peels off the three pieces of tape that form the last remaining obstacle between her and what's inside and pulls the gift from its wrapping.

It's a large jewellery box in polished mahogany, the wood gleaming with restorative pleasure. As Ellie lifts the lid, a drawer underneath opens automatically, revealing a labyrinth of individual compartments inside, each dressed decadently in deep red velvet. It really is a beautiful object.

'Your dad and I felt that now you're the custodian of all your mummy's jewellery, it was time you had a proper, grown-up jewellery box of your own to keep it all safe in.'

Ellie beams at her, as if understanding in an instant that this is a rite of passage, a moment of graduation in which she's been invited to join the world of adult responsibilities.

'Thank you so much. I love it. And I promise to take really good care of it, and of all Mummy's things.'

She flings her arms around Eve's neck and the hierarchy of appreciation is, I'm sure, completely justified. It's the most generous and poignant of gestures and one for which I'm sure both Ellie and I have Eve to thank. An act of generosity for which there's but a single way for me to reciprocate, I know.

'And that's not all, angel. There's one more surprise for you. Hold on there just a few seconds and I'll bring it up.'

Max disappears and Ellie looks up at Eve expectantly, who's unable to suppress the broad grin on her face. I think she's almost more excited than Ellie.

As Max opens the door, Ellie squeals with delight before I manage to catch a glimpse.

'A puppy! You got me a puppy? Oh my goodness, he's adorable.'

The chocolate-brown labrador springs out of Max's grasp and on to the bed where it's met by the over-excited arms of one very happy eight-year-old girl.

'Well, actually he's a she. I take it you like her then?'

'Like her? I love her! I love her so much already. Is she really all mine? I'm going to take such good care of her, you'll see. Thank you so so much. But you've been saying for ages that I'm not allowed a puppy. How come you changed your mind?'

'Well, you have Eve to thank for that. Turns out she's almost as mad keen on dogs as you are.'

Eve takes the puppy into her arms and holds her still so that Ellie can stroke her nose.

'I always wanted a puppy when I was younger and my mum and dad would never let me have one. So I knew just how you felt. And both your dad and I think you've been so grown-up lately that you're ready to look after her. You are, aren't you?'

'Of course I am. But, Dad, you said it wouldn't be fair to have a dog because we can't walk it during the day. Are you going to take her to school with you?'

Max laughs as he joins them on the bed.

'No, of course I'm not. Grandpa has very kindly said that he'll come and walk her every day while we're all at school. Although that still means we'll need to walk her before and after. Do you think you can do that with us?'

'I promise I'll do it every single day. And Grandpa can bring her to school when he comes to pick me up. All my friends are going to be so jealous. What do you think we should call her?'

'Well, I think that should be your decision, sweetheart, don't you? What name do you think might suit her?'

Ellie studies the puppy's face intently as if trying to read the name hidden in her warm, cocoa-coloured eyes.

'Dad, what was the name of that goddess we saw in that museum in Greece? The one who was really cool and really good at loads of different things and I told you at the end of the holiday that she was my favourite?'

'You mean Athena?'

'Athena. Yes. That's what I think we should call her. Because this puppy's going to be good at loads of things too and I'm going to teach her loads of tricks and she'll be the cleverest dog in London. We could call her Thena for short, like when we're chasing her in the park. What do you think?'

Max and Eve exchange smiles of quiet pride over the top of Ellie's head in a single, silent, affectionate communication.

'That, munchkin, is just about the best name I've ever heard for a dog. Athena it is.'

Ellie thanks Max with a smattering of kisses all over his face before turning her attention back to the most prized possession of the morning. As I watch the three of them romping on the bed with this newest addition to their clan, I finally understand that I've been deluding myself about this trio. They're not the make-shift community I've sometimes believed them to be. This is a family, a happy family, a family I'm no longer a part of. But it's also a different family to the one I knew and loved. And knowing that, seeing it with my own eyes, makes my exclusion from it bearable in a way I never imagined possible.

They were right before, Eve and Max: you can only ever have one mum and you can only ever have one first great love. And those are two achievements that even my untimely death can't take away from me.

As I watch this newly formed family unit collectively review Ellie's presents, I think forward to how the rest of their day will unfold.

I know that later on this morning, Max, Eve and Ellie will walk the ten-minute journey to Joan and Ralph's where Ellie's grandparents and uncle will shower her with yet more presents, such is the prerogative of an only child. I know that at lunch Ralph will sit Ellie to his left and Eve to his right, with Joan opposite him, and joke about how lucky he is to be surrounded by three such beautiful women. I know that Joan will light the Christmas pudding with only a drizzle of brandy, producing just the faintest flicker of a flame, and that Connor will insist they light it again, dousing it in so much alcohol that Joan will reprimand him as if still a child. I know that the grown-ups will play party games well into the early hours while Ellie will fall asleep from the excitement of it all, and that later Max will wrap her in a blanket to carry her the short distance back home. And I know that it's Eve who now has the leading role to play in this familial narrative, not me.

After all these months of worrying about my access – about when it might next be granted and when it might suddenly be denied – I begin to wonder just how valuable it is to me now. I used to feel compelled to watch the world below me, preoccupied during my temporary absences by speculations about what I might be missing. It was unbearable to me, once upon a time, the thought that one day my access might disappear permanently, never to return. But now I wonder whether I wouldn't be happier to be left alone with my memories, the restored recollections in glorious, emotive technicolour that have returned just in time to reassure me that my life wasn't, after all, meaningless.

It's funny really, when you think about it, all the lessons I've learnt about life by virtue of being dead.

I've learnt that work isn't about job titles or social status, it's not about precocious success or external approbation, nor about the acquisition of fame or money or power. Because unless we're the one-in-a-hundred-million who achieves something so exceptional that we may be remembered for generations – the composer or the playwright, the statesman or the politician, the inventor or the destroyer – it's about the quotidian pleasures we take in the work that we do, the value with which we imbue it and the satisfaction that we allow ourselves to take from it, day after day.

I've learnt that love isn't about our place at the centre of it, but about finding the generosity to allow those we care about to discover happiness wherever they so choose, with whomever they so desire, even if — for whatever reason — that isn't with us.

I've learnt that life's endeavours include the ability to die gracefully, graciously and with gratitude for the life that we lived, however long it lasted.

I've learnt that death is no impediment to love and that one of our greatest accomplishments is to be remembered well by those with whom we shared our days.

I've learnt that to be replaced doesn't mean to be forgotten and that even though life may go on without us, we each leave behind a legacy to influence generations to come, however seemingly quiet and inconsequential our lives may have been.

I've learnt, ultimately, that what's important is not what you know nor even who you know, not what you achieve nor even how successfully you achieve it, not the magnitude of recognition nor even by how many you're remembered. It's the quality of the imprint each of us leaves behind on those we have loved and who loved us in return.

Because I've learnt that the ripples of influence we each bequeath extend beyond the imaginable to people and places and times we cannot yet comprehend. All we can do is trust that those we encounter on our journey through life — the parents and children, the partners and siblings, the friends and colleagues — will transmit little pieces of us, from the snippets we taught and the things we said to the smallest inventions of our own making, through the generations, keeping the flame of our memory alive long after our bodies have died. And that this, after all, is life's great immortality project.

When I look back now on my thirty-six years of life what I see is not a catalogue of regrets but a succession of relationships that are each in possession of their own unique legacy.

I see a successful marriage to a loving husband, a marriage which made us both profoundly happy, a marriage in which each of us learnt from the other and from which Max's discoveries will undoubtedly contribute to this next big love of his life.

I see the beautiful, well-adjusted daughter I brought into the world, the child I taught to walk and to talk, to love and to learn, to play the piano and make roast potatoes and who, with a little help from her dad and her grandparents and the woman whom I strongly suspect will one day be her stepmother, will hopefully take a little part of our relationship with her wherever she goes in the future.

I see the mother whose grief I helped to bear, whose pride I was able to earn and for whom I provided the greatest gift of all in Ellie.

I see a best friend who allowed me into the core of her emotional world, with whom I shared some of life's greatest secrets and who has taken from my death her own desire to create life.

And now there's another woman, too, someone I never encountered when I was alive, someone who's getting to know me from beyond the grave and who seems to embrace the ripples of influence I've left cascading through the family she's inherited.

It doesn't sound too bad an existence when I put it like that. It's ironic, I know, that it's only in death that I've learnt how to live.

And I suppose, in a way, it's only now that I've learnt how to die, too. Because that's what this netherworld has been about, surely? All this time I've thought that the purpose of my access was to allow me to observe my family in mourning, to remain close to them and to watch over them as they come to terms with my absence from their lives. Now I see that it's been my own grieving process too, the space for me to learn how to be without them. The freedom to mourn the family I miss, the life that I've lost, and the life that I'll now never lead. Perhaps it's an opportunity afforded only to those who die young or unexpectedly or, in my case, both; an opportunity, like that of the terminally ill patient, to assess your past and to prepare yourself for a future that will evolve in your absence.

All this time I've been fearful of Max and Ellie moving on without me. Now I understand that it's my job to move on from them and that the time has come for me to do just that. Because if grief is the price we pay for love, then I think all of us have settled our debt now.

Max, Eve and Ellie have moved to the kitchen, where they're feasting on our traditional Christmas morning breakfast of smoked salmon and cream cheese bagels. It comforts me to see that some traditions never change.

Max selects an album of Christmas carols on the iPod and the high soprano voice rings out both in their world and mine. It's beautiful and peaceful and I feel dreamlike, as if I'm witnessing the world through the sepia spectacles of a life I can see is now in the past.

It's nearly time, I know, to leave. Not just for this morning, but for good. I know that the present is no longer mine to be a part of, even if only vicariously. It's time for them all to pursue their lives without my passive interference and time for me to face whatever comes next. I've no idea what might follow this netherworld if I willingly relinquish my access to the living. But I do know that I don't fear it, whatever it is. Because I understand that I've reconciled myself to the life that I led and the death that became me and that this acceptance was the only thing ever required of me here.

I'd assumed all this time that accepting my death would involve a recognition of the finiteness of existence, a confirmation that my past would perish with me and that all my relationships would be erased on my departure. I'd thought it would involve the acknowledgement that everything – every thought, feeling, hope, fear, desire, passion and memory – would expire with my body. I'd thought it was the acceptance that, in the end, nothing and no one can beat the transience of life.

But now I can see the sequence of imprints I've left indelibly behind me and I feel sure that all those I knew and loved will carry those legacies with them throughout their lives and will allow them to influence their own relationships, their own choices, their own journeys, whatever those journeys may entail and wherever they may lead.

It's the acceptance that my greatest bequest to the world was love, and that there's no legacy more enduring that anyone can leave rippling behind them.

And it's with this acceptance that I can now honestly say, hand on defunct heart, there's not a single thing I'd change about the way I lived my life, even if that mythical opportunity were available to me.

As the faintest of clouds begins to mist my view, I catch my final glimpse of Ellie, cream cheese smeared around her mouth, hungrily devouring the last of her bagel, curled up on Max's lap and giggling at a joke the three of them are sharing, the newest member of their clan bounding excitedly around her feet. She looks happy, relaxed, a child no longer burdened by grief but instead embracing the family she knows will take care of her.

I wonder whether my departure from this netherworld heralds the end of all access through time immemorial or whether I might, one day, be granted the occasional return passage to watch her graduate or get married or have children of her own. It would be lovely to think that I might. But it wouldn't be the end of the afterworld if I didn't. Because I know that she's going to be just fine, my little girl. They're all going to be just fine.

The bright clouds thicken and the whiteness gathers beneath me and I know, unequivocally, that they're eclipsing my view for the very last time.

# Acknowledgements

I'm indebted to various works on the nature of grief, death and dying for helping to shape my thoughts about Rachel's predicament: Elisabeth Kübler-Ross's *On Death and Dying*, Darian Leader's *The New Black: Mourning, Melancholia and Depression* and the truly inspiring *Staring at the Sun: Overcoming the Dread of Death* by Irvin D. Yalom.

My thanks go to everyone at Penguin: to Sarah Hunt Cooke, Kate Burton and the Rights team; to Joe Yule, Katie Sheldrake and Olivia Ovenden; and most notably to my editor, Hana Osman, for her incisive notes, editorial guidance and for spotting potential in characters that helped make their lives – and this story – so much richer.

My agent, Luigi Bonomi, is the kind of agent every writer dreams of but only a few of us are lucky enough to have; he took a punt on a single chapter and his editorial insights, commercial astuteness and belief in the narrative were fundamental to shaping what the book would eventually become. He also does a pretty good line in avuncular advice to first-time mums.

I'm indebted to Stephanie Jackson for reading everything I've ever written and for her steadfast encouragement that I'd one day be publishable.

Horatia Lawson and James Ingle do the world's greatest line in love, lunches and enduring friendship, and life would be immeasurably duller without them in it.

My nieces – Tamsin, Maddy, Jemima, Tilly, Esme and Lois – taught me so much about little girls before I had my own and inadvertently provided me with some of the better lines of dialogue contained herein.

My grandparents, Bidsa and Ronnie Beckerman, may no longer be alive to read this for themselves but their extensive ripples of influence – their love, pride and nourishment (both intellectual and culinary) – really will survive for generations.

My mum, Tania Bowler, has spent close to forty years walking the ten blocks (and back) for me more times than I can remember and I hope this book is, at least in part, testament to everything she's taught me about maternal commitment. And I'm delighted that she's had Jerry to keep her company (and make her happy) on her most recent journeys.

My beautiful daughter, Aurelia, arrived just in time to show me that parenthood is everything I'd imagined it would be (and more), and to open up an emotional world that's infinitely richer and considerably more fun than I would have dared hope.

And to my husband, Adam Jackson: saying a mere thank you seems woefully inadequate given that without his love, support, wise counsel and insightful readings – not to mention numerous weekends of solo childcare – the book would never have been finished. But thank you and I love you.

If you enjoyed

# The Dead Wife's Handbook

and would like to discuss it with your friends,
please turn over for our reading group questions.

# Reading Group Questions

1. The novel is narrated by a deceased character. Do you think this made you more critical of the living characters' actions than if the narrative was told from their point of view?

2. How do you think Max handled introducing Eve into Ellie's life? Did you think he let his new relationship distract him from other responsibilities?

3. Were you surprised when you learnt about Eve's infertility and estrangement from her parents? Did that knowledge make you more sympathetic to her? And do you think her parents should have behaved differently?

4. Did you feel that Harriet and Celia's initial reactions to Eve were justified?

5. Were you rooting for Max and Eve's relationship to be a success or were your sympathies with Rachel?

6. If you were in Rachel's position do you think you could ever feel comfortable with another woman taking your place?

Do you think that Eve would make a good stepmother for Ellie? What did you like or dislike about their relationship?

The novel implies that there may be a future romance between Harriet and Connor. Do you think they'd make a good couple?

Do you think the book paints an accurate portrayal of grief? Was the use of the seven stages of grief helpful in segmenting the narrative?

0. Rachel ultimately comes to terms with the fact that life will continue without her. Is that how you expected it to end and, if not, what had you been hoping for?

. One of the lasting messages of the book is that close relationships are more important than external achievements. Do you agree?

. The title of the novel is 'The Dead Wife's Handbook'. What did you think about the lessons Rachel feels she's learnt at the end of the novel? Did you agree with them?

# He just wanted a decent book to read ...

Not too much to ask, is it? It was in 1935 when Allen Lane, Managing Director of Bodley Head Publishers, stood on a platform at Exeter railway station looking for something good to read on his journey back to London. His choice was limited to popular magazines and poor-quality paperbacks – the same choice faced every day by the vast majority of readers, few of whom could afford hardbacks. Lane's disappointment and subsequent anger at the range of books generally available led him to found a company – and change the world.

*'We believed in the existence in this country of a vast reading public for intelligent books at a low price, and staked everything on it'*
**Sir Allen Lane, 1902–1970, founder of Penguin Books**

The quality paperback had arrived – and not just in bookshops. Lane was adamant that his Penguins should appear in chain stores and tobacconists, and should cost no more than a packet of cigarettes.

Reading habits (and cigarette prices) have changed since 1935, but Penguin still believes in publishing the best books for everybody to enjoy. We still believe that good design costs no more than bad design, and we still believe that quality books published passionately and responsibly make the world a better place.

So wherever you see the little bird – whether it's on a piece of prize-winning literary fiction or a celebrity autobiography, political tour de force or historical masterpiece, a serial-killer thriller, reference book, world classic or a piece of pure escapism – you can bet that it represents the very best that the genre has to offer.

## Whatever you like to read – trust Penguin.